Praise for

Beverly Brandt

The Tiara Club

"*Steel Magnolias* meets *The Sweet Potato Queens* in this book about friendship, beauty pageants, Southern living, deep dark secrets, and the sacrifices we make in the name of love. After laughing and crying along with Georgia Elliot and her friends, you'll wish you had a Tiara Club of your own. Don't miss this witty, charming novel!"
—*New York Times* bestselling author Joan Johnston

"A heartwarming tale of Southern love and friendship, which proves that retired beauty queens are more than meets the eye. It's the *Ya-Ya Sisterhood* with sizzle."
—Cara Lockwood,
bestselling author of *Dixieland Sushi*

Dream On

"No one in Brandt's tale is who or what they seem to be, and their journey involves one madcap situation after another, a powerful love attraction, and a whole lot of fun."
—*Booklist*

Room Service

"A fine, funny tale."   —*Booklist*

"Brandt dishes up another lighthearted office romance touched with humor and suspense . . . this is fun, breezy, beach reading."
—*Publishers Weekly*

continued . . .

Record Time

"A wonderfully entertaining book!"   —Elizabeth Bevarly,
author of *Take Me, I'm Yours*

"A sparkling, fast-paced romp. Witty and entertaining to
the satisfying end."   —Stephanie Bond,
author of *I Think I Love You*

"Brandt maintains a delightful balance between control
and confusion, and pads her story with a cast of well-
drawn ancillary characters . . . this fun, feel-good romance
is the perfect pick-me-up for rainy days."

—*Publishers Weekly*

True North

"Sassy and sexy with a touch of suspense! Beverly Brandt
makes sparks fly."   —Julie Ortolon,
bestselling author of *Dear Cupid*

Match
Game

Beverly Brandt

B

BERKLEY SENSATION, NEW YORK

THE BERKLEY PUBLISHING GROUP
Published by the Penguin Group
Penguin Group (USA) Inc.
375 Hudson Street, New York, New York 10014, USA
Penguin Group (Canada), 90 Eglinton Avenue East, Suite 700, Toronto, Ontario M4P 2Y3, Canada
(a division of Pearson Penguin Canada Inc.)
Penguin Books Ltd., 80 Strand, London WC2R 0RL, England
Penguin Group Ireland, 25 St. Stephen's Green, Dublin 2, Ireland (a division of Penguin Books Ltd.)
Penguin Group (Australia), 250 Camberwell Road, Camberwell, Victoria 3124, Australia
(a division of Pearson Australia Group Pty. Ltd.)
Penguin Books India Pvt. Ltd., 11 Community Centre, Panchsheel Park, New Delhi—110 017, India
Penguin Group (NZ), Cnr. Airborne and Rosedale Roads, Albany, Auckland 1310, New Zealand
(a division of Pearson New Zealand Ltd.)
Penguin Books (South Africa) (Pty.) Ltd., 24 Sturdee Avenue, Rosebank, Johannesburg 2196,
South Africa

Penguin Books Ltd., Registered Offices: 80 Strand, London WC2R 0RL, England

This is a work of fiction. Names, characters, places, and incidents either are the product of the author's imagination or are used fictitiously, and any resemblance to actual persons, living or dead, business establishments, events, or locales is entirely coincidental. The publisher does not have any control over and does not assume any responsibility for author or third-party websites or their content.

MATCH GAME

A Berkley Sensation Book / published by arrangement with the author

PRINTING HISTORY
Berkley Sensation trade paperback edition / October 2005
Berkley Sensation mass market edition / June 2006

Copyright © 2005 by Beverly Brandt.
Cover art by Kim Johnson Lindgren/Smith.
Cover design by George Long.
Interior text design by Kristin del Rosario.

ISBN: 0-425-20828-1

BERKLEY SENSATION®
Berkley Sensation Books are published by The Berkley Publishing Group,
a division of Penguin Group (USA) Inc.,
375 Hudson Street, New York, New York 10014.
BERKLEY SENSATION is a registered trademark of Penguin Group (USA) Inc.
The "B" design is a trademark belonging to Penguin Group (USA) Inc.

PRINTED IN THE UNITED STATES OF AMERICA

10 9 8 7 6 5 4 3 2 1

To my sister, Kelley, who is nothing like Miranda.
Well, except for the bossy part.
But I love you just the way you are,
and I hate to think what my life would
have been like without you.

•ACKNOWLEDGMENTS•

I'd like to thank my agent, Deidre Knight, for everything!

Also, my thanks to Cindy Hwang and Susan McCarty at Berkley for shepherding this book through the process, for being so understanding, and for being such enthusiastic readers.

A huge "thank-you" to fellow writer Laron Glover for her insightful feedback on this story. You are a goddess among critique partners!

Are You a Bad Bride?

Your big day has finally arrived and you've handled all the ups and downs of pulling together the perfect wedding with aplomb . . . or have you? Take this quiz to find out if wedding-day jitters have transformed you from serene to psychotic.

The freshly delivered flowers clash with the groom's cummerbund, you just found out the cake was left in the caterer's van overnight and is frozen solid, and it's T-minus two to picture time and one of your bridesmaids is MIA. What do you do?

a· Embrace your inner two-year-old and throw yourself down on the floor in a sobbing, kicking tantrum. Surely someone will step in and fix this mess for you.

b· Just keep smiling and weaving dainty white baby's breath through your elaborate hairdo. Things will work out the way they are meant to—as Guru Ramu says, there's no use resisting that which you cannot change.

c· Button up the groom's jacket while calling the nearest Baskin-Robbins for turtle fudge ice cream to go with your trend-setting icebox wedding cake and sending hand signals to your former K-9 unit pet "Wolfie" to go sniff out the missing bridesmaid and bring her to heel.

continues on next page . . .

If you chose A, congratulations! You win the Bad Bride prize. Grow up, Scarlett, and learn to deal with your own problems. You B brides out there need to get real! Sell the flower-power VW bus, take a clue from Clinton and inhale just a little less, and stop trusting the world to be a better place just because you and your chanting, hand-holding, incense-sniffing pals want it to be. For those of you who chose C, you are every wedding planner's dream client—smart, efficient, and reasonable. If your marriage runs as smoothly as your wedding, you and your groom will truly live happily ever after!

{one}

It all started with the September issue of *All About Brides* magazine.

Newly engaged Savannah Taylor had run down to the Super ShopMart on her lunch hour to pick up a six-pack of Diet Sprite and a jug of Chardonnay for predinner drinks with her friends that evening when she spotted the 720-page special edition sitting in the rack next to *Glamour* and *Cosmo* and the latest *National Enquirer* (which claimed to have actual photos of aliens abducting Julia Roberts, but Savannah guessed the aliens in question were just a pair of Julia's normal, non-movie-star friends). .

"Everything You Need to Make Your Wedding Perfect," the banner read, and Savannah thought, *Wow, everything I need in one place*. Since she was an accountant and the IRS had over a hundred publications to explain the proper filing of one simple tax return, she was thrilled to think that everything she needed to plan her wedding could be found in this one edition of *All About Brides*. She didn't even balk at the $16.99 price tag—more than the oversize bottle of wine and six-pack of soda put together.

When she got back to the Maple Rapids, Michigan, branch of Refund City—a nationwide accounting firm that specialized in completing tax returns for their mostly walk-in clien-

tele who squeezed tax planning in between trips to Ra-
dioShack and picking up two-for-one gallons of milk at the
new Super ShopMart—Savannah put the Chardonnay and the
soda in the overpacked fridge in the employee lunchroom to
chill. Then, knowing her coworkers as she did, she grabbed a
pad of yellow sticky-notes from the counter, wrote "Touch
this and die," and stuck the Post-it on the bottle of wine. The
Diet Sprite, she figured, was safe.

Her best friend, Peggy, used to drink regular Sprite with
her vodka, but she'd switched to diet when Savannah had
asked her to be a bridesmaid in Savannah's wedding. Savannah thought the whole idea of losing weight for a wedding was
ridiculous. A reunion, she could understand. You wanted to
show off to people you hadn't seen for years that you were no
longer the chubby geek you were in high school. That made
sense. But, presumably, the people at the wedding had seen
you recently and they knew you were carrying around an extra
ten pounds. It didn't make sense to try to lose weight for *them*.

Savannah was happy to have her theory confirmed in the
article "Wedding Dos and Don'ts." Number 4 on the "Don't"
list was "Don't buy a too-tight dress and promise yourself
you'll lose that extra padding in time for the wedding. Instead, buy a dress that fits a little loose and schedule your final fitting no more than one week before the big day. The last
thing you need is to exhale right before your groom says 'I
do' and end up blinding him with a popped button flying at
him at the speed of light." Solid advice, as far as Savannah
was concerned.

She had lost track of time that day, sitting at the wobbly
table in the lunchroom poring over all that needed to be done
in the next five months. Savannah was surprised to discover
that she was already behind schedule. Who knew that you
were supposed to reserve both the church and the reception
hall a year before the wedding? Or that most caterers expected
a 25 percent deposit six months in advance of the big day?

Feeling nervous that she had missed these deadlines without even realizing it, Savannah took the magazine back to her
desk and, hiding it in between the pages of IRS Publication
1212 (List of Original Issue Discount Instruments), she carefully marked the articles she wanted to keep with colored

flags. After a while it occurred to her that she should color-code the flags. Maybe red for anything to do with flowers, green for bridal gowns, yellow for the reception, and blue for the wedding itself. After another twenty minutes she decided that four categories weren't enough. *All About Brides* was filled with information about photographers, flowers, brides-maids' dresses, bridal gowns, tuxes, musicians, caterers, cakes, rings, and wedding planners. And although she didn't know anyone who had ever hired a wedding planner (wasn't that what mothers were for?), Savannah thought it was important to at least know what one could do for her.

In the end she took off work a few minutes early—God knew she'd make up the lost time once tax season got in full swing—and walked over to the Kinko's next to the Super ShopMart, where she used the industrial-sized paper cutter to cut the spine off the magazine. Before leaving work, she had "borrowed" a three-ring binder, a set of tab dividers, and a handful of plastic sheet protectors to put together her new wedding bible. Okay. She hadn't exactly borrowed them, since she didn't plan on giving them back. But it wasn't like she had taken a stapler or something really expensive.

"You're not going to go to hell for lifting a few office supplies," she assured herself, carefully binder-clipping the now-loose pages together so they wouldn't go flying everywhere as she stuffed the magazine into her bag along with the loot she'd taken from the office.

Loot. As in stolen goods.

Savannah sighed as she walked over to the office supply section of the copy shop and picked up a large three-ring binder, a set of tab dividers, and a box of plastic sheet protectors. She could almost see her former Sunday School teacher nodding approvingly as she dropped her items on the counter and waited the requisite six and a half minutes for an employee to notice her and amble over to the cash register so she could pay for her purchases. She'd return the stolen goods to the supply room tomorrow, hoping her boss wouldn't notice her petty larceny and fire her on the spot.

That night Savannah shared her find with Peggy and the rest of her friends. To Savannah, the "Step-by-Step Guide to a Flawless Wedding" (pp. 623–37) alone was worth the cost of the magazine. It even had boxes she could check off as each task was completed. Each section was broken up by a time period: a year before the wedding, eight months before, six months, four months, two months, one month, two weeks, seven days, six days, etc., until it actually started counting down the hours until the big event. She had slipped these pages into protective plastic sleeves and given them a tab all to themselves, right in the front of her binder. As the months passed, other sections got cluttered up with articles from other bridal magazines and pockets for swatches and samples and pictures Savannah found while waiting at the doctor or the dentist or the minister's office (she and Todd were required to complete eight hours of premarital counseling before Reverend Black would perform the ceremony), but the "Step-by-Step Guide to a Flawless Wedding" section remained pristine, marred only by Savannah's neatly penciled checkmarks.

The wedding was set for the afternoon of February 14. Todd had joked that this date had received his vote because, as he put it, "Now I won't have to buy gifts for both our anniversary and Valentine's Day." As much as she loved him, Savannah feared that Todd wasn't kidding. As a matter of fact, she suspected that if it were possible, he'd ask her to change her birthday from April 15 (her oldest sister Miranda often said this was a sign that Savannah had emerged from the womb destined to become an accountant) to February 14 so he could kill all three birds with one stone. Truthfully, by the time April 15 rolled around, Savannah was so exhausted from working around the clock to get people's taxes filed on time that it didn't take much in terms of gifts to impress her. Which worked out well for Todd, who, for the three years they'd been dating, had taken her to the Olive Garden for her "special" birthday dinner.

"All the salad and breadsticks you can eat," he always said, grinning as if he'd made some sort of joke.

Savannah often found herself thinking that it was a good thing she loved Todd.

Of course, she'd *better* love him, she reminded herself as she nervously checked her "Step-by-Step Guide to a Flawless Wedding" to make sure everything was on schedule. With just over an hour to go before the exchanging of "I do's," it was a bit late to be questioning her feelings for her fiancé. Not that she needed to. Todd was nice, safe. Reliable. He'd never cheat on her. And he'd asked her to marry him. No other man she'd ever dated had done that. What more could a woman ask for?

"How are you holding up?"

Savannah took a calming breath and turned to answer her sister Belinda, who looked great wearing nothing but matching pink bra and panties. Before Savannah could say anything, Belinda's cell phone rang—a not uncommon occurrence. Belinda held up a finger as if to say, "Back to you in one," as she flipped open her phone and answered, "Hello."

There was a slight pause before Belinda said, "I know your parents' thirtieth wedding anniversary is tonight, but that allocation needs to be ready for the Monday morning meeting in Phoenix. Maybe we should meet later tonight and work through the night to get it done. I'll limit myself to one glass of champagne if you will."

Belinda never let anything stand in the way of work, not even her baby sister's wedding.

Savannah sighed and looked around the vestibule at the back of the church that had been set aside for the estrogen-producing half of the wedding party. It looked as if Macy's had exploded. Assorted makeup and hair accessories were strewn about the room, curling irons and hot rollers plugged in and ready to go. The clothes Savannah, Belinda, Peggy, and Todd's best man's girlfriend Trish had worn into the church that morning were draped atop tables and chairs, some neatly folded, and others tossed down without care.

"The florist just arrived and the flowers aren't right. They clash with Todd's cummerbund. Didn't you take swatches with you when you went to pick out the flowers?"

Savannah turned to find her oldest sister Miranda peering around the vestibule door, looking like a fairy-tale princess with her shiny black hair and pale skin and large green eyes. All three of the Taylor girls had the same coloring, but it was almost as though Belinda and Savannah were muted replicas of their older sister, each of them successively less stunning than the previous sibling.

"Of course I did," Savannah said, gathering up her train to go check out the extent of the floral crisis.

She grabbed her three-ring binder from a table and felt a

draft of cold air wash over her as she stepped out of the quiet back room. The First Baptist Church that Savannah had attended all her life had a high, peaked ceiling that made it difficult to heat. Once the pews were full, the church would warm up, but for now, the chilly atmosphere made Savannah shiver.

She followed the sound of raised voices and found the florist at the front of the church, crouched over a box behind the wooden altar.

"This just won't do," Savannah heard her mother's familiar voice say. "These flowers are violet, not magenta."

Savannah stepped up onto the raised dais where Reverend Black delivered his sermons every Sunday to find her mother and the florist squatting on the orangish carpet, staring in a dejected manner at the box of various corsages, boutonnieres, and bouquets.

"I'm certain I ordered the right color," the florist said.

"Oh, Savannah honey, there you are. Didn't you take a swatch with you when you picked out the flowers?" her mother asked.

Savannah swallowed a sigh before answering, "Of course I did, Mom." It was no use reminding her mother that she was not a baby anymore. Her protest would only fall on deaf ears. Savannah set her wedding notebook on the pulpit, flipped to the tab marked "Bridesmaids' Dresses," and pulled out a piece of fabric.

"Here, the flowers are supposed to match this," she said, holding out the scrap of magenta cloth.

The florist took the swatch and held it against the flowers.

Savannah cringed.

"It doesn't match," the florist said glumly.

"No, it doesn't," Miranda agreed from behind her little sister.

"Are you sure these are the flowers for the Everard-Taylor wedding?" Savannah asked, hoping the florist would smack her wide forehead with her hand and say, "What? This isn't the Miller-Tompkins wedding? Silly me, I must have switched the deliveries." Instead, the woman nodded and said, "Yes. This is the only wedding we have this weekend. We were too busy with Valentine bouquets to take on another wedding."

"I don't suppose there's any way you could swap out the violet flowers with something that isn't quite so . . . purple?" Savannah asked.

Again, the florist shook her head. "I'm sorry, but by the time I took these all back to the shop and fixed them, you'd already be on your honeymoon."

Savannah closed her eyes and put two fingers against her throbbing left temple. How could this have happened? Hadn't she followed her "Step-by-Step Guide to a Flawless Wedding" exactly? Opening her eyes again, she flipped to the front section of her notebook and slid her French-manicured finger down the second page, stopping when she got to the heading that read "Two Months Before the Wedding." There, next to the line about placing an order with the florist (with the accompanying note about making certain to bring a sample of the bridesmaids' dresses to ensure proper color-matching), was a neat check mark.

She flipped the book closed heavily and turned back to the group gathered around the offending floral arrangements. "Well, there's nothing we can do but try to make the best of it. At least it won't make a difference in the black-and-white photos."

"No, they'll look lovely," her mother agreed, patting her youngest daughter's back comfortingly.

Miranda refused to meet her eyes, and Savannah knew her sister was dying to tell her what she should do to fix this problem. That was Miranda's assigned role in the family. She was the adviser—the one who knew the right thing to do in every situation. At least she thought she did. As a child Savannah found herself giving in to Miranda because every time she tried to do something for herself, Miranda would stand back and shake her head as if to say, "If you would just listen to me, I could tell you how to do that. Here, I'll just do it for you." It was either engage in a constant battle for independence or let Miranda have her way. Since Savannah looked up to her big sister, she chose the path of least resistance, which earned her the label of being passive and unable to stand up for herself. Which was fine, Savannah supposed. That was *her* role in the family.

Miranda was the bossy oldest, Belinda the overachieving middle kid, and Savannah the placid youngest.

On her way back to the vestibule in the rear of the church, Savannah gave a little snort. She was thirty-one years old, owned her own home, had a responsible position as a CPA, yet still struggled to get her family to see her as anything but a helpless baby.

Halfway down the hall she was stopped again, this time by the photographer, a thin young man whose cameras looked as if they weighed more than he did. He'd come highly recommended by her mom's best friend, and Savannah had been impressed by his portfolio (tip #6 in "Twelve Tips to Pulling Off the Perfect Wedding" was to check out the photographer's portfolio, no matter how many referrals he had), so she assumed that he wouldn't collapse under the weight of his equipment mid-photo shoot.

"Are you girls about ready?" he asked, apparently eager to get this over with.

Savannah couldn't say she blamed him. Despite her organized approach to planning this wedding, the potential for disaster was enormous. It would only take one clumsy guest bumping against the cake table to turn her elegant reception into a joke that would be told and retold thousands of times for the rest of her life. Or one hung-over groomsman to throw up on a bridesmaid's shoes. Or one unity candle to catch her dress on fire. Or . . .

Savannah shuddered. No, she had to stop thinking like that. Everything was going to turn out perfectly. Hadn't she followed the instructions in her wedding planner down to the very last detail? Well, with the tiny exception of this morning, when her "Step-by-Step Guide" said she was supposed to be getting a manicure and pedicure with her bridesmaids and she was actually at work, going through Mrs. Jackson's receipts one last time so that her client could face her audit on Tuesday without worrying that the IRS would find something amiss.

Savannah hadn't filed Mrs. Jackson's return—the woman had actually done her taxes herself, which was something Savannah always discouraged. "You wouldn't perform brain surgery on yourself, so why do your own taxes?" was her motto.

But Mrs. Jackson had used some supposedly foolproof software to calculate her taxes, turning to a professional only after her return had been chosen for an audit. At that point she'd dropped by Refund City, loaded down with a Palm Pilot box (shoeboxes were *so* last millennium) bubbling over with receipts. She'd dropped the mess on Savannah's desk, nearly in tears as she explained about the letter she'd received from the IRS telling her to report to the IRS office in Flint on Tuesday, February 17 at 1:00 P.M.

"Why did they pick me? I haven't done anything wrong," Mrs. Jackson had wailed.

Savannah had murmured soothingly to the older woman as she brought her some hot tea. She assured Mrs. Jackson that the IRS was not picking on her, nor were they suspicious that she was hiding anything. It was merely a routine record check, probably brought on by Mrs. Jackson's claim that she used her personal vehicle in her home business.

"Self-employed taxpayers are audited much more frequently than those with regular jobs," Savannah had said, calmly dumping the receipts out onto her desk and beginning to sort them into neat little piles.

"You seem to be very good at this," Mrs. Jackson had remarked after raising her teacup to her mouth with shaking hands.

"I am," Savannah answered. "Now, there's nothing to worry about. Let's just get this all organized for the big bad auditor, shall we?"

That's when Mrs. Jackson had set down her cup and rummaged around in her handbag for a Kleenex to wipe away the tears that had sprung into her eyes. "I'm sorry," she apologized gruffly. "I lost my husband two years ago, and some days it feels as if the whole world is against me."

Savannah reached out and squeezed the other woman's hand. "Believe me, this audit is nothing personal. The IRS probably just selected your return at random. They do that to a small percentage of the total returns filed in any given year just to keep taxpayers honest."

Mrs. Jackson had been so grateful that Savannah felt compelled to go to the office this morning and check for the third and final time that everything was in order for Mrs. Jackson's audit. She didn't want to suddenly realize that she'd missed something crucial while sunning herself on the sandy beaches of Cozumel next to her new husband. Besides, she'd taken care of the mani/pedi task yesterday, for once springing for the acrylic tips on her fingernails that she loved, but which tended to get stuck in between the keys on her keyboard, making her clients' "Wages, Salaries, Tips, etc." come out as something like $27,4855555555555555 instead of $27,485. Obviously, from an income tax perspective, this was not a good thing.

So, three hours before the wedding, satisfied that everything was in order, Savannah had reclipped Mrs. Jackson's receipts together and put everything back in the file her coworker Josh would take to the audit on Tuesday. But just because Savannah had deviated from the plan didn't mean that disaster was imminent.

Right?

Savannah took a deep breath and pushed open the door to the vestibule to see if her bridesmaids were ready for their photos. She'd left Miranda up at the altar—probably muttering to their mother that if Savannah had let *her* be in charge of the flowers, this wouldn't have happened. Belinda still had her cell phone attached to her ear and was helping Peggy zip up her dress, but Trish seemed to have disappeared.

"Where's Trish? The photographer is ready to get started with the pictures," Savannah asked, speaking softly so as to not interfere with Belinda's call. She supposed it should annoy her that her sister was absorbed with work on Savannah's wedding day, but the truth was, she accepted her sister's workaholic tendencies. It was just the way Belinda was. Getting angry with her for it would be like getting angry at Miranda for being bossy, or at Mom for being incapable of balancing a checkbook, or at Dad for his inability to work common household appliances like dishwashers and irons.

Ugh, we're the Cliché family, Savannah thought with a surprised chuckle.

"I don't know," Peggy answered, interrupting Savannah's thoughts. "She got a call on her cell five minutes ago and dashed out without saying anything. You look gorgeous, by the way."

Savannah checked herself out in the mirror on the opposite wall, running a critical eye over hair, makeup, and dress. She was willing to admit that she looked pretty good, her makeup slathered on heavier than usual, her dark hair shiny and healthy after the previous day's visit to the beauty salon. And she loved her dress—a shimmery white silk with beaded lace at the hem and sheer long sleeves that were perfect for a winter wedding.

"It's my wedding day," Savannah said, turning from the mirror. "I have to look good. It's one of those unwritten laws of the universe, like the one that says you must lose at least one sock per month in the dryer."

Peggy laughed and Belinda finally hung up her phone and asked, "What's so funny?"

"Nothing. Are you ready for pictures?"

Belinda fluffed her hands through her hair, tossed her cell phone into her purse, and looped her arm through Savannah's. "Let's go," she said.

Just then the vestibule door flew open and an out-of-breath Trish nearly fell into the room. Her formerly neat dress was rumpled and there was a dark spot near her left hip.

"What's wrong?" Savannah asked, afraid that Trish had gone outside and slipped on the icy sidewalk and hurt herself.

"What? Nothing. Why do you ask?" Trish nervously ran her hands down the front of her dress.

"No reason," Savannah said with a shrug. "Here, your dress got a little wrinkled. Let me steam it for you." She was glad she'd paid close attention to the article "Ten Things No Bride Should Be Without" and made sure to bring clear nail polish (to fix runs in pantyhose), extra tissues (for obvious reasons), a steamer (the article actually said to bring an iron, but Savannah loved her little portable steamer, so she'd brought that instead), Tums, aspirin, Super Glue (in case one of the bridal party broke a heel), a curling iron, Band-Aids, Saltine crackers, and baby wipes (to wipe frosting and other sticky substances off people's fingers).

Trish quickly shucked off her dress and held it out for Savannah to work her magic on. Savannah frowned at the spot, which didn't seem to be drying very quickly. Hmm. She should write to the editor of *All About Brides* and tell them to add a blow-dryer to their list of "Ten Things No Bride Should Be Without." Of course, that would make it "Eleven Things

No Bride Should Be Without," which probably wasn't as catchy a title, but still . . .

She handed the dress back to Trish, who hurriedly smoothed it back into place and presented her back to Savannah for zipping.

"Okay, looks like we're all ready. Time to say cheese," Savannah said, ushering her bridesmaids out into the church, where Todd and his groomsmen were waiting. Besides Todd's best friend Robert, Todd had asked his cousin Ryan and Miranda's husband, Alex, to stand up with him. Savannah's gaze fixed on Todd, who looked suave in his black tuxedo with a crisp white shirt and magenta—he never would have agreed to wear this color if she'd mentioned the word *pink*—cummerbund.

Normally, Todd wasn't the sort of man who would attract a lot of female attention. Not that he was unattractive. More like unassuming. He had what would be referred to in nonbeauty salon circles as dishwater blond hair and brown eyes that were not a dark chocolate brown or brown with golden flecks or anything like that. They were just plain old brown. Todd liked to joke that his appearance worked to his advantage down at his dad's car lot. He said people saw him and expected him to be a pushover.

"They don't see the shark underneath the sheep's clothing," he'd told Savannah once, and she hadn't had the heart to tell him that he'd mangled the saying. He had a habit of doing that. One time he'd called Savannah at work to tell her that he'd just managed to sell a loaded Toyota Camry to a woman who had come in looking for basic transportation.

"She bought it all—the six-disc CD player, the $800 undercoating package, extended five-year warranty—the whole Chihuahua."

Savannah had nearly snorted root beer out her nose at that. But mangled sayings aside, Todd looked every inch the handsome groom today in his tux and tails.

She heard someone giggle and turned her head to see that Trish's cheeks were as bright as her dress. When she followed Trish's gaze to Robert and saw the smug look on his face, she swallowed a shocked gasp. Her gaze flew back to Trish.

Oh, for God's sake.

Robert and Trish had just had premarital sex. Very satisfying premarital sex, too, by the look of things. And that spot on Trish's dress . . .

No, she didn't even want to think about that. Her mother was coming down the aisle, laden down with flowers, so Savannah grabbed a bouquet and pushed it toward Trish with a whispered, "Use this to hide that spot on your dress."

If anything, Trish's blush got even pinker as she looked down, realizing that she was inadvertently wearing a little token of her boyfriend's affection. "I'm sorry," she whispered back. "I'll just go to the ladies' room and see if I can get this out."

"Hurry," Savannah encouraged, noting that her photographer had now disappeared.

Quickly counting heads to make sure she hadn't lost another bridesmaid to prewedding lust, Savannah satisfied herself that all were present and accounted for just as the photographer came from the direction of the men's room, looking a little green.

Great, just what she needed. Something else to clash with the bridesmaids' dresses.

She got as far as "Are you feel—" before the look on his face warned her that no, he was not. Without thinking, Savannah grabbed the photographer's arm, jerked him through the waiting wedding party, and pushed him into the vestibule just in time to hear the telltale sounds of retching. She stepped back, pulling the door closed as she fought her own instantaneous gag reflex.

Ugh. There was nothing worse than hearing someone throwing up. Unless it was *smelling*—Savannah quickly plugged her nose and backed away from the door. No, she was not going to be sick at her own wedding.

Aargh. What else could go wrong today?

The thought entered her consciousness before she had the chance to stop it. Savannah closed her eyes, knowing she had just cursed her own wedding. Now all bets were off.

She dropped her forehead into her hands, moaning, "No, no, no," under her breath.

"Do you want me to do anything?" Miranda asked, clearly eager to be allowed to manage *something* today.

"No," Savannah said, straightening her shoulders and tak-

ing a deep, calming breath. "Everything's going to be all
right. I can get Uncle Dave to take photos after the ceremony
if the photographer hasn't recovered by then. He took pictures
at Cousin Jerry's graduation last year and they turned out
great." She scrunched up her nose, thinking. People would
start arriving soon, and the wedding party needed to disappear. But with the vestibule . . . um, otherwise occupied, they
were going to need to go somewhere else.

"All right," Savannah said, taking charge and shooing
everyone with her hands like a border collie with a herd of re-
calcitrant sheep. "Everyone downstairs. Robert, you and Trish
stay where I can see you. Belinda, get away from the vestibule
door. I'm sure Todd will let you borrow his phone. If we get a
whiff of that odor, we're all going down."

Savannah was surprised when everyone, including Miranda, allowed her to shepherd them toward the back stairs,
and she smiled with pleasure when Todd pulled away from his
friends to come walk beside her.

"Hey, you look great," he said, as if it had just occurred to
him that today was a special occasion.

"Thank you. You do, too."

Todd's chest seemed to swell with pride as he smoothed
his hands down the lapels of his jacket. "Yeah, this is a good
look for me. I might try to convince my dad that all the salesmen down at the lot should dress like this. Give the place a little class, you know?"

Savannah blinked at the image of a bunch of tux-clad used-
car salesmen wandering Mr. Everard's lot. She wasn't quite as
convinced as Todd that it was a good idea, but figured she
wouldn't tell him how to sell cars if he didn't try to do her taxes.

The wedding party traipsed down the narrow stairs and
into the basement of the church, through the kitchen, where
potluck suppers were held every Wednesday night, and into
the first of several Sunday School classrooms filled with
child-sized multicolored plastic chairs and the felt boards Savannah remembered from her childhood. Her Sunday School
teacher would tell Bible stories by moving felt people around
on the board, the fabric sticking to it as if by magic.

Soon the sound of footsteps could be heard from upstairs,
along with the faint strains of the organist playing Muzak

versions of standard wedding fare such as "I Will Always Love You" and "The Wind Beneath My Wings." Savannah, who had a fondness for eighties hard rock, had jokingly suggested that "Love Bites" by Def Leppard be included in the medley, but the disapproving looks from both her mother and Todd had quashed that idea. Still, Savannah found herself humming "Love bites, love bleeds" under her breath as she sat with her friends and family in the cluttered K-2nd Grade room, listening to muffled voices overhead and waiting for her wedding to begin.

When her father opened the classroom door and poked his head inside the room, Savannah felt her stomach do a slow roll. Up until that moment she hadn't been nervous about getting married, despite the mini-disasters that had marred her perfect day. After all, it wasn't like she and Todd were rushing into this. They'd been dating for three years—if Todd had a foot fetish or a penchant for wearing ladies' underwear, Savannah would have discovered it by now.

No, there were no surprises awaiting either one of them after today. So why was her stomach lurching like a zombie in *Night of the Living Dead*?

Just normal prewedding jitters, she assured herself, putting a hand against her stomach to stop it from gurgling.

"All right, gang. It's time," her father announced.

Next to her, Todd stood up and straightened his shoulders, nodding as if he'd just been given some critical mission to complete. "See you up there," he said solemnly, then patted her hand.

Her father stepped back to let Todd and his groomsmen pass him in the hall. When Savannah heard their low, muttered conversation, she figured Dad was giving Todd the required "You'd better treat my daughter right or you'll have to answer to me" speech. Since Dad was a pudgy insurance executive and not some slick *Sopranos* type, Savannah didn't figure this threat struck much fear in Todd's heart, but she appreciated the gesture.

And then it was time.

Peggy left first, followed by Belinda and then Miranda, who stopped at the doorway and turned back, her eyes moist with unshed tears.

Savannah waited for her big sister to say something touching or profound, but instead she said, "Remember, wait until the organist begins the Wedding March before you start down the aisle."

Resisting the urge to say, "You're not the boss of me," Savannah sighed and said, "I *know*," as patiently as she could manage, and without even so much as a slight rolling of her eyes.

Her father waited until Miranda was out of earshot before offering Savannah his arm and saying, "She means well."

Savannah took her dad's arm, the rented tux scratchy beneath her fingers. "I know, and I love her for it. I just wish sometimes that she would stop treating me like a baby."

"You'll always be my baby," her father said, squeezing Savannah's arm against his side. He was warm and soft and he smiled down at her with such affection that Savannah had to blink back the tears that threatened to spill over her lashes.

"Don't say things like that. You'll make me cry," she said.

"It's your wedding. You're supposed to cry." He squeezed her arm again, and then the look on his face turned serious. "Are you sure you're ready to do this?" he asked.

"Of course I am, Dad," Savannah answered, briefly resting her head on his shoulder and suddenly wanting very much to curl up in his lap and feel coddled and completely safe again.

Reg Taylor cleared his throat and blinked away a suspicious wetness from his eyes. "Sorry for asking, but I'm your father. It's my job to question decisions like these."

Savannah pressed her nose into her dad's chest, inhaling the scent of the Old Spice he still insisted he loved, which was a good thing because his three daughters had bought enough of the stuff over the years to keep him smelling like a dad for several decades to come. Taking a deep breath, Savannah finally released her father, shook out her dress, picked up her bouquet, and said, "I'm ready."

She and her father slowly made their way up the basement steps, Savannah being careful not to trip on her own dress. When they appeared in the back doorway of the church, the organist gave a sharp nod and took his fingers off the keyboard, presumably to add an air of suspense to the proceedings.

There was a short, anticipatory silence before the familiar notes of the Wedding March sounded. On cue, the congregation stood up and looked toward the back of the church, gasping as if they'd never expected to find a bride and her father standing there. Savannah fought the urge to laugh and wondered if her attack of nerves was making her hysterical.

They started down the aisle, Savannah feeling a bit ridiculous with everyone staring at her. Finally they reached the front of the church, where her father handed her over to Todd after kissing her on the cheek with a murmured, "Your mother and I love you," which inexplicably made Savannah want to cry again. She knew her parents loved her. What was it about weddings that made everyone so emotional?

And then Reverend Black began the ceremony, his familiar deep voice doing that "love is a never-ending circle which cannot be broken" thing that he did at every wedding here in the First Baptist Church. When that was over, he did Savannah's favorite bit—the part where he turned to the congregation and asked, "If anyone here can show just cause why these two should not be joined, speak now or forever hold your peace."

Savannah loved that line and she had to admit that a part of her (the part that loved to watch old Doris Day–Cary Grant movies and sighed from deep in her soul every time Colin Firth wrapped his coat around a half-naked Renée Zellweger at the end of *Bridget Jones's Diary*) wished that the church doors would be flung open to reveal a dark and tortured hero who had fallen in love with her from afar and had nobly tried to stay away from her but could no longer deny his feelings. Then he'd sweep her off her feet and carry her back down the aisle to his waiting black Ferrari and Savannah would look back and shrug apologetically, as if to say, "What was I supposed to do? I had no choice."

Oddly, she didn't imagine Todd putting up much of a fight as she was whisked away by another man, her silky white train scattering the violet rose petals that her niece had strewn along the aisle.

"Well then," Reverend Black began, clearing his throat and bringing Savannah's attention back to her less-than-swashbuckling fiancé. Obviously, there would be no objections to the Everard-Taylor nuptials—no dark, conquering hero coming in from the cold to sweep Savannah off her feet.

Only, before the pastor could continue, the church doors were flung open, letting in a blast of frigid air from outside. With a gasp Savannah dropped Todd's hand and turned toward the back of the church, dreading that she may have actually conjured up a broodingly mysterious man with her silly fantasies.

And—ohmigod!—not one, but *three* broodingly mysterious men stormed the church, their hard faces impassive, their navy suits crisply pressed.

Savannah's mouth hung open as she watched the men stalk toward her. Had her fantasy man sent these henchmen to bring her to him? She shivered and closed her eyes, telling herself to stop being ridiculous. There was no fantasy man. She loved Todd and she was marrying him and that was that.

Her father stepped forward, halting the men before they could reach the altar.

"Here now, what's this all about?" her father asked.

The man Savannah assumed was the leader pushed aside his suit jacket, and Savannah's eyes widened at the sight of the gun he had holstered at his left side. The congregation began to buzz with whispered questions.

The man unclipped something from his belt and showed it to her father, who automatically took a step back. "I'm Special Agent John Harrison with the Federal Bureau of Investigation," the man announced, turning his head to look at Savannah, whose hands had started to shake, dislodging several of the flowers in her bouquet. Purple and white petals wafted to the floor in front of her, forming a little pile that looked like a grape-flavored Sno-kone at her feet.

"Savannah Taylor?" Agent Harrison asked, looking into her eyes as if he could read all her secrets there.

Savannah tried reminding herself that she couldn't possibly be in trouble with the law. She didn't have so much as an unpaid parking ticket on her rap sheet.

She swallowed, trying to moisten her parched mouth. "Yes," she croaked, waiting for the punchline. Maybe these guys were really strippers that Peggy had hired to come to the bachelorette party, but they'd somehow mixed up their schedule and arrived here at the wedding instead. Or maybe . . .

maybe . . . Savannah's stunned brain couldn't come up with any other scenarios.

Agent Harrison nodded and his two cohorts stepped forward until they were flanking her, their bodies so close that Savannah could have reached out her hands and touched them both. *Okay,* she silently willed them, *go ahead and tear off your pants now. Let's hear the Velcro rip. Give the people of Maple Rapids a reason to talk about my wedding for years to come.*

The FBI agent complied with her request—but not in the way she had meant—when he announced flatly, "You are under arrest for tax evasion and money laundering. You'll have to come with us."

Is He About to Dump You?

You and your fella have been together for a while and that first heat of passion has become more of a flicker than a flame. Still, that's bound to happen in every relationship, right? So how do you tell if this drop in intensity is just your love life running its natural course or whether he's about to say hasta la vista, baby? Take this quiz and find out!

You've just had one of the worst days of your life. Your boss publicly berated you for missing a deadline when you've been waiting on her input for three months, your best friend just announced that she's met Mr. Rich and Perfect, you went to a new hairdresser and your hair looks like something out of *Mad* magazine, *and* you just got your period. When you come home in tears, your own Mr. Not So Rich and Perfect:

a. Laughs and asks if you got your finger caught in a light socket.

b. Cuts you off in the middle of your tearful rant about your bad day and says, "That's nothing. Let me tell you about what happened to *me* today."

c. Pours you a bubble bath and a big glass of wine and rubs your tired feet while listening to you pour your heart out.

If you chose A, we have bad news for you. This guy is a dump truck and he's carrying a full load of manure that's about to land right on your head! If B was your answer, your fella might not be getting ready to walk away, but that may not be good news, either. Who wants a guy whose troubles always trump yours? For you gals with C guys, you're making our hard little hearts go pitter-patter. You'd better start working out so you can hold on to this Mr. Right with all your might!

{two}

"You're not worth the trouble."

Todd's words would have made a great magazine article. "Five Little Words to Break Your Lover's Heart."

Savannah sat at the chrome-and-Formica table in her condo and stared blindly at the piles of paper in front of her. Seven days ago Todd had sat across from her, wincing as she explained the significance of each pile.

"These are credit card statements. The person—I'm assuming it's a woman based on the charges to spas, boutiques, and shoe stores—took out over fifty thousand dollars of credit in my name and maxed out all of these cards. Agent Harrison said I'll need to contact the issuing banks to get this sorted out. In the meantime, my credit is ruined."

Savannah had waved to another pile of papers. "Those are W-2s that were filed under my Social Security number, and over there are copies of bank statements that were mailed to a post office box in Naples, Florida, that had been rented under my name. Agent Harrison believes that the woman who is using my identity is running some sort of money-laundering scheme. When the FBI discovered that I was an accountant, they assumed I was the one who set this up. But after questioning me, Agent Harrison said it was obvious that I was not involved." Savannah paused, then tried to make light of a dark situation. "I'm not sure if I should be flattered or insulted by that."

Todd hadn't laughed. Instead, he wiped a palm down his face, as if trying to wipe away the shock and disbelief clouding his eyes. "So you still have your job, right?" he asked.

"Yes, of course. I haven't done anything wrong. It will just take a while to sort this all out with the banks and the IRS."

She waited for Todd to take her hand and tell her that everything was going to be okay, but he didn't. He'd been distant ever since her father had brought her back to Maple Rapids from the FBI office in Flint the Sunday after their ill-fated wedding ceremony, as if he was worried that if he got too close, her troubles would rub off on him. Which, she supposed, they would. Once they were married, her credit problems became his, too. But wasn't that what marriage was all about? Sticking together through the bad times as well as the good?

Apparently, Todd was one of those people who wanted to rewrite the wedding vows to say, "In fitness and in health, for richer or even richer, until someone better comes along," because when Savannah broached the subject of rescheduling the wedding, his gaze had swept the cluttered table between them as he blurted, "I'm sorry, Savannah, but I can't do this. It's not worth the trouble."

But what he really meant was "*You're* not worth the trouble."

Even now, more than a week later, she couldn't get the words out of her mind.

Savannah laid her head down on the table, the credit-card statements rustling beneath her, the paper cool against her cheek. All her life she'd secretly felt she wasn't fill-in-the-blank enough—not *smart* enough or *pretty* enough or *organized* enough or *ambitious* enough. She wasn't the type of person whom bosses begged to stay when she announced that it was time to move on. Men didn't cross crowded bars to talk to her. Children and dogs didn't leap into her lap when she sat down.

And Todd's defection had just confirmed her suspicions. She wasn't *whatever* enough to keep Todd from leaving when things got tough.

Tears dripped from her eyes and splashed on the pages cradling her cheek. She was supposed to have been back at work yesterday, but not even the news of Mrs. Jackson's successful audit last week could cheer her enough to leave home. Ever since Todd had said those words to her, she had been filled with a lung-squeezing hopelessness that wouldn't let her go. It followed her around everywhere she went, asking "Why bother?" when she half-heartedly contemplated taking a shower or making herself something to eat. Her answer was a despair-filled shrug. The voice was right. Why bother?

She wasn't worth it.

More tears soaked the paper beneath her cheek and she didn't even move her head when a loud knock sounded on her door. Whoever it was would go away soon enough if she didn't answer.

"Savannah, it's Peggy. I know you're in there. Mr. Thorson downstairs says you haven't left your condo for days." Peggy rapped louder on the door, the sound echoing in Savannah's head. She tried to get up—really she did—but her weakened legs didn't have the strength to raise her up out of the chair.

She had a sudden vision of herself, still lying on the table a week from now, credit-card bills and fraudulent bank statements glued to her face with dried-up tears. Her neighbors, alerted by the smell, getting a locksmith to unlock the door and finding her there. The coroner telling her friends and family that she'd died from a broken heart. How romantic it all sounded, as if she were the ill-fated heroine in some old movie.

Savannah heard the deadbolt slide open just before the front door swung inward. Peggy stood in the doorway, juggling a sack of groceries, the glossy bright covers of several of Savannah's favorite magazines poking out the top.

"Go away," Savannah muttered, the words muted by the papers stuck to the side of her face.

Peggy stepped into the condo and looked around at the disarray. Usually, Savannah was a very neat housekeeper. She loved buying organizers from the Hold Everything and Pottery Barn catalogues to keep all of her stuff in order. But ever since Todd had ripped her heart out through her throat, sliced it into tiny pieces, and stomped it to death on the dining room floor, she hadn't had the energy to tidy up. Half-empty bowls of cereal sat atop sticky milk rings on her glass-topped coffee table. Discarded Def Leppard, Bon Jovi, Van Halen, and Poison CDs—all testaments to love gone wrong—were scattered on the oatmeal-colored berber carpeting in front of her new stereo. The two hundred and forty-three remote controls she needed to run the TiVo, TV, DVD, VCR, CD player, and stereo (which she usually kept in a partitioned wicker basket with neatly typed labels to indicate where each remote should go) had disappeared. Savannah vaguely remembered last seeing the TiVo remote in the medicine cabinet in her bathroom, though she had no idea how it had gotten there.

She simply didn't care anymore.

"It's even worse than your mother thought," Peggy muttered to herself as she closed the door behind her and walked into the galley kitchen to set her grocery bag on the Corian countertop.

Savannah blinked, but still didn't move.

The legs of the chrome diner-style chair scraped across the floor as Peggy pulled out the chair Todd had sat in the day he had walked out on Savannah and her problems. Savannah squeezed her eyes shut again as a batch of fresh, hot tears were served up by her overproductive tear ducts. What was so wrong with her? Why couldn't she be the type of woman who *was* worth the trouble? She'd give anything to be that person if only she knew how to change.

"I can't go on living like this," she whispered, finally getting up the strength to pull her head off the table. The top page of a credit-card statement stuck to her wet cheek, and Savannah peeled it off and put it back on the pile.

Peggy stood up and walked around the table, throwing her arms around Savannah's shoulders and squeezing her tight. "It's going to be okay."

Savannah shook her head as she sobbed against her best friend's shoulder and wished that she could believe that.

"Shh," Peggy said, patting Savannah's back comfortingly. "You just can't see that everything will work out right now because you're upset. Besides, this thing with Todd . . . It's not permanent. He's just confused right now. He'll be back. You two are meant for each other."

"I don't think so. He hasn't even called since the day he walked out." Savannah took a shuddering breath and pushed her chair back, letting Peggy give her one last squeeze before ending her hug. Unexpectedly thirsty, she stepped into the kitchen and poured herself a large glass of water. She drank the entire glass before refilling it and bringing it back to the table with her.

Sitting back down, she stared at the two-inch stack of credit-card statements in front of her, statements she'd shuffled through a few times but hadn't really paid much attention to until now.

"I know it seems hard, but things will get better. You'll see," Peggy said as she went into the kitchen to unload the groceries she'd brought. Out of the sack came a handful of magazines, a big bottle of wine, two Lean Cuisines, a bag of grapes, and a Caesar-salad-in-a-bag kit.

"That's just it," Savannah said, shaking her head. "They won't. If I don't change, don't become the sort of woman who *is* worth the trouble, I'm destined to repeat this pattern forever."

The utensils in Savannah's silverware drawer clattered noisily as Peggy rummaged around for a corkscrew to open the bottle of wine. "What are you going to do?" she asked. "It's not like we can just snap our fingers and become someone different."

Savannah picked the credit-card statements up off the table. "Why not? This woman did. She took me—boring accountant Savannah Taylor—and made me over into someone else. Look at this stuff. Five-hundred-dollar Kate Spade boots. Eight hundred dollars' worth of underwear from a fancy lingerie shop in Naples. Expensive dinners, astronomical bar tabs on a Wednesday night. *This* Savannah Taylor isn't like me at all. She has fun. She goes out. I'll bet no man has ever walked out on her." Savannah paused, intently studying the charges marching down page after page. She looked up and met her best friend's gaze before saying softly, "This Savannah Taylor knows how to live. And I am going to go find her."

"What?" Peggy gaped, her mouth open wide as she blinked at Savannah. "Are you nuts?"

"No," Savannah said, suddenly feeling more sure of herself than ever before in her life. This woman, this other Savannah, she grabbed what she wanted, and she didn't care what others thought. And, while Savannah didn't exactly admire that "I'll take what I want and to hell with you" attitude, she *did* envy the other woman's determination to lead a more interesting life.

"I'll bet no man's ever told her *she's* not worth the trouble," Savannah muttered, trying to picture what her alter ego looked like. She envisioned silk thong panties and knee-high boots, a short leather skirt and matching black bustier. When *that* Savannah walked into a crowded bar, men probably abandoned their dates and flocked to her in droves. And it wouldn't just be the clothes that made them stick around, it would be the woman's entire attitude that said, "You'd be lucky to have me." And she wouldn't go by the boring name of Savannah, either. No, she'd be known in her circle as the sexy Vanna T.

"Here, drink this. It'll make you feel better," Peggy said, setting a glass of Chardonnay on top of the credit-card statements in front of Savannah. Then, in an obvious attempt to distract her friend from her misery, she pushed several magazines across the table. The glossy magazines slid over one another, *Cosmo* jockeying for top position with *Glamour* and *Marie Claire,* their headlines teasing readers into believing that within these pages could be found the answers to all of life's problems.

Want a better sex life? *Cosmo* gave you "42 Secrets for Scintillating Sex."

More energy? *Marie Claire* promised "Two Weeks to a Healthier New You."

A more rewarding job? Then take *Glamour*'s monthly quiz to "Find the Right Job for You!"

The funny thing was, right before Todd broke up with her, Savannah had taken a relationship quiz and had been convinced that their bond was strong. No, Todd didn't pour her scented bubble baths or expensive glasses of wine, but that was okay. He was reliable. Dependable. Predictable.

Words that now made Savannah cringe.

Because suddenly she realized that those words best described her. Words that ad executives used to describe washing machines and adult diapers also applied to her.

God, no wonder Todd had walked out on her. Men didn't

want reliable, dependable, and predictable. They wanted sexy, fun, and adventurous. They wanted women like Vanna T.

"Oh, look. Here's one of those quizzes you like so much." Peggy's voice was infused with just the right amount of phony enthusiasm—the sort that Savannah always used when trying to get her three-year-old niece to stop trying to bite the cat and come watch *Monsters, Inc.* for the four thousandth time instead. "Come on, let's take it together."

Savannah let Peggy pull her up out of the dining room chair and followed her best friend over to the couch, where Peggy made quick work of clearing up the dishes and wiping sticky milk off the coffee table.

"Here, this will be fun," Peggy said, plopping down on Savannah's prized off-white leather couch. Savannah loved this couch, loved how the cool leather warmed to her skin and how she could change the look of her living room just by switching the pillows or the knickknacks arranged neatly on the coffee table. Right now the pillows were a soft chocolate brown with tiny red diamonds patterned into the fabric. A set of red candles with burnished brass holders were scattered about the room, and Savannah had draped the softest red chenille blanket over one edge of the couch.

Normally Savannah felt comfortably at home in her three-bedroom, two-bath condo, a home she'd purchased just two years out of college. But now she couldn't help thinking how sad it was that she'd lived in the same place since she was twenty-four years old. Sad . . . and boring.

Boring, boring, boring.

She didn't need some magazine quiz to tell her that.

"This quiz will tell you which goddess you are," Peggy said, still with that same fake enthusiasm she'd used earlier. "Okay, here's the first question. What is most important to you? A, romance and passion. B, your career. C, learning new things. Or, D, children?" Peggy seemed to think about it for a moment before saying, "That's easy. D. I really want to have kids." Peggy searched around for a pen and then marked her answer on the thin page of the magazine. Then she asked, "What's your answer? I'll bet it's B."

"I don't know," Savannah said, although B had been her

first choice. She knew it sounded silly, but she actually liked her job, liked knowing how much it helped people to have someone who knew what they were doing to file their taxes or help prepare for an audit. But she was tired of being predictable, so she clutched a pillow to her chest and said, "A, romance and passion."

"Really?" Peggy looked at her, her eyes wide with surprise.

"Yes. That's what I said," Savannah snapped. Was it so hard to believe that she had a passionate side?

"Sor-r-ry," Peggy muttered as she marked Savannah's answer in the magazine.

Savannah closed her eyes and shook her head at herself. "No, I'm sorry. I shouldn't have snapped at you. I've had a rough couple of weeks."

Peggy reached out and squeezed her hand. "I know."

"What's the next question?" Savannah asked, trying to muster up some interest in this for Peggy's sake.

"Are you sure you want to do this? I mean, we can watch a movie or something instead."

"No, it's all right. This is fun," Savannah lied, setting aside her pillow as she leaned forward to pick up her wine. She took a large swallow and sat back, letting the couch envelop her in its comforting embrace.

"Okay, this is a good one. When it comes to sex, you: A, can't get enough of it; B, have a hard time relaxing at first but end up enjoying it; C, could take it or leave it; or, D, enjoy pleasing your partner more than yourself."

Savannah took another swig of wine and tried not to blush. She and Peggy had been best friends since the third grade, and of course they had talked about sex over the years, but Savannah never felt all that comfortable around the topic. So, okay, she knew her answer was B, but that wasn't the answer she wanted to give. She *wanted* to say "A." She wanted to feel so comfortable in her own body that sex was not something she was vaguely embarrassed about. And really, she liked sex. She just had to distract her brain from thinking about how ridiculous she looked and sounded to enjoy it.

But maybe that was the key. If she could convince herself that she couldn't get enough of sex instead of worrying about what she was doing, then she could actually answer "A" to this question. Maybe then she could become the confident woman she wanted to be.

"Could I see that?" Savannah asked, gripped by a new idea.

"Uh, sure," Peggy said as she let the magazine go.

Savannah flipped to the end of the quiz and quickly read the key. This one was easy because all the A answers went with one type of goddess, all the B's with another, and so on. Savannah scanned the four goddess types: Aphrodite, goddess of love; Athena, ruled by her head and not her heart; Persephone, spiritual and independent; and Demeter, giver of life. Aphrodite was the goddess she most wanted to be like— feminine, full of unbridled passion and sexuality. The clincher, however, was when Savannah read, "Men are drawn to you Aphrodite gals like bears to honey."

That was the thing. They weren't, but Savannah wanted them to be. If only Aphrodite were her goddess, Todd would never have left her.

And this, this magazine quiz, was going to tell her exactly what to do to transform herself into that type of woman. Romance and passion were going to become vitally important to her. Sex was going to become something she couldn't live without.

She was going to transform herself into a sex goddess, a woman who drew men to her, a woman who was worth any amount of trouble she put a man through, if it was the last thing she ever did.

What Your Car Reveals About You

Okay, let's see a show of hands here—who was surprised when Susan Sarandon and Geena Davis drove their Thunderbird convertible off the cliff at the end of Thelma & Louise? I'll bet not one of you has your paw in the air, because you all know that girls who drive convertibles are fun and exciting and live life to its fullest . . . and to hell with the consequences. Want to know what your car says about you? Read on!

You just inherited a large sum of money from your dear aunt Mildred, and one of the stipulations is that you have to use at least half of your windfall to buy yourself a new set of wheels. You stuff your purse full of hundred-dollar bills and you're off to the car lot. When you drive off the lot two hours later, you're driving:

a. A sensible tan sedan with plenty of trunk space and lots of leg room in the backseat for your friends.

b. A green hybrid with a cramped interior that makes it impossible for you to drive without wrapping your right leg up around your neck to get it out of the way—but who cares? It has low emissions, will help save the environment, and will funnel the smallest amount of money possible to the big bad oil companies.

c. A metallic blue convertible with gray leather interior and an engine that'll take you from zero to eighty in three-point-two seconds without even mussing your hair.

continues on next page . . .

You A gals are so dull, we're surprised you're not asleep at the wheel! What's next for you? A minivan? Goldfish? A nice little house in the suburbs with two-and-a-half kids and a Labrador retriever? Yeah, sounds like an exciting life to us. Not! Those of you who chose B are to be commended on your environmental consciousness . . . but come on, do you really think you're going to change the world one little Kermit-the-frog car at a time? In a few years the world's entire oil reserves are going to be depleted and single-occupant vehicles are going to go the way of the dinosaur. You might as well enjoy the ride for now like the rest of us! As for you C girls . . . do you mind if we hitch a ride? We'll bet you have more adventures on your way to the grocery store than those A and B gals have during their entire lifetimes!

{three}

So far, Savannah wasn't having much luck convincing the people around her that she had become a new person.

On Wednesday, the day after she'd made her decision to transform herself into someone exciting and sexy and irresistible, she'd bought out Super ShopMart's entire selection of women's magazines. On her lunch break she'd taken *Stylish* magazine's "Seven Sexiest New Looks" to the department store next to her office and had enlisted the aid of a commission-smelling salesperson to help her replicate all seven looks. She'd donned look #1 on Thursday morning, squinting at herself in the full-length mirror hanging on the back of her bedroom door.

Look #1 was Casual Chic—a below-the-knee-length dark purple-and-green plaid skirt topped with a white T-shirt and fitted denim blouse. Savannah felt fairly confident about the hiking boots that *Stylish*'s fashionistas had paired with the ensemble, but she wasn't quite so sure about the large furry hat covering her hair. It looked like a giant beaver had curled up on her head and died.

She turned around, trying to get a glimpse of what she looked like from the back.

"Mirror, mirror, on the wall, please tell me this doesn't look ridiculous after all," she said to her reflection.

The magazine lay open on her bed, the pages showing a

model wearing nearly the same outfit as Savannah standing at the edge of a mountain lake looking pensively off into the distance. Savannah wondered why the model looked so thoughtful. Perhaps she was contemplating what would happen if the beaver awoke from the dead and mistook her skinny neck for a tasty sapling.

Shaking her head ruefully, Savannah pulled the hat off her head. No way could she wear that into the office. She felt like an idiot . . . and now she couldn't seem to stop humming a song about Davy Crockett that she'd learned as a Girl Scout. The words of the childhood song echoed through her head as she ran her fingers through her hair to unflatten it. Then she pushed aside the dead-beaver hat, grabbed her purse, and left for work.

She entered the office, pausing to see if any of her coworkers would notice her trendy new look. When no one said anything except "good morning," Savannah chalked it up to everyone being so busy that they just didn't notice. Not that it mattered, she told herself as she made her way to her desk. What was important was that *she* could feel the transformation inside herself. Others would pick up on the changes in her personality soon enough.

On Friday Savannah tested out Look #2—Parisian Romance—which consisted of a pair of slim-fitting black pants, a sheer blouse that showed off the model's trim waistline but that Savannah wore over a tank top to hide her not-so-slender stomach, and knee-high boots with green, orange, and pink flowers appliquéd all over them. This look, too, came with a fuzzy hat—apparently, hats were hot this season—a doughnut-shaped black one that had a much lower dead-beaver quotient than yesterday's had.

"I'll bet Vanna would feel perfectly comfortable in something like this," Savannah assured herself as she twisted first to the left and then to the right in order to get a 360-degree view of herself in her bedroom mirror. And, actually, she didn't look all that bad. The hat was maybe a bit *haute couture* for Maple Rapids, but it was sort of Audrey Hepburn-ish, which wasn't exactly a bad thing.

With a reassuring nod to her reflection, she left her condo and headed to work, again pausing in the doorway to see if anyone would comment on her glamorous new look. She even went so far as to pirouette in front of the front window, raising her arms wide as if to welcome in the weak, late winter sun.

"Hey, Savannah. Your mother dropped by a few minutes ago on her way to the mall. She said to remind you to pick up the cake for your niece's birthday party tomorrow," her coworker Josh said without looking up from his computer screen.

"As if I could forget," Savannah muttered under her breath. Her mother had left a message on Savannah's voice mail at home last night and had sent her two e-mails yesterday to remind her to pick up the cake before the party on Saturday. It wasn't like Savannah was particularly forgetful, but no matter how many times she protested the constant reminders, her mother still treated her as if she were eight years old and prone to leaving her lunch on the kitchen counter every morning when she left for school.

With a loud sigh Savannah pushed the hat out of her eyes and clomped noisily back to her desk in her new boots, which were cute but weren't exactly practical given that there was still a foot of snow on the ground outside. She wiggled her toes and grimaced when she realized that the suede was damp and cold with melting slush. She reached down and turned on the small floor heater that all the women in the office had sitting under their desks. It didn't seem fair that the guys were always warm no matter what temperature it was inside the office, while the women froze throughout most of the winter and spring. The building manager had banned the heaters last year when Savannah had turned hers on one frigid November morning, only to blow out half the computers in the office when the power surge overloaded the circuits. But slowly, like mold spots appearing on a block of cheddar cheese, the heaters had returned.

Savannah shivered as the warm air finally managed to penetrate her wet boots and hoped the suede wouldn't shrink-wrap itself to her feet as it dried.

The next morning she got up at the same time as usual, even though it was Saturday and it wasn't her weekend to go into the office. She'd brought her laptop home, along with several of her clients' files. With just seven weeks to go until

April 15, she was working long hours to get tax returns filed on time. She yawned as she pulled back the curtain after her shower and stepped out into the steamy bathroom.

"So much for my exciting new life," she said to herself as she wiped a clean spot on the mirror so she could do her makeup. She'd worked past midnight last night, quitting only when she realized that she'd entered the client's wages, salary, and tips into lines 7, 8a, and 10, thereby tripling his income . . . and his anticipated tax burden. She planned to work for a few hours this morning, then go pick up the clown cake her mother had ordered for her niece's birthday party before heading to her parents' house.

Savannah yawned again as she finished drying her hair, ruthlessly straightening out the dark locks' natural inclination to curl. When she was finished, she padded out into the bedroom and contemplated the clothes hanging in her closet.

If she were to follow the "Seven Sexiest New Looks" article to the number, she'd be wearing look #3—Ski Bunny—today. The problem, however, was that Ski Bunny consisted of form-fitting white pants with a silver chain around the waist and a fur-trimmed white cardigan with a matching tank. Savannah figured it would take less than four minutes for her niece, Amanda, to wipe blue or red frosting on her all-white outfit—most likely on the crotch or butt for full comedic effect.

"No, thank you," she said, shaking her head at the vision of sticky fingerprints all over her ass. Instead, she decided to go with Look #4, Little Red Riding Hood. First, she pulled a pair of thick black tights on over her white Jockeys. Then she slid on a red-and-black tartan skirt that seemed shorter today than it had when she'd tried it on on Wednesday. Why was it that new clothes always seemed tighter or shorter or more revealing once you got them home?

Next, she tugged a thin red sweater on over her head and straightened the hem, then added the *pièce de résistance*—a hooded knit capelet dyed to match her sweater. The capelet had a hook-and-eye closure at the neck and a drawstring that ran around the hood so she could close it around her nose like she and her sisters had done with their ski jackets when they were kids. At each end of the drawstring were two large pom-poms that would send her parents' cat to kitty heaven.

As she turned back toward the closet to get the black boots that would complete her ensemble, Savannah found herself twirling the strings of her capelet, making the pom-poms fly in front of her face until they crashed together.

She could tell that it wasn't going to be easy to resist playing with those things throughout the day.

She set off to the kitchen, feeling very much like Little Red Riding Hood in her little red cape, and finding it difficult not to skip. She couldn't wait to see her family's reaction to her new look when she arrived this afternoon. If her mother disapproved, Savannah figured she was on the right track.

She hid her smile as she made herself a pot of coffee and picked up the latest edition of *Cosmo* as she waited for the coffee to finish brewing. She was flipping to an article about "Awesome Sex Tricks That Will Triple His Pleasure"—not that it looked like she'd need those tips anytime soon, unfortunately—when she passed a quiz that was supposed to be able to predict your personality based on the kind of car you drove.

"I can just imagine what they have to say about my beige Toyota," Savannah said with a grimace as she slid her thumb into the magazine to mark her place while pouring herself a cup of coffee.

She brought her cup and the magazine to the dining room table and pushed out a chair with the tip of her boot, scanning the quiz. As she suspected, *Cosmo*'s quiz masters didn't pull any punches about telling her how dull she was to own a tan sedan.

"Like I don't know that already," she said, taking a sip of her hot coffee and nearly falling off her chair when her phone rang.

"Mom, if that's you calling to remind me about the cake again, I'm going to hang up on you," she warned as she crossed the room to find the receiver. She looked at the caller ID display and rolled her eyes heavenward, praying for patience when she saw that it was her parents' number. "I won't forget to pick up the cake," she said by way of greeting.

Her father cleared his throat. "Uh, good. We'll expect you around noon, then."

Savannah shook her head disgustedly and ended the call.

She was going to have to find a way to put a stop to this constant nagging. Maybe *Cosmo* had a quiz for it.

She was halfway back to the dining room when the phone rang again. Savannah clenched her teeth in anticipation of yet another call about the blasted birthday cake, then unclenched them again when she saw that it was Todd calling, not her mother. She took a deep breath and stared at the number on the display.

What could he be calling about? She'd already packed up the things he'd left at her condo over the years and left the boxes on the stairs leading up to the apartment his parents had built for him over their garage. Was it possible that maybe, just maybe, he wanted her back?

Savannah took a deep breath and willed herself to answer the phone, unsure of what her response would be if Todd asked her to forgive him. He had really hurt her by not standing by her when she got arrested. But maybe he had realized what a mistake he had made by letting her go. Maybe being without her all this time had made him see that she *was* worth the trouble.

Well, she'd never know if she didn't take his call.

With trembling fingers Savannah pressed the Talk button on her phone and croaked out a hoarse, "Hello."

"Savannah? Is that you?"

She closed her eyes. His voice was so familiar. Before this week they'd talked at least once or twice a day every day since they'd first started dating. God, she missed that closeness, that intimacy that they had shared.

"Yes, Todd. It's me," she whispered.

"Oh. Well, are you all right? You sound kind of funny," he said.

Savannah opened her eyes and pressed the phone more tightly to her ear. "I'm fine," she said. "How are you?"

"Good, good," Todd answered, sounding a bit uncomfortable.

Savannah had read enough women's magazines in her lifetime to know that she should make Todd grovel and beg to get back together with her . . . but she didn't have it in her heart to make him suffer. The truth was, she missed their relationship, and, besides, she still hadn't returned any of the wedding gifts. Now maybe she wouldn't have to.

Todd cleared his throat. "I, uh, stopped at your office on my way to work this morning, but you weren't there."

Savannah tried to stem the rising tide of hope welling up in her chest and making her feel light-headed. "No," she said, swallowing to get some saliva back into her suddenly dry mouth. "I'm not going in to the office today."

"Ah. Well, I needed to talk to you." Todd cleared his throat again and Savannah frowned. She'd forgotten about Todd's constant throat-clearing. He really ought to go see someone about that.

"About what?" she asked. She held her breath, waiting for Todd to ask her if she'd take him back and knowing—despite what the magazines might advise—that her answer would be yes.

"About my taxes," Todd answered. "I need you to do them again this year. They're really complicated. I made a lot of money last year, you know. I was top salesman in all of upper Michigan," he announced proudly.

Savannah felt the phone slip from her grasp and tightened her grip. He wanted her to do his taxes? After dumping her in her hour of need? Why that stupid, selfish, no-good—

"I think I'm getting a refund, so I was hoping you could file my return by Monday. Robert wants me to go to Vegas with him, and I think that's just what the doctor ordered after all I've been through this past month," Todd continued.

"After all *you've* been through?" Savannah repeated incredulously.

"Well, yeah. Watching you get hauled off at the altar wasn't exactly easy for me, you know."

Todd sounded hurt. Savannah wished he were here so she could show him what hurt really was. The rat bastard.

"I'm not doing your taxes for you," she said through teeth clenched so tightly together that she was certain her molars would be ground flat.

"That's ridiculous. You've done them for years. You have all the history. It'll be a snap."

"I'd like to snap something. Your neck!" Savannah nearly yelled.

"Geez, forget it. I never expected you to get emotional about this. It's only my taxes."

"Not get emotional?" Savannah sputtered. "You think we're just going to have a business relationship after you dumped me like that?"

"Well, yeah. Why not? I mean, if you were in the market for a new car, I wouldn't hesitate to give you a good deal. But maybe that's just the kind of guy I am," Todd said, sounding so sanctimonious that Savannah wished she could reach through the phone line and yank his tonsils out through his nose.

"You know what, Todd? I *am* in the market for a new car. And you can bet your tax refund that I'm sure as hell not buying it from you." With that, Savannah slammed the phone back down on its charger. Seething with rage, she grabbed her purse and the magazine with the car quiz in it and marched out into the snow.

By the time she turned her sedan onto Maple Rapids' version of auto row (there were only two car dealers in the entire town—one owned by Todd's father and the other by Chip Hadley, whose son Barry had graduated from high school with Savannah), Savannah had cooled down enough to realize that she wasn't so much angry at Todd and his request that she do his taxes as she was hurt that he didn't want her back. She felt foolish for even thinking for one moment that he might.

"How many times does he have to tell you that it's over before you get it into your thick skull?" she asked her reflection in the rearview mirror as she turned into Chip Hadley's car lot.

Mr. Hadley kept his lot free of the hard, icy snow that packed the ground, and Savannah figured some poor high school kid had the job of cleaning frost from the cars' windshields every morning, because they, too, were frost-free. She parked her Toyota in the middle of the lot and stepped out of her car. When a blast of chill wind hit her bare-but-for-a-pair-of-thick-tights legs, she wished her hooded capelet was longer. It might be cute, but it was no match for Michigan's winter weather.

As soon as her booted feet hit the ground, a salesman came through the front door, cupping his hands and blowing into them before pushing them into the pockets of his dark gray overcoat.

"Hello, ma'am. Can I help you?" the salesman asked.

Savannah turned to find that the salesman was none other

than her old classmate, Barry Hadley. "Hey, Barry," she said. "I'm looking for something less . . . beige." She waved dismissively toward the reliable car she'd purchased used eight years ago and that still showed no sign of breaking down anytime soon. She reminded herself that her sexy new persona would not drive a brown car, and that Todd's earlier dismissal of her only hammered home once more the fact that, in order to be unforgettable to the opposite sex, she had to do something drastic to change who she was. Otherwise, she'd never find a man who was willing to walk through fire for her.

"Hi, Savannah. How are you?" Barry asked, taking one large hand out of his pocket to clap her on the shoulder.

"I'm good. I'm looking for a new car." She laughed a little nervously. "Obviously, I mean, what else would I be here for? To buy a refrigerator?"

Barry smiled and Savannah waited for him to lead her to one of the sleek sports cars near the front of the lot, but, instead, Barry led her over to a row of sedans that looked nearly identical to the car she owned now and said, "We have a nice selection of vehicles this time of year. Now, you can't go wrong with any of these models. They're fuel efficient, reliable, low maintenance—"

"No, wait," Savannah interrupted, holding up her hand to stop him before he could get too far into his spiel. "I don't want reliable and low maintenance. I want fun. Sporty. Sexy. You know . . . hot. Do you have something in red?"

Barry's dark brows drew together when he frowned. He scratched the back of his head. "Red's not very practical. Studies have shown that people who own red cars get nearly twice the number of speeding tickets."

"I don't want practical," Savannah protested. "I've had practical all my life, and, to be honest, it sucks."

Barry pursed his lips. "What's your price range?"

Savannah thought about her dwindling bank account— sorely depleted after the wedding that had ended in such disaster plus her recent shopping spree. And with her identity thief out there racking up enormous bills in Savannah's name, she couldn't rely on credit. Even if she could get a loan right now, the interest rate would be exorbitant. "I've got my trade-in," she said with a nod toward the sedan. "That plus four thousand two hundred and fifty-two dollars is all I've got left."

Barry rubbed his chin thoughtfully for a moment. "You say you want something fun and sporty, huh?" he asked.

Savannah nodded.

"And you don't care if it's high maintenance?" he asked.

Savannah shook her head.

"All right. Follow me," Barry said and took off toward the far corner of the lot with Savannah at his heels.

When he stopped and stepped to one side, Savannah gasped. He waved grandly at a red-and-white Thunderbird convertible with gleaming chrome trim. "There she is," he announced.

"It's perfect," Savannah whispered.

"It's not practical," Barry argued.

"I know," Savannah answered.

"And it doesn't come with any of the options you'd expect with a newer car. No heated seats, no GPS, no CD player. I'm not even sure it has air-conditioning," he warned.

"I love it," Savannah said, taking a step closer and tentatively reaching out her hand to touch the smooth chrome. Now, this was a car that said something about a woman. She pictured herself driving around town on a warm summer day, the top down, her hair blowing wildly in the breeze, waving to Todd as she passed by his father's car lot as if to say, "All of this could have been yours, if only you'd stuck with me."

"She's in good condition for as old as she is, and you can buy the extended warranty, but it's not going to be cheap."

Savannah pulled open the heavy door and slid into the driver's seat. The worn leather grabbed hold of her and held her tight, as if the car wanted her as much as she wanted it. She caressed the steering wheel longingly. This was her car. She could feel it.

"Let me just get the key. I'll be right back." Barry obviously smelled a sale and trotted back to the sales office, returning in short order with the key to the T-bird. It only took him a few minutes to show her how to raise and lower the roof, and they discovered that the car did have air-conditioning.

Barry backed the car off the lot and then stepped out, holding the door open for her. He'd left the top down despite the cold and cranked the heater on high. "Have fun," he said with a grin.

Savannah slipped back into the driver's seat and tilted her head up to gaze at the overcast sky overhead. Hot air blew from the heater, warming her legs as she pulled out of the lot. As she passed the Everard's dealership, she saw a familiar figure waving at her, trying to get her attention.

Todd. Probably annoyed at seeing the potential commission slip through his fingers.

She ignored him and kept going, past the Dairy Queen where she'd worked during high school and the elementary school she'd attended as a child. The chill wind nipped her face, turning her nose red, but Savannah didn't care. She felt free for the first time in a long time, as if by shedding her old car, she really was shedding at least some part of her old, boring self.

The temptation to raise her hands in the air and yell with abandon was almost too great to resist, but Savannah managed to keep both hands on the wheel. Still, she couldn't stifle her grin as she passed the park at Main Street and returned the wave from a dark-haired little girl who had stopped to stare when Savannah drove by.

With the wind ruffling her hair and the heavy car beneath her, Savannah began to think that maybe—just maybe—becoming the person she wanted to be might not be impossible after all.

Your Family

Should You Take 'Em or Leave 'Em?

Ah, family ties. As humorist Erma Bombeck once said, these are the ties that bind . . . and gag! Does your mother constantly nag you about giving her grandchildren before she gasps her final breath? Do you run to Daddy every time your kitchen pipes spring a leak? Is your little sister still stealing your money, your clothes, and your boyfriends? And how can you tell if this is just normal behavior or if it qualifies your relatives for the Dysfunctional Family Hall of Shame? Take our quiz, of course!

Your big sister is getting married to the perfect guy—he's handsome, he's gainfully employed, and he's even nice to your horrible aunt Gertrude—but they've made it clear that they aren't having children. You dumped your boyfriend a week ago when you mentioned that you'd gained five pounds from sampling all those wedding cakes with your sister and the b-friend told you that you looked like a giant eggplant in your purple bridesmaid dress. At the rehearsal dinner your mother takes you aside and says:

a· She can't believe you'd embarrass your sister by showing up to her wedding without a date. Then she reminds you that she's counting on you to keep the family name alive and encourages you to hook up with the groom's uncle, who is about forty years older than you but can't seem to keep his eyes off your breasts.

b· It just figures that you got dumped. Your big sister is the only one in the family whom she and your dad ever expected would amount to anything. This is just like the time back in kindergarten when you—(You stop listen-

continues on next page . . .

ing at this point because you've heard this refrain so many times.)

c· She's so happy that both of her girls are so well adjusted. She knows that you don't need a man to make you complete, and she would rather see you alone than in an unhealthy relationship. Besides, she has a full life of her own and grandchildren just aren't that important to her.

If you picked A or B . . . Well, we're sorry for the cliché, but your family puts the "fun" in dysfunctional! Have you ever thought of moving? We've heard that Siberia is nice this time of year. For those of you who picked C, do you think your parents are interested in adopting? We know several gals who would be interested in being your sisters!

{ four }

After twenty minutes with her family, Savannah began to realize that the problem with trying to become someone new in a place where you've lived your whole life is that the people you've grown up with just don't seem to be capable of letting the old you go.

She set the white carton containing her niece's birthday cake on the counter in her parents' newly remodeled kitchen and pretended that she couldn't hear her mother and Miranda whispering about her as they dished mashed potatoes and creamed peas into serving dishes. She could hear snippets of their conversation—phrases like "just a stage she's going through" and "how can she sit in that short skirt" and "been acting strange ever since Todd left her" were muttered as though they thought they were speaking in some foreign language that Savannah couldn't understand.

She wondered if Vanna had a close family. Probably not, since Savannah hadn't seen any charges to mental health counselors on the credit-card bills Agent Harrison had given her.

The lucky bitch.

Savannah sighed, adjusted the capelet that *Stylish* magazine had proclaimed "the season's can't-do-without piece," and helped ferry serving dishes from the kitchen out to the dining room table where the rest of her family was seated. The ties of her capelet were a bit too long so she pulled the loops of the bow wider so the pom-poms wouldn't drag in the gravy.

She supposed she shouldn't be so annoyed. At least her family had noticed her new look.

Savannah sat down at her usual place on the left side of the table as Mom and Miranda brought out the last of the food from the kitchen.

"Are you sure you're not cold?" her mother asked for what had to be the hundredth time since Savannah had arrived. The question was asked with a pointed glance toward the skirt Savannah was wearing. When she was standing up, it was a relatively demure mid-thigh length, but when she sat down, it crept way closer to her crotch than she had expected. Good thing her tights kept her legs warm.

"I'm fine, Mom," she answered.

There was a slight silence around the table, and Savannah shifted uncomfortably in her seat. She knew what was coming next.

"So, you bought yourself a new car," Miranda said in that mock-innocent voice that made Savannah want to hurl peas across the table at her.

"Yes. Yes, I did," Savannah said.

"You should have taken Dad with you," her mother admonished, passing the mashed potatoes to her right.

Savannah looked over at her father, who appeared to be counting the number of pearl onions on his fork. Miranda busied herself with cutting her daughter Amanda's roast beef into tiny bite-sized pieces while her husband Alex craned his neck to watch the Pistons versus the Lakers game that was silently playing on the TV set beyond Miranda's head. Belinda had excused herself a few minutes ago when her cell phone rang. Savannah was really beginning to envy her sister's built-in escape route.

She took a huge bite of potatoes smothered in gravy and, because she knew it would annoy her mother, said, "I'm capable of buying a new car by myself," around the food in her mouth.

Her mother frowned but didn't mention the breach in her daughter's table manners. "You never told your father and me that you were thinking of buying a new car."

"And did you factor in maintenance and fuel costs when comparing prices to a newer vehicle? I mean, that thing you bought is just going to eat up your savings with repair bills," Miranda said, looking up from her daughter's neatly cut-up food.

Savannah swallowed her mashed potatoes and wiped her mouth with a paper napkin. "What savings?" she asked, reaching for one of her mother's yeast rolls. "I used the last of my money to buy the car. I guess I'll just have to pray that it doesn't fall apart on me."

Miranda gasped and her mother put a hand to her chest as if Savannah had just announced that she'd intentionally run over a basket full of kittens. Nobody in their family did rash, impractical things like spending their entire savings on a hot car. But Savannah couldn't hold back a smile. The thrill of driving around this afternoon with the top down and the heater (and stereo) blasting had been worth it.

"You didn't?" her mother gasped.

Savannah straightened her shoulders, barely catching her capelet as it slid sideways and nearly ended up in her plate. "Yes, I did," she said proudly. "I handed Barry Hadley a check this afternoon."

"But we've bought our cars from the Everards since before you were even born. Al Everard would never have let you spend your entire savings on a car. That Mr. Hadley doesn't even know us." Her mother looked around the table at the shocked faces of the rest of her family.

Savannah scowled. "Well, after Al's son dumped me practically at the altar, I hardly think we owe him any more loyalty, do you?"

"It wasn't like that, and you know it," her mother protested.

"Besides, the Everards always give us a discount. That Hadley boy probably charged you full price," her father added, apparently so horrified at her defection that he felt it necessary to join the conversation at last.

"At least tell us that you researched prices on the Internet first," Miranda chimed in.

"And you *had* to have checked out *Consumer Reports*," her brother-in-law said, shaking his head as if to say that he just knew this never would have occurred to her.

Savannah pushed her plate away and stared open-mouthed

at her family. Did they think she was totally incompetent? That she couldn't even do something as simple as buying a car without their guidance?

How was she ever going to change—to become someone who was fun-loving and confident and brash—if she continually had to fight her family's low expectations?

At that moment Belinda came out of the kitchen, where she had taken her phone call, her arms laden down with the brightly colored clown-shaped birthday cake Savannah had picked up at the Super ShopMart on her way over. Belinda had lit the four sparkler candles that the bakery had included with the cake and, unaware of the tension in the dining room, stepped through the swinging door brightly singing "Happy Birthday" to their niece.

After an awkward pause, everyone joined in, including Savannah, who—annoyed as she might be—wouldn't hurt four-year-old Amanda's feelings for anything. Belinda set the cake down in front of the girl, who was sitting across from Savannah, and said, "Okay, make a wish and blow out the candles."

Amanda closed her eyes and moved her lips as if she were reading to herself. Savannah wondered what her niece was wishing for—probably a horse, since that's what was always on the top of her wish list at every gift-giving occasion. Amanda was smiling when she opened her eyes again and drew in a deep breath. Then she blew with all her might. The candles flickered and went out, and Amanda grinned.

"You blew them all out," Miranda said approvingly, patting her daughter on the back. "That means you get what you—"

At that moment the candles lit back up again. The bakery had obviously given Savannah those trick candles that you couldn't blow out. Unfortunately, what was supposed to be a joke wasn't exactly funny to the four-year-old, who obviously thought that since she hadn't managed to blow out the candles, she wouldn't be getting her wish after all.

Amanda started to wail. "I wanna horsey!"

Miranda shot Savannah an accusing glare as she gathered her daughter in her arms. "I know you do, baby. Don't cry. Auntie Savannah didn't mean to pull a trick on you. She just doesn't know any better."

"I didn't pick out the candles," Savannah protested, scooting her chair back and leaning over to take the offending items off her niece's cake.

"You should have checked them," Miranda scolded, still rubbing her daughter's back.

It was at that exact moment that Savannah knew she could not continue living like this. She loved her family—really, she did. But they were making it impossible for her to change her life and become the person she wanted to be. If she remained here, she would always be exactly what she was now: incompetent, obedient . . . and alone.

She had to leave. Now. Or she'd be trapped like this forever.

And she knew exactly where she was going to go. Naples. Where her alter ego had charged up thousands of dollars in Savannah's name. Agent Harrison had told her that it would be nearly impossible to successfully bring Vanna to trial, even if they did manage to catch her. It was more likely that they would never find anything to tie her to the crime. Plus, since 9/11, the FBI just didn't have the manpower to commit to these nonviolent criminals. But Savannah wasn't interested in bringing Vanna to justice. She just wanted to meet the woman who had taken her identity and done so much more with it than Savannah ever had.

She grabbed all four still-lit candles off the cake and blew them out, wondering how many lives had been transformed as a direct result of family dinners.

Then she squealed and raced from the room when she realized that the candles had sprung to life again, catching the pom-poms on her capelet on fire. She refused to take this as an omen that her dreams of a new life were about to go up in smoke.

Home Sweet Home

Who says that where you live doesn't say a lot about who you are?
Not us! We believe your address—not your eyes—is the window to
your soul. So, what does where you live say about you? Take this quiz
and find out!

Say you could reside anywhere your little heart desired.
Which would you choose?

a· **The house you grew up in, which is the same house**
    where your mother and her mother before her were
    raised.

b· **A tent in some mosquito-infested country where you**
    moved when you dedicated your life to the Peace Corps.

c· **A condo overlooking the beach in Ft. Lauderdale with a**
    dozen trendy bars and restaurants on the first floor and
    plenty of great shopping nearby.

We pity you gals who picked A—don't you know there's a whole wide
world out there to explore? For those of you who chose B, we com-
mend you on your altruistic nature, but come on! You can't live off of
granola and tree bark forever. One of these days you're going to have
to move out of the commune and get your own place! You C girls un-
derstand just what we're talking about. Life is meant to be enjoyed, so
grab that glass of Chardonnay and your brand-new Coach purse and
let's party!

{five}

Two weeks, two days, and one hour later, Savannah got her wish: She was *hot*. As she stepped out of the T-bird in the parking lot of the quaintly named but not so quaint-looking Sand Dunes Motel tucked just off the touristy Sunshine Parkway in Naples, Florida, she wiped the sweat off her upper lip. How in the world could it be eighty degrees here when the snow was barely beginning to melt back in Maple Rapids?

Leaving home had been surprisingly easy. Savannah hadn't wanted to bring anything that would hinder her transformation (like her tattered but comfortable Michigan State sweats or her old furniture), so she'd limited herself to only those things that would fit with her new lifestyle. Which pretty much meant she'd loaded only a few necessary items of clothing in addition to her "Seven Sexiest New Looks" into the trunk of her new car and had left everything else behind. She'd rented her furnished condo to Peggy, who had been looking to move from her one-bedroom apartment for months, but just hadn't found the right place. Savannah knew Peggy would take care of her stuff, and Peggy was thrilled to move into a place that she couldn't afford to buy on her salary, so they were both happy.

Savannah's family had, of course, tried to talk her out of leaving, but she wouldn't budge. She was determined to strike out on her own—with or without her family's blessing. And so, on the cold but clear Saturday morning after Savannah had worked out her two weeks' notice (and despite the fact that her boss had actually gone down on his knees and begged her not to leave), Savannah set off to find herself. Or rather, to find Vanna, who was herself, only better.

On the journey south on Interstate 75, Savannah shed layer after layer of clothing, losing her sweaters outside of Lexington, her jeans in Chattanooga, and her long-sleeved shirts around Macon. She had seen more sunshine in the last three days than she had in three months back home. For her arrival in Naples, Savannah had decided to dress for the occasion. This was going to be a day she'd remember for the rest of her life, and she wanted to be dressed appropriately.

Unfortunately, all of her new clothes were more suitable for the cold weather in Michigan than early spring in the tropics. So Savannah improvised, swapping out a red T-shirt for the sweater that had gone with her Little Red Riding Hood look and forgoing the capelet that had gotten her here in the first place. (She'd cut the half-burnt pom-poms off after the birthday candle incident and tied the ends in knots so they wouldn't fray. No need to throw the baby out with the bathwater, as the saying went.) She felt a little strange wearing her black boots with no tights, but the thought of trying to struggle into pantyhose in eighty-degree weather was worse than the sight of her bare, pasty white legs reflecting back at her in the front window as she headed toward the office of the Sand Dunes Motel.

She'd chosen this location carefully after studying a map of Naples on MapQuest last night at a no-name motel south of Tampa. She'd wanted to arrive in Naples fresh and ready to take everything in, so instead of pushing herself to drive the last few hours last night, she'd stopped early enough to get a real dinner at the motel's restaurant instead of grabbing something from a bag and continuing on her journey. Her room had been nice enough; it was clean and Savannah could still smell faint traces of fresh paint when she first stepped into the room. Best of all, the motel provided Internet service at a reasonable $9.99 per day, so with Vanna's credit-card statements strewn all over the bed, Savannah pulled up a map of Naples and located each business that her alter ego had frequented. One street name popped up over and over again: Sunshine Parkway. Savannah assumed this was a major shopping area—an assumption that proved to be correct when she had cruised down it just a few moments earlier, watching people walk up and down the sun-dappled sidewalks as she drove by.

She had called last night and reserved a room at the Sand Dunes Motel after chatting for a while with the friendly desk clerk. Savannah figured the place must not be very busy since the woman had kept her on the line for over ten minutes after asking how long Savannah planned to be in town.

When Savannah stammered that she really didn't know, the clerk said she was only asking because she could give Savannah a nice discount if she planned to stay for more than a month.

Savannah wasn't certain how long this complete life makeover might take, but she was fairly sure that she'd be in Naples for at least a month, so she told the clerk she planned to stay through the end of April and was given the "long-term" rate. After living in her condo for so many years, Savannah found it amusing that the clerk considered thirty days long-term.

Smoothing her skirt over her thighs, Savannah stepped up over the curb and reached for the door. She tugged, but it didn't budge. She cupped her hands around her eyes and pressed her nose against the glass to peer into the darkened office, but couldn't see anyone moving about in the shadows. Then she took a step back and noticed that someone had placed a sign to the right of the door.

"Back at 8 P.M. For emergencies, call Lillian at 555-3777," Savannah read. Hmm. Roasting on the sidewalk probably didn't count as an emergency, but it was just past two o'clock in the afternoon and there was no way she was going to sit around and wait for six hours for the clerk to come back and give her a room key, so she whipped out her cell phone and called the number on the sign.

"Rules of Engagement," a perky woman on the other end of the line answered after two rings.

"Yes, can I speak to Lillian, please?"

"Certainly. Can I tell her who's calling?"

"This is Savannah Taylor. I have a reservation at the Sand

Dunes Motel, but there's nobody here and the sign on the door says to call this number."

"Oh. Just a second and I'll get Lillian for you," the woman said.

Savannah walked back to the car and wedged her cell phone between her shoulder and her ear as she pulled open the heavy door of her car. She needed air-conditioning, and fast. Even her toes were sweating.

"Savannah? This is Lillian Bryson. We talked last night. I'm so sorry I wasn't able to be at the motel to greet you, but my schedule is pretty full today and I wasn't sure when you'd arrive. Would you mind coming by my office to pick up your key? I've got the paperwork and everything ready for you. We're just around the corner from the motel—100 Sunshine Parkway. Suite A."

Savannah blinked at the rapid-fire barrage of information being tossed at her. "Uh, sure. I can be there in just a minute," she said.

"Wonderful. I've got an appointment in about ten minutes, but at least we'll have a few seconds to chat," Lillian answered.

"Okay," Savannah said, since that seemed to be the appropriate response. Then she ended the call and carefully backed the T-bird out of its parking space. She hadn't realized how much longer and wider the car was than her old Toyota until the first time she tried to wedge it into a compact space. She managed to get the car into the spot, but then realized that she could only open the door about six inches, which, had she not gained fifteen pounds since graduating from college, she might have been able to squeeze through. But she was foiled by one too many Krispy Kremes that had managed to pass through her iips and onto her hips, so she'd had to back the car up and park it out in the far reaches of the Super ShopMart's lot where all the Suburbans and Navigators were banished.

She didn't get why parking spaces seemed to be getting smaller while cars were only getting bigger. She also wondered when the trend toward enormous vehicles would stop. As it was, Peggy had an SUV that was larger than their dorm room back at Michigan State. Every time Savannah hauled herself up into her best friend's vehicle, she felt as if they were on their way to invade Canada.

The T-bird might be big and heavy, but at least it didn't have that same paramilitary feel to it.

Savannah cruised toward Sunshine Parkway, keeping her eye out for any empty head-in parking spaces along the way. She wasn't all that confident about her parallel parking skills, and would rather pay to park in a lot than have a bunch of giggling tourists watch her try to shimmy back-and-forth into a too-tight spot. But luck was on her side because just as she spotted a cheery yellow building with "100 Sunshine Parkway" written in black script on the overhanging second story, a gray Porsche pulled out of an end spot on her side of the street. Savannah easily maneuvered the convertible into the empty spot and turned off the engine.

She sat for a moment under the shade of a leafy oak tree and studied her surroundings. She was certain that, like all cities, Naples probably had its drab areas where people on the fringes of society lived; neighborhoods with squat, ugly houses seven years overdue for a coat of paint where even straggly weeds had to struggle to survive. But here on Sunshine Parkway, everything and everyone gleamed with an almost golden glow that reflected off the stucco buildings filled with happy tourists. Here, parents gazed indulgently at children splashing in a shallow fountain outside a four-dollar-per-latte coffee shop, lazy dogs sleeping in the shade at their feet. Slender women with hair the color of wheat meandered in and out of shops, shopping bags with braided rope handles looped around their wrists.

This was not like Key West or Miami's South Beach, with a party-all-night and sleep-all-day sort of feel. No, Naples was expensive candlelit dinners on balconies overlooking the Gulf of Mexico and tissue-wrapped souvenirs that you brought home to cherish. It was not sand dollar ashtrays and extra-large T-shirts stenciled with thong bikinis.

And as Savannah sat in her car and soaked it all in, she thought, *This feels like home to me.*

Then, a few moments later, she realized that if she didn't get in to see Lillian Bryson and get her room key, her car was literally going to feel like home to her because she wasn't going to have anywhere else to sleep tonight. She waited until there was a break in traffic before opening her door and stepping out of the car. She grabbed her purse from the floor of the backseat and headed toward the two-story building that in any other city would have been considered a strip mall.

As she pulled open the door to Suite A, she briefly wondered what sort of business Rules of Engagement was. A dating service, maybe? A set of bells tied to the door jingled merrily as Savannah stepped inside the office and looked around. It was fairly unremarkable, with what appeared to be a waiting area off to one side and a hallway leading to several offices, one of which had an opening overlooking the waiting area.

A well-groomed woman with curly brown hair looked up from a desk behind the opening and smiled as Savannah approached.

"Hello. You must be Savannah. Lillian's expecting you," the receptionist said, waving toward the hallway to indicate that Savannah should just go on back.

"Thank you," Savannah said, feeling suddenly very self-conscious in her too-short skirt with her too-white legs. She tried tugging her skirt down a bit, but it wouldn't budge so, instead, she tried channeling Vanna, who Savannah guessed never felt underdressed.

She tapped lightly on the door of the first office down the hall, tentatively poking her head inside when she was told to come in.

"Hi. I'm Savannah," she said to the woman sitting behind a large cherry desk.

The woman smiled and stood up, making Savannah feel like a gargantuan next to her. Not that Savannah was particularly tall, but Lillian Bryson was probably no more than five-one, even with the two-inch sandals she was wearing. She was dressed in coral silk slacks with a brightly patterned matching blouse, and she was perfectly accessorized with gold-and-coral earrings, necklace, and bracelet.

Savannah shuffled into the room, clasping her hands behind her back. She didn't have much in the way of nice jewelry. It had always seemed so impractical to buy such things for herself, and Todd wasn't exactly the jewelry-buying type. She vowed that once she got settled in to her new life, she would go out and buy herself at least one nice bracelet or a pair of earrings that wouldn't tarnish in six months.

"It's very nice to meet you. I'm Lillian," the other woman said warmly, moving around her desk to greet Savannah.

For some reason, Savannah felt as if she were being studied and did her best not to squirm.

"So, you're an accountant," Lillian said, indicating that Savannah should sit down in one of the red-upholstered chairs across from her desk. Savannah took a seat and was surprised when Lillian sat down next to her rather than going back around her desk.

Savannah crossed her legs, then uncrossed them again, worried that she might be flashing her new landlord. "Um, no. I mean, I was, but I plan to look for a new line of work here in Naples."

"What sort of job are you looking for? I know quite a few people in town, and your boss back in Michigan couldn't recommend you highly enough."

"You called my boss?" Savannah asked with a slight frown.

"You gave me his name last night as a reference," Lillian reminded her.

Right. She'd forgotten about that. "I'm not certain what it is exactly that I'm looking for. I'm going to spend some time this afternoon looking at the want ads to see if anything sounds interesting. I've been an accountant for years. I thought it might be fun to try something new," Savannah explained, even though Lillian hadn't asked.

"Let me know if you need any help. Not that you'll need it with the glowing recommendation you've got from your old boss." Lillian laughed and patted Savannah's arm as if they'd been pals for years.

Savannah didn't think she'd ever met anyone so welcoming. "What sort of business is Rules of Engagement?" she asked. "Is it a dating service?"

Lillian's dark brown eyes sparkled as she laughed again and leaned toward Savannah as if she were about to confess a secret. "Heavens, no. As my boys will tell you, my attempts at matchmaking have always ended in utter disaster. The last girl I set my oldest son, Sam, up with turned out to be a transvestite. I had no idea. I mean, she—er, he, that is—had the most beautiful figure. And I met him down at Valeen's shoe shop trying on a gorgeous pair of silver strappy sandals." Lillian shook her head as if to say, *What a waste.* "Really, it was too bad he wasn't a woman. He would have been perfect for Sam."

Savannah chuckled as Lillian rolled her eyes heavenward and continued.

"And don't even get me started on poor Mike. I must confess that I have absolutely no idea what he's looking for in a mate. The ones he brings home are always the strong, silent type, but I think he needs to find someone more daring and less practical than himself. He's begged me to stop trying to set him up, so I've had to back off. What's a mother to do, though? I want to see my boys happy."

Savannah smiled and shrugged. Reading between the lines, she guessed that this Mike was probably gay, hence his penchant for the "strong, silent type." She was tempted to suggest that Lillian might want to introduce Mike to the transvestite she'd originally intended for Sam, but then she realized she was getting way too involved in the Bryson family saga and still had no key—and no idea what sort of business Lillian was running here.

"So if this isn't a dating service, what do you do?" she asked.

"We help people get married," Lillian answered.

"You're a wedding planner?"

"No. What we do is to take someone who wants to get married—whether or not she's in a relationship—and we analyze her behavior in order to figure out what she needs to do or not do to get a man to commit. I say 'she' because the majority of our clients are women. But we do get a few men in every now and then."

"I don't understand," Savannah said, frowning.

"Well, say you've been dating someone for several years and he just never seems to be ready to pop the question. There's a reason for that. Sometimes, he's just not that into you, and he's never going to be the right one. If that's the case, we help you to end that relationship and move on to someone else who will love you enough to get married. Other times we find that a woman has simply made it too easy on her man. She's allowed him to take advantage of her and he's never going to pop the question because he no longer sees her as a challenge. He has no incentive to take the next step because she's already made it clear that she's willing to stay by his side, with or without the ring. We fix that." Lillian gave her a knowing wink.

"Wow," Savannah said. "I've never heard of a service like this."

"I haven't, either. Mike's after me to franchise before someone else comes up with the idea, but I'm not so sure I'm cut out to run an empire at this stage of my life. Besides, I enjoy working with my clients, and the sort of venture he envisions would require a lot more management than I'd like."

"Lillian? Your two-thirty is here," the receptionist said over the intercom.

"Ah, time to get back to work." Lillian unfolded herself from the chair next to Savannah. "It was nice talking with you. I really do hope you'll call if you need anything. Maddie has your key and the paperwork we need you to fill out. It's just a formality. After talking to your former boss and the president of your homeowner's association back in Michigan, I feel certain we're going to be as happy with you as you'll be with us. Our little motel may not be glamorous, but it is homey. We've got some children of friends of the family coming to stay during their break from school for the next week, but the place is usually very quiet. And I'm sure the kids will be respectful of everyone else. Their parents are dear friends of mine."

Savannah got such a warm feeling from Lillian Bryson that she was tempted to hug her. Weird. She wasn't really the hugging type. "Thank you," she said as she stood up to leave, then felt herself being enfolded in Lillian's arms. Apparently, she wasn't the only one who felt the need for a hug.

It only took her five minutes to fill out the rental application and get her key from the pretty receptionist, and soon Savannah was on her way back to the Sand Dunes Motel. She smiled when the white stucco building with sea-green trim came into view. Lillian was right. The place wasn't glamorous. But, as of now, it was home.

What Do You Do When Someone Hot Hits on You?

Did you know that airplanes are the new meat market? Well, they are! And with so many young, successful people traveling on business these days, your Mr. Right could be sitting right beside you! So when that cute guy in 6C leans over and asks if you come here often, what do you do?

a· Glare pointedly at his left knee, which is invading *your* space, and then go back to the book you were reading before you were so rudely interrupted.

b· Tell him this is your nineteenth trip in twelve weeks and list, in detail, every reason you hate air travel.

c· Smile and say that one of the things you love most about business travel is how many interesting people you get to meet. Then you coyly mention that your meetings end at seven this evening and ask if he has any recommendations for dinner.

You A girls might just as well give up any hope of meeting your Mr. Right! You have to be open to new experiences. Remember, the book will wait—your life will not! Here's a newsflash for those of you who chose B: Everyone hates air travel. Stop your whining and make the best of the situation. Your leg room will not magically increase just because you complain to your seatmate about it. Congratulations to those of you who picked C! Even if Mr. 6C doesn't turn out to be Mr. Right, you'll still end up with a dinner date (and maybe even something more . . .) and not have to spend the evening sitting on your bed in your hotel room, watching old M*A*S*H reruns on TV and eating an overpriced hamburger from room service.

six

Mike Bryson was having a bad day, although in his line of work, the phrase *bad day* had been completely redefined by the events of September 11, 2001.

Like most days, this one hadn't started out any worse than usual. Get up, take a shower, shave. Drive out to Baxstrom airport just outside of Naples and take a short hop to Miami for his Miami to LaGuardia flight. Some of his friends thought it was strange that he didn't just move to Miami or Tampa with their larger international airports, but Mike liked living in Naples. Besides, as he always explained, the forty-five minute flight from Naples to Miami was no longer than most people's commutes by car. And being a U.S. air marshal meant that he could bypass the long security lines that regular travelers unfortunately had to face.

He'd been assigned the Miami to LaGuardia run that morning because three young men with student visas had booked the flight at the last minute and all three had purchased one-way tickets. Not surprisingly, this raised red flags with the Transportation Safety Administration, and Mike had been scheduled to accompany the men on their journey to ensure that it was a safe flight for everyone.

In the end, it hadn't been the students who were the problem, but a belligerent executive in first class who took advantage of the airline's free drink policy and proceeded to get obnoxiously drunk. He then got overly friendly with the first-class flight attendant, who firmly and politely told the man to take his seat after he cornered her in the galley and volunteered to initiate her into the Mile High Club. Apparently put out by the flight attendant's refusal to get it on in the 737's tiny lavatory, the man took out his annoyance on a pair of children from coach whose parents had sent them up to use the first-class cabin's bathroom since the aisle behind them was blocked by two beverage carts.

Mike, who was sitting in the aisle seat of the bulkhead row separating coach from first class, saw the man get up and push in front of the two little girls as he told them to get back to coach where they belonged. Mike calmly unbuckled his seat belt and stood up, stopping the frightened-looking kids as they obediently headed back to their seats.

"It's okay," he said quietly. "You can use the bathroom up here."

The asshole paused with his hand on the lavatory door and started to say something, but the dark look Mike shot him shut him up.

Mike waved toward the area near the front door of the aircraft, which was shielded from view of the passengers by the first-class bathroom. "Could I speak with you for a moment," he said, hoping the man realized that Mike wasn't asking.

The man let go of the bathroom door and stepped aside, and Mike indicated to the girls that they were free to use the facilities. He heard the door squeak shut as he followed the jerk around the corner and out of sight. The man turned on him, his cheeks mottled red with anger.

"Listen, buddy—" the passenger began.

"No," Mike interrupted. "You listen. Your first-class ticket does not entitle you to treat the flight attendants and other passengers on this plane with disrespect. We'll be in New York in less than an hour, so I suggest you go back to your seat, maybe read the *Wall Street Journal* or take a nap, and keep your hands—and your opinions—to yourself for the remainder of the flight."

The man's face got even redder, and Mike sighed, knowing what was going to happen next. Why did the airlines continue to serve alcohol on these flights? He'd be willing to bet that over eighty percent of the incidents he dealt with involved drunk passengers.

"Fu—"

"Stop," Mike interrupted again, holding up one hand, palm out like a crossing guard trying to halt a two-ton vehicle with his hand. "Before you do or say anything more, let me save you a lot of trouble." He pulled his credentials from the back pocket of his jeans and held his badge in front of the man's nose. "I'm a federal air marshal, and if you so much as squint in the wrong direction, I'm going to handcuff you and lock you in the lavatory for the rest of the flight." He paused, then added, "Back in coach."

"But—" the man sputtered.

Mike shook his head and pushed his sport jacket aside as if reaching for a set of handcuffs, a move meant to give the guy a glimpse of his shoulder holster—with his 9mm pistol securely in place. "Fine. Let's do this the hard way," he said.

But the man held his hands out in surrender and backed as far away from Mike as he could get. His watery blue eyes were round with fear, and Mike figured that no further scare tactics would be necessary.

"I'll sit down," the man said, and Mike stepped back to let him pass.

He heard the satisfying click of a seat belt being fastened and caught the amused eyebrow-raise of the first-class flight attendant who had been shamelessly eavesdropping on the conversation from the safety of the galley. As Mike stepped out into the aisle, he had to struggle to keep a straight face as the man he'd just spoken with closed his eyes and feigned sleep.

With that trouble averted, Mike made his way back to his seat, where he pretended to read the in-flight magazine while studying the three students across the aisle from him. They were speaking in low voices, their heads close together. The passengers around them eyed the group warily, and Mike could feel the tension as people twitched every time one of the students moved.

Man, he'd be glad when this flight was over. He'd just come off what felt like a decade of heavy international travel and had been promised a few weeks of less-intense domestic routes. And since it looked like he was actually going to be in Naples more than just a day or two this month, he'd set up a meeting with the contractors who were going to remodel the old motel he'd bought last year and turn the twenty-four-room motel into half as many spacious condominiums. Once the plans were finalized, the permits could be filed and, with luck, work would begin within the next four to six weeks. Mike couldn't wait. He wasn't cut out to run a motel and, even with his mother's help, keeping the mostly vacant place running day in and day out was starting to wear on him.

And it was only going to get worse over the next week. He had no idea what had possessed his mother to offer up rooms at the Sand Dunes when her friends, the Morriseys from Pennsylvania, mentioned that their kids were upset because they hadn't made plans for spring break until the last minute and hadn't been able to book rooms in Daytona Beach. His mother, the eternal optimist, assured Mike that she was certain the Morriseys' son and daughter and ten of their closest friends would be no trouble at all. Mike, the eternal skeptic, didn't believe that for a second.

He rubbed his forehead with one hand and tried to ease the tension pounding in his temples. His mother meant well, but she could be so naive sometimes. Like the time she'd set him up with a stripper that she'd met at the beach one day. The woman's three-year-old son had apparently seen something he liked in Mom's cooler, and, when the child's mother dashed over to apologize for the kid's behavior, she and Mike's mother had become instant friends. Stuff like that happened to his mother all the time. She didn't have a mean or distrustful bone in her body.

Not that Mike hadn't been impressed by Shayna's "I'm-an-exotic-dancer-not-a-stripper" body. And what bothered him wasn't even what she did for a living. No, it had taken him walking in on her snorting cocaine in front of her kid that made him run the other way . . . and shake his head at his own stupidity for not checking the woman out before agreeing to go out with her. He should know better by now. His mother was a nutjob magnet and every woman she tried to hook him up with ended up having some sort of serious issue.

Like the socialite Mom had met at a fundraiser who turned out to be a kleptomaniac. Or the—

Mike stopped reminiscing about his mother's failed attempts at matchmaking when the three students across the aisle unfastened their seat belts and rose. The first two headed toward the front of the plane, while the third made his way to the back. Mike caught several passengers exchanging worried glances as he, too, stood up, immediately assessing the situation.

The students had been checked out before the flight and none had anything more than a parking ticket. They weren't known to be affiliated with any terrorist organization and, just because they were traveling on last-minute, one-way tickets, that did not mean they had nefarious intentions. Still, Mike wasn't about to leave anything to chance.

He followed the two students who had headed into first class, catching the eye of the flight attendant and nodding surreptitiously toward the lone student walking down the aisle toward the galley located at the back of the plane. She dipped her chin and immediately disappeared to call the staff handling coach to tell them to keep their eyes on the passenger headed their way.

When Mike felt a presence behind him, he turned slightly to find that two men had followed him up to first class. They both had the hard, determined look of men who had served in the military and who, like him, had no intention of having anything go wrong on this flight. Still, as good as their intentions might be, it would only escalate the situation if they planned to act first and ask questions later. So now he had both the students *and* these men to deal with. Great.

The two young men stopped at the front of the plane, just outside the door leading to the cockpit. The door was locked, of course, and Mike knew the students had been subjected to extra screening at security since their names had been flagged before the flight. Still, he wasn't naive enough to think that it was impossible to sneak a weapon past the screening agents. It seemed that as soon as the good guys devised a way to spot the newest threat, the bad guys developed something even worse. Although Mike doubted that they'd smuggled a gun onboard, he didn't feel nearly as confident about explosives.

Some of the new compounds were virtually undetectable by their screening equipment and could be molded to look like everyday objects such as keychains or pens. And it wouldn't take a lot to blast through the cockpit door and take over control of the plane . . . or knock a hole in the plane's exterior and bring the whole thing down.

Mike shook his head. He'd rather deal with drunks than terrorists any day.

The first student entered the lavatory and Mike came up behind the second man and put himself between the student and the cockpit door. The other two men thankfully didn't appear to be hotheaded, because they simply got in line behind Mike, as if they, too, were waiting for the bathroom.

As the seconds ticked by, the student in front of Mike seemed to get more and more nervous, stealing glances at them out of the corner of his eye as sweat trickled down the back of his neck and dripped onto the collar of his dark blue polo shirt. When his friend came out of the bathroom, the second kid nearly knocked him over in his haste to get inside.

Mike held his breath, knowing that there was nothing he could do if the young man had an explosive hidden somewhere on his body that he planned to detonate once inside the lavatory. He could defend against an attack on the passengers and crew, he could immobilize anyone acting suspiciously or could, God forbid, even call for a fighter jet to shoot them out of the sky if hijackers got control of the plane and attempted to use it as a missile. But he couldn't arrest someone who had done nothing more suspect than perspire while waiting for a free toilet just because he was making the other passengers nervous.

Mike tensed and slowly reached for the gun at his side when the first student stopped at the entrance to the first-class galley, blocking the flight attendant's exit. He ran through possible scenarios in his head. The man could use the attendant as a human shield or as a hostage to keep the other passengers in their seats (although, since 9/11, that tactic wasn't likely to ever work again—passengers no longer believed their own lives would be spared if they cooperated with terrorists), but since Mike was standing behind the student, he was certain he could overtake the man before he could harm the attendant.

Then Mike closed his eyes and relaxed his grip on the handle of his pistol when he heard the student say, "Excuse me, ma'am. Would you have any Sprite or 7-Up? My friends and I were thrown a farewell party last evening, and I'm afraid the three of us aren't feeling too well this afternoon."

And that, Mike thought as he waited to board the flight back to Miami later that night, was exactly why his job was so difficult these days. It wasn't like the terrorists had giant red T's tattooed on their foreheads.

He was hopeful that his return flight to Miami would be uneventful. After all, with this one, he wasn't tailing anyone suspicious. He was just trying to get back home.

Unfortunately, Fate wasn't quite through with him for the day. On the packed flight back from New York—which left two hours late due to a mechanical problem—he got seated next to a lean man about his own age who was traveling with a six- or seven-year-old girl. Since he technically wasn't working, Mike pulled out the latest Michael Crichton thriller and settled in to read. Only the man next to him had other plans. A few minutes after the plane took off, he began a diatribe about his ex-wife, who had custody of their daughter during her spring break and who had insisted the man fly to New York to come pick her up. Mike was then regaled with tales of the ex's spending habits (she apparently had some sort of purse fixation and owned over 100 handbags, at the man's last count), her eating habits (she was a former Miss Idaho who ate only canned soup and Velveeta cheese), and—much to Mike's dismay—her sexual preferences. (Mike grimaced when the man jabbed him in the ribs and said, "She likes the oral stuff, ya know? A lot.")

Then, when the man's daughter excused herself to go to the lavatory for the third time in an hour, he confessed, "I don't know what that poor girl's mother feeds her when she's there. Whenever I get her back, she has diarrhea for two weeks. And the color! You wouldn't believe—"

Mike closed his eyes, rested his head on the back of his seat, and sighed. Did he look like the sort of guy who would be interested in this? Because he really, really wasn't.

Deciding he'd had enough of being trapped next to verbal diarrhea man, Mike excused himself and spent the remainder of the flight in the rear galley talking to the flight attendants.

As he walked to the boarding gate for the last leg of his journey, he figured the chances were good that he'd finally be able to get to his thriller. That is, until he walked down the jetway to the waiting Cessna and found himself surrounded by a group of women who apparently had started partying a few hours ago and did not intend to stop.

Mike took a seat in the very last row of the plane, but since this was a small plane, he was still pretty much in the middle of the party. He attempted to ignore the women, but found it impossible to concentrate with all the noise, so, after about five minutes, he gave up trying to read and stared out the window as the plane passed over the Everglades on its way from Miami to Naples. He looked up, startled, when someone sat down in the seat next to him and put her warm hand on his thigh.

The woman sitting next to him had long dark hair and expertly made-up green eyes. She had the trim body of someone who spent a lot of time at the gym and the firm breasts of someone who spent a lot of money at the plastic surgeon's. She was wearing a pair of form-fitting black pants and a green tank that was probably comfortable outside in the high-seventy-degree heat but obviously wasn't warm enough inside the air-conditioned aircraft.

"Hi, I'm Ashleigh. And you're cute," she said with a low, throaty giggle.

Mike laughed at the unexpected comment. "Thank you," he answered.

Ashleigh moved in closer, her face so close to his that he could see the tiny lines around her eyes that her makeup hid at a distance. "I'm drunk," she whispered, the smell of alcohol so strong on her breath that Mike was certain his own blood-alcohol level had just passed the legal limit by inhaling the fumes.

"Yes, you are," he agreed.

She squeezed his thigh, then made Mike jump when she cupped a hand over his crotch. "Wanna play?" she asked.

Mike removed her hand. O-kay. Well, this wasn't quite the

uneventful flight he'd been hoping for. "No. But, uh, thank you," he said. He was all for women going after what they wanted, but this was a bit extreme.

"You're welcome." Ashleigh reclined in her seat, seemingly unaffected by his rejection of her advances. "What's your name? What do you do?" She asked the questions in quick succession, but didn't wait for him to respond before saying, "My fiancé runs his own business, and he makes lots and lots of money. Isn't that wonderful? I *love* money." She closed her eyes and sighed contentedly.

Mike rolled his eyes. She obviously didn't love her fiancé as much as she loved his money. Otherwise, she wouldn't be hitting on a complete stranger.

"Ashleigh, come back up here. Kate has the most precious Coach boots to show you," one of the women in the front of the plane cooed. Ashleigh's eyes popped open as if someone had waved smelling salts under her nose.

"Ooh, Coach. I'll be right there," she said, then left without another glance at Mike, who shook his head with amused disgust and went back to looking out the window even though it was dark outside and the only thing he could see was the occasional headlight of a car headed east on Florida's famed Alligator Alley below.

Less than half an hour later he was home. Well, not that he exactly considered the Sand Dunes Motel "home," but it was where he was living for now. All of his money was currently sunk into real estate, and it didn't make sense for him to rent another place when he might just as well stay in one of the vacant efficiencies until the renovation began. He had already earmarked one of the twelve new condos for himself—a nice corner unit overlooking the interior courtyard, which was also getting a makeover, including all new landscaping and a new swimming pool.

The Sand Dunes Motel was built in a square, with three units up and three down on each side of the square. There were stairwells at each corner leading up to a walkway that ran along the inside perimeter of the second floor. When the remodel was complete, this walkway would be gone, replaced by second-floor balconies that would open up onto the courtyard. Entrances to the converted townhouses would be on the first floor. This meant that the twenty-four units would be reduced to twelve condos, less the one Mike planned to keep for himself. He was hopeful that he'd make enough money on the sale of the remaining eleven to make the investment of time and money worth his while.

Mike was mentally listing all that needed to be done before construction on the condos could start as he pulled into the normally half-empty parking lot of the motel and stopped. Although there were two dozen units, the original owner had only eked out enough parking spots for half that many cars. And tonight they were all full.

Well, correction. All but one was full. The remaining space—the one right in front of the office where Mike usually parked his pickup—was only a quarter full. An old red-and-white Thunderbird convertible was parked in the next space with its passenger-side tires four inches over the line.

Mike shook his head and grumbled, "Road hog," as he carefully backed his truck out of the lot and went to find parking on the street.

He found an empty spot about a block away and deftly maneuvered the truck into the space. The sidewalks were deserted, which didn't surprise Mike at all. Naples wasn't like Daytona or Pensacola, with their young, party-hearty spring-break crowds. MTV was not going to be filming any wild antics here, he thought as he locked his pickup and started back toward the motel.

Mike frowned as he turned the corner and heard the unrelenting boom-a-boom-a-boom-a of someone with their bass turned up way too loud. He hoped that whoever it was would turn it off . . . and soon. He also knew that, if they didn't, the Naples police department wouldn't take long to come out and address the problem.

But as he unlocked the door leading from the street into the interior of the Sand Dunes Motel, Mike's frown deepened. Rather than abating, the noise was getting louder.

He walked past the stairwell and stood, staring, at the sight greeting his eyes.

It was as if he had just stepped back fifteen years in time. Spring break. Daytona Beach. Nearly naked young men and women. Volleyball in the pool. Keg of the cheapest beer on earth flowing freely. Boom box booming. Couple going at it (most likely two people who had never been attracted to each other until this evening) in the shadows over by the ice machine. Two guys chasing each other with Super Soakers up on the second-floor walkway.

This was *not* supposed to be happening.

His mother had promised these kids would behave like . . . well *not* like coeds on spring break.

Mike knew he wouldn't be heard over the squealing laughter and rap music thumping out of the stereo, so he rubbed a weary hand across his forehead and made his way to the center of the courtyard to turn off the boom box. Everyone froze when the rap stopped, like children playing musical chairs. He could still hear a somewhat lower boom of another stereo cranked up several dozen decibels too loud, but figured he'd better deal with this crowd first.

With all eyes on him, Mike cleared his throat and said, "Hello. My name is Mike Bryson and I'm the owner of the Sand Dunes Motel. If we are going to coexist peacefully for the next week, there are some ground rules you need to follow. First, there will be no loud music after midnight. Second, there will be no underage consumption of alcohol anywhere where I can see it. Third, the parking spot outside the front door is mine. Whoever is taking up half the spot with your careless parking job, go out and move your car. Now."

Mike knew there was nothing more he could do. His mother would give him one of her patented you-can't-kick-them-out-where-will-they-go? looks if he tried to evict them, and, really, so long as they didn't hurt anybody, they had just as much right to be here as anyone else.

He turned around to go upstairs and the coeds—minus their music—came back to life. Mike followed his ears to unit twenty-three and stopped just outside the door. Unlike the music downstairs, he actually recognized this. Def Leppard's "Pyromania" vibrated through the door at an eardrum-breaking level.

Mike pounded on the door. "Turn the music off!" he shouted before anyone answered.

The music stopped. "What?" was yelled through the door.

"It's after midnight. Keep the music down," Mike ordered.

Then, because he was tired and had had enough drama for the day, he turned and walked away, not looking back even when a door opened behind him and he heard a woman say, "I will if you will."

What's Your Dream Job?

When you were a kid, did you dream of becoming a doctor? A lawyer? An insurance salesperson? We doubt it! Most of us had much more exciting ideas about what we'd be when we grew up, but we'll bet you didn't end up as a professional cheerleader or a rock star or an astronaut. But it's never too late to change careers. Which one of these dream jobs is right for you?

a. An accountant at a film studio—a job that blends the practical nature of number-crunching with the glamorous world of Hollywood.

b. An artist who spends her days alone in her studio creating and her nights at gallery shows and openings.

c. The CEO of a small but outrageously successful advertising agency.

If you chose A, what were you thinking? An accountant is an accountant is an accountant! When did you lose the ability to dream big? You B girls have the right idea. Just don't go off the deep end and do anything drastic like cutting off your ears! C sounds like the perfect dream job to us—you jet off to meet clients in places like New York, Rome, and Beijing, always wearing the latest fashions and presenting the most cutting-edge ideas. You go!

[seven]

When she was twelve, Savannah dreamed of being a rock star when she grew up. She figured her career would be off to a flying start the moment she was singled out at the talent fest that was held at the Maple Rapids Mall every August. Savannah and Peggy had spent that summer listening to Bon Jovi's *Slippery When Wet* album and had practiced a dance routine they'd choreographed every day until they could do the steps blindfolded. The day of the talent fest Savannah's voice was hoarse from singing "Livin' on a Prayer"—a selection she thought even Reverend Black would approve of—over and over again for nearly two hours just to make certain she knew all of the words by heart. With some effort she tugged on the red-and-black vinyl pants she'd bought at Kmart with the last of her allowance. The outfits she and Peggy had purchased were completely impractical. Neither of their mothers would let them wear the tight vinyl pants and sleeveless black tops to school . . . or anywhere else, for that matter. Which is why, although it was nearly eighty degrees outside, Savannah pulled on a pair of jeans that she'd taken from Belinda's laundry pile over her legs and covered the black top with the Mickey Mouse T-shirt she'd gotten earlier that year when they went to Disney World on vacation during spring break.

It turned out that she needn't have bothered with the disguise. Mom was watching *General Hospital* in the living room, and she didn't even turn her head when Savannah rushed down the hall and clumped down the stairs of their split-level in her mid-calf scrunched red boots.

"I'm going to the mall with Peggy!" she shouted up the stairs, pulling the front door open at the same time.

Back then, parents didn't drive their kids everywhere or treat every stranger as if he or she was a closet pedophile, so it was not unusual for Savannah to be allowed to bike or walk around town by herself. Which was just as well, because Mrs. Taylor was too engrossed with her soap opera—and nobody in the Taylor household knew how to program their new VCR to record the show except Belinda, who was too consumed with her fledgling dog-sitting business to lend her assistance—to have stopped watching TV long enough to drive Savannah and Peggy to the mall.

"Be home by six!" her mother shouted back, although Savannah knew very well what time she was expected home. You could leave home at three in the morning and spend your day doing all manner of things, just as long as you were back by six, in time for supper.

Savannah hurried out the door as she checked the Swatch her parents had given her for her birthday back in April. As usual, she was early. But that didn't matter, it only meant that she'd have time to get an Orange Julius at the mall while she waited for Peggy to arrive.

She grabbed her bike from the driveway where she'd left it propped up by the kickstand earlier and started off toward the mall. Just in case her mother was watching her from the living room window upstairs, Savannah waited until she'd turned the corner before stopping to shed the T-shirt and jeans that were making her sweat in the mid-August heat. She folded the clothes neatly and stowed them under Mr. and Mrs. Rotta's rhododendrons, where she'd retrieve them on her way home.

She arrived at the mall without incident and had plenty of time to purchase the aforementioned Orange Julius before Peggy arrived, sweating and out of breath. Unlike Savannah, Peggy was never early to anything.

Savannah took one final slurp of her drink and threw the

cup in the trash as she got up off the bench outside the Gap, where she and Peggy had arranged to meet. She ran her hands down the smooth vinyl pants, straightening out the creases. Excitement hummed through her veins. She was certain that superstardom was mere minutes away.

"Are you ready?" she asked as Peggy reached down to tug her boots up. Sears had been out of boots in Peggy's size, so she'd had to settle for a pair two sizes too big. Savannah dearly hoped that one of Peggy's boots wouldn't go flying into the audience when they did a kick during their big finish. That wouldn't exactly impress the talent scouts she was sure were in the crowd sitting on metal folding chairs in front of the blue-skirted stage.

Peggy stood up and straightened her shoulders before giving Savannah a serious look. "I'm ready," she answered.

"Remember to smile. And don't be nervous." Savannah was worried that Peggy was about to chicken out, so she grabbed her friend's arm and pushed her toward the curtains at the back of the stage. They were scheduled to go on next, right after some junior-high-school boys got done jumping around on the stage and crooning some stupid song about "didn't I blow your mind this time" in voices so high that they sounded like girls.

"What a dumb song. We're gonna blow these guys out of the water," she assured Peggy, whose arm had started to shake beneath Savannah's hand.

"All right, all right. Put your hands together for Donnie, Joey, Jordan, Danny, and Jon, also known as the New Kids on the Block," the emcee announced as the girls in the audience squealed and clapped and wriggled in their seats like excited puppies at the pet store.

Savannah peeked around the curtain and scowled at the crowd. "You've got to be kidding. They actually *liked* that?" she muttered as the boy band high-fived one another and showed off onstage until the emcee finally shooed them away.

"I don't know. They're kind of cute," Peggy said, her eyes glued to the stage.

Savannah rolled her eyes. There was no doubt about it. Over the summer Peggy had turned boy crazy.

"And next up, we've got Savannah Taylor and Peggy

O'Reilly, with "Livin' on a Prayer." Come on, give a big round of applause for these little ladies," the emcee announced.

Taking a deep breath to try to slow her fast-beating heart, Savannah started toward the stage.

"Hey, good luck out there," one of the New Kids—Savannah thought it might be Donnie, but she wasn't sure—said, patting her on the shoulder as the boys filed past.

"Thanks," Savannah murmured, immediately deciding that maybe they hadn't been so bad after all.

It was only as she stepped out on the stage amid the luke-warm applause of the audience that she realized she was alone. She turned to look behind her, thinking that perhaps Peggy was still ogling the New Kids. But that did not appear to be the problem. The guys had left, but Peggy remained standing right where Savannah had left her, gripping the handrail of the short flight of stairs leading onstage. Her eyes were wide and unblinking, her skin a color that Savannah had never seen on a person before.

Savannah knew in that instant that she was never going to get Peggy up on that stage.

Drawing a shaky breath, she turned to the emcee and whispered, "I'm ready."

The man glanced at Peggy and then looked back at Savannah. He gave her a sympathetic smile before nodding. "Okay, looks like this is going to be a solo and not a duet," he announced to the crowd, then stepped away from the microphone and moved to the edge of the stage as the music started to play.

Savannah lowered her head and closed her eyes. This was it. Her big chance at stardom. And just because Peggy couldn't go through with it, that didn't mean that Savannah had to give up on her dream, too.

She lifted her head.

"Once upon a time," she said softly.

And then she was doing it, just like she'd practiced, only without Peggy to sing backup or grab the microphone stand and twirl it around like the rock stars they wished to become. Four minutes and nine seconds later, she was finished, her arms outstretched to the crowd, out of breath, her heart beat-ing at five times its normal rate. She expected the people in the audience to leap to their feet and start wolf-whistling. She expected talent scouts to push their way to the front in a race to be the first to reach her. She expected stardom to rain down on her like the softest summer shower.

What she got was a smattering of applause from a mostly bored audience and a nice pat on the back from the emcee as he ushered her offstage.

Which, Savannah reflected nearly two decades later, is the not-so-happy ending of many a childhood dream.

Savannah sat in the puddle of sunshine coming in from the open curtains of her motel room, sipping a cup of coffee and wondering exactly how it was that she'd gone from expecting stardom to settling for a job with a dental plan and a 401(k).

"But that was the old me," she said to herself. She was going to begin her new life in Naples by finding her dream job.

Savannah took another sip of coffee, rubbed her eyes, and blinked at the magazine she'd propped up on the desk in her tiny, yet affordable, motel room. She was reading a special pullout section called "The Complete Moron's Guide to Acing Interviews." She had already scoured the article three times that morning, but figured a fourth time wouldn't hurt, especially since she had managed to set up two interviews today. Which was a miracle, since she'd slept till nearly ten because she'd been fuming until dawn about the high-handed way she'd been ordered to keep her music down after the college students had nearly blasted her out of her room for the previous four hours. She'd only had her own music on so loud to drown out the noise from the courtyard. So to have someone bang on her door and tell her to keep it down was infuriating.

She took another sip of coffee and tried to focus on the article, but soon gave up and decided to get in the shower. She was too tired to pay attention to the words and too nervous to sit still any longer. It had been six years since she'd gone on a job interview and, according to "The Complete Moron's Guide," it was a whole different world out there now. Gone were the days when you were asked to list your strengths and weaknesses, and for the latter, you could just make up something stupid like "My greatest weakness is that I care too much about my work. If I don't do my job well, I can't sleep at night." Which every hiring manager knew was total bullshit, but they dutifully noted that you had—in interviewese—just admitted that you were willing to forfeit all semblance of a personal life for the job.

No, in today's interviews, you were asked to list the original colors of M&M's or to give your theory about why manhole covers were round. Apparently, the answers you gave to these weird, non-job-related questions were supposed to show interviewers that you could think on your feet. If Savannah were doing the hiring, she'd be more impressed with the candidate who said he didn't know and would have to do some research before answering than one who just tried to wing it, but "The Complete Moron's Guide" said admitting you didn't know something was akin to standing up on your chair, mooning your prospective employer, and confessing that you'd been fired from your last job for hinting that you hated your boss and "knew where she lived."

Savannah took extra time in the lukewarm shower, conditioning her hair twice to make sure it would shine. She was excited about her first interview, which was for a job as an advertising sales associate. She'd been surprised when she called and the man on the other end of the line had asked if she could meet him at the Fat Cat restaurant for lunch. She'd never been to a lunch interview before, but "The Complete Moron's Guide" had gone over the finer points of being interviewed while picking at a salad, so she felt confident that she could handle it.

The second interview was for a management position at a local shoe boutique that, according to the charges on the credit-card statements Savannah had been given, Vanna had frequented. Although that job sounded interesting (who *wouldn't* want to spend the day surrounded by glittering sandals, high-heeled boots, and supple Italian leather?), Savannah was hoping to cancel the appointment after she aced her first interview.

But that would never happen if she didn't get out of the shower and get dressed. As she stepped out onto the bathmat she'd laid down on the slippery tile floor, the earth started to shake. At first Savannah thought it was an earthquake. Or maybe a sinkhole, since that was more likely to happen here in Southern Florida. It took a moment for her to realize that it was neither. No, it was just the pounding bass of the spring breakers' rap music that set Savannah's teeth on edge.

She did her best to unclench her teeth as she dried herself off. "It's only for a week," she muttered to herself. Besides, it wasn't like she was going to be here to listen to it all day. With any luck she'd have a job before the day was out, and within a few days she'd be so busy going out and having fun with new friends that the students' noise wouldn't even bother her.

This thought so cheered her that before long Savannah caught herself humming, "Ba boom, boom, boom, boom," and swaying to the music. She chuckled to herself and then nearly poked herself in the eye with her eyeliner when her phone rang. She'd given her mother and Peggy the motel's number, of course, but she figured if they needed her, they'd call on her cell phone.

"I guess not," she said as she pulled her lilac silk bathrobe closed and dashed for the phone next to the bed. Through her open curtains she could see several of the students running around the walkway on the second floor and could feel the vibration of their pounding feet as they ran past her room. Ah, to be young and silly again, she thought, shaking her head.

"Hello," she answered after the phone rang again.

"Savannah? This is Lillian. Lillian Bryson."

Savannah blinked, surprised. Why would Lillian Bryson be calling her? "Yes. Hello. How are you?" she said.

"I'm fine, dear. Thank you for asking. I just called to see if you've settled in all right. Do you have everything you need?"

Wow. Talk about great customer service, Savannah thought. There was no way she'd tattle on the students, not since they were children of Lillian's friends. "Yes. I've settled in fine. Got plenty of towels and those little soaps," she said.

"That's wonderful. Now, are you sure you don't want me to call someone about a job for you? I really do know quite a few people in town."

Savannah looked at her watch, thinking that she was going to have to hurry and get off the phone to make it to her interview in time. She had just under thirty minutes to finish her makeup, dry her hair, get dressed, and walk the two blocks to the restaurant on Sunshine Parkway. Not wanting to insult her new landlord, however, she said politely, "Thank you, but I've got a couple of things lined up already. I'll be sure to let you know if these don't work out, though."

"Where are you interviewing?" Lillian asked, sounding as if she had all the time in the world to chat.

"I've got a lunch appointment at the Fat Cat restaurant and then another interview at two down at Valeen's shoe shop. As a matter of fact, I'm running just a tad late, so I'm going to have to go. But thank you so much for calling."

"You're welcome, dear. You take care."

Savannah smiled as she hung the phone up and hurried into the bathroom to finish getting ready, all the while thinking what a nice person Lillian was.

"Of course, she could just be worried that I won't be able to pay the rent," Savannah said as she pulled on a pair of pantyhose and slipped into her favorite black skirt—one with a slit up her left thigh—and a magenta blouse with zebra-print shoes and handbags scattered across the fabric. She didn't wear a jacket, figuring that both jobs she was interviewing for today were far enough on the creative scale not to require such formal attire. Then she added a pair of pointy-toed Kate Spade knockoffs that she'd bought in New York's Chinatown last Christmas when her mom decided that they were taking everyone on a family trip instead of giving out presents that year.

Her outfit complete, Savannah took a deep breath and looked herself up and down one final time in the mirror.

"Oh, oh, you're halfway there," she sang to herself, remembering again that day on the stage and how determined she had felt to make something exciting of her life. Somewhere along the way, that determination . . . that courage to take risks . . . had deserted her. But now she was going to get it back.

She grabbed her purse and stepped outside, making her way toward the stairs. And as she descended, she ignored the whoops and yells of the other tenants, focusing instead on her own thoughts. She *was* halfway there. More than halfway, actually. She'd moved thousands of miles from home. Quit her secure job. Given up everything that was safe and comfortable in her life in order to be reborn.

Now, nothing could stop her from achieving her dreams.

"You're goin' down!" someone shouted, and Savannah

jerked her head up just in time to see two young men rounding the corner in front of her. The man in the lead ducked, and Savannah flattened herself back against the building, but she was too late.

A stream of warm liquid hit her full in the chest as the second man opened fire with his Super Soaker.

Funny, but her dreams had never included being doused with warm beer seven minutes before what she hoped would be the job interview that would change her life.

Who's Your Hero?

You're trapped in the evil villain's dungeon when suddenly the trapdoor flies open. Which of these dream men are you hoping has come to rescue you?

a· **Prince Charming**

b· **Robin Hood**

c· **Superman**

If you chose A, it's likely that you're a traditional romantic. You've taken a passive role in your dating life and deep down you expect a fairy godmother to one day appear and make your life perfect. If you chose B, you're likely attracted by dashing, fun-loving men. Remember, though, Robin and his band of Merry Men were quite content without a woman around. You might find yourself always coming in second place to "the guys." For those of you who chose C, you want it all—a guy who's smart and got a good job and can also single-handedly save the world. If you ever do find such a guy . . . could you give us his number?

{eight}

An hour later Savannah began to wonder how much humiliation Jon Bon Jovi had had to endure on *his* road to stardom as she stood on the sidewalk outside the Fat Cat restaurant with her legs sticking out of a grouper's ass.

She was tempted to throw her arms around the jacaranda tree beside her and sob into its bark, but she didn't, mostly because her arms were zipped tightly to her sides inside a fish costume, with only her hands loose inside the fins. When she and her sisters had been little, they used to tuck their arms into their T-shirts and put their hands in the sleeves and run after one another in a game of mutant tag. Savannah could always make her sisters scream with laughter when she would add a limp and say, in her best hunchback voice, "Yes, Master. I'm coming, Master."

Having her arms trapped inside this costume felt similar, but wasn't nearly as amusing. At least, not to her.

She'd arrived at the Fat Cat one minute early with her clothes damp and her shoes dripping with beer after deciding that it was better to be on time and pray that her interviewer couldn't smell the alcohol on her than to take the ten minutes she'd need to change. She had given her name to the hostess, who'd gotten Savannah's hopes up when she said immediately, "Yes, come on back."

After the disaster at the motel, she was looking forward to

a little star treatment, although she had hoped that Mr. Miller wouldn't be at the restaurant yet so she'd have a few minutes to go to the ladies' room and get the booze out of her shoes. Oh, well. She'd just have to keep her feet under the table and hope for the best.

The restaurant looked new, with maple tables, chairs upholstered in vibrant burgundies and greens, and earth-toned tiles on the floor. The smell of food cooking over a real wood fire made Savannah's stomach grumble hungrily, reminding her that she hadn't eaten anything today. She was still reeling a little from the Super Soaker incident, and she was careful to put one foot steadily in front of the other as she followed the hostess through the restaurant.

She expected the woman to show her to a table in the already crowded dining room, and was surprised when they passed the tables and the open kitchen and started down a quiet hallway. Savannah wondered if perhaps she was to meet Mr. Miller in a private dining room. If that were the case, this advertising sales associate position must be even more important than she'd thought.

The hostess opened a door and ushered Savannah into a room that was so cold it could have been used as a backup freezer.

"You can put that on over your clothes. I'll zip you up," the woman said, gesturing toward a row of hooks lining the far wall. Hanging on one of the hooks was a heap of fabric printed with an odd pattern of grays, greens, and blues.

"Pardon me?" Savannah asked, thinking the hostess must have her mixed up with someone else.

"You're here for the job, right?" the woman asked.

"Yes," Savannah answered.

"Then put that on. You can't exactly do the job without it." The hostess smiled as if she and Savannah were in on a private joke, but Savannah didn't get it.

Suddenly it dawned on her that this must be some kind of test, like what she'd read about in "The Complete Moron's Guide to Acing Interviews." The article had mentioned a company that made potential employees take part in skits as part of the interview process. They were known to pick historical events like when President Lincoln was shot and sometimes an interviewee would be asked to play Abe Lincoln and other times she'd be John Wilkes Booth. The company claimed this helped them assess a candidate's psychological makeup, but Savannah bet that all it really did was give HR something to laugh about in between corporate restructurings.

Still, sometimes you just had to play the game to get what you wanted. And she wanted a glamorous job in advertising. She could see herself sitting at a trendy bar after work sipping martinis with her chain-smoking new boss, who, in Savannah's imagination, looked like Sarah Jessica Parker in *Sex and the City*. The woman would be outfitted in whatever was the most fashionable, most expensive clothing du jour. Advertising was like that, right? Everyone so cutting-edge (or was *bleeding-edge* the right term these days?) and in the know about the newest, hottest trends.

So anyway, she'd be sitting at the bar, getting tips from her mentor, when a dark, brooding man would catch her eye from across the crowded room. And she'd completely ignore him, as if she were much too busy and important to flirt with *him,* but he would be so taken with her aloof attitude (because he was so gorgeous that women regularly swooned into his arms whenever he came near, so he would see Savannah as a challenge) that he would send over a round of drinks, which would impress her new boss enough to gesture the man over. And he'd come sauntering over . . . Savannah could just see the arrogance oozing off of him . . . and he'd pretend not to notice her while he made small talk with her boss. Then finally he'd turn to her, nonchalant as can be, and he'd say, "And what is it you do? No, wait. Let me guess. You're a model?"

Savannah would snort—delicately, of course, yet with all the disdain she could muster—as if being a model was just *so* beneath her, and she'd spear him with a haughty look and say, "Of course not. I'm in advertising."

And then he'd smile at her with a gleam in his unholy dark eyes and—

"Do you want the job or not?" The hostess interrupted Savannah's fantasy, sounding more than a little annoyed.

Savannah awoke to reality with a start. If she didn't do this, she'd have no chance of getting the job and meeting her fantasy man.

Hastily she grabbed the costume off the peg and shook it out, trying to figure out how to put it on. "Sorry," she mumbled as she shoved her feet through the hole at the bottom of the outfit. It took her a few minutes to realize what sort of costume it was that she was slipping into, but when she did, she turned to look at the hostess over her shoulder. "I'm a trout?" she asked dubiously.

"Grouper," the hostess corrected, tugging the zipper up the length of Savannah's spine. "This is a seafood restaurant. Get it—Fat Cat . . . seafood."

"Ah." Savannah nodded, still not quite certain how this all fit in with her dreams of selling products no one needed to people who couldn't afford them. But "The Complete Moron's Guide" couldn't be wrong. Could it?

She tried to turn around, but with her arms zipped tightly at her sides, she felt herself starting to topple sideways.

The hostess caught her by the back fin and gave her a stern look. "Are you going to be all right?" she asked.

Savannah would have straightened her shoulders with resolve, but she could barely do more than waddle in this fish getup, so she just nodded instead. "You can tell Mr. Miller that I'm up to any challenge," she said. Then, because she'd read in "The Complete Moron's Guide" that a sense of humor was imperative when interviewing, she added—without even cracking a smile—"I'm no Chicken of the Sea."

"Save it for the stand-up act," the hostess deadpanned, opening the door and gesturing for Savannah to follow her back out into the hall.

The restaurant's patrons didn't seem all that surprised to find a grouper in their midst, and Savannah was glad that not too many of the diners openly stared at her as she made her way toward the front door. The interview article she'd read this morning certainly had been titled correctly—she felt like a complete moron. Which, she supposed, might be why the advertising company was putting her through this. If a candidate was willing to totally humiliate herself like this even before she was hired, then they'd know they had found someone who really wanted the job. Or was really desperate for the money. Either of which meant that they had you exactly where they wanted you.

Savannah flipped her fins and tried to look eager. "Okay, so what do I do now?" she asked as the hostess returned to her safe perch (no pun intended) behind a wooden podium.

"You go out there and get people on the sidewalk to come in for lunch," the woman said, waving toward the glass doors that had been etched to make it look as if water were flowing through them. "Tell them we have great seafood."

Savannah took a deep breath and headed toward the doors. She had no idea how she was expected to open them since her wrists were trapped against her thighs, but she was determined not to fall on her face, figuratively or literally.

Fortunately, just then the doors were pulled open from the outside, and Savannah slipped through. Well, she didn't exactly slip through. She sort of lurched drunkenly through.

The glaring noonday sun blinded her for a moment, and Savannah would have kicked herself for not thinking to bring her sunglasses if only her feet weren't hobbled together in the asshole of a grouper. Oh, well, so what if she was blinded and humiliated? Sometimes you had to just reach out and grab what you wanted, rather than sitting back and waiting for exciting things to happen to you.

"Right. Carp diem," she muttered to herself, trying to make a joke to lighten her spirits as she faced the task ahead.

"Seize the carp?"

Savannah heard an amused male voice and blinked up into the sunlight, her eyes watering. She tilted her nose up in a mock-haughty gesture and said, "I, sir, am not a carp. I'm a—"

Just then a dark cloud passed over the sun, momentarily unblinding Savannah, who found herself staring into the grayish-blue eyes of the most handsome man she had ever seen. He had a six o'clock shadow even though it was only noon, a strong jaw, and thick dark blond hair, and Savannah just stood there gazing at him with her mouth open like a, well, like a fish out of water.

"You're a what?" the man asked, smiling down at her with his large, perfect white teeth.

Savannah wobbled on her shaky feet and he reached a hand out to steady her. *My God,* she thought, *his forearms are bigger than my calves.*

"I'm, uh, a grouper," she said when he released her, as if the loss of contact had given her back her powers of speech.

"That doesn't have quite the same ring to it, does it? Grouper diem. I suppose you could work around the 'per diem' thing, but I'm not sure it's worth the effort."

Savannah didn't hear a word he said. His lips kept moving, but her brain had stopped. Fortunately, in a few seconds the cloud moved away and the sun went back to blinding her. Otherwise, who knows how long she would have just stood there on the sidewalk, not thinking of her new career or her new life or anything but this man's biceps?

"You coming, Mike?" Savannah heard another man say.

With a self-deprecating smile, Savannah turned away from the sun, waved a flipper at the man she assumed was Mike, and said, "Well, I'd best be off to seize the customers."

A low-pitched chuckle followed her as she made her way farther down the sidewalk and tried to forget about Mr. Perfect. She paused briefly at a chalkboard that had been set up near the outdoor seating area of the restaurant. Today's specials at the Fat Cat were pan-seared grouper (Savannah winced) in a shallot-lemon–white wine reduction, a roasted root vegetable penne pasta with goat cheese and toasted pine nuts, crab bisque, and a lobster risotto with fricassee of wild mushrooms.

Savannah swallowed the drool that had gathered beneath her tongue. Man, was she hungry. Her stomach grumbled in protest as she walked past the diners sitting in the roped-off portion of the sidewalk that had been appropriated by the restaurant. She tried to motivate herself with the reminder that if she did this job with enthusiasm, it could be *her* sitting there eating expense-account lunches with her clients and coworkers.

She pasted a bright smile on her face as a well-dressed couple came toward her, pausing only briefly to look at the lunch specials before continuing on their way.

"Fat Cat has the freshest grouper in town," she announced with a flip of her fins.

The couple hurried past, barely sparing her a sideways glance.

Hmm. Maybe she needed a slogan. Ooh, maybe that was part of the test—to come up with a catchy jingle to lure customers in. That certainly made sense. Anyone who worked in advertising would need to be able to recognize a good jingle when she heard it, right?

"Try Fat Cat for the fattest fish in town?" Savannah muttered aloud, trying to see if that had a ring to it.

It didn't.

"Your cat would be fat if he ate at Fat Cat?" she tried again.

"No, that sounds stupid," she said, her forehead creasing as she frowned thoughtfully. She walked a way up the sidewalk, mumbling to herself. "Fat fish. Cat, fat, rat—no, that's not a very appetizing word. Be a fat cat when you eat at Fat Cat? Find the freshest fish at Fat Cat? That's not too bad, I guess."

"Are you all right?" A woman touched Savannah's shoulder, and she turned to find that she was being watched with concern. She looked back down the sidewalk to see that she'd wandered about two blocks from the restaurant. Obviously, people in Naples weren't accustomed to seeing grouper wandering their streets mumbling to themselves.

Savannah smiled and turned back toward the restaurant. "I'm fine, thank you," she said, still mulling over possible slogans.

By the time she reached the restaurant again, she was sweating inside the costume. Her black hair absorbed the heat from the noonday sun as if a solar panel had been strapped to her forehead. She was thankful that most of her hair was shaded by the grouper's head. Otherwise, she might spontaneously combust before she'd aced this interview.

A bead of sweat dripped down Savannah's back and past the waistband of her skirt. Ugh. She could only imagine what her clothes were going to look like when she emerged from this costume. And she wasn't going to have time to run back to her motel room to change after this interview was over or she'd be late to her next one at the shoe store just down the street. Well, with luck, after this ordeal, she'd be offered the advertising sales associate position, and she could politely cancel her next interview. She'd much rather be in advertising than shoe sales, although the idea of showing expensive shoes to wealthy women all day wasn't completely unappealing. The truth was, Savannah wasn't certain she had ever actually seen a pair of Jimmy Choos or Manolo Blahniks outside of the pages of a fashion magazine. It wasn't like there was much demand for $300-a-pair shoes in Maple Rapids.

"Excuse me, do they allow dogs here?"

Savannah blinked at a fashionably dressed young man holding two anorexic-looking greyhounds by matching silver leashes.

"Uh, I'm not sure," she answered. Then, since she figured her potential bosses would be impressed if she showed initiative in customer service, she said, "Let me go find out for you."

The hostess gave her a what-are-you-doing-back-here? look when Savannah poked her head inside the restaurant after struggling to open the heavy front door with her fins. "Do we allow dogs here?" she asked.

The hostess sniffed. "Of course not," she answered disdainfully.

"What about in the outside seating area?" Savannah asked, refusing to be daunted.

"No."

Savannah stepped back and let the door swing shut behind her. "I'm sorry," she told the man. "There are no dogs allowed at the Fat Cat."

The man sighed. "That's so unenlightened."

Not knowing what the appropriate response to that might be, Savannah just nodded and smiled. Then she turned her attention to another couple walking by and said, "The freshest fish in town are at Fat Cat."

The couple surprised Savannah by stopping to look at the specials board, then stunned her even more when, after a whispered conversation, they went inside. Wow. Her first success. She chalked up another point in her favor when the fashionable dog guy also entered the restaurant, sans dogs. She figured it was her "can do" attitude that had convinced him to give the Fat Cat a try, even though they weren't canine friendly.

Pumped up by her victories, Savannah spent the next forty-five minutes standing in the sun flapping her flippers and singsonging her slogan to increase lunch traffic at the Fat Cat. It was only when she spun around too quickly in an attempt to give herself a high five when she landed another customer that she realized how light-headed she was from lack of food. She nearly fell backward when the dizziness overtook her and attempted to put her head between her knees to keep from fainting—an impossible feat since her knees were clamped together inside her costume.

Not wanting to pass out right there on the sidewalk and equally loath to go back into the restaurant and admit defeat, Savannah figured she just needed to get out of the sun for a minute. Just beyond the area that had been roped off for the midday diners, she spied a jacaranda tree with a bench underneath it and waddled toward it.

Gratefully she sank onto the bench. It wasn't much cooler in the shade, but at least the sun wasn't quite as intense. Savannah closed her eyes and let the slight breeze wash over her cheeks.

When she felt something tickling her right ankle, she figured it was just a fly and wiggled her foot to get the insect to leave her alone. She lashed out again a few seconds later when the tickling resumed, surprised when her foot connected with something soft and large and very unbug-like. Her eyes jerked open to see the greyhounds with the silver collars crouched at her feet. One of them licked her shoe again with his long pink tongue and looked up at her with his soulful brown eyes.

Great. She'd forgotten about the beer in her shoes.

"Sorry, guys. I don't think your owner wants you two to be drinking," she said, scooting away from the dogs.

She was about to close her eyes again when she spied the hunky man who had joked with her outside the restaurant. Mike—that's what the other man had called him—was just exiting the restaurant with his friend. Savannah sighed. Wow, was he cute. Like a bigger, more solid version of Matthew McConaughey. Her sigh of longing turned to one of regret, however, when Mike turned to embrace his friend. It wasn't one of those brief, touch-as-few-body-parts-as-you-can-and-get-it-over-with hugs that heterosexual males gave to each other. Instead, it was a real hug. Like one Savannah might exchange with Peggy or one of her sisters.

Why were the cute ones always gay?

Savannah turned away from the scene when she felt that telltale tickling at her feet again. Now both dogs were licking her, their tongues lapping at her feet and ankles.

Suddenly it was all too much. The hunger, the sweat dripping down her back and into her skirt, the dogs treating her as their own personal lollipop, the humiliating costume. She was finished. If she hadn't already done enough to earn the advertising sales associate position, then she'd just have to ace her interview with the shoe store manager and be happy with that.

"I don't know why they can't just ask me about my strengths and weaknesses like normal people," she grumbled as she stood up.

As she took a step forward, she put a hand to her head and squeezed her eyes shut for the briefest of seconds to stem another wave of dizziness. Only, with her eyes closed, she didn't see that she had somehow managed to get her feet tangled up in the greyhounds' leashes. She felt herself lurching forward and flapped her fins to try to regain her balance, then squealed as she pitched forward into the path of an oncoming gelato cart that was being pushed down the sidewalk by an elderly man.

Startled at seeing a woman in a fish costume hurtling toward him, the ice-cream man gasped and pulled back on the cart, trying to get it to stop. But it was heavy and his hands were slick and the sudden move jerked the cart out of his grasp. It gained momentum on the slight slope as Savannah toppled to the sidewalk.

Savannah barely heard the vendor shouting for help as she tried to roll out of the way, hopelessly tangled up in the dogs' leashes. Out of the corner of one eye she could see the cart barreling down on her, and she couldn't believe she was going to meet her Maker covered with dog slobber and wearing a fish suit. Her glamorous new life, over before it had begun.

And then her world went dark. Not—as she had expected—because she'd been run over by the gelato cart, but because a man's body covered her own, his arms gripping her tightly as he rolled her out of the way just before she would have been crushed.

Her face smooshed against the man's heaving chest, Savannah lay still. She heard the clattering of something that sounded like glass breaking and silverware falling mixed with the noise of dogs yelping, but it all came to her ears as if filtered through a haze of fog. She inhaled deeply of her hero's scent, some expensive-smelling cologne mixed with soap and sunshine. He smelled like heaven to her.

It was only when he lifted himself partially off of her that Savannah realized who it was and felt a twinge of disappointment.

Great. It just figured that her knight in shining armor was looking for a prince, not a princess.

"Are you all right?" Mike asked, looking genuinely concerned.

Savannah felt something warm trickle into her costume at the neck. She shifted her gaze to see a large white bowl cracked in two just beside her left ear. Crab bisque was running in a little river toward her head. Other dishes and silverware littered the ground around them, and Savannah realized that they must have crashed into a tray of food when Mike rolled her out of the way of the gelato cart.

She stared up at the nearly cloudless blue sky beyond her rescuer's head, feeling more miserable than she had since being arrested back in Maple Rapids. She couldn't even go on a simple job interview without it ending in disaster.

Todd was right. She wasn't worth this trouble.

Savannah held back a sniffle as Mike rolled off her and pulled them both into a sitting position in one smooth movement. He was still looking at her as if wondering if she'd cracked her head when she fell. "Are you okay?" he asked again.

Savannah nodded and gave him a watery smile. "I'm fine," she said, then sniffed.

"I guess I shouldn't make any jokes about telling the waiter there's a snapper in my soup, huh?" he teased.

A lump of crabmeat dropped from her hair onto her lap. Staring fixedly at the white blob on her greenish-blue costume, Savannah sighed.

"I'm a grouper," she corrected him, then awkwardly lurched to her feet. She held out a fin as Mike also stood, dusting off the back of his jeans. "Thank you for . . . saving me," she said awkwardly, waving toward the retreating man with the gelato cart.

"It was my pleasure," Mike said with a smile that made Savannah's already weak knees wobble even more.

She had to get away from him before she did anything even more stupid than she'd already done. Not that it mattered. She wasn't exactly his type anyway. With a final nod, she turned away and weaved through the crowded tables, wondering the entire time if Vanna was here, eating an expensive lunch with her glamorous friends and laughing at the pathetic spectacle Savannah had made of herself.

What's Your Greatest Weakness?

We've all been asked this question a time or two, whether at a job interview or on a date with someone who likes to play twenty questions. Of course, we know how to spin the answer to our benefit when we have to. But, come on, tell the truth now. What *is* your greatest weakness?

a. You cry during sappy Hallmark commercials and chick flicks.

b. You can't resist chocolate and Krispy Kreme doughnuts.

c. Weakness? What weakness? Everything about you is perfect!

Newsflash to you A gals—everyone cries during Hallmark commercials and chick flicks. Duh. Those of you who chose B need to realize that eating fattening foods isn't a weakness—it's our God-given right! Once again, C is the correct answer. You know you're perfect just the way you are!

{nine}

So, how was your lunch at the Fat Cat?" Lillian Bryson asked innocently as her youngest son, Mike, sat down across from her, planting his booted feet on the carpet. Of her two boys, Mike was the more classically handsome. She loved both of her children equally, of course, but she and Mike were closer than she and Sam were, most likely because Sam had spent the last twenty years as a Navy SEAL stationed on the West Coast and often disappearing for long stretches to places he never talked about. Sam had already been in the Navy for four years when his father died suddenly, at forty-five, of a massive heart attack. Sixteen-year-old Mike had been the one to find his father, slumped over the breakfast table, when he'd come down to grab some Pop-Tarts before heading to school.

Lillian feared that Mike had been forced to grow up too soon—not because he had been thrust into the role of provider or anything so dramatic, but because she was afraid she'd not done a very good job at hiding her sorrow at the loss of her soul mate. She hadn't realized how her sadness was affecting her younger son until it was too late. And it wasn't like the changes were necessarily bad. Mike had gone from a decent student more interested in playing tennis and hanging out with his friends to a serious young man intent on earning scholarships so as not to be a burden on his mother. She never knew if his decision to go to the University of South Florida in St. Petersburg was because it was the school he truly wanted to attend or if he was simply going there to stay close to her. She had been so deep in the fog of her own grief, she had simply been grateful for Mike's bimonthly visits. Looking back, she wasn't certain how she would have survived that dark period of her life without him.

But now she worried that Mike was too responsible, too serious. He was always looking ahead, always working toward something in the future, but she feared this meant he wasn't enjoying the present. Which was why, despite her track record at matchmaking, she refused to give up trying to find a wife for her son—preferably a woman with good values and a sense of fun. Perhaps like their new tenant, Savannah Taylor, who Lillian had taken an instant liking to when they'd met yesterday afternoon . . . Which was why she'd suggested to Mike that he and Sam have lunch at the Fat Cat today, where Savannah had gone for her job interview. She planned to do everything in her power to throw Mike and Savannah together and see if they hit it off as she hoped they would.

"It was interesting," Mike answered with an enigmatic smile before he continued. "Sam said to say hello and to let you know that he'll be at your house around seven for dinner tomorrow night."

Lillian nodded and tapped the notepad in front of her with the tip of her pen. "Are you going to be able to make it?" she asked.

"Yeah. I've got an early flight tomorrow. Miami to Chicago and back. I should be home by five or six at the latest. I'll have to stop in after work and check on the motel to make sure those kids haven't torn the place apart in my absence. I don't know what possessed you to rent them rooms."

Lillian laughed at the dour look on her son's face and waved one hand dismissively. "Oh, they're just kids having a good time."

"Well, their music is shaking the roof tiles loose. If they're at it again tonight, *you* can come over and try to get them to quiet down."

"I'll do that," Lillian said, knowing that Mike wasn't as put out by the college students as he tried to make it seem. Then she changed the subject to the one she wanted to discuss with him in the first place. "Have you met our newest tenant? Savannah Taylor? I put her in twenty-three, right next to you."

Mike slouched back in his chair and crossed his feet at the ankle. "No, but she seems to fit right in with the kids," he said.

Lillian stopped tapping her pen. "What do you mean? She seems like a nice girl. Very responsible."

"Yeah, if you call blasting loud rock music with no regard for your neighbors 'responsible,'" Mike muttered. "Did you have Lainie or Jack run a background check on her? Since she's planning to stay so long, we really should know if we can expect any trouble. I don't suppose you got a damage deposit from her like you're supposed to do when you rent someone a room for over a week?"

Smoothing a hand over her hair, Lillian looked away from her son so he wouldn't see the guilt in her eyes. He never did trust her hunches about people, preferring cold hard proof instead.

"That's what I thought," Mike said, and Lillian glanced back in time to see him shaking his head.

"She had wonderful references," Lillian protested. "And she did pay this week's rent in advance."

"All right, Mom. I'm sure it'll be fine. But I'm still going to have Intrepid do a background check just in case," he said, referring to the private investigations firm housed next door to his mother's business. "Do you have the application? I'll drop it over on my way out."

Lillian handed her son the file she'd set up for Savannah, which contained records of her conversations with their new tenant's former boss and the president of her homeowners' association. As Mike took the file and stood up, Lillian steepled her fingers together on her desk. She just knew the investigation was a waste of time and money.

What could that nice Savannah Taylor possibly have to hide?

"What would you say is your greatest weakness?"

I'm a gullible moron? Savannah considered the answer, then discarded it. Surely her interviewer didn't expect her to be *that* honest. She pasted an earnest smile on her face and focused on Valeen Wright, the owner of Valeen's shoe shop,

which was just down the street from the Fat Cat restaurant—
an establishment Savannah vowed never to step foot in again.

She had been so stupid, thinking that the whole grouper
costume thing was some kind of test. After picking herself up
off the sidewalk and walking away from Mike, she'd high-
tailed it to the ladies' room to clean up before demanding to
know whether or not she'd landed the advertising sales associate position.

She'd studied herself in the mirror, noting that the heat and
humidity had turned her new Lush Lash mascara to paste. At
$14.99 a tube, she would have expected *Glamour*'s "Top
Beauty Pick for March" to hold up better under pressure.

"Maybe they should name it 'Backlash,'" Savannah ob-
served glumly as she used a paper towel to try to blot the black
clumps from her eyes without smearing them all over her
face. She heard the ladies' room door open but kept her eyes
closed as she continued removing mascara from her lashes.
She was past caring who might see her looking like a disaster
in her stained and wrinkled clothing, her hair damp with sweat
from being stuck inside that fish costume in the midday heat.

"Are you about done with your break? We need you back
outside."

Savannah pried her eyelashes apart and squinted at the
woman behind her. It was the hostess from out front, looking
as fresh and clean as she had when she'd first ushered Savannah inside and forced her into that costume. Fighting a wave
of despair, Savannah chanced a glance at her watch. She had
less than twenty minutes before her next interview. She'd
done her best to prove what a valuable asset she would be.
Now it was time for her potential employer to fish or cut bait.

Perhaps, she thought, this was just another interview test to
see how much abuse a potential employee would take before
putting her foot down and saying, "No more." It was important to set limits in business, to give your best but not be a
doormat.

Inhaling a deep, calming breath to center herself (a tip
from *Cosmo*'s "Five Ways to De-Stress in Five Seconds or
Less"), Savannah turned away from the mirror and said, "I'm
not going back out there until I know whether or not I have
the job."

The hostess scowled at her. "Were you out in the sun too long or something?" she asked.

Savannah's gaze darted to the mirror. Was her nose sunburned? Well, maybe it was a little, but what did that have to do with the job? "I'm fine," she answered with a dismissive wave of her hand. "Did I get the job or not?"

"Of course you have the job. What the hell do you think you've been doing for the past two hours?"

Savannah's mouth fell open as she took a step back, away from the bathroom door. No. No, no, no. The hostess had to be kidding. Or playing some sort of cruel joke at Savannah's expense. "But . . . but . . . but I wasn't being an advertising sales associate. I was a talking fish," Savannah spluttered.

"No," the hostess said, looking down her nose at Savannah as if she were just about the stupidest person she'd ever encountered. "You were *advertising* our restaurant to increase our *sales*. Advertising. Sales. Associate. Get it?"

Savannah's back hit the bathroom wall with a loud *thunk*. Oh, God. How could she have been so naive? Closing her eyes with despair, she clutched her head in her hands. How in the world could she have thought that dressing up in a dorky costume was some kind of an interview test for a better, cooler job?

She was such a moron.

"I'm going to take this and leave you alone for a minute," the hostess said, speaking softly as if she thought that Savannah might snap and go on a rampage at any moment.

Savannah heard a faint rustling as the hostess slowly lifted the grouper costume off the peg in the handicapped stall where Savannah had hung it. She opened her eyes and peered through her fingers as the hostess backed away, holding the costume up like a shield just in case Savannah gave in to the urge to lunge for her throat. Then she slipped through the bathroom door, leaving Savannah alone in the silent lavatory.

Savannah remained motionless against the wall for what seemed like a long time. She knew that this was one of those pick-yourself-up-by-your-bootstraps moments, but she couldn't force her weary mind to make her limbs work. Besides, it was peaceful in here. And cool. A self-contained waterfall gurgled and splashed on the granite countertop and Savannah was tempted to stay in here forever.

But she couldn't. It was time to move on.

"You've got some sense of humor all right," she mumbled, looking heavenward as she pushed herself away from the wall. It was time to end this pity party. Otherwise, she'd miss her next interview.

An interview that, fortunately, was going exactly as Savannah had expected—not an M&M or manhole question in the bunch.

Savannah tried to look thoughtful as she gave her standard answer to Valeen's "greatest weakness" question. "I'd say my greatest weakness is that I care too much about my work. I can't sleep knowing I haven't done my very best at my job," she said.

Valeen, a slender chain-smoking blonde of indeterminate age, seemed pleased by her response.

Savannah sat back in her chair. Now, this was how interviews were supposed to work.

"Why did you leave your last position?" Valeen asked after taking a deep drag of her slim cigarette. Her words came out accompanied by a cloud of smoke and Savannah had to clear her throat to cover the urge to cough.

She had practiced her answer for this question several times this morning and it came out easily now. "The work was too easy because I'd been doing the same job for too long. I wanted to do something different. To challenge myself," she added.

Valeen's red-lipsticked mouth twitched with a smile as she made another note on Savannah's application. "I think it's important that we don't allow ourselves to stagnate," she said, her voice throaty as only a lifelong smoker's could be. "When can you start?"

Savannah blinked at the unexpected question. "Um, right away?" she answered, cringing inside when she realized that she'd made it sound like a question.

"That's fabulous. Be here tomorrow at nine A.M." Valeen stood to signal the end of the interview, then frowned when Savannah got out of her chair. "Oh, and about your shoes . . ." She paused, staring down at Savannah's feet, a distasteful look hovering about her pursed lips.

Savannah felt her cheeks flush with embarrassment. Could

Valeen smell the beer that had dribbled into her pumps? She hoped not.

"You get a forty percent discount on all shoes in stock. Our customers expect you to know the merchandise, and they can smell a fake at forty feet."

Well, as long as they couldn't smell booze, Savannah figured she'd do just fine. With a grin she held out her hand to her new boss and said, "Understood. I'll see you tomorrow at nine."

Valeen shook her hand with her own cold, bony one before ushering Savannah out of her office and onto the sales floor filled with expensive footwear. Savannah lingered a moment, letting her hand glide over the supple leather of a sexy high-heeled boot, then fingered the heart-shaped charm attached to one red strappy sandal. These were the shoes that graced the pages of *Vogue* and *Marie Claire* and *Cosmo,* shoes that confident women wore every day, unmindful that they might get dirty or wet or that their heel might get caught in a crack in the sidewalk and break off. These women didn't worry about such things because they never happened to *them*. Women who wore shoes like the ones at Valeen's didn't fall in front of gelato carts or get arrested at the altar, and they sure as hell didn't have fiancés who told them that they weren't worth the trouble. Savannah wanted so much to be one of them that she closed her eyes, her fingers closing convulsively over the heart-shaped charm she'd been fondling.

"Please. Please turn me into someone different," she whispered silently, almost reverently, as if praying to some sort of footwear fairy godmother for help with her transformation.

Then the buzzer on the front door squawked as a potential customer entered the shop. As she wafted by Savannah in a cloud of Chanel No. 5, Savannah inhaled deeply and let her hand drop to her side. She had just landed her dream job. Now all she could do was hope that some of whatever magic these women possessed would rub off on her.

How Sexy Are You?

You can tell a lot about a woman by the clothes she wears closest to her skin. Come on, girls, it's time to take a peek in your underwear drawer! Pull it open. What do you see?

a. Plain white cotton panties as far as the eye can see.

b. Mostly sensible undies with a flash of color and a daring red crotchless number you've got stashed away just in case.

c. One of everything from the latest Victoria's Secret catalog—and none of it in white!

Do we really need to tell you A gals that your lingerie is bo-ring . . . and most likely, your love life is, too! If B was your answer, your man is comfortable around you and enjoys that you occasionally surprise him in bed with a new move or a sexy striptease just for fun. Those of you who chose C, you're hot, hot, hot in the bedroom and your lovers appreciate you for it!

{ten}

Despite—or perhaps because of—her success at Valeen's, Savannah felt restless that evening, dissatisfied with her sad little dinner of frozen Lean Cuisine and a celebratory glass of wine from a Styrofoam cup.

"Face it. You're lonely," she said wistfully to her reflection in the front window of her motel room as she stared out over the courtyard below. Moving here had been the right decision. She was certain of it. Here in Naples she was free to become anyone she wanted to be, to do anything she wanted to do. But she hadn't realized that the cost of that freedom was loneliness. Yes, she no longer had her family's expectations to live up (or down) to. As a matter of fact, no one here cared at all what she did. And that was the problem. No one cared about her at all.

She put one hand against the warm window and watched the students outside for a moment. They were so carefree, so happy. Savannah supposed she'd felt the same way at that age. Back when she was in college, the world had seemed full of endless possibilities. Which had been the cause of her downfall—with so much to choose from, how did you pick? She thought back to those days, wondering if she could pinpoint the exact moment when her big dreams came crashing to the ground. Did the answer lie in one seemingly unimportant decision, like when she'd decided to take an accounting course instead of art history, or was it something more ingrained in her personality, something about her that had doomed her to an insignificant life from the very beginning?

Savannah took a deep, shuddering breath and closed her eyes, surprised when a tear dripped into her Chardonnay. Watching the students outside filled her with such a sense of longing and regret for her own wasted life that she was tempted to open her door and shout a warning to them not to play it safe or they'd end up like her: alone, unloved, and unfulfilled in a dingy motel room far from home.

And then a mattress passed by her window, sending all her self-pitying thoughts fleeing from her mind.

Savannah pressed her face to the glass to see the mattress, carried by two young men, continue down the walkway. She laughed and shook her head at their antics. Best not to ask what they were up to.

Instead, she plopped down on the lumpy floral-patterned chair near the window and opened the magazine she'd picked up at the mini-mart along with her wine and frozen dinner. She flipped randomly through the magazine, stopping to see which style of little black dress would best suit her figure (fitted top with slender straps to enhance her small chest and a flowy bottom to hide her not-so-trim hips), then moved on to a quiz that promised to determine how sexy you were by what was in your underwear drawer.

Savannah winced, knowing she was probably about to take another beating.

She followed the quiz's directions, going over to the dresser with a television perched on top and opening the middle drawer, where she'd stashed her underwear. The sight that met her eyes reminded her of a joke in the art appreciation class she'd taken when the instructor, while trying to explain modern art, held up a blank sheet of paper.

"What do you see here?" she had asked.

Several people had raised their hands, all pretty much giving the same answer: nothing.

The teacher had smiled. "Well," she replied, "that's what *you* see. The modern artist, however, sees a helpless white rabbit trapped in a vicious blizzard while ghosts of those who died here before look on. The artist has titled this piece 'Doom.'"

The class had laughed, but Savannah had learned a lesson that day. Life was all about your perspective. Although perhaps the lesson should have been about the depths artists would go to in order to seem clever. Or to sell a piece and pay the rent.

Well, whatever the message was supposed to have been, she looked at her drawer full of stark white cotton panties and thought, *"Doom."*

But, unlike that poor rabbit, she was not helpless. She saw the storm coming to wipe her out, to doom her to a life of boredom, and she chose to step out of its path. She may have let life happen to her, to let events shape what she'd become and get her to this point, but no more. Now *she* was taking control.

And if getting rid of her dull underwear would help to make her sexy, then she'd do it.

Savannah grabbed a handful of panties, raising them to the sky like a sword. "You are not going to beat me," she vowed, scooping up all but one remaining pair of her white undies. Then, knowing that she'd never be motivated to buy new underwear if the old ones weren't completely gone (she knew her practical nature would try to put off buying new panties until the old ones wore out), she went into the kitchenette and grabbed the thin plastic bag the clerk at the mini-mart had used to wrap her purchases earlier that evening and stuffed her panties in it.

These babies were Dumpster-bound.

With her bag of undies in one hand and her room key in the other, Savannah stepped outside into the warm Florida evening. Even in mid-March it was humid, though she'd been told that this was nothing compared to what it would be like in the summer, when the air was so damp you couldn't step outside without feeling as if you'd stepped into a steam bath. This information was always followed by a laugh and the assurance that it was even worse elsewhere in the state, although she wasn't certain why that would make a difference. It was like having your plane crash in the middle of the ocean and being surrounded by hungry bull sharks and having someone tell you that at least these weren't great whites. She figured if you were about to be eaten by sharks, it didn't much matter which ones were worse.

But for now the weather was quite pleasant, with temperatures in the high seventies and humidity at a bearable fifty percent. It certainly beat the subzero temperatures back in upper Michigan at this time of year.

The trash bins were located across the courtyard from Savannah's room, and she hesitated for a moment before deciding to walk through the crowd of students hanging around the kidney-shaped swimming pool instead of skulking in the shadows to reach her destination. After all, she was paying the same nightly rate as they were. Why shouldn't she roam freely about the premises?

She straightened her shoulders and refused to feel self-conscious as she crossed the courtyard. She was skirting the edge of the pool when one of the young women in the group stepped in front of her and said, "Hey."

At five-four Savannah had to look up to meet the girl's gaze. "Yes?" she asked, squashing her initial burst of jealousy at the younger woman's appearance. Even at nineteen Savannah had not looked like this woman, with her smooth brown hair, flat stomach, and endlessly long legs exposed by her tight pink shorts.

"Would you like a drink?" the student asked, surprising Savannah. She didn't know why she had expected the other woman to be mean or rude, but she had.

"Uh, no, thanks. I was just on my way to the trash," Savannah said, holding up her bag as if to prove it.

The woman smiled, exposing small, even white teeth. "You could take it with you," she said, then held out her hand. "I'm Christina, by the way."

"Savannah," Savannah said, shifting the grocery bag to her left hand as she took Christina's hand with her right.

Both women looked up, startled, when they heard a loud "Yee-haw!" from up above. They watched in horror, their feet rooted to the concrete, as a mattress, straddled by a young man, flew off the sloped tile roof and headed straight for them.

* * *

Mike Bryson pulled into the motel parking lot and saw that the red Thunderbird was still hogging more than its fair share of parking spaces. He made a mental note to find out which of his renters owned the vehicle so he could ask that they be a little more considerate of others and move the car so it wasn't taking up so much room, but then he realized that it wasn't really the T-bird's fault. The car parked next to the red behemoth was parked over its line, as was the next one down the row.

"All right. I'll cut you some slack," Mike said to the convertible as he once again backed his pickup out of the lot and cruised around to find parking on the street. He locked the truck and grabbed the grocery bags from the back, careful not to drop anything as he headed back to the motel.

He half-expected to hear the thudding bass of the students' rap music as he neared the white building. It was only nine o'-clock, but even if it were later, he really didn't expect them to heed his warning to keep it down. He was fully aware that, as an authority figure, he was the enemy.

Fortunately, with his job, he was accustomed to this attitude . . . even from people who should know better.

Mike pushed open the door leading to the interior of the motel just in time to hear a bloodcurdling scream. He dropped his groceries in the stairwell and sprinted toward the noise, wondering what the hell was going on. As he emerged into the courtyard, his eyes took in a bizarre scene. Two women, standing by the edge of the pool. A flying mattress, like Aladdin's magic carpet, hurtling toward them. Mike charged, sprinting across the patio like a bodyguard determined to stop a bullet from reaching his charge. He tackled the women, grabbing them around the waists and pushing them into the deep end of the pool just before the missile would have smashed into their chests.

Savannah didn't know what had hit her. She wasn't even sure if it had been her or Christina who had screamed right before they were unceremoniously shoved into the swimming pool. But what she was certain of as she came up spluttering was that whoever had pushed them into the pool had a very firm chest. She knew this because her nose was currently pressed into that chest as the man who had shoved her into the deep end hauled her to the side of the pool.

"I can swim," she protested into the man's wet shirt, since he was holding her so tightly that she couldn't look up without knocking the top of her head into his chin. Secretly, however, she had to admit that it was nice to be held this close. She could feel the warmth of the man's hard stomach pressed against her belly, the caress of his jeans against her bare legs as he pulled her into the shallow end.

Savannah closed her eyes and relaxed against him, glad that he didn't let her go until her feet were resting safely on the bottom of the pool. She had to force herself to step away from him, only to look up and find herself gazing into the same gray-blue eyes that had so mesmerized her earlier that day.

Her heart dropped to the pit of her stomach. "My hero," she breathed.

His mouth quirked up at the corners, as though he was trying not to laugh. "Are you okay?"

Savannah shook her head, clearing the water out of her brain. "Yes. Sorry. I'm fine. What are *you* doing here?"

A lock of hair flopped onto his forehead and water dripped into his eyes. Savannah noticed that his hair got darker when it was wet, the blond highlights nearly disappearing. He pushed the hair off his face and smiled down at her. "I manage this place," he explained, then added, "I almost didn't recognize you without your grouper costume."

At that moment Savannah wanted to wail at Fate for being so cruel. Of course. This must be Lillian Bryson's son, Mike. The one she was certain was gay after Lillian mentioned the sort of mate he always brought home—and even more certain about his sexual preference after seeing him hug his friend at the restaurant that afternoon. How could she be so attracted to a man that she could never have? She wanted to stomp her feet and throw herself on the ground and thrash her arms like a spoiled two-year-old whose mother wouldn't let her have a lollipop.

Yeah, I'd like to lick him all over. The thought came out of nowhere, startling Savannah. Whoa. That kind of stuff never entered her mind. She was an accountant, for God's sake.

Hmm. But maybe this new Savannah thing was really

working. Maybe she really was becoming someone sexy and adventurous, a real love goddess.

Great. And the guy who brings out the goddess in you just happens to be gay.

"Shut up," Savannah muttered to that mocking voice in her head.

"Pardon me?" Mike asked.

Savannah pushed a lock of hair behind her ear and said, "Nothing. I was just . . . talking to myself."

"You're sure you're all right?"

"Yes. I'm fine," Savannah answered, wondering what he'd do if she put a hand to her head and faked a swoon. Would he carry her up to her room like Rhett Butler to her Scarlett O'Hara? The thought of that nearly made her knees collapse for real.

Engrossed in her fantasy, Savannah clutched the side of the pool as Mike turned to survey the scene of the crime. Christina had already hauled herself up and out of the pool and was smiling down at the idiot who had nearly decapitated her and Savannah with the flying mattress. The mattress had floated to the far end of the pool, where the boy clung to it, grinning at Christina and no doubt enjoying the view as her wet clothes clung to every curve of her perfect body. Savannah glanced down at her own soggy clothes and sighed. It was obvious she wasn't hiding a perfect body under there. But what did it matter? It wasn't like—

A white scrap of fabric drifted toward Mike's waist and Savannah gasped. She had forgotten all about her underwear.

Oh, no, she thought, shoving herself away from the edge of the pool and lunging toward the panties. *Don't let him pick those up!*

"What are—" Mike began as he reached out and took hold of a pair of her undies.

Her cheeks burning with embarrassment, Savannah grabbed the panties from Mike's hand at the same moment he realized what he was holding. "Those are mine," she mumbled, balling the panties up and attempting to hide them behind her back.

"Well, uh." Mike cleared his throat as if he were trying not to laugh. "Let me get them out of the pool before they clog the filter."

Savannah refused to meet his eyes as he hauled himself up out of the swimming pool and then reached down to help her out. She, of course, could have just as easily swum to the stairs on the other side of the pool, but when he held one strong, warm hand down to her, she didn't resist.

Clutching her lone pair of panties to her chest, she sighed as she watched Mike walk away, his jeans clinging to one of the finest asses she'd ever seen. Life was so not fair.

He returned a few moments later with a bright blue net at the end of a long pole.

"James, get out of the pool," he ordered to the student who was still clinging to the mattress in the pool. "And get that mattress out of there, too. I don't know what the hell you were thinking, but you could have killed someone with that stupid stunt. You can bet that your parents are going to hear about this."

Savannah watched as Mike fished her underwear out of the pool, the students—male and female alike—watching him with a mixture of admiration and respect. When he was done, he walked back to her, reached into the net, and handed her her underwear. Despite her embarrassment, Savannah whispered, "You don't sound all that upset."

Mike shrugged and leaned closer to her, so close she could smell a faint trace of cologne on his wet shirt. "Boys this age are idiots. They think they're invincible. I knew when my mother rented rooms to them that something like this would happen. It was only a matter of time."

"Do they ever grow out of it? Being idiots, I mean?" Savannah asked with a laugh to let him know that she was only joking. The guys she'd always hung out with had been the serious, studious types—not prone to flying off rooftops riding stolen mattresses.

Mike grinned and shocked Savannah when he bent down and kissed the tip of her nose. He looked as surprised as she felt when he pulled back, his lips just inches from hers, and said, "Apparently not."

Will You Ever Be Rich?

You walk into the ladies' room at your local department store and find an envelope bulging with cash. There's nothing that identifies who the money belongs to, only a phone number written in black pen on the envelope itself. What do you do?

a. Duh! Call the number and tell whoever answers that you've found their missing loot.

b. Leave it there. You don't want to get involved. With this amount of cash, it could be drug money and you don't want your fingerprints anywhere near it.

c. What a dumb question! No one is going to see you take the money. You casually slip the cash into your purse and head straight to your bank to open an investment account.

What? Are you A girls looking for a special pass into heaven? Stop trying to make the rest of us look bad and take the money already! Those of you who chose B watched The Sopranos one too many times. You'll never be rich because you're too afraid of your own shadow to take the necessary risks. You C gals win again! Wisely invest those windfalls, and we'll see you on your yacht on the Riviera. You deserve more out of life and you know it!

{eleven}

Mike lay in bed that night, staring at the wall that separated his room from Savannah Taylor's, marveling at his own behavior. He couldn't believe he'd kissed her out of the blue like that. For God's sake, he didn't even know her. She certainly didn't appear to be his type—he liked practical, responsible women, not ones who dressed like fish or wandered around motels carrying their underwear.

But that didn't mean he wasn't attracted to her. Mike rubbed his forehead with a thumb and forefinger and tried to coax himself to stop thinking about how cute she'd looked with her green eyes round with horror as he'd fished her panties out of the pool. She had been so embarrassed. Definitely not the type of girl who'd grab a guy's crotch the first time they met like that woman . . . what was her name? Tiffany? No. Ashleigh. Yeah, that was it. Ashleigh, who'd come on to him on the flight from Miami with a fiancé waiting for her back home in Naples.

Mike closed his eyes and tried to imagine Savannah doing something like that, then swore when he realized that his imagination was all too happy to serve up that fantasy. Great, how was he supposed to sleep now?

With a sigh he got out of bed, pulled on a pair of swimming

trunks, and grabbed a towel. And as he went down to the pool for a calming midnight swim, he made a vow. As soon as Intrepid Investigations finished with Savannah's background check, he would ask her out and see if she even came close to the woman in his dreams.

With all that had happened that day, Savannah expected to toss and turn all night, reliving her humiliation over and over again well into the wee hours of the morning. Instead, after Mike had fished her key out of the pool's skimmer basket, she went up to her room, curled up into a ball in the middle of her bed, pulled the thin blanket over her shoulders, and slept like a contented cat until the alarm clock on the nightstand by the bed rang at seven-thirty the next morning.

She opened her eyes immediately and turned off the alarm, never one to hit the snooze button for hours when she was supposed to be getting ready for work. She pushed back the covers, feeling a little stiff, but surprisingly optimistic about the day ahead.

"Probably because it couldn't get any worse than yesterday," she said with a self-deprecating laugh. Then she dragged herself into the kitchen to make coffee, frowning when she realized that she'd been spending way too much time talking to herself lately.

"Maybe I need to get a cat," she said as her toes touched the chilly linoleum. She wondered if talking to a pet would make her seem any less crazy.

She took her time getting ready for her first day as "Savannah Taylor, Shoe Saleswoman to the Stars." She repeated the phrase to herself a few times, lowering her voice as if she were a TV announcer, liking how it made her sound important—like Spiderman or Wonder Woman or something.

The front door to Valeen's was locked when she arrived at fifteen minutes to nine, so Savannah took a seat on a bench on the sidewalk and indulged in a bit of people-watching. Everyone here looked so happy, even the ones balancing cups of coffee in their hands as they pulled open doors to the various offices, art galleries, and boutiques lining the street. Savannah wondered if they really were happy, or if it was just all this sunshine that made them glow.

When she spied a tall, thin man hurrying down the sidewalk toward her, his skin a grayish-white color that she hadn't seen on anyone in Naples except for herself, Savannah watched him out of the corner of her eyes. He was not glowing. As a matter of fact, he was glowering.

He marched past her without acknowledging her presence, too intent upon his mission to notice the other people on the sidewalk. When he opened the door to an office half a block from where she was sitting, Savannah read the lettering on the window and said, "Ah. That explains it." The man worked for her old company, Refund City. And with just a month to go until April 15, she knew the reason for the man's pallor. He probably hadn't seen the sun for two months, and wouldn't get to do so for another thirty days. Accountants at tax time were like moles, poking their heads up out of the ground only when flushed out by hunger or predators.

She assumed there would be some seasonality in the shoe business, but guessed it was nothing like being an accountant at a firm like Refund City, where the vast majority of business was transacted from mid-February until midnight on April 15.

Savannah turned when she heard the door behind her being unlocked. Her new boss, Valeen, stood framed in the doorway, looking like some 1940s movie star. Her dark green felt hat was adorned with speckled feathers, and her nylons had seams that ran down the backs of her calves. Her crocodile shoes were the same dark green as her hat and had a squared toe, a chunky heel, and a burnished brass buckle across the top. She was wearing one of those slim, Doris Day movie suits—the skirt so binding at the knees that it forced her to walk with an exaggerated hip sway. On Savannah the outfit would have looked silly, but on tall blond Valeen, it was glamorous.

For her first day Savannah had chosen to christen Ski Bunny—Look #3 on her "Seven Sexiest New Looks" list. She even felt a little glamorous in her all-white outfit with the silver belt around her waist. The white, fur-trimmed cardigan was a bit warm for south Florida, but she figured that once inside the air-conditioned boutique, she'd be comfortable. Her only problem had been with her shoes. The magazine had paired the outfit with a pair of white sherpa boots that would have looked completely wrong here in sunny Naples. Instead,

Savannah had "borrowed" a pair of metallic sandals from Look #6—Hot City Nights—but bare toes with a fur-trimmed cardigan just didn't look right.

Savannah was hopeful that Valeen would have some advice for her, so as they entered the shop, she figured she might as well address the issue before her boss did and said, "I realized this morning that these shoes just don't go with this outfit. Do you have any suggestions?"

Valeen stowed her handbag in one of the drawers beneath the cash register in the middle of the boutique and turned to study Savannah's feet. Narrowing her eyes, she pursed her lips and tapped her full bottom lip with the tip of one index finger and said, "Hmm."

Finally she nodded and spun around. "Yes, I have the perfect thing. You're a what? Six and a half?"

"Wow, you're good," Savannah said, sliding her purse into the drawer next to Valeen's.

"Here. Come with me," Valeen said. "I'll show you how to find the inventory."

Thus, Savannah began her new career wearing a pair of silver ankle boots with four-inch heels that made her wobble when she walked but made her feel like a true sex goddess whenever she caught a glimpse of herself in one of the many mirrors scattered throughout the shop. The boots—even with her forty percent employee discount—set her back over a hundred dollars. With less than two hundred dollars left in her bank account, she was almost completely broke. Having her identity stolen and then coming here to find Vanna had brought her to the brink of financial ruin, but Savannah no longer cared. At least she was doing something unexpected for a change.

And speaking of unexpected, Savannah wondered if the woman who had stolen her identity ever expected one of her victims to try to find her. Most likely she knew that if she kept the monetary value of her crime low and covered her tracks reasonably well, the FBI wouldn't bother to come after her. As Agent Harrison had explained, law enforcement treated identity theft as a sort of victimless crime since all an innocent party had to do was to protest the fraudulent charges made in their name in order to get them expunged from her records. It wasn't an easy or quick process to clean up your credit report once your identity was stolen, but it wasn't impossible, either. So who paid for the crime? Savannah had wanted to know. Agent Harrison told her that the credit-card companies and merchants paid initially, but, of course, they passed their expenses along to the consumer in the form of higher interest rates and elevated prices. In some ways, Savannah thought, it was like crime laundering. You take a crime, remove the victim, and voilá—no more crime.

But Savannah wasn't giving up so easy. She wanted to meet the woman who had dropped thousands of dollars here at Valeen's on shoes just like the ones Savannah herself was now wearing. She wasn't certain what she'd do once she found Vanna, but she just knew she had to meet her, to see if all those expensive dinners and fancy footwear made her the type of woman Savannah dreamed of becoming.

"Ah, your first customer," Valeen murmured beside her as the buzzer on the door beeped and a dark-haired woman stepped in, followed by a miniature version of herself. Valeen favored Savannah with a slight smile and slid silently back into the stockroom.

Savannah knew that Valeen would be watching to see how she handled the customers, so she gave them her brightest smile and cheerfully said, "Good morning. How can I help you?"

"Byrony, you look around here. I'm going across the street. I'll come get you when I'm finished." The woman—who Savannah assumed was the girl's mother—didn't even bother to address Savannah.

Then the woman turned and left. The girl, seemingly unconcerned about being ditched, slowly walked to the artfully arranged display near the front of the boutique.

Valeen displayed her shoes on clear acrylic pedestals of varying heights. Track lighting along the ceiling illuminated each cluster of pedestals, making it appear as if they were lit from within. It was all very "shoes as objects to be revered," Savannah thought.

Byrony, who was probably no more than eleven or twelve, was obviously not in a reverential mood, however, because she nonchalantly picked up a Swarovski-crystal-beaded Stuart Weitzman sandal, tossed it to the floor, stuck her foot inside it without bothering to take off her Adidas spa shoes first, and clumped around the boutique like Captain Hook on his pegleg.

"Um, we don't really have any children's shoes," Savannah said hesitantly after the girl had made one round and started on a second. She glanced back toward the stockroom to see what Valeen thought about this, but her boss had disappeared.

"I'm looking for a gift," Byrony said with a haughty look from under her lashes as if Savannah were some kind of idiot.

Not wanting to offend the girl in case that were really true, Savannah didn't say what she was thinking, which was *What kind of kid spends $365 on a pair of shoes—even if they* are *a gift?* Instead, she said, "Okay. Who is this gift for?"

Byrony continued circling the room, her feet making a *clomp*-step, *clomp*-step noise as she walked. "My nanny," she answered.

"Oh," Savannah said. "Was that your nanny who came in with you?"

The girl stopped and looked at her with a contempt that Savannah reserved for child molesters or people who tortured animals. "No-o," Byrony answered. "That was my mother. Carmina was sick today."

"Is that why you're buying her the gift? So she'll feel better?" Savannah asked, wondering how it was that this skinny girl with attitude could make her feel so hopelessly inferior.

Byrony stared at her for a long moment before breathing out a disgusted "Duh" under her breath and saying only "Birthday," as if she were completely out of patience.

But Savannah refused to let this child intimidate her any further, so she reminded herself that nobody could make her feel like an idiot. Only *she* could do that. She flashed the girl a perky smile and walked over to some pastel-colored, shearling-lined slip-ons adorned with the Nike swoosh. "These would be a nice gift for someone who spends a lot of time on her feet," she said, then added, "And they're only $89.95."

Byrony didn't even bother to glance at the slippers as she *clomp*-stepped past Savannah.

Savannah put the shoe back on its pedestal. "No? Something with a little more attitude perhaps?" She looked around the store, her gaze alighting on a shoe that Valeen had told her had just come in last weekend. They were black clogs with white stitching along the toe, adorned with a choice of white, purple, pink, or blue leather flowers. "These are cute," she said, holding out one for Byrony's inspection. She turned the shoe over to check the handwritten price on the label affixed to the sole. "And even more reasonable at $79.95."

Byrony just scoffed, but Savannah refused to give up.

Over the next half hour she picked out antiqued-leather boots, hand-beaded moccasins, high-heeled strappy sandals, slingbacks, sensible loafers, mules, and plain old pumps. All were disdainfully dismissed.

"If this was how Peter Pan acted, I can understand why Captain Hook wanted him dead," she muttered under her breath, about to lose her patience and tell the kid to sit down, shut up, and give her that damn shoe back when the door beeped open and Byrony's mother stepped in.

"Did you behave? Did she behave?" The woman first asked her daughter and then, without waiting for an answer, turned to Savannah.

"I didn't realize I was her baby-sitter," Savannah grumbled.

"Pardon me?" the woman asked, pushing the strap of her $900 Louis Vuitton purse over her shoulder. (Savannah knew how much it cost because she'd seen that very purse in *Glamour* the night before in their "Can't Afford This? Try This Instead" feature.)

Byrony looked over at Savannah for the first time and smiled sweetly. "Carmina would *love* these," she said, pointing to the glittering sandal she'd been abusing for the last forty minutes.

"Oh, yes. Those are darling," the girl's mother said absently, glancing at her watch as if she had just remembered a previous engagement.

"What size would you like?" Savannah asked, determined not to lose this sale after all her effort.

"We'll keep them in mind as we do our shopping. Come along, Byrony. We've got to go."

Savannah gritted her teeth when the girl looked up at her and blinked her eyes coquettishly. "Yes, we must go," she singsonged. Then she flicked her foot and the sandal fell to the carpeted floor, teetering for a moment before toppling over on its side. She followed her mother out the door, pausing to flutter her fingers at Savannah and say "Ba-bye" before letting the door close behind her.

How Are You at Managing Conflict?

For some reason, conflict is a word that's gotten a bad rap these days. Why is it that women, in particular, seem to have difficulty when others express opposing views on an issue? So someone doesn't agree with you? Big deal! Take our quiz to find out how good you are at handling conflict.

A coworker who is only slightly senior to you always seems to grab the best assignments for herself, leaving you with the dogs. During a meeting, your boss brings up a project that suits your skill set perfectly, but—as usual—your coworker raises her hand first. What do you do?

a. Go grab another raspberry cream cheese muffin from the box of baked goods you fetched before the meeting and stuff it in your mouth, seething the entire time.

b. Give your boss an ultimatum: either you get this project or you quit.

c. Calmly state the reasons you believe you'd be better suited to run with this assignment. If your boss still decides to give the job to your coworker, offer to be her second-in-command. Everyone likes a team player!

If A was your answer, we predict that Weight Watchers and ulcers feature heavily in your future. Stop being such a wuss and stick up for yourself every once in a while. If you chose B, how many times do you have to walk off the job in a huff before you realize that acting like a spoiled prima donna only works if you're an actor or an opera singer? You C girls are destined to go far. You're smart, you're calm, you're reasonable—what more could an employer ask for?

{twelve}

Savannah stared at the shoe on the floor, seething. That little brat. Treating her as if she were the hired help. She hadn't been so insulted in ... in ... God, she couldn't remember ever feeling so insulted. As an accountant, people were grateful for her help. Yes, they might not like the tax codes or how much of their income they had to pay to the government, but she had never had a client treat her with so little respect.

"So how'd you do?" Valeen asked, breezing out of the stockroom as if she'd only been gone for a few seconds.

Taking a deep, calming breath, Savannah turned to face her new boss. She hated to admit failure, but—as she always said when a client expressed consternation over his tax liability—the numbers didn't lie. She shook her head sadly. "I didn't get the sale. I guess I should have been nicer to the kid, but she had such an attitude."

Valeen surprised her by patting her on the back and laughing. "Don't blame yourself. They weren't here to buy anything."

"What do you mean?" Savannah asked, her eyebrows drawing together in a puzzled frown.

"Mrs. Goldman never buys anything when she brings her daughter here. It's just, every once in a while, her nanny calls in sick and she doesn't know what to do with her kid. So she brings her down here and fobs her off on the shopkeepers while she goes about her business."

"Oh," Savannah said, taken aback. What kind of mother didn't know how to entertain her own child? "What sort of business is Mrs. Goldman in, then?" she asked.

Valeen laughed again, humorlessly this time. She dipped her chin toward the front window. "You see that man there, coming out of the insurance agency?"

Savannah looked across the street, where a handsome young man had just stepped out of an office and was straightening his tie. "Yes."

"That's Mrs. Goldman's stepson. He runs the family business now that his father is retired."

"And?" Savannah asked, raising her eyebrows when Valeen didn't continue.

"And let's just say that young Mr. Goldman is sharing more than just his father's client list these days."

Savannah groaned. "Ugh. So you mean Mrs. Goldman comes and drops her daughter off while she and her stepson are busy going at it on top of the auto ID cards?"

"Precisely," Valeen answered. "And none of the shopkeepers complain about this arrangement because on the days Mrs. Goldman's nanny *isn't* ill and she comes shopping by herself, she makes our cash registers very, very happy." Valeen delicately shrugged one slim shoulder. "Byrony Goldman may be an insufferable brat, but she's a *rich* insufferable brat with influential parents, so she is tolerated. That's just the way it is."

Ah. Yet another reality Savannah hadn't faced as an accountant. At Refund City, her clients were mostly middle-class folks who didn't have enough money to worry about sheltering their income from the IRS. The few residents of Maple Rapids in the upper income tax brackets used the services of George Billings down on Seventh Street because George had once worked for PricewaterhouseCoopers in Detroit and they thought they were getting better service since George charged four times as much as the accountants at Refund City.

Yes, she'd had one or two clients over the years who demanded more of her time because of the complexity of their

returns, but they were billed at the same hourly rate as everyone else . . . and they sure as heck didn't bring their kids in for
her to baby-sit while they were off screwing around with the
clerks at the Super ShopMart. If anyone had ever tried to do
such a thing, her boss would have set them straight immediately. He wouldn't have nodded and shrugged and acted as if
it were all just a part of Savannah's job.

Perhaps that was the key to this whole glamour thing, Savannah thought as she went to work replacing the shoes on
their pedestals. It was only fun and exciting if you were the
one on the moneyed side of the equation.

A steady stream of customers wandered in and out of the shop
that morning. Some walked out with the sturdy paper bags
custom printed with Valeen's logo on them and others did not.
Most were polite, a few were imperious, and one or two
merely oblivious, treating Savannah as if she were no more
important than the little bags of silica gel in each shoe box,
put there to keep the mold away.

By lunchtime her feet ached. Her silver sparkling boots
may have been pretty, but they sure weren't practical. Valeen
let her take her half-hour lunch break first, so at one-thirty,
Savannah dashed as quickly as she could in her high heels
down to the coffee shop two doors down from Valeen's. She
purchased a regular coffee (on her new budget, she was going
to have to forgo the two-dollar Americanos she liked in favor
of the eighty-five-cent cup of regular coffee that really wasn't
so bad) and a tomato, basil, and mozzarella sandwich, since
that was the cheapest, most filling meal on the menu. After
paying for her lunch, she went back outside to sit on the coffee
shop's patio, trying not to be discouraged about her financial
situation. She'd thought her Top Ramen and potato salad days
were over.

She sat down and unwrapped her sandwich, nibbling on
one corner to try to make it last as she looked around the seating area. Tables and heavy wrought-iron chairs spilled out
onto the sidewalk, where well-groomed people and their
equally well-groomed pets lolled in the sun, sipping chai
lattes and three-dollar iced teas.

Savannah moved the plate holding her sandwich to the

edge of the table and thought about her new job. She had thought that being a "Shoe Saleswoman to the Stars" would be more glamorous than it actually was. She wasn't quite sure why she'd thought so—maybe because she'd imagined everything associated with Vanna would be exciting and fun.

She squinted as a woman's gold wristwatch caught the sun and temporarily blinded her. Well, so maybe selling shoes wasn't as thrilling as she'd hoped, but she wasn't going to give it up yet. With her bank account dwindling, she had to stick it out. Besides, it was only her first day. It *had* to get better. And she couldn't go back to being an accountant. She'd had enough of playing it safe. The new Savannah had to be open to trying new experiences.

"Spirulina smoothie?" A young man with unruly brown hair and holes in his earlobes large enough for her to have stuck a twig through pushed a tray of small plastic cups under her nose.

The cups were filled with a cement-colored mixture that made Savannah shudder and swallow so she wouldn't gag. She pressed her spine against the back of her chair and held her palms out in front of her chest. "No, thank you," she said, hoping the man would remove the vile-looking concoction before she lost what little she'd eaten of her sandwich.

"It's algae and wheat grass and blueberries. It's good for you," the man added, as if that might sway her.

"Even more reason not to try it," Savannah said, before looking at her watch and realizing she'd better hurry and eat her sandwich. It was nearly time for her to get back to the store.

She hadn't finished her coffee by the time her break was over, so she took it with her, hoping that the "No Food or Drink" policy wouldn't pertain to her. When she arrived back at the shop, Valeen was nowhere around, so Savannah tucked her coffee under the cash register before raising her voice and calling out, "I'm back."

Valeen sauntered out of the stockroom a few seconds later wearing a different pair of shoes than she'd had on when Savannah had left.

"Those are cute," Savannah remarked, waving toward

Valeen's shoes, which were, indeed, a very cute forest green suede pump.

"Do you like them better than the others?" Valeen asked, turning her ankle one way and then another to show off the shoe from all angles.

Savannah pursed her lips, considering the question. "Hmm. I like that pair better on its own, but I think the ones you were wearing before look better with that outfit."

Valeen frowned but said nothing for a long moment. Then she nodded once, decisively, and said, "I believe you're right." But Savannah noticed that she didn't change back into the previous pair before she went on her lunch break.

"Maybe that was her version of the manhole question," Savannah said as she took a sip of lukewarm coffee and pressed the Z key on the computer to get it out of screen-saver mode. Now that she was alone, she could search the shoe store's sales history for Vanna's address. Perhaps she'd had a pair of shoes delivered or asked to be added to Valeen's mailing list. If so, now was Savannah's chance to find out.

She logged into the system and searched for her own name, surprised when the computer immediately returned several records. She'd expected it to be much more difficult than this. With a furtive glance in the direction of the clock hanging above the door to see how long Valeen had been gone, Savannah clicked on the first record. Back in December of last year, Vanna had bought two pairs of Salvatore Ferragamos and some Donald J Pliner boots. Savannah wrote down the credit-card number that was used for the purchase so she could match it with the statements in her motel room just to make sure there wasn't *another* credit account out there that she didn't know about yet. She pulled up the remaining records, but found no more new information. When she was finished, she selected the mailing-list-management option and searched again, but Vanna had not requested to be added to Valeen's mailing list.

Savannah hurriedly logged out when the buzzer on the front door beeped. She wasn't exactly sure why she felt guilty for snooping in Valeen's records. It wasn't like she was doing anything wrong. Still, some overdeveloped guilt complex had her escaping out of the system and trying to look innocent as a woman who resembled the Asian version of a Barbie doll stepped through the door.

She was tall and slender, with impossibly long legs and sleek dark hair that fell to her waist. She wore so much jewelry that she literally glittered, and it wasn't until Savannah stepped closer that she realized that the glowing effect wasn't from the jewelry but from the hair and body glitter the woman had slathered on from the tips of her gold-painted toenails to the ends of her shiny black hair. When the woman turned slightly, Savannah saw the tiny black nose of an apricot-colored Pomeranian emerge from the oversized bag slung over the woman's shoulder.

Ah, yes. The tiny dog. This season's hottest fashion accessory, according to *Cosmo.*

"Good afternoon," Savannah said as she moved out from behind the cash register. "Can I help you find something?"

"Yes. I need some shoes to wear at an evening wedding I'm attending on April sixteenth. My dress is gold."

Naturally, Savannah thought, but was smart enough not to say it aloud. "Is the dress short or long?" she asked, as if that would help her know what to suggest. The truth was, she didn't have any ideas what to pair with a gold dress aside from gold shoes. What else could possibly work? Unless there was some new trend she was missing that said it was okay to mix gold with black or silver, she didn't think there were all that many options.

"It's long. Floor-length. With a slit in front so the shoes will be visible when I'm walking or standing." The woman shrugged and sat down on one of the red velvet sofas Valeen had placed around the sales floor for customers to sit on and relax while the clerks waited on them foot and foot. She set her bag beside her and the Pomeranian stuck its head out, its pointy little black nose and dark whiskers reminding Savannah of a mouse. The dog, like its master, had a glittery sheen and Savannah wondered what *Cosmo* would have to say about people who rubbed glitter on their dogs.

Well, it wasn't her job to judge people and their pets. Her job was to sell shoes.

"I think we've got exactly what you're looking for," she

said, then looked down at the woman's feet, which looked to be at least two sizes bigger than Savannah's six-and-a-halfs. "What size are you? Eight? Eight and a half?" she asked.

"I'm a six," the woman answered, narrowing her eyes at Savannah as if she'd just accused her of having ugly children.

Savannah looked at the woman's feet again. No way was she a half size smaller than Savannah. "Um, I meant your shoe size," she said hesitantly.

"I'm a six," the woman repeated in a tone so glacial that Savannah was certain she'd set global warming back a good ten years.

"Yes, ma'am. I apologize for the misunderstanding." Savannah backed away, giving the woman her best obsequious smile as she slunk back into the stockroom to fetch all the size six gold shoes in the store. "This is so much harder than filling out 1040s," Savannah muttered to herself as she reached up on her tiptoes to grab a pair of Prada sandals that laced up the calf. She was beginning to wonder when the glamorous part of the job would kick in, when she'd make friends with some of the customers who would invite her to become a part of their fun, fast-paced world. Because so far, selling shoes—even the expensive ones here at Valeen's—wasn't exactly what Savannah would consider a fulfilling life's work. Not that calculating people's taxes was all that great, either, but at least she felt she was really helping people. Baby-sitting rich women's children while they were off screwing their stepkids and finding just the right shade of gold to match someone's gown wasn't as rewarding as she had thought it would be.

Savannah emerged from the stockroom, her arms so laden with boxes of metallic shoes that she had to crane her neck to see over the stack.

The woman had let her little glittery dog out of her bag, and it was now wandering the carpeted sales floor, sniffing around the pedestals Valeen used to display her wares. As she set the boxes on the floor, Savannah watched the dog out of the corner of her eye. She hoped it didn't feel the need to tinkle, because if Valeen expected her to clean up dog pee, she was going to quit, employee discount or not. She was beginning to realize that there was only so much she was willing to do in order to become a new person. Scrubbing dog pee off of plastic pedestals was definitely on that "not even if hell freezes over" list.

Keeping one eye on the dog, she pulled a stool up next to the other woman's legs and took the lid off of the first box of shoes. The tissue paper rustled as she gently moved it aside to reveal a pair of gold sandals with straps at the toes and ankles so delicate that they looked as if they'd fall apart if you so much as touched them. This style was her favorite of all the shoes she'd brought for the woman to try on, and she caressed one shoe reverently as she pulled it out of the box. "Aren't these beautiful?" she breathed.

The woman looked bored, though, so Savannah decided she'd better just keep her opinions to herself. She pulled the cardboard spacers that helped the shoes retain their shape out from under the toe straps and slid the sandal onto the woman's waiting foot.

No surprise. It didn't fit.

"Uh," Savannah began, not quite sure how to politely point out that the woman's heel was hanging a good two inches off the back of the shoe and that the circulation to her toes was being cut off by the too-tight toe straps.

"These are hideous. Try something else," the woman ordered with a haughty wave of her manicured hand.

Savannah swallowed her despair. None of these shoes were going to fit, and she was going to spend the next hour taking all the little sticks and cardboard shapers out of them and then having to put them all back again even though there was nothing wrong with any of them except that the number printed on the box wasn't deemed acceptable according to some standard in this woman's glittering head.

What difference did it make if the shoes were size six or size fifteen? As long as they didn't scrunch your toes or rub blisters into the back of your heels, who cared what the number on the box said?

Hmm. What an interesting thought. Savannah narrowed her eyes as she speculatively eyed the boxes on the floor. This was one instance where size really didn't matter. What mattered was selling this woman a pair of shoes.

Abruptly she stood up and grabbed the boxes from off the floor. Ignoring the woman's surprised look, she said, "I'll be right back." Then she hurried into the stockroom and swapped sixes for nines on some of her favorite styles. If the woman bought a pair of the "wrong" sized shoes, they could simply change the size printed on the box of the other pair. It wasn't like *most* people cared what number was written on the damn shoebox.

Satisfied that her plan might work, Savannah reemerged a few minutes later to find the Pomeranian noshing on the straps of the shoes she'd left on the floor while the customer talked on her cell phone and ignored her pet.

"Bad dog," Savannah admonished as she whipped the shoes off the floor. There were tiny teeth marks on one of the straps, and another was bitten clean through. The shoes were ruined.

Savannah didn't wait for the woman to end her call before sliding the next pair of shoes on her feet. The customer muttered the occasional "uh-huh" as she considered the metallic gold slingbacks before shaking her head at Savannah to indicate that she didn't like them. They finally hit pay dirt on the sixth pair—a three-and-a-half-inch Lucite-heeled sandal with gold beading at the toe and instep. For these, the woman stood up and glided over to the mirror, the Pomeranian trotting enthusiastically at her heels. She studied her feet for a moment, then sauntered back to the couch.

"I'll take them," she mouthed to Savannah.

Savannah was careful to pick all the discarded shoes up off the floor as she went to the cash register to ring up the woman's purchase. She wished Valeen would get back so she could ask what to do about the sandals the Pomeranian had chewed up. There was no way they could sell the shoes for full price now—not with one of the straps broken and teeth marks in the other. It didn't seem fair that Valeen's should take a financial hit, especially since the woman had sat and watched her dog chew on the shoes without even trying to stop it.

Just as Savannah was about to present the customer with a bill for both pairs of shoes, Valeen breezed through the front door. She and the customer air-kissed and raised their voices in the high-pitched manner of women who barely knew each other but were pretending to be bosom buddies.

While Valeen and the customer chatted about the wedding

the customer was attending next month, Savannah slid the credit card slip across the counter at her.

"What's this?" the woman said, her voice no longer friendly and her almond-shaped brown eyes narrowed to dangerous slits.

"Um, your charge slip?" Savannah said, wincing when the words came out sounding like a question.

"This is for two pairs of shoes. I'm only buying the one. Are you trying to rob me?" the woman accused.

Valeen grabbed the receipt from the woman's hands and laughed lightly. "I'm sorry, Yasmine. Savannah's new. She must have made a mistake."

"Um." Savannah cleared her throat and coughed, then looked toward the front door as if pondering an escape. "Actually, it's not a mistake. Her dog chewed the straps on a pair of Prada sandals, and I assumed that she would be responsible for the damage. We can't sell them like this," she said, holding up the ruined shoe for Valeen's inspection.

"My little Mooshie didn't do that," the customer lied. What's worse, she gave Savannah a look that said, "I know that you know I'm lying. Too bad you can't do anything about it."

"Yes, he—" Savannah began, but Valeen cut her off with another of those phony laughs.

"Don't worry about it," she said, then pushed Savannah aside so she could void the transaction and begin again.

Savannah tried to keep a pleasant look on her face, but inside she was fuming. It was so wrong to just let this woman off the hook, but if Valeen was prepared to pay for it, she supposed she should just let it go. But it wasn't easy.

"Bye, Yasmine. Have a great time at that wedding," Valeen said as the woman took her pair of shoes and her annoying little dog and left the shop.

The front door whooshed shut and Savannah inhaled deeply and turned to face her new boss. "Her dog *did* chew up these shoes," she said, her sense of fairness making it impossible for her just to let the matter drop.

"Yes," Valeen said, seeming very serene about the loss of a pair of two-hundred-and-fifty-dollar shoes. "And someone will pay for that damage. You see, Savannah, when you're managing the store, you're responsible for what happens to the shoes in your care. Therefore, I'll expect a check from you before the end of the day. Of course, your forty-percent employee discount will apply."

And with that, Valeen sashayed into the stockroom, leaving Savannah gaping at her retreating back and wondering how many hours she was going to have to work just to break even in her glamorous new job.

Get a Life!

You're new in town and haven't had the opportunity to meet new people. It's Friday night and you're all dressed up with no place to go. What do you do?

a. Change into sweats and spend the night with your cat watching old romantic movies.

b. Grab a book and take yourself out to dinner at some quiet Italian restaurant you've been wanting to try.

c. You're in the mood to dance, so you stop at a trendy new bar. Who cares if you don't have a date? You know you'll be surrounded by men in no time!

If you chose A, girl, you need to get a life! You B gals are on your way—you just need to put the book down and look around every once in a while. You never know, Mr. Right might be sitting at the next table! For those of you who chose C, you don't need any advice from us. You've grabbed life by the horns and are enjoying the ride!

{thirteen}

Savannah's feet were killing her—both literally and figuratively. She'd forgotten how difficult it was to be on her feet all day. And the ankle boots that she'd bought that morning were a great match for her Ski Bunny look, but weren't exactly the most comfortable shoes she'd ever worn. Plus, after buying both the boots and the damaged sandals, she was nearly dead broke.

As she slipped the fur-trimmed cardigan off her shoulders, she tried to ignore the doubts rattling around in her brain. This new job was supposed to make her feel better about herself, not worse. It was supposed to make her feel fashionable and hip and trendy, but instead all she felt was fatigued from being on her feet all day and annoyed that Valeen had made her pay for the damaged sandals. So far, her transformation from ugly caterpillar to beautiful butterfly didn't seem to be going very well, and Savannah couldn't believe she'd moved fourteen hundred miles away from everything she'd ever known just to end up failing as miserably here in Naples as she had back in Maple Rapids.

Her shoulders slumped and Savannah had to force herself to keep walking. "Okay, stop it. One bad day does not make you a failure," she whispered to herself as the sloping sea-green roof of the Sand Dunes Motel came into sight. She wasn't certain why she suddenly felt comforted—it wasn't like she thought of the motel as home or anything—but, for some reason, she found her steps quickening. Perhaps it was that her feet knew that a hot soak was just a few hundred yards away.

Savannah let herself into the courtyard, pausing to listen for any shouts or strange noises that might warn her that she was once again the deer in danger's headlights. But all she heard was the heavy thumping of one of the students' boom boxes and laughter and splashing coming from the pool. She stepped out of the shadows to see a game of bikini beach ball in full swing. It was girls against the guys, and it appeared that the major objective was for everyone to show off as much skin as possible as they tried to hit a black beach ball with a giant number eight on the side over a two-foot-high net.

"Hey, Savannah," Christina called from the pool, bobbing up out of the water to return the ball that James had lobbed her way. Her bright yellow bikini was patterned with pink hibiscus flowers and did a fine job of showing off her ample cleavage as she raised her arms to hit the ball.

Savannah wished that she had even a small percentage of Christina's self-confidence when it came to her body.

"Hi, Christina," she called back, giving the group a friendly wave before turning to trudge up the stairs.

She unlocked the door to her room and breathed in the stale air-conditioned air as she threw her purse and a shopping bag from Valeen's on the bed. She sat down on the thin bedspread with its seashell motif and pulled off her new boots. Her feet felt as though they'd swollen to twice their normal size, and she groaned as she rubbed her aching toes.

"You'll get used to it," she encouraged herself as she limped into the bathroom to fill the tub up with enough water to give her feet a nice hot soak. As the tub filled, she spread a towel across the side so she wouldn't slip in and then rolled up the hem of her white pants so they would stay dry. Then she went back out into the room to grab something to read while her feet soaked. She'd left her magazines in a neat stack next to the pile of Vanna's credit-card statements on top of the counter that separated the kitchenette from the rest of the room. Green and blue Post-its marked articles she was particularly interested in reading. Savannah picked the top magazine off the pile and straightened the stack again. Her gaze briefly landed on the credit-card statements, with their pages and pages of charges.

Now that she'd been in Naples for a few days, she recognized many of the establishments Vanna frequented. The Fat Cat, Valeen's, Mason's Furniture, Elite Jewelry, Cock Tails bar, Flair Boutique, Jilly's Lingerie—all shops that looked out over tree-lined Sunshine Parkway. Savannah just knew that if she worked in the area for a little longer, she'd find her alter ego.

And when she did . . . Well, she wasn't quite sure what exactly she expected would happen. She knew she should be angry at Vanna for ruining her credit and implicating her in a crime. But the truth was, some part of her admired Vanna for knowing what she wanted out of life and taking it, and to hell with the consequences. Maybe if they met, just a little of that determination would wear off on her.

Savannah hugged the magazine to her chest and closed her eyes, allowing herself to believe that the new life she longed for so badly was out there, just waiting for her to come and get it. The vision was so clear—she could see herself dressed in white silky clothing, her feet bare on the smooth warm tiles of a house on the beach. Waves crashed on the shore beyond the open French doors, endlessly advancing and retreating. Children squealed with laughter as they played tag with the waves and chased the sea birds that feasted on the ocean's bounty. Sunlight streamed in through the large, hurricane-proof windows (okay, that was her sensible side intruding into her fantasy), making the soft blues, greens, and yellows of the walls glow. From behind her, she heard a man's voice, calling her name. She smiled and turned to see her dark and mysterious dream man, but when she opened her eyes, all she saw was the avocado green refrigerator in her motel room.

Savannah sighed and curled her toes in the thin green wall-to-wall carpeting.

"This is not exactly my dream life," she said, trying not to grimace at the difference between her fantasy and reality. As she walked back to the bathroom, Savannah wondered where Vanna lived. Did her alter ego live in a cozy beachfront bungalow or an imposing waterfront mansion? Or maybe a pent-house where she had her own private elevator?

She sat down on the edge of the tub and swung her legs over the side, wiggling her toes in the tepid water as she stretched out her feet. She was fairly certain that Vanna didn't spend too many of *her* evenings stuck in a tiny motel room soaking her aching feet.

Shaking her head with self-disgust, Savannah twisted the hot water faucet and then flipped the magazine open on her lap to take her mind off her own inadequacies. Unfortunately, the magazine opened to a quiz about how she'd spend her time if she were a stranger in a new town. Reading in the tub wasn't one of the choices, but Savannah guessed that what she was doing this evening was equivalent to watching old movies in her sweats. According to the quiz, what she *should* want to do was go to a trendy bar. Alone.

Ugh. She'd never been to a bar alone in her life and the thought of doing so was completely unappealing. Most likely because she'd listened too carefully when her mother lectured her about the sorts of girls who went to bars alone. To put it politely, Mom's opinion was that those were not the type of women guys wanted for anything but a good time.

But, according to *Stylish* magazine, there was nothing wrong with that. And maybe they were right. Maybe women who went to strange bars by themselves had lots of fun and grabbed life by the horns and all that, but the idea of it still made Savannah slightly sick to her stomach.

"Chicken," she accused her reflection in the bathroom mirror.

She closed the magazine and was just about to turn off the hot water when a knock sounded on her door. "Who is it?" she called, knowing the walls were thin enough for even the slightest whisper of sound to carry.

"It's Christina. From downstairs," the girl added, as if Savannah might not remember her.

Savannah hurriedly wiped off her feet and padded to the door to open it. "Come on in," she said, and then went back to the bathroom. She normally wouldn't entertain guests in there, but she figured that she and the student shared a bond after nearly being killed by a flying mattress. She turned the water off and twisted around to find Christina standing in the doorway, a wisp of see-through pink fabric tied sarong-style around her waist. "What's up?" she asked.

Christina sat down on the toilet and stretched her long, tanned legs out in front of her. Her toenails were painted a bright pink that matched her bathing suit, and she wore a crystal toe ring on the second toe of her left foot that depicted two sparkling red cherries attached by a bright green stem.

"That's a cute outfit," Christina said, waving toward Savannah's white tank top.

"Thanks. I had to take the cardigan off because it was too hot. Hard to believe the snow has barely melted back in Michigan, but it's too hot for a light sweater here in Naples." She laughed.

Christina smoothed the hem of her cover-up on her thighs. "Yeah, it's still cold in New Jersey, where I go to school."

Savannah wondered why the girl was up here talking to her when she could be down cavorting with her friends, but she didn't mind the company, so she continued to make small talk. "Oh?" she said. "I thought you all were from Pennsylvania?"

Christina smiled, exposing a row of even, white teeth. "Well, we are. But I go to Princeton. My best friend Liz is a year behind her brother James at Penn State. James is the one who was . . . uh, riding the mattress the other day. His best friend, Nathan, helped him get it up to the roof. I haven't seen James since we all went back to school in the fall. Uh, I mean, I haven't seen any of the gang since then," she corrected, her cheeks flushing beneath her tan.

That was Savannah's second clue that Christina had a crush on James. The first, of course, had been her cheerful attitude about James's mattress ride, even though he had nearly killed both her and Savannah with the prank.

"Weren't you all at home together at Christmas?" Savannah asked, finally deciding that her feet had had enough soaking since her skin was turning all pruney.

"No. I have an older brother who lives up in Connecticut with his wife, so my parents went there over the holidays. I spent most of the break working at an investment banking firm in New York where I interned last summer. I had to earn some money for spring break and . . . uh, some other things that I needed."

The younger woman's blush deepened and Savannah's curiosity grew. "Like what other things?" she asked as she used the bathmat to dry off her feet.

Christina laughed sheepishly and lowered her gaze to stare at the black plastic toilet plunger sitting in the corner of the bathroom that had obviously been provided by management to cut down on midnight calls to fix clogs. "If I tell you, will you promise not to say anything about it to anyone?" she asked, not taking her eyes off the plunger.

Now, why would she tell me something she hasn't already told her best friend? Savannah wondered. But she just nodded and said, "Sure."

Christina wrapped her slender arms around her waist and rubbed her upper arms as if she'd suddenly gone cold. "We-ell," she began, dragging the word out as if reluctant to spill her secret. "I'm thinking about getting breast implants," she blurted.

Savannah's gaze dipped briefly to Christina's very adequately sized chest before she looked back up into the other woman's eyes. "Why would you do that?" she asked.

"I'm trying to get someone to notice me. Someone I've been in love with for a long time," she added wistfully.

Savannah reached out and squeezed the younger woman's arm. "Christina, you're lovely. I'm not against people getting plastic surgery if it would make them feel better about themselves, but you shouldn't change for somebody else. Especially when there's nothing wrong with you to begin with."

"Well, I'm trying something less drastic first. I'm hoping it works." Christina shrugged and looked away uncomfortably, and Savannah was afraid she'd alienated the student with her preachy Oprah answer.

And really, who was she to talk? She'd done everything but resort to plastic surgery to change her own life . . . although she did feel that she was making these changes to be happier for herself, and not for someone else.

"Look," Savannah said, scooting forward until she was balanced on the very edge of the tub. "I understand what it's like to want to feel better about yourself. Just make sure you've thought through all the consequences before you do something you can't take back, okay?"

Christina gave her a weak smile. "Sure," she said, in that voice younger people used on those more than four years older than themselves when they didn't agree with a word you'd said but didn't want to argue.

Savannah sighed, then frowned, remembering an article she'd read in *Glamour* about the pitfalls of breast implants in young women. Maybe if Christina wouldn't listen to her, she'd listen to the experts at *Glamour.* Savannah stood and hurriedly rolled her pants down. "Wait just a second. Let me get you something."

She went to her stack of magazines and searched the covers for the issue she was looking for. She found it near the bottom of the stack.

"Ah, here it is," she murmured, pulling the magazine out of the pile. The teaser on the cover read "My Breast Implants Are Killing Me!"

Savannah turned to find that Christina had followed her out into the living room. She handed the magazine to the younger woman, surprised for a moment when she felt a slight reluctance to let it go. Okay, she was spending *way* too much time alone with her magazines if she felt a sense of loss at the thought of one leaving her possession. She silently rolled her eyes and forced herself to let it go.

"There's an article in here about the dangers of implants. At least take a look at it before you decide," she said.

Christina's smile seemed warmer when she looked at Savannah again. "Thanks. I will," she said.

"You're welcome," Savannah said. And then, because she really was starting to worry about all the time she spent alone talking to herself, she asked in a faux-casual tone of voice, "Hey, what are you guys doing tonight? Is it going to be safe for me to come out of my room?" she joked.

"We're going out. I guess there's a couple of cool bars over on Sunshine Parkway that we're going to check out. Would you like to come with us?"

"But you're not old enough to drink," Savannah protested.

Christina's smile turned to a grin as she winked at Savannah. "Ah, but I have an ID that says I am," she said.

Savannah chewed on the inside of her lip. Hmm. If the students were going bar-hopping in the tourist district, that
would give Savannah a chance to do some asking around
about Vanna. Plus, she could keep an eye on Christina and her
underage friends to make sure they stayed out of trouble. Perfect. She could kill two birds with one stone and feel like a
nice person for doing it. Plus, she didn't have to sit here in her
motel room all alone like the loser the *Stylish* quiz accused her
of being.

Sounded like a win-win for everybody.

Besides, it was a Wednesday night in sleepy Naples. How
wild could things possibly get?

Are You a Wet Blanket?

You and your friends go out to a hot new bar in town to check out the scene. You've had a hard day at work and your feet are killing you, but you agree to go because you don't want your pals to think you're boring. Only, when you get there, you discover that the place draws such huge crowds because its wait staff delivers drinks to the patrons . . . on their bodies! When a hunky waiter lays down on your table and pours your martini on his concave abdomen for you to slurp up, you:

a· Offer to pay an extra $5 to get your drink served in a glass.

b· Run for the bathroom, hoping you'll get there before you lose the turkey sandwich you had for lunch. After all, you have no idea where that guy's stomach has been!

c· Cool drink, hot guy. What more could a girl ask for?

You A gals might not be wet blankets, but you sure are damp. What's the fun in drinking out of plain ol' glass when you could slurp gin off a cute guy's washboard abs instead? Those of you who answered B could put out fires with your wet-blanket attitudes. It's a wonder you have any friends to go out with in the first place! You C girls understand that it's a lot more fun to be a part of the entertainment when you go out. The only thing wet about you is . . . Well, we'll leave that up to your imaginations!

{fourteen}

Cock Tails apparently got away with its risqué name by pretending that the "cock" in question was a rooster. Four-foot wooden roosters perched on the two front corners of the bar, peering out at the noisy Wednesday-night crowd with their beady black eyes. Standing at the bar, Savannah ducked when a waitress carrying a tray laden with drinks nearly took her out. She bumped the back of her head on one of the cocks' tail feathers and glared at the waitress who had been ignoring their table for the last hour—probably because the students had pooled their money to buy two of the cheapest pitchers of beer on the menu and had only given her a ten-percent tip. Savannah had opted for the house Chardonnay, a bargain at $4.50 a glass. She'd tipped the waitress a buck, but that was obviously not enough to keep the server coming back.

So, while the four students who had come out tonight were busy pouring their third round, she'd headed out into enemy territory alone to buy herself another drink.

"Can I help you?" the bartender asked as Savannah moved to the front of the line and away from the glowering rooster.

"I'll have a house Chardonnay, please," she said, telling herself to stand up straight and stop feeling uncomfortable. Bars always made her feel this way, as if everyone were staring at her. It made her feel even worse to turn and discover that no one was staring at her. Or paying her any attention at all.

"Yep, that's me. Invisible Accountant Girl." She smiled at the image that conjured up—her with red tights and a blue cape with a big yellow A on the back.

"Anything else?" the bartender asked as he set a wineglass in front of her.

"Um, well yes, actually. It's not a drink, though," Savannah said with a wink, attempting to be charming.

The bartender just looked bored. And impatient.

Savannah sighed.

"I was wondering if you know a woman who goes by the name Savannah Taylor?" she asked. "I know she used to come here a lot. At least, as of a month ago, she did."

Savannah had to give the guy credit, he appeared to give the question some thought before shaking his head and saying, "Sorry. Doesn't ring a bell."

He didn't look like the type of person who would help her out any more than that, so Savannah didn't bother giving him a card and asking him to call if someone using her name happened to drop by. As a matter of fact, he looked like the type who would take her card and rip it to shreds in the blender as soon as she turned her back.

By the time Savannah made it back to the table, the second pitcher of beer was gone . . . and so were all the students but Christina.

"Where'd everyone go?" Savannah asked, sliding into the red vinyl booth next to Christina. The music was so loud she had to lean in to hear what the other woman said, and Savannah feared the loud *boom-boom-boom* was going to be echoing in her head tomorrow.

"They thought this place was kind of lame. Too many old people," Christina added, without malice.

Since Savannah figured she was the same age as most of the bar's patrons, she tried not to take offense. "Yeah, just look at all the canes and wheelchairs in here," she said wryly.

Christina turned, a horrified look in her eyes. "Omigod, I'm sorry. I shouldn't have said that."

Savannah laughed and took a sip of her wine. "That's all

right. I understand. I can remember when thirty seemed old. So, did they leave without you? That wasn't very nice."

"Oh, no. I told them I'd wait for you to come back and finish your drink, and we'd meet up with them at another place a couple doors down. It's supposed to have karaoke."

"That was nice of you, but maybe I'd better call it a night. Why don't you go meet your friends and I'll go back to the motel. I don't need this anyway," Savannah said, waving at her wine. She didn't want to get in the way of the students' fun. And the truth was, she *did* feel old compared to them. Liz giggled all the time and sat on Nathan's lap every chance she got. Her brother James was flunking out of Penn State and didn't have a clue what he wanted to do with his life aside from drinking and partying and acting like every day should be spring break. His best friend Nathan seemed a bit more mature, but not much, since he was obviously willing to go along with James's silly pranks. It wasn't that Savannah disliked them, it was more that she realized the things that were fun when you were nineteen weren't so entertaining when you got to be thirty.

Or maybe it was that life was so much more serious than it had been back then. You realized that it wasn't going to last forever, so all those things you figured you had plenty of time to do a decade ago became all the things you knew you'd never accomplish now.

"No," Christina said, jerking Savannah out of her philosophical revelation. "I think you need to come with me."

Savannah tucked a lock of hair behind her ear and stared at her drink. "Why do you say that?" she asked.

Christina pushed her out of the booth with a surprisingly strong nudge. "Because you look sad, and you should be having fun. It's hump day." She raised her arms in the air and giggled, grinding her hips against Savannah's until Savannah started laughing and told her to knock it off.

Once outside, Christina threw an arm around Savannah's shoulders as if they were the best of friends and not people who had only met two days ago. That was another thing Savannah remembered about college—the easy friendships that came with being so young and alone for the first time in your

life. Everyone had so much in common: long hours of studying, pressure to pass your courses without someone watching
over your shoulder every week to make sure you were keeping
up, tough teachers who sometimes acted as if it were their job
to get you to drop out. And, of course, learning when to say
"enough" when presented with limitless opportunities to party
and have fun.

They walked a few doors down to a bar with people
spilling out the front door and onto the sidewalk. The front of
the bar was open to the warm night breeze, the walls rolled up
like garage doors. Inside, there were whoops and catcalls as a
young blond man in a cowboy hat and boots sang "Achy
Breaky Heart" while the words of the song scrolled slowly
across a television screen.

"I didn't think you guys would like a country bar," Savannah said as she and Christina snaked their way around to
where the rest of the students were sitting.

"Country's okay," Christina said with a shrug. "But we're
really here for the karaoke. Do you sing?"

Savannah snorted. "Not since I was twelve. At least, not in
public," she amended, remembering her humiliation at the
Maple Rapids Mall talent fest.

"What kind of music do you like?" Christina asked, as they
paused for a moment in front of the stage.

"Eighties rock. You know, Bon Jovi, Van Halen, Def Leppard, Poison. I like the softer stuff, too. Air Supply, REO
Speedwagon, Rick Springfield. I grew up listening to that kind
of music with my sisters. We used to put on shows for my parents and sing together. It was stupid, but we didn't have a
thousand channels on TV like you guys do. We had to make
our own entertainment," Savannah joked.

"You old people all think we have it so good," Christina
joked right back. "But we didn't get satellite TV until I was
nearly ten. You can't imagine the emotional scar that left."
She sniffled and Savannah punched her on the arm.

"Very funny."

Christina picked up a clipboard that was hanging on a
chain and scribbled something. Then she turned to grin at Savannah. "We've got the song after next," she announced.

"What?" Savannah inhaled so quickly that she nearly choked on her own saliva.

"It'll be fun. I know some of those eighties songs, too, you know. They used to play them back in high school when we had 'oldies' day."

Savannah coughed. She was so busy trying to get her breath back that she couldn't smack the younger woman. Only, once she was able to breathe again, she found that she was actually looking forward to getting up on stage. So what if she was a little rusty? It wasn't like she was naive enough to think that there were talent scouts out in the audience like she had when she was a kid.

"Do you know Bon Jovi's 'Livin' on a Prayer'?" Savannah whispered to Christina when a man wearing headphones called their names and waved them up on stage.

"Sure," Christina said, grinning as she took a microphone. "Let's do it."

Savannah looked at the other woman and nodded, determinedly squaring her shoulders as she prepared herself to conquer her age-old demon. "Yeah, let's do it," she muttered under her breath.

Then the lights dimmed and it might have been Savannah's imagination, but it seemed as though the crowd quieted as the first strains of the song came over the speakers. "Wa-ooh-wa-ooh-ah. Wa-ooh-wa-ooh-ah."

Savannah closed her eyes, worried that when she opened them again, she'd be back on that stage in Maple Rapids, alone in her bid for stardom. Instead, as she raised her head and started singing, her voice was joined by another. She turned to look at Christina and then started in on the routine she and Peggy had practiced so many times that Savannah would never forget how to do it. Christina looked surprised for just a moment, then did her best to follow along as the song built to its finale. After the last note was sung, Savannah stood on the stage, her chest heaving. She raised her head and looked out over the audience, hearing nothing but silence for one heartbeat.

And then . . .

A smatter of applause and a couple of wolf whistles and

Christina was laughing as she bounded off the stage. Savannah followed, handing her microphone to the next wannabe as they passed on the rickety steps.

"That was so fun," Christina announced as she and Savannah plopped down in the seats the other students had saved for them. Her eyes sparkled as she looked toward James, so obviously hoping for a compliment that Savannah felt her heart squeeze in her chest.

Come on, James. Say something nice, she silently willed.

He belched. Loudly. Savannah was tempted to kick him, so she did. Hard.

"Ouch!" he yelped, reaching down to rub his bruised shin.

"Oh, sorry. I thought that was the table," Savannah said in as bland a tone as she could muster.

The server at this bar was a bit more attentive, and he came around just then to check on the table and take drink orders from Savannah and Christina. This didn't seem like the sort of place Vanna would frequent, and Savannah hadn't seen any charges from here, so she decided not to bother asking the waiter if he knew anyone by Savannah's name. Instead, she splurged on one more glass of wine, not certain she'd be able to refrain from kicking James again without the Chardonnay's soothing effect. Christina helped herself to the pitcher of cold beer in the middle of the table, and Savannah sat back and listened to the students as they talked about their different campuses, music, and their families.

She sipped her wine slowly, enjoying being out and not sitting alone in her motel room feeling sorry for herself. *See, I have a life,* she thought with a mental toast to whoever had written that *Stylish* quiz.

Just then Christina got up to use the rest room. Savannah absently watched her new friend weave through the crowd and frowned when she realized that Christina was actually *weaving*. She hadn't paid attention to how much Christina was drinking, but it was obvious that the girl had had more than she should.

She hurried to the bathroom to see if Christina was okay and found her slumped against the bathroom wall, looking pissed off as only a cross-eyed drunk could look.

"Hey. Are you all right?" Savannah asked as she skidded to

a stop in front of Christina. Her feet were starting to ache again in her impractical silver ankle boots and she took a second to squash the dread of how her feet were going to feel tomorrow.

"No, I'm *not* all right." Christina pounded the plaster behind her with her fists and pushed herself away from the faux–beach scene painted on the wall. "I spent half of the money I earned over Christmas break on new clothes for this week. I went to a salon in New York and spent *three hundred dollars* on a haircut. I've been pedicured and waxed to within an inch of my life. And James *still* doesn't notice me. I've been outgoing and fun and acted just like all those girls he stares at on MTV's *Spring Break*. What more do I have to do to get him to look at me as someone other than his little sister's geeky friend?"

Savannah blinked, uncertain which point to address first. "Um, geeky?" she repeated, looking at the tall slender woman with sleek chestnut hair, smooth tanned skin, and looks that Savannah would kill for. *Geek* was definitely not a word she'd apply to Christina.

Christina waved one manicured hand in the air angrily, narrowly missing a woman who had stepped out of a stall and was heading to the sink to wash her hands. "Yes, geeky. I was a dork in high school, all right? I was good at math. And science. And I had braces. And glasses. But I'm not that person anymore. Why can't James see that?"

Christina sounded dangerously close to tears, and Savannah was afraid to be too comforting, because that was always her downfall. She could be stoic in the face of any amount of adversity, but the second someone was nice to her, she lost it. So, hoping that she was doing the right thing, she said matter-of-factly, "James is just an immature kid who wouldn't recognize true love if it . . . if it came up, grabbed him by the front of the shirt, and kicked him in the balls. If you really love him, you're going to have to wait until he's as mature as you are and can see what's right under his nose."

"Mature?" Christina gaped. "Are you calling me mature? Haven't you seen me playing beach ball in the pool when I should have been studying for my finals this semester? I've been drinking and spending my money irresponsibly. I saw James and Nathan take that mattress up to the roof and didn't even try to stop them. And just look what I am wearing. Does this outfit say 'mature' to you?" She turned to the mirror and pointed to herself in her navel-baring top and short skirt.

Well, Savannah had hoped her response wouldn't cause Christina to cry, and it looked as though she had gotten her wish. Christina's face was red with anger as she stomped her foot in her impractical—and very immature, Savannah conceded—three-inch-high platform sandals.

"I'm sor—" Savannah began, but Christina interrupted her.

"No. Forget it. I'll show you—and James—just how *mature* I am." With that, Christina pushed past Savannah and went back out into the bar with Savannah following hot on her heels.

Savannah could feel an embarrassing moment of epic proportions coming on, and she knew she had to do whatever she could to stop it. In everyone's life there was that one event that you wished later someone would have stepped in to prevent. That time you went braless in the school production of Cleopatra and that idiot Greg Fisher stepped on the train of your toga. That time at the eighth grade dance when Tiffany Mastrioanni told you she'd overheard Heather McLinn telling Crystal Jean Monroe that Heather's brother Bobby had a crush on you and wished you'd go over to where he was standing there with all his friends and ask him to dance. And you did, only to have him laugh right in your face. Or that time— the first time you really drank—when Kim Johnson and Karin Roche were doing Coke and MacNaughton's shooters and you kept up with them, drink for drink, until you ended up passing out on the bathroom floor and throwing up all over yourself at the local underage dance club where everyone from school hung out.

In the interest of sparing Christina one of "those" moments, Savannah chased after her, not pausing to think what Christina might have in mind as she grabbed two full pitchers of beer from the table closest to the stage. Ignoring the protests of the group seated there, Christina continued up the stairs and onto center stage where a young man with a squeaky voice was singing "I Will Survive."

"Hey," the man protested as Christina stepped in front of him, blocking his view of the prompter.

Savannah walked to the bottom of the stage and cupped her hands around her mouth. "Psst," she said, trying to get Christina's attention.

But Christina ignored her, so Savannah tried to think of something else that would coax her down off the stage. Before she could think up a plan, however, James—the idiot—let out a loud wolf whistle and shouted, "Go, baby!"

Savannah wished he were closer so she could kick him again.

Christina, however, grinned and started bumping and grinding to the song. Beer sloshed over the edge of the pitchers in her hands as she gyrated, her words slurring as she sang, " 'As long as I know how to love, I know I'll stay alive.' "

Savannah cringed. She had to get that beer away from Christina before she did something stupid. Like drink any more of it.

So she stepped up on stage, hoping that if Christina thought she was coming up to be part of the act, she might let Savannah have the beer. Instead, Savannah ended up right smack-dab in the middle of her own embarrassing moment of epic proportions when Christina warbled out the last word of the song, wiggled her ass at the audience, and then raised both pitchers of beer to shoulder level and doused herself. Since Savannah was standing so close, she caught a full pitcher of beer in the face. Her eyes closed and she raised her hands instinctively to ward off the attack, but she was too late. She gasped as the cold liquid dripped down her neck.

As people started hooting, Savannah kept her eyes closed. She could only imagine what she looked like with her hair plastered to her face and her makeup running down her cheeks.

It was only when Christina shouted, "Wet T-shirt Contest!" that Savannah's eyes popped open and she looked down at her chest, just then realizing that her white tank top was soaked . . . and that she hadn't bothered with a bra that morning.

What Are You Hiding?

We've all got something in our closets tucked away behind the Manolo Blahniks and that sequin dress we bought on sale ten years ago and are saving for just the right occasion. So when you open those doors and a bone or two falls out, don't be ashamed of your sins—be proud. Those skeletons made you who you are today!

Come on, it's time for a little honesty here! No one will see this quiz but you. So, tell us, what's hiding in the back of *your* closet?

a· A Liz Claiborne sweater that you shoplifted back when you were fifteen. You've been too ashamed all these years to actually wear it, but you couldn't work up the courage to take it back, either.

b· Nothing. Really.

c· Well, hmm. Behind that stack of homemade porn starring you and three of your previous boyfriends is a little baggie filled with—No, forget it. Time to plead the Fifth Amendment.

Oh, pu-leeze. If you chose A, get over it already! You are not going to hell for that stolen sweater. The darn thing is hopelessly out of date by now and so is your guilt trip. Give them both to Goodwill and go out and get some real skeletons to fill up the back of your closet! If B is truly your answer, boy, do we feel sorry for you. Everyone should have at least a little something in her life that she wants to keep secret. You naughty C gals sure do know how to live! Just be sure to keep your stash—ahem—stashed if you ever decide to date one of those hunky law-enforcement types!

{ fifteen }

Because of a flight delay in Chicago, Mike missed dinner with his mother and brother. Sam had ribbed him about intentionally taking a later flight so he wouldn't have to endure the usual game of Twenty Questions: the Love Life Version—to which Mike responded, "Can you blame me?" Of course, he hadn't *voluntarily* spent five extra hours in the Chicago airport. No sane person did such a thing, although during his years as an air marshal, Mike had learned to be prepared for flight delays and cancellations. But, to be honest, he wasn't particularly upset about missing dinner. Since they all lived in Naples now, he saw his family more often than most people did. And, yeah, his mom did try her best to interfere with Mike's love life.

So he wasn't in a bad mood when he approached the Sand Dunes Motel that night at eleven, one ear cocked for the strains of loud music or screeches of out-of-control young people. But as he pushed open the door leading to the courtyard of the motel, his expectant ears were met only with blessed silence. Mike figured it was probably too much to expect that the students had simply turned in early. More likely, he guessed, they were out wreaking havoc on the town.

"It won't take them long to realize that Naples isn't Daytona Beach," he snorted to himself as he checked the courtyard for any signs of life. Daytona during spring break was a madhouse—with college students bunked six or eight or even ten to a room. Mike had no idea whose bright idea it had been to try to lure that demographic to their town—probably the same sort of brilliant city leaders who in another popular Florida town had made their city a haven for the elderly, even going so far as to install green benches every ten or so feet so there would be plenty of places for the city residents to rest. Unfortunately, those city leaders hadn't asked themselves what sort of town they'd end up with if eighty percent of their population were on fixed incomes. Want nice shops and restaurants? Movie theaters and marinas? Live shows and concerts? Not with people raking in five hundred a month on Social Security. So the city had found themselves with a quiet population that didn't overly tax their police force or schools, but that had no interest in investing in the city's future.

Similarly, Daytona Beach's spring-break crowd was both a blessing and a curse. Yes, they brought tourism to the city, but it was a tourism centered around getting wasted, hanging out at the beach all day, and buying cheap food and liquor at the grocery store because who needed to go out to a bar or restaurant when the entire place was one giant party? The hotel staffs were overburdened trying to keep their properties maintained, and the police were kept busy with trying to keep the streets safe for everyone. Unfortunately, by the time the city leaders and business owners realized that the financial and emotional cost of hosting this demographic wasn't offset by the income they brought in, it was too late. Spring break in Daytona Beach had become a tradition and there was nothing they could do to stop it.

Naples, fortunately, had been spared the same fate. Partially, this was because hotels in Naples charged way too much to appeal to the average struggling college student. Also, it wasn't within easy driving distance of the big universities in the south. After spending just a few days with the kids in his motel, Mike was even more grateful that this was the case. No way could he deal with ten times as many students as this. Not with their crazy antics.

He could only hope that they mellowed out as the days wore on. All that drinking and sitting in the sun *had* to get tiring after a while, right?

Mike walked past the two units on the upper level on the way to his own room. The first room, a long-term rental infrequently inhabited by a quiet German couple who paid their rent on the first day of the month without fail, was dark and the shades were drawn. But that was no different than when they were here. Aside from the occasional Schmidt sighting, the only way Mike could tell the couple was in residence was when they requested maid service. They were the perfect tenants—the sort that Mike would not be surprised to discover were professional assassins or international jewel thieves or serial killers who hacked their victims into small pieces and buried them in buckets of concrete at the local Shurgard storage or something.

Savannah Taylor, on the other hand, had left her curtains wide open and the light on in the kitchen, so he had a clear view into her room. However, not being the nosy sort, he didn't even pause except to note that there didn't seem to be anything interesting to note. There was no sign of the underwear she'd been carrying around yesterday, her bed was neatly made, and she hadn't thrown any red lingerie over any lamps, as far as he could tell.

Doesn't look like she's got anything to hide, Mike thought as he continued on to his room. As he opened the door, he noticed the light on his message machine was blinking. Odd. Since he traveled so much and worked such erratic hours, almost no one ever called him at home.

He slung his travel bag down on the bed and reached for the phone. He had one message from Lainie Ames at Intrepid Investigations, the firm he used to perform background checks on prospective tenants. While his mother preferred to rely on hunches, Mike only trusted the facts. Unlike people, facts didn't have any reason to lie.

"Hey, Mike. It's Lainie. I have some information for you on Savannah Taylor, and I think you'll find it pretty interesting. I'm faxing a report to you at the motel's number, and I'll send a duplicate over to your mom. I understand that you've already rented her a room for a while and . . . I'm sorry."

Mike took the receiver away from his ear and looked down at it and groaned. Oh, great. Now what?

He'd told his mother a thousand times that she couldn't just have people sign long-term rental agreements without checking them out first. Once the agreement was signed, that person was protected from eviction by the law. But he supposed he couldn't really blame his mom too much for this one. His gut had told him that Savannah Taylor was all right, too. Matter of fact, his gut had told him that Savannah Taylor was more than all right. Now to find out that she was . . . well, he didn't exactly know what she was. Maybe all Lainie's report would tell him was that Savannah had overdrawn her checking account a few times or was late paying her electric bill. Figures that he'd jumped to the conclusion that she was some sort of criminal. He supposed it came from too much worst-case-scenarioing at his job, playing the "what if" game with passengers who seemed too jumpy or sweated too profusely or clutched their bags too tightly. These days everyone was a potential terrorist, and Mike wondered if he was letting that attitude seep into his personal life, too.

"What you need is a good long swim," he told himself, rubbing the back of his neck as he took a Corona out of his fridge. He popped off the top and drank nearly half of the beer in one long swallow, then changed into his swimming trunks, grabbed a towel and what was left of his beer, and headed back downstairs with his keys. First, he'd check out the fax from Lainie, and then he'd work off his tension in the pool. With any luck Lainie's report wouldn't implicate Savannah Taylor in anything more sinister than a few bounced checks, and he could act on his impulse to ask his tenant out. Because, unbalanced checkbook or not, he found Savannah Taylor very attractive.

Which was surprising, because she wasn't his usual type. For one thing, she was shorter than the women he typically dated. She couldn't be more than five-three or -four at the most. But he liked the feeling of towering over her, even though he was just shy of six-one himself. There was also something about her that appealed to him. He couldn't name exactly what it was, but he'd felt it the first time they'd met

outside the Fat Cat restaurant, when she'd been wearing that
silly fish costume and had made a joke about it.

Mike unlocked the door of the motel's tiny office. Back in
its heyday, he supposed the desk had been manned 24/7, but
since the Sand Dunes had fallen into disrepair, business had
slowly dropped off, and the families who had once vacationed
there moved to the newer La Quintas and Days Inns off of
Highway 41 or the more upscale hotels along Vanderbilt
Beach. Now he or his mother fielded the infrequent calls to
the motel's front desk. And soon, once construction began to
convert the place into condos, the Sand Dunes Motel would
be no more.

For some reason, that made Mike a bit sad. Not that he had
any fond childhood memories of the place himself, but in
some way it signaled the end of an era.

Mike shook his head and laughed at his temporary foray
into nostalgia. He wasn't usually the sentimental sort.

Unfortunately, reading the report Lainie had faxed over
pretty much ended any feelings of nostalgia Mike felt. He
locked the office door behind him and headed back out to the
courtyard, plopping down in a lounge chair as he read.

"Jesus. Tax evasion. Money laundering," he muttered,
scowling at the report. He reached out for his beer and continued scanning the dirt Lainie had dug up. To be fair, the
charges had been dropped, although Lainie's sources weren't
able on such short notice to discover the reason why.

So, technically, Ms. Taylor had not lied on her rental application. She had not been *convicted* of a felony—or even a
misdemeanor. And an arrest without a conviction wasn't supposed to count against a person, but still, it certainly went a
long way to discrediting his mother's hunches.

"Guess I should be glad she's not a murderer," Mike said,
glumly dropping the report on top of his towel as he got up off
the chair. And so much for his fleeting attraction to his cute
tenant. No way was he getting involved with a suspected criminal, no matter how tempted he was to try to convince himself
that someone, somewhere, in the criminal justice system had
royally screwed up. He'd been in law enforcement long
enough to know that the jails were full of people who claimed

they were innocent—and 99.999999 percent of them were not. He wasn't going to chance that Savannah was that one in a million who had truly been falsely accused.

Sadly, that left his libido in a hell of a state, so Mike dove into the deep end of the swimming pool in an attempt to work off his sexual tension by tiring himself out in another way.

He was on his ninth lap, enjoying the rhythmic splashing of his own arms and legs as he propelled himself through the cool water, when he saw a flash of white out of the corner of his eye. He kept his head down, ignoring the frustrated anger that welled up in his gut when he thought of how tempted he'd been last night to give Savannah more than just a chaste kiss on her nose after he'd fished her—and her panties—out of the pool.

His feet slapped the wall of the pool as he pushed himself off for another lap. But by the time he was on his eleventh round, Mike realized that he could be at this all night and still not have worked off his irritation that he'd let himself entertain romantic notions about Savannah before checking her out first. Although, to cut himself some slack, he wasn't in the habit of running background checks on his dates, so who knew? He could have dated several convicted felons without even knowing it.

Whoever had said that ignorance was bliss was right, Mike thought as he heaved himself up and out of the pool. The laps weren't relaxing him, so maybe another Corona and some mindless channel-surfing would do the trick. He doubted it, but it was worth a try.

He quickly toweled off and headed for the nearest stair-well, his empty bottle and Lainie's report in hand. His feet slowed as he approached a well-lit room on the second floor, on the opposite side of the building, facing his unit. From inside the room came the unmistakable sound of female wailing.

Mike cringed. Like every man on the planet, he *hated* that noise. It was a noise to be avoided at all costs, and his body immediately went into flight mode. He flattened his back against the warm stucco wall. Perhaps if he remained motion-less, the noise would stop and he could safely continue on his journey.

But no, the crying continued.

"Look, Christina," he heard Savannah say, her voice calm and emotionless. "You can't jump him tonight. Wait until tomorrow morning, when he's not expecting it. You'll have the element of surprise on your side."

Mike's eyes narrowed. What was she talking about? Was Savannah planning a robbery with one of the students? Lainie's report hadn't mentioned anything about robbery or breaking and entering. And who was their intended victim? He'd noticed yesterday that the students pretty much left their doors wide open, so there would be no need to jump anyone in order to steal anything. All they'd have to do was to wait until their target was distracted and go ransack his room without having to worry about retaliation.

Then Mike blinked. Was *he* the potential victim? He had an expensive stereo in his motel room, plus a new forty-two-inch plasma TV that he'd splurged on last Christmas when one of his investments paid off unexpectedly. He was fairly certain he'd left his curtains open a time or two—often enough for someone interested in casing the motel to see what was inside.

The sounds of crying inside the room subsided somewhat, but Mike was busy mentally inventorying his possessions, so he was surprised when the door opened and Savannah stepped out into the breezeway, nearly stepping on his toes with her sparkly high-heeled boots. She gasped and her hands flew to her throat as if she'd just seen a ghost.

Mike's job was to defuse conflict. He did so by giving people options in a firm, yet polite, manner. *Please sit down or I will be forced to handcuff you and lock you in the lavatory. If you do not calm down, you will face possible jail time and a ten-thousand-dollar fine.* Simple, clear, easy to understand. Be reasonable. Give the perp a choice so he or she does not feel that they've lost control.

His training, however, flew out the proverbial window at the thought that this cute-but-deadly woman was plotting to rob him blind.

He dropped the stuff he was holding, grabbed Savannah's wrists, and dragged her behind him into the room she had just exited.

Once inside the enclosed space, Mike sniffed and then frowned. What *was* that smell? He sniffed again and looked over at a pile of clothes that had been abandoned on the floor. Someone was desperately overdue for a trip to the laundromat.

A dark-haired woman wearing pink silk pajamas with pastel polka dots sat on the bed, her face devoid of makeup and her eyes swollen from crying. It was the same woman Mike had saved yesterday by shoving her out of the way of the flying mattress and into the pool.

"What's going on here?" he asked, in his best don't-give-me-any-shit voice.

The woman on the bed looked up, startled, and rubbed her eyes with the heels of her hands. "Wh-what are you talking about?" she said.

"Let go of me," Savannah protested, trying vainly to tug her hands out of his grasp.

Mike held tight and shot her a look that had quelled many a more hardened crook, but seemed to have no effect on her because she continued to struggle. "I overheard you talking," he said, ignoring her thrashing. "Who are you two planning to rob?"

The corners of Savannah's eyes crinkled when she frowned. She stopped struggling, more, Mike figured, out of shock that he was on to her than out of any real fright for her physical safety. So, yeah, he wasn't really going to do anything to harm her, but would it have hurt her to act at least a little intimidated? He let her go, but remained in the doorway to block her exit just in case she took it in her head to try to escape. Instead, she backed up until her head thumped against the wall, her hands wrapped protectively around her neck. For just a second, Mike wondered why she was doing that—did she think he was going to strangle her or something?—but then he got back to the issue at hand.

"Well?" he asked, crossing his arms over his chest and glaring at the women.

"I have no idea what you're talking about," Savannah said. "And I really don't appreciate being manhandled. Just because you manage this motel doesn't mean you have the right to burst into someone's room like this. And, what did you mean, you overheard us talking? What are you doing skulking around people's doors?"

Mike frowned. "I wasn't skulking. I was returning to my room after a swim."

"Then what are you doing on this side of the building? Your room is over there," Savannah said, jerking her chin in the direction of his room.

"This stairwell was closer and—" Mike began to explain, then cut himself off with a shake of his head. What the hell was he doing explaining himself to *her*? "Forget it. I don't just manage this place, I own it. And I have every right to confront a tenant if I see her engaging in suspicious behavior. Now, I heard you talking about jumping someone and I will warn you right now that I'm on to you. If there's so much as an ashtray missing from anyone's motel room, I'm having you arrested. Do you understand me?"

Savannah's mouth dropped open and she stood there, her back against the wall, rapidly blinking her pretty green eyes. Then, to Mike's surprise, she burst out laughing. And when Christina joined in, Mike began to feel uncomfortable. He uncrossed his arms and scratched the side of his nose.

"What's so funny?" he asked.

Savannah looked at him through the tears of mirth clouding her eyes. The tip of her pink tongue came out and moistened her bottom lip and Mike had to pull his gaze away from the sight or he feared he'd throw her over his shoulder and drag her off to his room—and to hell with her criminal record. But as his gaze dropped from her face, Savannah's arms dropped from around her chest and Mike found himself staring instead at her breasts, peeking out at him from behind her wet tank top. When she realized that she'd exposed herself to him, she immediately recrossed her arms in front of her chest again, all signs of laughter gone as her creamy white skin flooded with color.

Mike reached down and grabbed his towel off the floor and held it out to Savannah with a mumbled, "Sorry," although for the life of him, he didn't know what he needed to apologize for. It just seemed like the appropriate response.

"Thank you," she said, taking the towel and wrapping it around her shoulders. She clutched the ends together in front of her chest as she studied the worn carpeting in Christina's motel room and explained, "We were talking about Christina's . . . uh, impulse to . . . um . . ."

Her tongue came out again and Mike nearly groaned with frustration. If she did that again, he was going to have to grab the towel back to hide a body part of his own. *Think about foot fungus,* he told himself, trying to get his mind off of sex and all the delightful things that little pink tongue might do to— *Okay, stop it.* Mike cleared his throat and sank down in the chair next to the door, rearranging himself as discreetly as possible.

"Christina has a crush on James," Savannah began again in a businesslike tone. "I was encouraging her to keep that information to herself until tomorrow morning. When perhaps she'll be a little more clear-headed than she is right now."

Mike looked over at the girl on the bed, who had closed her eyes but was still smiling. She hiccupped and said, "James is so-o-o-o cute."

Mike glanced at Savannah, who shrugged one shoulder as if to say, "Kids these days. What can you do?"

"And what about . . ." Mike waved toward Savannah's chest, although that really had nothing to do with anything, but he was curious as to why her shirt was all wet.

Savannah winced and clutched the towel tighter to her chest. "Christina thought James's opinion of her might be, uh, enhanced if she did something a little outrageous. Like take part in a wet T-shirt contest. Where she was the only contestant," Savannah added with a wobbly smile.

"But then why are *you* . . ." Mike waved at her again, starting to think he sounded like an idiot who couldn't form a complete sentence.

Savannah slumped against the wall. With her free hand, she pushed her dark hair out of her face and sighed. "Me?" she asked, with a self-deprecating roll of her eyes. "Once again I seem to have gotten caught in the crossfire of love."

How Bad Do You Want It?

Getting to the top takes lots of hard work and sacrifice. If you want to succeed at anything in life, you're going to have to be willing to put up with long hours, pride-swallowing run-ins with bosses and clients, and, most likely, the complete forfeiture of your personal life. So, do you have what it takes to make it to the top? Take our quiz and see!

You've worked your ass off the last two weeks on a big presentation for your company's most important client. Three days before the presentation, your boss casually mentions that there are too many attendees, so your name got cut from the list. You're crushed because you know this means you won't get any credit for your work and you'll be stuck working for your asshole boss forever. Then, the next day, your boss says you're back in again. You're thrilled, assuming it was your professional demeanor that got you added back to the guest list. Only, the morning before the presentation, you're in the ladies' room when you overhear two of your boss's peers laughing about some bimbo the client has a crush on so he insisted she be included in the meeting today. It's only after the meeting begins and the client, who just happens to be seated next to you, squeezes your knee that you realize the bimbo they were talking about is you! After the meeting, you:

a· Write up your resignation and have it waiting on your boss's desk when he gets back from his two-martini lunch with the client. This job is one big dead-end and you don't need any more signs to tell you that.

continues on next page . . .

b. Go back into the ladies' room and cry your heart out. You deserved to be at that meeting because of your brains, not because some jerk has the hots for you.

c. Slip a note in the client's pocket letting him know you'd like to meet him for a drink after work today. What's wrong with using every advantage you've got to get ahead?

You're really willing to give up your job because some jerk in a position of power is championing you? Sorry to tell you this, but those of you who chose A are never going to make it to the top! The only way you B gals are going to make it big is if you buy stock in Kleenex. If you chose C, you don't need us to tell you that you're headed for bigger and better things. Hold on, baby! It's gonna be a wild ride!

{sixteen}

Savannah sat in a puddle of sunshine on the bench outside of Valeen's and tried to pretend that she hadn't just seen the Help Wanted sign taped to the door of Refund City.

The tall thin man who had scurried past her yesterday morning had done the same thing a minute ago as he hurried to the accounting office. He was one of those people who appeared to walk around with a dark wool coat of gloom wrapped protectively around himself.

"Like Scrooge," Savannah muttered, turning her attention to the tourists just starting their day at the coffee shop across the street. She wondered why the pull of the accounting profession was so strong. Just because she was good at it, that didn't mean it was the only thing she could do for a living. Why was she so tempted to leap off of the bench and follow Mr. Scrooge to his dark, dingy office surrounded by his tax forms and IRS demands for payment and audit notices?

Perhaps it was simply the lure of a predictable paycheck. There certainly was something appealing about that.

"Good morning, Savannah," Valeen said from behind her, twisting open the lock on the door to her shop.

Sure, *she* was cheerful. She hadn't spent more money than she'd made yesterday. Even worse, Savannah had awoken abruptly from a sound sleep this morning with the realization

buzzing in her brain that Valeen had dumped the worst clients
on her. When someone came in who Valeen knew would have
her running back and forth to the stockroom with no intention
of buying anything, she had found "something urgent" she
needed to take care of in the back. Not a very nice thing for
her new boss to do, but Savannah figured that Valeen's strat-
egy was to saddle her with the worst customers to see if she
could hack it. Then, once she passed that probationary period,
Valeen would treat her as more of an equal. At least, Savannah
hoped that was the plan. There was no way she could survive
in the supposedly glamorous business of high-end shoe sales
if every day went like yesterday.

Savannah followed Valeen into the store, smothering a
yawn with the back of her hand. She hated to admit this, but
the thought of spending a quiet night curled up with a good
book sounded far more appealing to her right now than going
out to another of Vanna's haunts in an attempt to ferret out her
alter ego. She didn't know how the other woman did it—
hitting bars and restaurants every night of the week. *Probably
doesn't have a job she has to get up and go to,* Savannah
thought. And why should she? She was living pretty darn well
off of other people's credit.

It didn't take much to get the boutique ready for their first
customer. Valeen powered up the sales system while Savannah
straightened a heel here and there that they'd missed last night
while closing up shop. At 9 A.M. on the dot, Valeen flipped the
sign on the door to indicate that they were open as Savannah
practiced her best customer-service smile. By ten they'd only
had one browser in, a plump middle-aged woman wearing
khaki shorts, white tennis shoes, and a green polo shirt. When
the woman first paused outside their front window and looked
at Valeen's display of spring footwear, Savannah heard Valeen
mutter something under her breath that sounded distinctly like
"Unfashionable loser."

The buzzer on the front door beeped when the woman
stepped inside, and Savannah watched out of the corner of her
eye as Valeen slowly slipped toward the back room like vapor
vanishing in a puff of wind.

Great, another dud.

Savannah tried out her smile on the woman, who smiled

back and said good morning. Savannah began to think that maybe she was going to make an easy sale, after all, but then the woman picked up a pair of red boots near the front of the store and gasped when she saw the price tag.

"Oh, my gosh," the woman said. "Are these really four hundred and eighty-five dollars?"

"Yes," Savannah answered, knowing by the woman's reaction that there would be no sale—easy or hard.

The woman shook her head, but her short gray hair barely moved. She set the boots down carefully, as if afraid she might break them and then have to buy them. Savannah wryly wondered if she should tell the woman not to worry. Any damage she inflicted would come out of Savannah's account, not hers.

"I can go to Payless and get something similar for thirty dollars. I don't understand it. How do you manage to stay in business?" the woman asked, shaking her head again.

Savannah figured it was a rhetorical question, but answered it anyway. "We carry only the finest designer footwear here at Valeen's, made from the best materials in the world. Those boots were imported from Italy. They're handmade." Of course that didn't really answer the question, so Savannah added, "Our customers expect to pay more for that kind of quality."

The woman laughed and backed toward the door. "Not me," she said. "With shoes that expensive, I'd be afraid to actually wear them."

"Well. Um. Have a nice day," Savannah said as the woman retreated. If Valeen expected her to have some magic spell that would convince a person like that to plunk down what was likely a week's take-home salary on a pair of boots, she was going to be sadly disappointed. For most people, $485 *was* a ridiculous amount of money to spend on a pair of shoes. Yes, these boots were of the finest quality, but at what point did that become moot? Would a five-hundred-dollar pair of shoes last that much longer than one that cost two hundred dollars? How much better could the five-hundred-dollar-a-pair cows have been, after all?

When the door jangled again and a redhead who could have graced the cover of a Victoria's Secret catalog stepped inside the shop, Savannah knew she had a big spender because Valeen emerged from the stockroom.

But before Valeen could scoop her first big sale, Savannah decided she'd had enough of being stuck with the duds. She needed a hefty commission to make up for the loss she'd taken yesterday, and, besides, she was sick of waiting on customers who never bought anything. If Valeen had come out of hiding, Savannah was certain it was because her boss smelled a sale.

So Savannah took a step toward the redhead, smiled obsequiously, and said, "Good morning. That shade of blue is lovely on you. It really brings out the color of your eyes."

The customer smiled back—oh, joy!—and said, "Why, thank you. Isn't that sweet of you to say?"

Savannah tried to look humble. "Just telling the truth. Now, is there something *I* can help you with?" She made sure her emphasis on *I* wasn't too overt. No sense offending Valeen if she could help it. Savannah turned her smile on Valeen just to show that there were no hard feelings and was surprised when her boss surreptitiously ran a hand across her neck in the international "cut" gesture.

How rude was that? The first time Savannah got close to a big sale and Valeen was trying to cut her out of it. Well, Savannah wasn't going to give in that easily. She had to prove to Valeen that she wasn't a pushover. Otherwise, her new boss would never stop taking advantage of her.

Ignoring Valeen, Savannah walked over to the customer and introduced herself. Then she asked, "Is there something in particular you were looking for today?"

"Actually, there is," the woman said, eyeing Savannah appreciatively.

Savannah's chest puffed with pride. Wow, maybe she *was* good at this Shoe Saleswoman to the Stars thing.

The woman held out her hand and said, "I'm Lindsay, by the way. Lindsay Baxstrom. My family owns half of Naples." This last was said with a mocking laugh that Savannah interpreted to mean that it was true, but that Lindsay didn't put much stock in it. Still, it was a strange way to introduce oneself.

"My family owns half of a 2003 Dodge Dakota. I'm sure we have similar issues," Savannah said, taking the other woman's hand and shaking it lightly.

Lindsay laughed and peered around Savannah. "I like this

girl," she said to Valeen, who had taken up a spot near the cash register.

"I'm sure you do," Valeen answered dryly.

Savannah thought Valeen was just being a poor loser, so she continued to ignore her as she focused her attention on Lindsay Baxstrom. "So, what can I help you find today?"

"Well, I'm looking for a couple of things. First, I've got a charity event coming up next week—you know, one of those boring cocktail parties where all the city's wealthy get together and decide who's dick is bigger by the amount of their donation. Shoes are my favorite thing in the whole world, so I figured I'd buy something fabulous here first and then go down to Flair Boutique to find a dress to go with them. That's just so much more fun than doing it the other way around, don't you think?" Lindsay trilled, laying her hand lightly on Savannah's forearm.

"That's a great idea. I don't think I've ever done that," Savannah said, then waved toward the velvet couch near where they were standing. "Why don't you sit down and relax and I'll bring you some of my favorite styles? Just think of me as your personal shopper."

Lindsay's blue eyes glittered as she squeezed Savannah's arm. "That sounds wonderful. I'm a size eight."

She let go of Savannah's arm and sank down on the couch with a little sigh of pleasure. Meanwhile, Savannah quickly looked around the shop to assess her choices. Her very favorite shoes were a pair of red sandals with a bow at the toe and a crystal heart charm attached to the strap across the instep. She would show Lindsay those first, along with a pair of magenta stilettos with sparkling rhinestone buckles at the ankle and toe.

"I'll be right back," Savannah murmured, already trying to decide if she'd buy herself one pair of new panties with her commission or splurge on two. After Mike had fished her boring white granny panties out of the pool two nights ago, she'd had second thoughts about tossing them out, but had forced herself to throw them in the trash can underneath the sink in her motel room's tiny kitchen. Unfortunately, since she hadn't had the time—or the money—to buy new ones yesterday, she'd had to fish them out last night after the whole wet T-shirt fiasco and had washed them out in the bathroom sink and hung them over the shower rod to dry.

Sexy new persona or not, she *refused* to go commando at work. It just wasn't professional.

"Here, let me help you." Valeen interrupted Savannah's contemplation of her undergarment situation, a strange note of urgency in her voice.

"Actually, I need to talk to you, Val. Can you hold up just a second?" Lindsay asked in a way that didn't make it sound like a question.

Savannah heard Valeen slowly release her breath, but didn't stop to wonder what that might mean as she hurried to the stockroom to gather up some fun party shoes for her new favorite client. It didn't take her long to choose five pairs of the cutest—and most expensive—shoes Valeen had in stock. When she got back to the sales floor, Valeen was standing by the couch, her hands clasped behind her back while she stared uncomfortably at the floor.

"I think you'll love these," Savannah announced into the awkward silence. Geez, Valeen was really taking this hard. Maybe she shouldn't have been so aggressive.

"I've . . . uh, I've got to check on something for Ms. Baxstrom. Holler if you need anything." Valeen swallowed audibly and sidestepped Savannah like a crab scurrying under a rock.

Weird, Savannah thought, her forehead furrowing. But she dismissed Valeen's odd behavior when Lindsay all but purred, "Now, come over here and show me what you've got."

It was nice to help someone who had an appreciation for what Savannah was selling. She set the shoe boxes on the floor and wheeled over a stool so she could help Lindsay try on the shoes she had brought. She was a little surprised to discover that Lindsay hadn't taken off her own shoes, but, hey, she didn't mind being a full-service Shoe Saleswoman to the Stars. Before Savannah could take out the first pair of shoes and prep them to be tried on, Lindsay lifted her right foot up and put it in Savannah's lap. The short, neon blue skirt she was wearing crept up her thigh, and from her vantage point on the stool, Savannah could see much more of Lindsay

Baxstrom's red thong undies than she was certain the woman intended.

Thank God Lindsay had not gone commando, Savannah thought as she directed her smile to the empty spot just beyond her customer's left ear. There was no point in letting on that she'd just been flashed. It would just embarrass them both, and Savannah was sure that would not be conducive to making a big sale.

Since the heel of Lindsay's blue pump was digging into her thigh, Savannah first removed the other woman's shoes before turning to the boxes at her side. She had thought that Lindsay would put her feet back on the floor, but she didn't, keeping them nestled comfortably in Savannah's lap, instead.

Probably didn't want to get her feet dirty, Savannah figured. Not that the floor was dirty. Savannah herself had run the vacuum cleaner over the carpet last night. But, no matter.

Savannah pulled the first red sandal out of the box and de-tissued it.

"Ooh, yes. That's lovely," Lindsay purred.

Savannah nearly jumped three feet when Lindsay's toes curled into her thigh, but she forced herself to relax. *It was just an involuntary reaction to the sight of the shoes,* she told herself. She slipped her hand under Lindsay's right heel and lifted her foot up so she could slide the sandal on, but it seemed to stick around Lindsay's toes.

"Hmm," Savannah said. "It looks like you may need a bigger size."

"Sometimes my feet swell when I've been walking. It might help if you rub them for a minute," Lindsay suggested in a strangely husky voice.

What? Did she look like a masseuse?

Okay, she would never, ever disparage being an accountant again.

Savannah rubbed her forehead just above her left eye, which was starting to twitch. She couldn't give up now. She needed this commission. Besides, really, it wasn't so bad. It was only a little foot rub, right?

She gave Lindsay a weak smile and said, "Sure. No problem." Then she set the shoe back in its box and, with a deep breath, she pressed her thumbs into Lindsay Baxstrom's insteps and started to rub.

Lindsay's feet were smooth and smelled faintly of some expensive brand of lotion like the ones given out in little foil-packaged samples at the Nordstrom perfume counter. Savannah guessed that Lindsay actually bought the lotion, however. That was the sort of thing you could afford when your family owned half a city.

Maybe with her commission check, she could buy a small bottle of the stuff for herself. Just for special occasions, Savannah thought as her fingers moved up to Lindsay's toes. Like maybe if Mike Bryson decided the moment he'd seen her breasts last night that the whole gay thing was a big mistake. For just a second when he had hauled her into Christina's room and was standing so close she could see the pulse throbbing in his neck, Savannah had thought she felt a spark pass between them. No matter how often her brain told her that she wasn't his type, her body didn't seem to be getting the message. Because every time they were within five feet of each other, her inner sex goddess screamed, "Yeah, baby. That's what I want."

Her mind was so focused on Mike Bryson and how he made her feel that Savannah wasn't paying any attention to Lindsay Baxstrom and the effect her foot rub was having on the other woman.

It was only when the front door of Valeen's flew open and the woman in the doorway gasped, "Omigod," that Savannah was jerked back to reality. Her gaze flew from the front door to Lindsay, who had rested her head on the back of the red velvet couch and was thrashing her long red hair, her legs slightly parted as she screamed, "Oh, for fuck's sake, don't stop now!"

Savannah realized at that moment that she was just not cut out for this kind of customer service.

"That's it," she announced, abruptly sliding off the stool, uncaring that Lindsay's heels banged on the carpeted floor as the redhead spluttered with frustration. "I quit. There's something wrong with you people." She marched to the center of the room and grabbed her purse from the drawer beneath the cash register. Then she made her way to the door, pausing for just a second to turn back to Lindsay and say, "You need serious professional help."

Then she stomped out into the warm morning, knowing she'd just abandoned her dreams of a glamorous new career, but feeling inexplicably happier than she had in months.

Does Your Guy Have a Hot Job?

Let's face it, women like men who have sexy jobs. There's a reason that all those ugly rock stars (money and fame) and those aging captains of industry (money and power) get all the hot chicks! But even guys with less impressive bank balances can be attractive, too. Take this quiz to find out if what your man does qualifies him as a certified hottie!

So tell us, what does your fella do to bring home the bacon?

a. He's a flight attendant, but he assures you that he's not gay. He insists that in recent years, the job has become more about flight safety and less about giving away those little packets of pretzels . . . and you believe him.

b. He's, uh, currently between jobs. He's always, uh, currently between jobs. Good thing you don't mind working night and day to support him!

c. He owns his own construction company and both designs and builds custom homes. And, no, when he fixes your pipes, there's no butt cleavage in sight.

A, A, A. We're shaking our heads with pity here. Even if your guy isn't swinging the other way, he spends his days acting as a flying waiter. Can we be any clearer? No, he does not have a hot job. If your guy falls into the B category, we pity you even more. Hot guys do not let their women pay the bills. Haven't you read The Rules? He pays. If he doesn't, he's just taking advantage of you until someone better (that's his opinion, not ours, mind you) comes along. Okay, girls, admit it.

continues on next page . . .

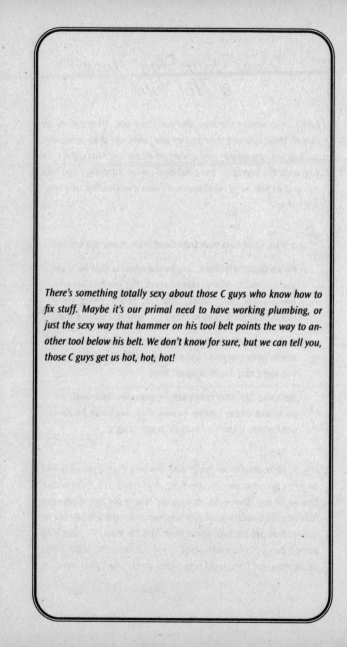

There's something totally sexy about those C guys who know how to fix stuff. Maybe it's our primal need to have working plumbing, or just the sexy way that hammer on his tool belt points the way to another tool below his belt. We don't know for sure, but we can tell you, those C guys get us hot, hot, hot!

{seventeen}

I assume you saw this report about Savannah Taylor?" Mike asked, raising the sheaf of papers and then letting them fall back to his lap. He was sitting in his mother's office, having stopped to say hello before heading out to the airport for what was supposed to be a short hop from Naples down to Key West. There had been an increase in drug trafficking into Naples in the past year, and the local police suspected it might be coming from Key West. Not that a cautious drug trafficker couldn't have his mules make the drive from Key West up to Naples or even deliver the goods by speedboat, where they wouldn't have to pass through any sort of security and risk getting caught. But sometimes traffickers weren't cautious. Sometimes they were cocky assholes who thought they could get away with anything—and it was part of Mike's job to disabuse them of that notion. There were rumors about a large air delivery in the works, so Mike was assigned to take a few runs down to Key West and check out security at the airport.

He was actually looking forward to it. The Naples–Key West run was an easy one, with very little chance of any major delays. With any luck he'd make a couple of runs and still be back home before ten P.M.

"Yes, I saw it," his mother answered glumly, bringing him

back to the matter at hand. "I just can't believe I was so wrong
about her."

Mike couldn't help but chuckle softly at his mother's dejected demeanor. "You're taking this way too hard," he said.

Lillian Bryson shook her head. Her son . . . She loved him,
but he was so clueless. Didn't he realize that every woman
who stepped through the entrance of her marriage-preparatory
service was assessed as a potential mate for her sons?

It wasn't that she was desperate for grandchildren (although a few babies around the house would certainly be welcome); it was more that she wanted to see her boys as happy
as she and their father had been. Even now, sixteen years after
Tom's death, Lillian missed him. She hadn't been interested
in dating again because she knew she'd never find that kind of
love with another man. She also knew that her boys would
never get to experience that same kind of joy if they didn't
find their soul mates. The problem was, neither of them took
her quest seriously. They didn't seem to understand that their
lives would not go on forever and that if they didn't take a
more proactive role in finding that one woman out there who
was right for them, they might lose the opportunity for all
eternity.

And for some reason, when Savannah Taylor had showed
up here in her office three days ago, Lillian had thought she'd
found *the one*. So, yes. She *was* taking it hard that the woman
she had thought was so right for Mike turned out to be a crook.

Lillian propped one elbow up on her desk and rested her
chin in her hand as she studied her son. He was handsome,
with his father's dark blond hair and gray-blue eyes. He had
Tom's dimples, too. Those dangerous dimples that made you
fall in love with him the moment he smiled. Not only that, but
Mike was financially stable. He'd always been a bit too serious about money, mostly, Lillian feared, because she'd con-
fided in him after his father died. He'd known about their
precarious financial situation and had never once complained
about having to buy bargain clothes or not getting a car on
graduation like most of his friends.

Her business hadn't started to make a profit until after
Mike had graduated from college, and no amount of insisting
that she help retire his student loans had made him relent. Lil-

lian blinked back tears as she marveled at what a wonderful man her son had turned out to be.

What was so wrong with trying to find him a woman who would appreciate him and love him and make his life that much happier?

"If it's any consolation, I had a hard time believing this myself," Mike said, tapping the report on his lap. "I'm still not one hundred percent sure that I do."

But there was no way Lillian was going to take risks with her son's future happiness, so she tried to discourage him by cautioning, "Well, you know that old saying about smoke and fire."

Mike pushed himself off the chair and stretched, his light gray shirt untucking slightly at his waist. His gun rested in its holster, and Lillian forced herself not to focus on it. She hated thinking of her baby—who was over six feet tall and probably weighed a good two hundred pounds—putting himself in danger, but he loved his job, so she kept her thoughts to herself.

That is, until he shot her a devilish grin and said, "Yeah, but sometimes you need a little fire to keep things hot."

Lillian raised her eyes heavenward. "Don't come crying to me when you get burned," she warned, only half in jest. She was starting to worry that maybe for once her matchmaking efforts with her son had actually worked.

Mike leaned over and kissed her forehead, then chucked her on the chin. "Don't worry, Mom. I can handle Savannah Taylor," he said, before shrugging into his sport coat and heading out the door.

Lillian cringed. Oh, didn't he know he was just asking for trouble by saying such a thing?

She heard the sound of voices from out in the front reception area and walked over to the door to see who was there, just in case Maddie had stepped out while she and Mike were talking. She didn't have an appointment until after lunch, and she wasn't expecting anyone, but one of her clients could have stopped in for an emergency session. That happened all too frequently. If only her clients would be strong and follow her instructions, she could have them all married off within twelve to eighteen months.

Sadly, though, no matter how many times she told a brokenhearted woman not to repeatedly call the man she loved to try to convince him to take her back or tried to persuade a man that his fiancée's reluctance to set a wedding date really did mean that she didn't want to get married, at least fifty percent of the time, they didn't listen. And so they did silly, counterproductive things—like leaving forty-three messages on their ex's cell phone or handing out ultimatums they wouldn't follow through on—that then required her to take more drastic measures.

But when Lillian poked her head out into the waiting area, she wasn't met by a wayward client looking for premarital advice, but the woman she and Mike had been discussing just moments before. Lillian looked on in silence as Mike and Savannah chatted, and she didn't even need to hear what was being said to know that her earlier fears were grounded. Savannah's cheeks were flushed with color as she batted her eyelashes up at Mike's. As for her son, he was leaning toward the shorter woman, his voice rumbling low in his throat as he talked.

This was not good. Mike was going to get his heart broken by this cunning criminal who had fooled them both. But Lillian couldn't lay the blame at Mike's door. From the first moment she and Savannah had talked, Lillian had been plotting this very thing. Only now she had to stop it.

She stepped out into the hallway and cleared her throat, watching with dismay as Mike and Savannah leaped back like teenagers who had been caught necking at school.

It was worse than she thought. But what could she do to break it up?

She didn't know exactly, but she'd figure something out.

"Why, hello, Savannah. What can I do for you?" she asked, hoping her cheery tone didn't sound too phony. She insinuated herself between Savannah and her son, holding out her hands in greeting as she turned her head to Mike and said, "Don't you have to be going? You don't want to be late for work."

She took it as a sign of Mike's befuddled state when he didn't protest her intrusion, instead saying, "Right. Yes. See you later," before he left.

Lillian turned back to Savannah, trying to smile without baring her teeth. "How can I help you?" she asked.

Savannah seemed nervous, looking first to the right and then to the left before answering, "Um, could we go back to your office? I need to ask you for a favor."

"Certainly," Lillian said, leading the way down the hall. When she got to her doorway, she stepped aside and indicated that Savannah should precede her into the room. Savannah did, taking a seat on the chair nearest the door.

Lillian crossed the room and sat down behind her desk, pulling out a pad of paper and a silver pen that Mike had given her for her last birthday, as if this were a business meeting. "What can I do for you?" she asked.

Savannah appeared to be chewing on the inside of her cheek and she looked vaguely uncomfortable. Lillian wondered just what sort of favor the girl was here to ask. Surely, she wouldn't expect Lillian to do anything illegal?

Finally, Savannah answered. "That job at the Fat Cat didn't work out and I just quit my job over at Valeen's and I . . . Well, I really hate to do this, but I wonder if I could take you up on your offer to put in a few calls for me? I'm smart, I'm resourceful, I'm a really hard worker." Savannah leaned forward as if pleading her case to a hostile judge.

Lillian almost felt sorry for her. That is, until she spied the report Lainie had dropped over that morning. This woman was a suspected felon with over fifty thousand dollars of unsecured debt. Lillian had no idea how someone of Savannah's age and income bracket could have convinced banks to make those loans, but she was certain it was not on the up-and-up. Most likely, she'd applied for ten or twelve cards simultaneously, hoping that no one would catch on to her scheme. And it looked as though she'd succeeded—probably using one card to make payments on the next and so on until her financial house of cards collapsed because it had no foundation.

This was not the sort of person she would refer to her friends for employment, but she didn't want to cause Savannah to lose her temper and go on some sort of crime spree, so she smiled and made a note on her pad and said, "I'll make some calls and get back to you on that. Maybe early next week?"

Savannah looked crushed as she slid back in her chair,
closed her eyes, and let out a heartfelt sigh. "I was hoping you
could help me find something a little sooner. I'm running a little low on cash, you see," she admitted quietly, as if it pained
her to do so.

"Well, I hadn't really given it much thought. There's one
person I could call right now if you like. He owns a furniture
store just down the street."

Savannah opened her eyes and gave Lillian an Oscar-
worthy look of gratitude. "Thank you so much."

Lillian reminded herself that this innocent act was just
that—an act. She picked up the phone and dialed her friend
down at Mason's Furniture. They exchanged the usual pleas-
antries while Savannah looked on and Lillian smiled encour-
agingly. Once the small talk was over, Lillian said, "By the
way, did you fill that sales position you were telling me about?
I have someone here in my office who might be interested in
the job."

Lillian mentally practiced looking disappointed, but she
feared that she was nowhere near as good an actress as Savannah. Her sympathetic tone seemed a bit forced when she said,
"Oh, no. I forgot you'd told me yesterday that you'd hired
someone. I'm so sorry to have bothered you." Then she hung
up the phone before her friend could suggest another job that
might still be available. She shrugged and tried to stay in the
role as she turned to Savannah. "I'm so sorry. The job was
filled yesterday. I guess I forgot. You know how it is when you
get older. Your mind turns into a sieve." Lillian jiggled her
head as if to prove that there was nothing but dry old dust bun-
nies up there, although she'd never had one moment of trouble
remembering anything in her life.

Savannah's shoulders slumped disappointedly. "Thank you
for trying."

"Certainly, certainly. I have another friend or two I can
call, but they're out of town this week vacationing with their
families. It's spring break, you know."

That drew an amused snort from Savannah, who muttered,
"Yes, I know," but didn't elaborate.

Lillian pushed herself up out of her chair, hoping that

would signal the end of this meeting. "I'll be sure to let you know what I find out," she said.

Savannah took the hint and stood, and Lillian couldn't believe how easily she had won this battle. With no job, Savannah wouldn't be able to pay next week's rent and they'd have the grounds to evict her. If there was one thing Lillian knew about her son, it was that he did not have a soft heart where finances were concerned. No way would he let Savannah live at the motel if her rent wasn't paid in full and on time.

When Savannah faux-casually asked her next question, though, Lillian started to sweat.

"So, I never have asked Mike what he does for a living. You said earlier that he was just leaving for work. He must work odd hours."

Lillian's eyes narrowed. No way was she telling Savannah that Mike was a federal air marshal. She'd seen the effect that had on some women, who went all weak in the knees and googly-eyed about men in law enforcement. It was even worse with Sam, a retired Navy SEAL who had had his share of starry-eyed groupies falling for him. Or, rather, for his uniform.

"He works for the airlines," Lillian hedged, studying a chipped spot on the door to her office and trying not to chew the inside of her own cheek now.

"Is he a pilot?" Savannah asked, sounding hopeful.

Suddenly Lillian was struck with an evil thought. She felt like the Grinch, eyeing her little dog Max to figure out how to attach a set of antlers to his head. She knew what the implications would be if she answered Savannah's question this way. Savannah would never look at her son the same way again. Which was exactly what Lillian wanted.

Mike would kill her if he knew she'd done this, but if she was lucky, he would never find out.

Lillian blinked and pasted on her sweetest smile. Then she looked up at Savannah and said, "Why no, dear. He's more like a . . . a part of the flight crew."

Savannah tried to hide her disappointment, but Lillian could tell that she was crushed—though she didn't seem as surprised as Lillian had expected.

"You mean," Savannah said, her voice full of resignation, "he's a flight attendant."

And Lillian, who didn't like to outright lie, merely smiled and shrugged, letting Savannah draw her own conclusions as to what that might mean.

Do You Make a Good First Impression?

You've heard the old saying that first impressions are everything? Well, we believe it! How many times have you met someone you took an instant disliking to and then ended up becoming that person's best friend? Never, right? It just doesn't happen. So, what sort of first impression do you make?

When you first meet people, their typical reaction is to:

a· Smile and nod, but their eye contact usually lasts no more than two seconds.

b· Take a small step backward and put their hands in their pockets.

c· Smile and lean toward you, then touch you somewhere (i.e., on your shoulder or your hand).

You A girls aren't doing awful in the first impressions department, but you could do better. Your problem is that you're not memorable enough for that other person to bother learning your name or anything about you. What are you doing wrong? Maybe you need to work on your smile or make sure to pop a mint before meeting someone new. Give it a try—it could work miracles! If you chose B, we're sorry, but you make a terrible first impression. The only way it could be worse is if the other person screamed and ran away from you! We don't know what you're doing wrong but you might want to try your greeting skills out on a trusted friend . . . if you have any, that is! For those of you who chose C, you're charmers and, what's more, you know it! Keep up the good work—and the good first impressions!

{eighteen}

Savannah had run out of options. She'd called on half a dozen want ads and heard nothing but the typical, "E-mail us your résumé and we'll get back to you next week." She couldn't wait until next week. She was down to her last fifty dollars, and, although she could always ask her parents for money, she hated to do that. It seemed so irresponsible, especially when all she had to do to get a job was to make the one call she'd been dreading.

In the end, what had pushed her over the edge was her strange encounter with Lillian Bryson that afternoon. Why had Lillian gone out of her way to offer assistance with Savannah's job hunt and then seemed so reluctant to help when Savannah took her up on her offer?

Savannah scowled at the cell phone in her hand as if it had somehow offended her. "I hate asking for help," she said to the phone, which didn't respond.

From where she was sitting on a bench under an oak tree on Sunshine Parkway, she could clearly see Refund City's phone number stenciled in white lettering on the front window across the street. The number taunted her, daring her to make that call, yet Savannah hesitated.

It felt as if she were giving up, as if by going back to a "safe" job in accounting, she was admitting defeat.

"But if you have more money, you can afford to go out to the bars and restaurants that Vanna frequented. You can shop where she shopped. Think about it this way, you're actually *increasing* your chances of finding Vanna and creating a glamorous new life if you do this," she told herself.

Yes. That was a better way to look at it. She wasn't giving up at all.

Her decision made, Savannah dialed the number for Refund City and in less than five minutes had secured herself an interview within the hour with a Mr. Leonard, who managed the Naples office. She hadn't had lunch yet, so she hurried over to the coffee shop and got herself an iced tea and a turkey bagel sandwich and brought her food back to the bench to eat.

Worried that she'd be late to her interview, Savannah wolfed down her sandwich and washed it down with Mango-Passionfruit-Ginseng-St. John's Wort-Wheat Grass iced tea.

"What ever happened to plain iced tea?" she wondered aloud after draining the last of the drink. She tossed the plastic cup and sandwich wrapper into the trash can beside the bench and felt a sliver prick her thigh as she nervously checked her watch. She was early. It figured.

Vowing never to be early again—punctuality wasn't sexy or mysterious and certainly didn't fit with the image she wanted to portray—she pushed her sunglasses up the bridge of her nose with her index finger and did her best to ooze bored glamour at the tourists who sauntered by.

After a few minutes she checked her watch again, sighing with relief when she realized that she could finally go get this interview over with. She didn't know why she was nervous. It wasn't like she didn't have the qualifications to do the job. Perhaps it was just that her last two employment experiences had her spooked. In the past three days she'd been attacked by dogs, nearly run over by a gelato cart, doused with crab bisque, enlisted as a nursemaid to a spoiled preteen, and preyed upon by a foot fetishist. And that was just the work-related incidents.

Was it any wonder she had some trepidations about this next encounter?

Savannah stood and tugged her red-and-black tartan skirt into place, doing her best not to swelter in the heat.

"Okay, exude confidence," she mumbled to herself as she slung the strap of her purse over her shoulder and headed across the street.

If events were to continue along in the same vein as they had this past week, Savannah figured that as she stepped off the curb, a large dark car—most likely a Mercedes, since the bad guys in movies always drove the expensive German cars—would come barreling around a corner and send her flying through the front window of Refund City. Nearly every bone in her body would be broken, and her parents would rush to her side and she'd discover, through painful recovery and a romance with her physical therapist, that her fatal flaw had been in looking for happiness somewhere else when it had been right under her nose in Maple Rapids the entire time. The story would end as she and Dr. Whoever said "I do" in the waiting room of Maple Rapids General Hospital, and they'd flash forward five years later to show two little Whoevers toddling around Savannah's feet with another one on the way while Doc waved Disney World tickets in front of the camera and beamed.

For some reason, however, that vision of her future made Savannah shudder, and, fortunately, no ominous screeching of tires met her ears as she trotted across the street and pulled open the door of the accounting firm. The air was filled with the tense sound of a dozen accountants entering tax return data as quickly and accurately as possible. Savannah could almost smell their exhaustion. She knew that as April 15 approached, their hours would only increase. And they knew it, too, which is most likely why only one of them looked up from her work as Savannah stepped into the office.

Ah, the junior accountant, Savannah thought, smiling at the young woman with the platinum blond hair. This was not a Big Six accounting firm, with a highly paid receptionist sitting in a glass-enclosed booth and barring entry to the hallowed halls within. Instead, the accountant with the fewest years out of college got stuck having to juggle not only her own workload but the receptionist duties as well. If this office worked anything like the one back in Maple Rapids, the woman would keep a log of walk-ins who would be assigned to the staff based on a rolling roster that ensured everyone got his or her share of the workload. For the first year the junior accountant would be assigned only the most routine returns.

"I'm Savannah Taylor. I'm here to see Mr. Leonard," Savannah said.

The woman shot Savannah a relieved smile when she realized that she hadn't come bearing W-2s. "Great. I'll let him know you're here," she said. Then she surprised Savannah by turning her head and yelling, "Hey, Len! Someone's here to see you."

The other people in the office were apparently accustomed to her outbursts because they didn't even pause in their data entry. Several seconds later the gloomy man Savannah had noticed hurrying past her for the last two mornings stuck his head out of the office farthest from the door. He motioned for Savannah to come back and then popped back inside his office again like a prairie dog.

Savannah nodded politely to the junior accountant before making her way to the back of the building. She hesitated in the doorway of Mr. Leonard's office because it seemed as if he had disappeared. She looked to the left, and then to the right, and then peered around the door to see if he was hiding there, waiting to jump out and yell "Boo" in some sort of weird interview test like the ones she'd read about in "The Complete Moron's Guide to Acing Interviews."

"Come in, come in," Mr. Leonard said, emerging from behind an enormous stack of files perched precariously on his desk.

Relieved that he wasn't trying to scare her as some sort of measure of her mental stability or reflexes, Savannah stepped inside the office and turned to close the door behind her, but stopped when he said, "You can leave it open."

Blinking, Savannah looked at the thin, wiry man who was nearly buried beneath the paperwork on his desk. "But I'm here for an interview," she said, thinking that perhaps Mr. Leonard didn't realize why she was here. After all, Blondie out there hadn't exactly given them a proper introduction.

Mr. Leonard stood up and waved one arm at the lone chair across from his desk. It, too, was overflowing with papers. "I have an open-door policy. You know, 'My door's always open.'" He gave her a frightening sort of smile that made her wonder how close he might be to garroting her with the cord of his adding machine, and then said, "Come in. Sit down."

Savannah sidled toward the chair, afraid of turning around and leaving her back exposed. "Um, okay." She pushed the papers to the back of the chair and balanced on the edge, keeping her feet flat on the floor in case she had to bolt.

"When can you start?" Mr. Leonard asked, pulling a manila file from the top of the stack on his desk and turning to his computer as if she wasn't even there.

"Well . . . um . . ." Savannah stammered. What the hell was going on here?

Mr. Leonard peered at her from behind his monitor, only a slit of his face visible from between the computer screen to his right and the mound of paper to his left. Savannah was surprised by the intensity of his gaze. His eyes—well, the one she could see anyway—were a luminous blue. "What? You want a raise? They all want raises," he muttered to himself. Without even looking down, he plucked a piece of paper from the top of his desk and continued, "All right. Cost of living here is higher by 16.3 percent than where you're from. I'll give you a twenty-five hundred dollar a year raise, but not a penny more."

Savannah's gaze flew to the open door. Was he really going to discuss her salary within hearing of everyone else in the office?

"You know how much space we got here?" Mr. Leonard asked, apparently apropos of nothing.

What? Was this one of those why-are-manhole-covers-round sort of questions? "No. But I'm sure I could contact the landlord and find out," she answered.

"One thousand forty," Mr. Leonard said, sounding amused. "Did that on purpose when they were subdividing the office space. Get it—one thousand forty. 1040."

Savannah slowly lifted herself off the chair and backed up, stopping only when the cool glass enclosing the manager's office was at her back. "Clever," she said with a nod and a fake smile.

"Yeah, I thought so. And in an office this small, you and I both know there's just no point in trying to keep anything secret. All it takes is one person leaving their pay stub at the Xerox machine and everybody's all up in arms. This way it's all out in the open. Everyone in the office except for Dani, who just started here three months ago, makes roughly the same salary. Everyone pulls their own weight. And if they don't . . ." Mr. Leonard paused, shrugged. "It's not like everyone else doesn't know it. We have what I like to think of as a self-correcting society here. One person starts slacking off and everyone else has to pick up the burden. And you know what happens then, don't you?" He nodded knowingly, as if to say that of course she knew. But she didn't.

Savannah was almost afraid to ask, but she gave a brief shake of her head and did anyway. "No. What happens then?"

Mr. Leonard drew in a deep breath and let it out loudly before answering. "Let's just say that we have a way of weeding out the slackers."

"Okay," Savannah answered hesitantly.

With that, Mr. Leonard ducked his head back behind his monitor and started muttering again. "Besides, I've already checked up on you and we don't have anything to worry about. So when can you start? Got any plans this afternoon?"

Slowly Savannah sank back into her chair. This was the weirdest interview she'd ever experienced. Well, maybe not *the* weirdest. That prize had to go to the one at the Fat Cat Restaurant on Monday. But this was still pretty strange. Where were the questions about her long-term and short-term goals? What about her strengths and weaknesses? Her ability to work independently as part of a team?

Instead, here she was with the Karl Marx of the accounting world, who figured that his employees would sort out any hiring mistakes he might happen to make by quote—weeding out—unquote anyone who didn't fit in.

Scary in a very Stepford Wives sort of way.

But she needed the job. Besides, if Mr. Leonard and his self-correcting employees were too much for her, she'd keep her job here while looking for another one somewhere else. It seemed that she'd used up all of her capacity for risk-taking in the past four days.

She was coming to realize that the financially responsible part of her was too deeply ingrained to change . . . at least not in such a short timeframe. Maybe next year, when her transformation was complete and she had men falling all over her to take her on exotic vacations or buy her expensive jewelry, maybe then she could start loosening up a bit on the whole practicality thing. Until then she needed a way to pay her bills, and Mr. Leonard here seemed only too eager to get her settled in behind a desk.

"All right. I'll do it," she said.

"Great," Len Leonard said without looking up from his computer. "Ashleigh Van Dyke will get you settled in. She's getting married on April sixteenth, and the fifteenth will be her last day here. She's been here for five years and I hate to lose her. Figures she'd go out and find herself a man with money. Shoulda figured she'd up and do something like that."

Savannah had to bite her lip to keep from laughing at the "woe is me" tone of her Mr. Leonard's voice. She picked up her purse and stood to leave, figuring she'd ask the junior accountant to point her in the direction of this Ashleigh person. It turned out that wasn't necessary, however, because just as Savannah stepped out into the main office, the front door breezed open and a slender woman with long dark hair and green eyes blew in, her cheeks bright with color and her arms loaded down with packages.

"Hey, Ashleigh," the junior accountant said, in the manner of a geeky high school girl greeting a cheerleader.

Ashleigh Van Dyke expertly tossed her curtain of silky hair over her left shoulder. "Hello, Danielle. You wouldn't believe the bargains to be had down at Elite Jewelry's annual spring sale. Look at these earrings. They were only two thousand dollars. Can you imagine? I almost feel like I *stole* them."

Dani seemed duly impressed and fawned over the earrings as it appeared Ashleigh expected her to. Savannah noticed that the rest of the accountants blatantly ignored their coworker's arrival, and wondered if Ashleigh Van Dyke had done more to alienate them than just showing off her expensive jewelry.

She stepped forward, in part to get a closer look at the other woman's outfit of green velvet pants with a lingerie-style blouse, but also to introduce herself and get down to work. Ashleigh began what appeared was going to be a lengthy discussion about a Coach handbag she'd bought when Savannah—as politely as possible—interrupted.

"Uh, hi," she said, holding out her right hand in greeting.

Ashleigh and Dani turned to look at her, both seeming shocked that she'd intruded on their tête-à-tête.

"Sorry to interrupt," Savannah said, telling herself she shouldn't feel guilty for trying to do the job she'd been hired to do. "Mr. Leonard said you could get me started. If you give me a computer and some files, I'll get down to work and leave you two alone."

Ashleigh executed another artful hair toss and sighed loudly as if she felt very put upon to actually have to *work* at work. "Well, all right. Just let me put these things in my car and I'll be right back. What did you say your name was?" She sniffed as if to say that it was inconsequential anyway, but that she expected a few karmic points for at least pretending to care.

Savannah reached out her hand in greeting and said, "Savannah Taylor, from Maple Rapids, Michigan." Then she blinked with surprise when Ashleigh's face turned a strange grayish color right before she fell, unconscious, at Savannah's feet.

Do You See Dead People?

Ever since the movie *The Sixth Sense*, there's been a sort of cachet associated with those who claim to be able to see ghosts. We're open-minded enough to believe that there are some people who have certain "gifts"—astrologers, psychics, and those people on the cop shows on TV who can find someone's murderer by speaking to them from beyond the grave. Spooky, yes, but also kind of cool, don't you think? So, when you're all alone in your grandmother's creaky old house and you see a strange light coming from the doorway, do you:

a. Go to the bathroom and swallow a couple of Tums. The pepperoni pizza you had just before bedtime must be making you see things.

b. Cover your head with the blanket and start rocking yourself back to sleep, chanting, "There's no such thing as ghosts. There's no such thing as ghosts."

c. Calmly thank the apparition for allowing you to share her space, then ask if there's something you can do for her. After all, she's been trapped somewhere between the world of the living and the dead for God only knows how long. It seems the least you can do to try to help free her.

Those of you who chose A need to get a crowbar (or maybe a yoga mat and some incense) and try to open your mind just a little bit to the possibility that our world might just be made up of more than only that which we can see and touch. You B girls need more than a crowbar—you need a spine. Stop shaking under the covers and get out there and confront your demons! If you chose C, you rate a 10 on our coolness scale. Let's roast marshmallows around a campfire sometime and swap some real ghost stories!

{ nineteen }

Ashleigh blamed her fainting spell on too much sun and lack of food and used the goose egg on her forehead as an excuse to leave at two after dumping the majority of her files on Savannah. Savannah didn't really mind, though. She was getting paid to do people's taxes, so that's what she'd do.

She opened the first of Ashleigh's files, expecting to see a completed checklist that would indicate that Ashleigh had interviewed the client and gathered all the required information to complete a return. Instead, all she saw were a handful of loose receipts and some sticky notes. Savannah wondered if perhaps Ashleigh had begun the switchover to Refund City's new paperless system, which was supposed to be fully implemented by next year. Once the rollout was complete, paper files would cease to exist. Savannah was all for the system—it promised greater security, since only the employee working the file and his or her supervisor would have access to it. As it was now, everyone in the office had keys to the filing cabinets. Savannah could, if she desired, go through anyone's files. She could be fired if she were caught nosing around without a good reason, but it wasn't like anyone paid all that much attention to the files on other employees' desks.

Not that she was distrustful of her coworkers, but Savannah much preferred a system with a few more safeguards for her clients' privacy. Perhaps Ashleigh felt the same and had already begun using the new system for all of her clients.

After logging into the system, Savannah searched the database for the Social Security number matching the W-2 in the file Ashleigh had given her. When no records were found, Savannah flipped open a few more of her new files, then shook her head and sighed. None of them had completed checklists or any method of organization that Savannah could decipher. That meant she was going to have to comb through every file to make certain she had all of the necessary information before even beginning the returns.

Well, she had two choices. She could: A) sit here sighing about the extra work, or B) just jump in and do it. She chose B.

Finally a quiz that she got right!

Savannah chuckled to herself as she opened a new client record and began making order out of the chaos of Ashleigh's files.

Six hours later Savannah rubbed her aching forehead as she spoke slowly and patiently into her phone. "Yes, Mrs. Reinhart, I understand that Jack is like your very own child, but under our current tax code, you are not allowed to claim pets as dependents." She listened for a moment, then said, "No, I'm sorry. The vet bills are not deductible as medical expenses, either."

Savannah only wished that this were the first time she'd had to deal with the "pets as dependents" issue. Typically, it came up at least three times a year. Sometimes more.

"Yes, Mrs. Reinhart, there is someone you can talk to about this. If you'd like to see pets become tax deductible, you should write a letter to the President and let him know how you feel about the issue. But even without claiming your dog as a dependent, you are due a refund of $261.64. Would you like me to file this for you electronically? If so, I can have your check here for you tomorrow when you drop by the office to sign the return."

That seemed to make the woman happy, despite the disappointing news about her Jack Russell terrier. Savannah clicked the "e-file" button to process Mrs. Reinhart's return as she ended the call. The clock on the bottom right hand of her computer screen showed that it was 8:51, and she looked up to see that everyone but Dani had already left for the evening. She wished she could join them. Unfortunately, her name was next on the walk-in roster, so if anyone walked in in the next nine minutes, Savannah would be assigned a new client. She didn't really mind working late, but preferred to do so at home with her laptop instead of in a mostly deserted office.

The whole vibe in the office was weird. With less than a month to go until April 15, the entire staff should be working late. Back in Maple Rapids, they'd have pizza or Chinese delivered, with the promise of a big party—including copious amounts of alcohol—after tax season was officially over. Here, the accountants had started disappearing around six o'-clock, as soon as their names were moved to the end of the walk-in roster. Most had taken files with them, so Savannah assumed they'd work from home, but it seemed strange to her that Len didn't try to foster a sense of camaraderie by enticing people to stay and work together.

Oh, well, what did it matter? Working here might not be full of friendship and excitement and glamour, but at least she wasn't dressed in a fish costume or staring up some pervert's skirt. Savannah shrugged as she opened another of the files Ashleigh had assigned to her, but looked up when the front door opened and a man with a medium build walked in. He scanned the office, as if searching for something, before approaching Dani.

"I'd like to talk to someone about getting my taxes done," he said in a low voice.

"We get that a lot," Dani joked, but the man didn't even crack a smile.

"I can take you," Savannah offered, more to rescue Dani than because she was eager to take on a new client two minutes before closing.

The man nodded and looked around again, scanning the darkened corners of the room. Savannah found herself doing the same thing, although she had no idea what she was looking for. This was just an ordinary office, with four rows of desks stacked three across and a large, locked filing cabinet covering the entire back wall.

When the man reached her desk, he leaned down and whispered, "Is there someplace we can go to talk in private?"

"Yes, we have a consultation room," Savannah said, indicating the room next to Len's and grabbing one of the new file kits she'd put together earlier, which included a document checklist and several sheets of blank paper for taking notes.

After entering the room and closing the door behind them, Savannah pulled out a chair at the small egg-shaped table in the consultation room and took a seat, indicating that the client should do the same. He startled her by first walking over to the Venetian blinds covering the window between the main office and the conference room and closing them. Savannah hoped that Dani could still hear her if she screamed . . . and that she had 911 on speed dial.

Telling herself she was overreacting, Savannah nevertheless scooted her chair back so that she was safely wedged in a corner of the room and asked, "So, what can I do for you?"

The man leaned forward, his dark eyes hooded and mysterious. "I want to file my taxes," he said.

"Well, you've come to the right place," Savannah said in her most cheerful tone. She clicked the button on her mechanical pencil to advance the lead and opened her new client file. "First, I'll need your Social Security number. If you have a W-2, I can get it off of that."

The man put his palms on the table and speared Savannah with an intense look. "I can't give you that information," he whispered.

Okay, this was getting weird. Savannah swallowed hard. And shivered. "I can't file a return if you don't provide me with your Social Security number. That's what the IRS uses to make sure you've paid your taxes," she explained patiently.

"I don't mind paying my taxes. I just don't want them to be able to find me." This was said with a furtive glance around the room, as if the man were looking for cameras or listening devices.

O-key do-key. Savannah decided the best way to handle this situation was to just play it straight. "If you pay your taxes but don't give the IRS your Social Security number, how will they know who the money is from? They have to keep track of that, you know. To make sure everyone who should pay, does."

"It doesn't matter if they know who the money is from. Trust me, I do this every year," the man said with a knowing look as he crossed his arms over his chest and leaned back in his chair.

Savannah pursed her lips. Hmm. What could she say to convince him that the system didn't work this way? "You do know that your employer is required to file their copy of your W-2 with the IRS, right? I mean, they would already have your information from that. Not to mention the 1098s your bank files if you have a mortgage on your home and your interest income statements if you earned any money on your investments this year."

The man waved one hand dismissively. "I have that all taken care of. I only work for cash and I don't deal with banks," he announced.

There was no winning this battle, but Savannah was starting to get curious as to why this man was so concerned about the IRS not knowing who he was, so she asked, "What are you so afraid of?"

The man hunched down in his chair and indicated that she should come closer. Savannah glanced up to see if Dani was watching, but all she could see was the faint glow of light from the lamp on her own desk. She decided to chance it and huddled in closer. "Tell me," she whispered conspiratorially.

"I'm dead," the man mouthed.

Savannah blinked three times in rapid succession. "Huh?"

Reaching into the back pocket of his jeans, the man took out a folded sheet of yellow paper and pushed it across the table at her. Savannah looked at it, but didn't pick it up. "That's a record of my income and expenses. I made nearly twenty thousand this year, doing lawn care and handyman work. I need to pay my fair share of taxes, but I'm not going to give them a way to trace me. Believe me, I'm better off dead."

Savannah cleared her throat and tugged at her earlobe. "But . . . you're not dead," she said.

For the first time the man seemed to relax as he chuckled and said, "No, but my wife thinks I am."

Wearily Savannah rubbed the back of her neck. "Okay. But be that as it may, I can't file an income tax return without a Social Security number."

Now the man seemed to really be getting excited. He stood up and stretched his arms out and grinned. "So go through your files until you find someone who died last year and won't have any income. Then you can file my information under their Social Security number and everything will work out okay. I *have* to pay my taxes. You go to hell if you don't carry your own load," he said, his eyes suddenly going out of focus as if he were replaying some oft-repeated sermon in his head.

Savannah closed her eyes and groaned inwardly. This was wrong on so many levels. "I can't do that," she said. "It's not right."

The man's eyes narrowed as he put his hands on the back of the chair he'd just vacated and glowered down at her. "I don't know why you're making this so difficult. The woman I talked to last year didn't have any problem with the idea."

Savannah's jaw dropped open. "What are you talking about? Did someone in this office file your taxes for you last year? Who was it? What name did you file under?"

He eyed her suspiciously for a moment, then suddenly grabbed for her neck. Savannah squeaked, dug her heels into the carpet, and tried to roll away. Her chair banged against the wall and one of the plaques perched precariously on a small nail wobbled and then crashed down, the corner of it hitting her on the head before it landed on her lap.

"Ouch," Savannah yelped, leaping up out of her chair and thrusting the 1999 Southeast Region President's Club award out like a shield to ward off the man's assault. Only he was still standing on the other side of the table, holding the sheet of yellow paper he'd pulled from his pocket earlier and looking at her as if she had lost her mind.

"You ask too many questions. I think maybe you're one of *them*," he said ominously, making Savannah shiver.

Without another word, he stomped out of the consultation room, paused to wish Dani a good evening . . . and then he was gone.

Savannah's encounter with Creepy Nameless Guy freaked her out so much she considered calling a cab to take her back to the Sand Dunes Motel instead of walking the block and a half in the dark. Despite the fact that Sunshine Parkway was well lit, Savannah kept imagining him jumping out of some dark alley, putting a knife to her throat, and ordering her to take him to "them." Trouble was, she didn't know who "they" were, unless maybe he meant the IRS, whose nearest office was an hour and a half away in Miami.

She would have asked Dani for a ride, but by the time she'd finished locking up her files and logging off her computer, Dani had disappeared, leaving her alone in the deserted office. As she left the office Savannah tried to convince herself she'd be safe. The sidewalks weren't exactly crowded with tourists, but they weren't empty, either. She'd just stick close to the street and away from the entrances to any alleys, and she'd be fine.

Still, her stomach fluttered nervously as she stepped out into the warm, sultry evening. She stood for a moment, looking first to her left and then to her right to make sure Creepy Nameless Guy wasn't lurking in wait for her.

When she saw that the coast was clear, she scurried out of the shadows and over to the curb, her steps quickening as she raced to catch up to a young couple about twenty feet ahead of her. Once she did, she slowed down to stay a few paces behind as they strolled along.

When they finally reached the corner where Savannah had to turn, she gazed intently down the street toward the Sand Dunes Motel. Sweat broke out on her upper lip as she realized that there were no streetlights on the side street.

She was going to have to make a run for it.

She paused for a moment to dig her motel key out of the bottom of her purse. Then she took one last look behind her at the safely lit tourist area, took a deep breath, and started running.

Running in high heels was not nearly as easy as they made it look in the movies. Savannah nearly broke her ankle when the heel of her right shoe stuck in a crack in the sidewalk and she ran right out of it, stumbling when her stocking-clad foot landed hard on a pebble. She caught her balance, then limped back to get her shoe, her heel throbbing. She clumped the rest of the way to the motel, sending uneasy glances over her shoulder as she hurried to the courtyard door.

She unlocked the door and slipped through the doorway. Leaning her forehead on the cool glass, she let out a deep sigh of relief when the lock slid back into place. Whew. She was home safe.

It was only as she started limping toward the stairwell that she began to think again about what Creepy had said about the woman who had filed his taxes last year. Had someone really filed a bogus return, hoping that she wouldn't get caught? And, even worse, had she filed the return using the identity of a dead person? Ugh.

The thought made the tiny hairs on the back of Savannah's neck stand on end, and she wrapped her arms around herself as she hobbled up the stairs in the chilly stairwell. For some reason—call it feminine intuition or just an overactive imagination—Savannah hesitated as she reached the top step. Instead of stepping out into the breezeway, she flattened herself against the wall to her right, the concrete cold and damp against her bare upper arm. Slowly she inched forward, until she could just see down the hall.

Much to her surprise, the breezeway was empty.

She put a hand to her chest, willing her racing heart to slow. "You're getting paranoid," she chided herself, stepping out onto the walkway.

But as she neared the door to her motel room, she had to force her unwilling feet to continue. Something was trying to warn her that all was not as it should be.

She took another step toward her room and felt a crunch under her foot. Savannah nearly screamed when she stepped back and realized she'd just stepped on a giant brown cockroach. God, she hated those things. They gave her the willies. She closed her eyes, trying to shut out that scene in *Indiana Jones and the Temple of Doom* when the heroine shines her torch on the floor beneath her feet and realizes she's walking on a living carpet of giant cockroaches.

Savannah shivered despite the warm night air and reminded herself that there was nothing amiss about seeing cockroaches in southern Florida. The bugs were a mild annoyance, not a portent of doom.

With a mental promise to sweep up the dead roach later, she took another step toward her room . . . and stopped dead in her tracks when she saw a sliver of light shining out from between the doorjamb and the door of her room, which stood slightly ajar. Savannah knew she had not left her door open that morning when she'd gone to work. She didn't do things like that. And if she hadn't left it open, that could only mean one thing.

Someone had been in her room.

Or, even worse, someone was *still* in her room.

Savannah heard more crunching under her feet as she backed away from her door, but she didn't look down to see if she'd taken out another cockroach. Instead, she focused intently on the door to her room, silently willing whoever was in there to stay put long enough for her to get out of there and call the police. She took another step backward, and then another.

Just three more feet and she'd be back to the comforting darkness of the stairwell.

Another step back. Two more feet.

Then one more.

And then—

When a man's hand landed heavily on her shoulder, Savannah nearly did one of those cartoon tricks where the coyote leaps in the air, leaving its skin in a heap on the ground.

"Where do you think you're going?" he said.

Rub a Dub Dub,
What's in Your Tub?

Ah, the bathtub. A place of serenity where you can soak for hours amidst flickering candles and frothy bubbles. What? That's not what it's like for you? Quick, go open your bathroom door and throw aside the shower curtain. Now, tell us. What's in your tub?

a· A sliver of Irish Spring and a half-empty bottle of shampoo.

b· A rubber duckie, three wet washcloths of indeterminate age, a pair of pantyhose that was drying over the shower curtain rod but slipped into the tub, and a soap-scum ring that won't go away.

c· A bath pillow that your sister gave you for your birthday, a chrome holder that spans the width of the tub and holds a book, a glass of wine, and a loofah, and plenty of fabulous-smelling bath salts.

Since when did bath time become so boring for you A girls? Don't you remember being kids and playing in the Mr. Bubble until your toes started to look like raisins? You need to bring some fun back into your bath time. Get a few candles, at least! Those of you who chose B need to stake a claim to the tub. This is your space to wash away the day's cares and relax. It's time for you to reclaim it! When those of you who answered C are done soaking, could we have a turn in your tub? All we can say is, "Ahhhh."

{twenty}

Mike was so taken off guard when Savannah turned and threw her arms around his waist with a heartily whispered, "Oh, thank God you're here," that he nearly fell down the stairs, taking her with him. He reached out one palm and flattened it against the wall to steady himself while he curled his other arm around her waist protectively. She was shaking so hard that her teeth were chattering, and Mike frowned, wondering what the hell had frightened her so badly.

He told himself that he was only giving her a moment to regain her composure before he loosened his grip on her, but that wasn't exactly the whole truth. The whole truth was that he enjoyed the feel of her soft body pressed against his and he didn't want to let her go until he had to.

He removed his hand from the wall and touched her hair, something he'd wanted to do since the day he'd pulled her out of the way of that ice-cream cart outside the Fat Cat restaurant. It even *felt* shiny under his fingertips as he smoothed his hand down over her silky locks.

"Shh," he murmured soothingly. "Everything's going to be okay."

She buried her nose in his chest, and Mike felt as if someone were squeezing the air out of his lungs when he felt her tremble again. At that moment Lainie's report and the incriminating evidence she'd found completely slipped his mind, and Mike was so tempted to crush Savannah even closer to him and kiss her until she forgot her own name that the intensity of his desire scared even him. It was even worse when she finally lifted her head and looked up at him with her big green eyes still filled with fright. Now he was ready to kill for her—not a good feeling since his gun was still holstered just under his left armpit and he could actually act upon that urge.

Mike took a deep breath and smoothed his hand down Savannah's hair one last time before taking a sanity-inducing step away from her. Whatever kind of spell she had over him, it seemed to be getting stronger. Despite every instinct that warned him she was trouble, he couldn't seem to convince himself to forget her.

He scratched his chest and cleared his throat. "So, do you want to tell me what's wrong?" he asked.

Savannah nodded, her eyes wide.

Mike waited for a moment, but she didn't speak, so he prompted, "Would you like to go to your room? You might be more comfortable sitting down."

She shook her head vigorously, the tips of her black hair tickling the tops of her shoulders. "He might still be there," she whispered.

"He, who?" Mike asked with a frown. Did she have a disgruntled boyfriend stalking her? Or, worse, a husband? Mike clenched his teeth at the thought, not sure if he was more angry at himself for not even considering the possibility before this or more annoyed with her for not letting him know she was off-limits.

She leaned forward and put a hand on his arm, her fingers squeezing him with surprising strength. "I don't know his name. He came into my office tonight and wouldn't tell me who he was."

Mike had no idea what she was talking about, but he felt much more relieved than he should have to know that she wasn't being hunted by an angry husband. Of course, that didn't mean she wasn't married, a topic Mike decided to table until this latest crisis was resolved.

"So you think there's someone in your room?" he asked, just to be sure that he understood the problem.

Savannah nodded without releasing her grip on his arm.

"But you don't know who it is or how many there might be?" She shook her head.

"Have you called the police?" he asked.

"No," she finally spoke. "I was going to go downstairs and do that when I ran into you."

"Okay. You stay back here and I'll go in and check out your room. If there's trouble, do *not* come in and try to show off your latest kickboxing move. Get out of here and call the police immediately. You got it?"

She nodded, but looked down at the cement walkway, which told Mike she was probably lying. Figured.

He wasn't too worried, though. He could handle most trouble life threw his way.

Mike pried Savannah's fingers off his arm and told her to stay put. With his right hand on the butt of his gun, he crept toward her room. He frowned when he noticed a trail of red ants marching in a neat, single-file line down the center of the breezeway. At Savannah's door, they curved inward, crawling up over the inch-high concrete lip, through the open doorway, and into the room. He grimaced when a three-inch-long cockroach skittered from the dark shadows behind him and slithered into the room ahead of the ants.

What the hell was going on here?

When Mike got to Savannah's door, he nudged aside his jacket and freed his gun from its holster. Then he bumped the door open with his toe and shouted, "All right. Whoever you are, come out with your hands up."

He waited several seconds, listening intently for any sound of movement from inside. Hearing nothing, he glanced over his shoulder to make sure that Savannah was still safe by the stairwell, then turned back around and slowly entered her room.

As Mike disappeared into her motel room, Savannah dug her cell phone out of her purse and dialed 911. She kept her finger poised over the Send button, ready to hit it the second she heard gunshots or shouting or any sort of commotion from inside her room.

She should never have let him go in there without her. He was a flight attendant, for heaven's sake, not a cop or some macho Kung Fu guy. He was no more qualified to battle an intruder than she was. So why had she just stood back and let him put himself in harm's way?

Savannah closed her eyes, remembering his strong arms around her and how safe she had felt in his embrace. She had allowed herself to be lulled by his bravado, and if he got hurt, it would be all her fault.

Keeping her finger on the Send button of her cell phone, Savannah opened her eyes, straightened her shoulders, and started toward her room. She couldn't let Mike put himself in danger on her account. He had done a good job of sounding threatening a moment ago, but what would happen once the intruder realized Mike was bluffing and didn't have a weapon or anything to defend himself?

As she stepped out onto the breezeway, Savannah heard a door slam open and a woman's high-pitched scream. Had Creepy grabbed Liz or Christina? Was he torturing one of them in order to get Savannah to come out of hiding?

With a gasp, Savannah hit the Send button on her phone and raced toward her room. When she saw Christina and Liz on the walkway outside her room, both holding red plastic cups and looking fine from where she stood, she felt a wave of relief wash over her. But then who had screamed?

It had sounded like a woman's high-pitched voice, but could it have been Mike?

Savannah was almost to her door when James came up behind Christina and did something that made her emit that screechy squeal again.

"James, stop it!" she shrieked, reaching behind her to fish out the piece of ice he'd dropped down her bikini bottom. She laughed as she started chasing after him, holding the ice cube out like a gun.

Liz and Nathan ignored the pair as they blithely walked into Savannah's room, not knowing the danger that lurked there.

"No!" Savannah screamed as she dived in after them, just as the emergency operator answered her call.

"This is 911. What is the nature of your emergency?"

"There's an intruder in my motel room," Savannah said breathlessly as she careened into Nathan's back.

"Hey, we're not intruders. Christina said you wouldn't mind if we borrowed your tub," Liz explained, her voice sounding fuzzy, as if she were speaking around a mouthful of cotton balls.

"My tub? Why would you need my tub?"

"Dude. Marcus is passed out in Liz's. Mine and Nathan's . . . well, I'm not drinking anything out of there. And Christina said we couldn't use hers because she wants to take a bath later. So we used yours," James explained from the doorway.

Savannah had no idea what they were talking about; so she pushed past Liz and Nathan to find Mike sitting on her toilet with his head in his hands, his shoulders shaking. What was wrong? Was he hurt? And where was Creepy Nameless Guy?

Tentatively Savannah put a hand on Mike's back. "Are you all right?" she asked.

Mike slowly raised his head and Savannah saw that he was laughing, not crying. He pointed to her bathtub, which, she realized, was swarming with ants. Savannah frowned and pushed back the shower curtain and a pair of the panties she'd hung to dry fell into the tub. Or, rather, fell into the dark pink liquid in the tub. Something floated by her right hand and she reached down to pick it up.

"Is this a maraschino cherry?" she asked, incredulous.

Mike's shoulders started to shake again but he manfully coughed and tried to contain his mirth.

"Hey, do you mind if we fill up our glasses now? We're getting thirsty," James said, crowding into the tiny bathroom as if it were Mike and Savannah who were intruding and not the other way around.

"Ma'am? Do you need the police?" the emergency operator asked, sounding more than a little peeved.

Savannah looked from Mike to James and the rest of the students and then to her bathtub full of drunk ants, floating fruit, and what smelled like some form of rum punch. "Yeah, you'd better send an ambulance in about five minutes, because I think I'm going to kill somebody," she muttered under her breath.

"Pardon me?" the operator asked.

"I'm sorry, nothing. It was just a mistake," Savannah said,

scowling when James shoved the shower curtain open even farther and her remaining two pairs of panties fell into the drink.

"Dude, are those clean?" James asked, frowning distastefully at her underwear as she fished the now-pink panties out of the tub.

"Right, like you have standards?" Savannah asked. "I took a shower in that tub this morning. Did you think of that?"

"Well, yeah, but Christina said the alcohol would sterilize it." James shrugged and filled his glass, then reached out to take Nathan's cup and fill his, too.

Savannah turned to Christina, who teetered to one side before grabbing the doorjamb to steady herself. One of her bikini straps had fallen from her shoulder and seemed dangerously close to sliding off altogether. Savannah shook her head at the adoring look the girl sent James as he refilled her glass.

"I can't believe you let them do this," she said.

Christina flinched at the disapproval in Savannah's voice and pushed herself away from the doorjamb, which only served to make her bikini strap slip down a bit farther. "I didn't just *let* them do this," she said, the wobbliness of her knees belying the steadiness of her voice. "It was my idea. I bought the rum and everything." She stood even straighter, defiant, trying to prove to them all that she was just as immature and irresponsible as the rest of them.

And while Savannah was annoyed that Christina had broken into her room, she understood what had driven her to do so. So, rather than being angry, she just let out a disappointed sigh and turned to fish another pair of her underwear out of the tub.

James dipped Christina's cup into the punch and reached out to hand it to her, but Nathan intercepted it. He smiled kindly at Christina and raised his elbow to point to her bikini strap. "You might want to, uh, fix that first," he suggested.

Christina's cheeks spotted with bright red as she slid the strap back up onto her shoulder. She didn't meet Nathan's eyes as she thanked him and took her cup.

"All right, you guys. That's enough. We're draining the tub—" Mike stopped to scowl at the students when they all groaned, then held up his hand for silence and began again.

"Yes, we're draining it. You can't just go around breaking into people's rooms. Besides, just look at these bugs. I'm going to have to call the exterminator and get him out here tonight to take care of this mess. Now, you guys are only here until Monday—that's four more days. I don't want any more trouble from you, you got it?"

The students mumbled like naughty children being sent to the corner, and if Savannah weren't so disgusted that they'd scared her half to death (not to mention that they'd ruined her underwear, forcing her to have to buy more when she really couldn't afford them), she'd have been amused. As it was, she just fished the last pair of dripping pink panties out of the tub, then shrieked when she realized that at least two dozen ants were swarming all over them. Hastily, she threw them back into the tub.

Her eyes narrowed when James snickered, raised his cup in a mocking salute, and said, "Dude. It looks like you've got ants in your pants."

It took every ounce of willpower Savannah possessed not to reach out, put her hands around his skinny neck, and drown him in the bathtub full of rum punch.

Are You a Rule Breaker?

There are some rules that are just made to be broken. Like those pesky little speed limit signs on the freeway. They're more like guidelines than actual rules, aren't they? And what about that "10 items or less" lane at the supermarket? Thirteen items is close enough, don't you think? We know some women wouldn't dream of even bending a rule now and then. What sort of gal are you?

It's tax time and you own your own business. You and your girlfriends just got back from a fabulous weekend trip to the Atlantis Resort in the Bahamas and one of your friends laughingly mentions that you complained about your least favorite client for an hour while sunning yourself on the beach, so you should deduct the trip on your return. You give it some thought and then you:

a. **Decide she's partially right. You did spend an hour discussing business, so you'll deduct 1/48 of the trip on your return.**

b. **Forget the whole thing. You don't want to risk getting audited.**

c. **Figure that it's only wrong to deduct the trip if someone at the IRS catches you. After all, you *did* go on the trip to destress because of business. So, why not call it a business trip? You can bet the old white guys running all those Fortune 500 companies write off the fifty-thousand-dollar birthday parties they throw for their wives and the yearly trips to London they take with their families!**

continues on next page . . .

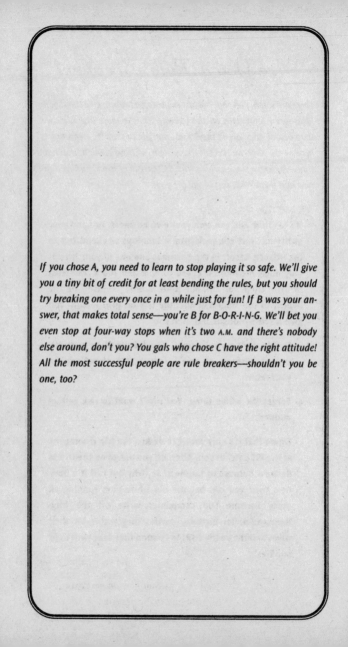

If you chose A, you need to learn to stop playing it so safe. We'll give you a tiny bit of credit for at least bending the rules, but you should try breaking one every once in a while just for fun! If B was your answer, that makes total sense—you're B for B-O-R-I-N-G. We'll bet you even stop at four-way stops when it's two A.M. and there's nobody else around, don't you? You gals who chose C have the right attitude! All the most successful people are rule breakers—shouldn't you be one, too?

{twenty-one}

Friday started off with dead cockroaches, progressed to prostitution, and ended in treachery.

The night before, after the students left her motel room, Mike had helped Savannah clean up the mess in her bathroom and waited up for Harv from Harv's Pest Control to show up and fumigate the room. Mike apologized for not just giving her another room, but until the students left, the Sand Dunes Motel was fully booked. He did offer to sleep on his couch and let her have his bed if she wanted, a chivalrous gesture that would have had Savannah falling half in love with him if only she didn't know that his inclinations ran in another direction. So she thanked him and decided to brave out the bugs.

When she'd opened the shower curtain that morning, it was to find two cockroaches lying on their backs with their feet up in the air and their antennae twitching. Her squeal of fright brought Mike to her door, wearing nothing but dark blue pajama bottoms and looking so good that Savannah wanted to cry because it wasn't fair that she was so attracted to a guy she could never have. When he got rid of the bugs for her with a grin and a joke that this was just part of the service here at the Sand Dunes Motel, Savannah wanted to throw herself down on her bed and scream into her pillow with frustration.

She *had* to get out tonight and do something more to make

a new life for herself. Sitting alone in her motel room pining away for Mike Bryson would be too sad for words.

As she was brushing her teeth, Savannah realized that, despite all her efforts to change, she was no better off than she had been in Maple Rapids. As a matter of fact, she was worse off. Instead of having *no* man, she was falling for a gay guy who could never return her feelings. Her closest friend here was a confused teen who was leaving in three days. And the only meaningful conversations she was having lately were with herself.

"On the flipside, your family's not driving you crazy," she said, trying to look on the bright side.

Savannah put on her makeup and started to get dressed, then grimaced when she tentatively sniffed a pair of her panties and realized that they reeked of rum. Not to mention they were so stiff Savannah could have used them to turn flapjacks. There was no way she could wear them.

Savannah chose a slim-fitting black skirt and put on a pair of black tights, but as she walked into the office that morning, she was certain that everyone could tell she wasn't wearing underwear. For courage, she'd read an article in *Stylish* titled "Dare to Go Bare," which featured stories of women who had chucked their undergarments in an attempt to celebrate their femininity. Savannah wasn't quite sure what one had to do with the other, but the women in the article seemed to feel some sense of power and liberation in their naked state. Savannah, on the other hand, just felt itchy and uncomfortable.

Fortunately, she'd had the foresight to grab Vanna's credit-card statements off the counter of her motel room before leaving for work. One of the keys to feeling at your most sexy and powerful, the "Dare to Go Bare" article had said, was that if you were going to wear underwear, it should be fun and daring and should express your true self. The white Jockey briefs she usually got at Target for $12.99 a three-pack did not express Savannah's true self, at least not the true self she was striving to be. So today, during her lunch hour, she was going to use the last of her cash to buy some hot underwear. And since Vanna obviously knew where to purchase such things, Savannah was going to follow in her alter ego's footsteps.

She arrived at the office a few minutes before nine and was

surprised to find that she was the first one there. Figured. She'd probably get labeled a brown-noser for being on time.

She sat down at her desk and powered up her computer, then looked around helplessly when the office phone began to ring. Back in Maple Rapids, she wouldn't have hesitated to answer the phone, but she didn't want to offend anyone by breaching protocol.

By the third ring she was sweating. She couldn't just let the call go unanswered. It would be unprofessional.

On the fourth ring she snatched up the phone on Dani's desk.

"Refund City. Savannah Taylor speaking," she answered, feeling as if someone had just removed a gun from her temple.

"Hi," a woman said. "I need to make an appointment with someone for first thing tomorrow morning to get my return filed. I'm expecting a refund and I need the money right away."

Savannah looked up at the walk-in board to see who was next in line for a client. She hesitated when she saw that it was Ashleigh Van Dyke, but wasn't sure why she didn't just book the appointment. So what if Ashleigh got upset at being assigned a nine A.M. appointment on Saturday? They all had to pull their weight, right?

Uh huh. Like she was going to piss off Len's pet employee on her second day of work.

"I'll take you," Savannah said, feeling every inch the martyr. "We open at nine."

"Thank you. My name's Jane Smith. I'll see you tomorrow morning," the woman said after giving Savannah her phone number, sounding relieved that Savannah hadn't turned her away.

"She must not realize that we don't turn anyone away. Not even dead people," Savannah muttered as she hung up the phone.

"What's that?" Dani asked as she breezed through the door at eighteen minutes past nine, unconcerned that she was late.

"Nothing," Savannah answered and wrote the appointment down in her book. She worked without taking a break for the next hour and a half, the other accountants drifting in apparently whenever they felt like it. So much for Len's self-correcting workforce, she thought as Ashleigh, the last to arrive, wafted in at half past ten, talking on her cell phone to someone named Victoria about how tacky it had been when someone else named Kate had served Moët champagne ("from a *fountain,* for God's sake," Ashleigh added with a distasteful crinkle of her pert little nose) instead of Dom Pérignon at a wedding last month.

Savannah tried to focus on the file in front of her, but it was difficult with Ashleigh twittering and whispering and gossiping right beside her. Everyone else seemed to be able to ignore it, their fingers busily tapping their keyboards as they entered one figure after another.

I need a drink, Savannah thought to herself as Ashleigh launched into a discussion about the merits of a horse-drawn carriage ("Romantic, but what about the shit?") versus a Hummer limousine ("Do you think Hummers are just so over? Maybe we should get a Navigator instead?") to transport her and her fiancé to the main ballroom at the country club from the beach where the wedding ceremony would take place on April 16.

As she walked back to the lunchroom to get a drink of water, Savannah noticed something odd. Her coworkers' hands all seemed to move from the alpha keys on their keyboards to the 10-key pad over on the right-hand side as she passed. Telling herself she was just imagining things, Savannah decided to stop in the rest room first before getting something to drink.

Then, to prove that she wasn't hallucinating, she slowly pushed the bathroom door open, cringing when the hinges made a faint squeaking sound. She slipped through the doorway and pressed her back against the wall, creeping toward the office. She stood in the shadows, squinting at the computer screen of the coworker nearest where she was standing.

Her eyes narrowed even further when she saw the unmistakable Instant Messenger box in the middle of his screen. He turned to make sure no one was behind him, and Savannah ducked back into the hall, crossing her fingers in the hopes that she hadn't been busted. She waited a second and then crept forward again.

She stood very still and tried to read the words on his screen.

I don't know, Bert, I think the doves we release should be wearing matching diamond tiaras, don't you?

Bert coughed and took a sip of the dark coffee on his desk before moving his hands to his keyboard.

No, Lucy. Diamonds are so *last year. We need to go with rubies.*

Savannah realized then that her coworkers were as annoyed and distracted by Ashleigh's conversation as she was. Which would have been comforting if only they'd asked her to join in their fun. Instead, she'd been left out. And, suddenly, she felt more alone than she had since leaving Maple Rapids.

No, she hadn't expected her new coworkers to bond with her instantly, but it would have been nice if one of them—just one—had said good morning to her today. Or asked how she was settling in. Or . . . or anything. Instead, they treated her as if she didn't exist.

Savannah cleared her throat as she stepped out of the hall and noticed that at least three people surreptitiously minimized their IM program so she couldn't see what they'd written. Well fine. Let them treat her like an outsider. She *was* an outsider. Wasn't that why she'd left Maple Rapids in the first place? To be someone different than these people were? To have a more exciting and glamorous life than they did?

That's right. Let them make fun of Ashleigh—wasn't that how people acted when they were jealous of someone else's success? Savannah wanted to be just like her, with her Cinderella-like wedding and champagne and caviar life. What did these accountants know anyway?

Savannah smiled at Ashleigh as she brought a glass of water back to her desk. The other woman seemed surprised for a second, and then nodded in return. Not exactly the friendly response Savannah was hoping for, but it was a start. She felt a wave of anticipation when Ashleigh said, "Just a second, Victoria," into her phone and leaned toward Savannah.

Savannah waited. Was Ashleigh going to invite her to lunch? Maybe ask her opinion on the Hummer vs. horse-drawn carriage issue?

Ashleigh smiled, her teeth whitened, smoothed, and straightened to perfection. "I need you to take this next client for me. I'm on an important call. Business, you know," she said, pointing to her phone as if she were on the phone with the President.

"She's a repeat from last year," Ashleigh continued, handing over a cocoa-colored file that contained the client's previous year's tax return.

Savannah's shoulders slumped as Ashleigh dumped another of her files on her. What would it be this time? Another person wanting to take her pet as a deduction? Some kook who read an article about how his taxes were spent and only wanted to pay for those things he deemed important? A tax protestor who insisted the IRS was unconstitutional and wanted to know what forms he needed to fill out to remove himself from the IRS's records?

Savannah opened the file Ashleigh had handed her before going back to her "important call" about whether or not pasties would work under her strapless wedding gown.

Ashleigh's eleven o'clock appointment was, according to the file, a professional sex therapist. Great, Savannah groaned. Would the woman take one look at her and know she wasn't wearing panties? But when the client walked in the door, Savannah took one look at *her* and knew *she* wasn't wearing panties. Or a bra, either.

"I'm Justine," the client announced softly as every eye turned in her direction.

She was pure sex poured into a red leather pantsuit. Her full, tanned breasts pushed at the zipper of her top as if trying to escape. She had softly curling chestnut hair and the darkest brown eyes Savannah had ever seen. There was something earthy and yet classy about her—an odd mix of come-fuck-me-baby and don't-even-think-about-it—that Savannah imagined men went wild for.

Savannah stood up, the client file and her mechanical pencil in hand.

"Hi," she said. "I'm Savannah Taylor. I'll be preparing your taxes today."

"Great," the woman said, turning her seductive smile on Savannah.

Wow. It seemed to work as well on women as it did on men, Savannah thought as she stood rooted to the carpet, mesmerized by Justine's eyes. Savannah cleared her throat and swallowed to break the spell. "Come on back. We can meet in the consultation room. Can I get you anything to drink? Water? Coffee?"

"No, thank you. I'm fine," Justine said.

Savannah led the way back to the small conference room, its far wall covered with Southeast Region President's Club awards. "Take a seat," she said, closing the door behind her.

Justine sat, sliding her purse off her shoulder as gracefully as a panther stretching its limbs. Then she folded her hands on the table and waited patiently for Savannah to begin.

Feeling awkward and ungainly next to Justine, Savannah pushed a lock of hair behind her ear and absorbed herself with lining up last year's return with the blank file she'd brought in to use for this year.

"So. You're a sex therapist," Savannah said, clicking the top of her mechanical pencil.

Justine seemed amused, but answered only, "Yes."

Savannah flipped to the Schedule C (Profit or Loss From Business) that was filed last year. "And you work out of your home, I see."

"Yes."

"You're still at 1215 West Gulf Drive?"

"Yes," Justine answered again.

"Okay. Then let's get down to details. Do you have receipts for your business expenses or did you bring a report from Quicken or some other financial management software?"

"I have receipts," Justine said, reaching over to pick her purse up off the chair where she'd left it. "One of my customers has offered to set me up on Quicken, but I don't really see the need."

"You might find it more useful than you think," Savannah said, trying not to overenthuse. The truth was, she loved financial management software—it made paying bills effortless, and she could see with one click of the mouse where her money was being spent. But sometimes she gushed too much and all it did was make her seem like a geek, so she tried to keep her voice even as she continued. "Especially for someone with a small business, a program like Quicken can be invaluable. You can set it up to record expected income and expenses so you can manage your cash flow, plus you can categorize each expense to make completing your tax returns a cinch."

Justine smiled indulgently. "Yes, that's what Jason tells me," she said, then pulled a red, rectangular box out of her purse. "For now, however, I'm still low-tech."

Savannah reached out to take the box. "You're not alone. Most of our clients prefer shoe boxes to software." Only, as she set the box down in front of her, she realized that this was *not* a shoe box. Instead, the picture on the top of the box showed a set of fur-lined handcuffs.

Savannah felt a blush creeping up her neck and told herself to get a grip. *The woman's a sex therapist,* she reminded herself as she opened the lid and pulled out the first receipt. Besides, there was nothing kinky about fur-lined handcuffs. At least it wasn't something more sinister, like—

She slapped her hand over the receipt from Whips 'n' Lace Manufacturing.

"Um," she stuttered, knowing her eyes had gone wide like an innocent cowgirl just off the farm. "I don't think you can deduct elbow-length latex gloves."

The corners of Justine's perfect eyes crinkled the tiniest bit when she frowned. "What do you mean?" she asked, obviously puzzled. "Occasionally, one of my clients enjoys—"

Savannah held her palms up to make Justine stop. She didn't want to know. She'd received enough porn spam to get the gist of what someone might need elbow-length latex gloves for. "Are you a *licensed* sex therapist?" she asked, almost afraid to hear the answer.

"Licensed by whom?" Justine asked with a tilt of her heart-shaped face.

"The State of Florida," Savannah suggested. "I mean, you have some sort of training, right?"

Justine laughed. "Training? To have sex? Who needs training for that?"

Savannah laid her head in her hands and groaned. "Please tell me you don't have sex with people for a living."

"What's wrong with that?" Justine asked.

"First of all, it's against the law," Savannah mumbled through her fingers.

"Not if I'm a sex therapist, it's not. That's what the girl told me last year."

"But if you're not licensed, you're not a sex therapist," Savannah argued, raising her head to look at Justine. "You're someone who has sex with people for money."

Justine reached out and patted Savannah's hand, her fingers cool and smooth on Savannah's. "That's just semantics. Besides, it's not like the IRS is going to cross-check their records with the state's licensing board, right? So, why not let me pay taxes like everyone else? I'll be in more trouble if I *don't* file. My bank has recorded my interest income, and I set myself up as a limited liability corporation like the accountant from last year suggested I do. So what's the problem?" Justine shrugged.

"The problem," Savannah said, "is that this is unethical. I can't file a tax return for you, knowing that you're running an illegal operation. It would be like a drug dealer telling me he wanted to deduct the expense for hiring assassins to kill his competition. I just can't do it."

That comparison garnered an unpleasant reaction from Justine, whose cheeks turned a mottled red under her tan as she stood up and grabbed the handcuff box off the table. "I'm not a drug dealer," she said.

"I didn't say you were," Savannah protested. "But prostitution is just as illegal as drug dealing, and I can't file a tax return for either occupation."

Justine's movements were jerky as she stuffed her box back into her bag and stomped over to the conference room door. She paused at the doorway to spear Savannah with a venomous look. "If you won't do it, you can bet I'll find someone else who will," she hissed, her perfectly manicured hand resting on the doorknob.

"I'm sure you will," Savannah said coolly. "But my integrity is not for sale."

"Whatever," Justine scoffed, then yanked the door open and flounced out.

Alone in the consultation room, Savannah ignored the eerie silence from out in the office as she flipped through the pages of Justine's tax return from last year, her eyes narrowing when she found the name of the accountant who had prepared her 1040 the year before.

What Party Animal Are You?

On Friday at one P.M., a wealthy friend invites you to her beach house for the weekend. You:

a. Say no. You don't have enough time to pack, shave your legs, wash your hair, and water your plants. Maybe this will teach your friend to give you more time to prepare next time.

b. Say yes, but you'll need to know what sorts of activities are planned and exactly what time you'll be back on Sunday. There's an important segment of *60 Minutes* on that you can't miss.

c. Are already out the door, your emergency weekend party bag in hand. Let the fun begin!

If you chose A, your party animal is a slug! Come on, stop being such a dud and live a little. For those of you who chose B, your party animal is a skunk. You'll stink up everyone else's fun weekend by trying to have everything your way . . . and our guess is you won't be invited back! You C girls are the ultimate party animals and people love having you around. Never change, darlings!

{twenty-two}

Ashleigh had left for lunch by the time Savannah closed Justine's file and left the conference room. It was already twelve-fifteen, and Savannah had a one o'clock appointment, so she was going to have to hurry if she wanted to have time to eat after buying some new underwear at Jilly's Lingerie, one of the many shops that Vanna had frequented.

Savannah locked the files she was working on in her desk drawer and grabbed her purse, pausing for a moment to speak to Dani on her way out. Everyone else had already left the office except Bert and Lucy, whose names were next on the walk-in list, but Savannah still lowered her voice as she asked, "Who was Mary Coltrane?"

Dani wrinkled her nose. "She was a junior accountant. She was let go right before I started."

"Who was her supervisor?" Savannah asked, wondering if anyone in management knew that she'd filed a client's taxes under false pretenses.

"Well, Len, I guess," Dani answered with a shrug.

Savannah frowned. "Len checked her day-to-day work?"

"No. I would expect that Ashleigh did. She gets all the new trainees."

"Why is that?" Savannah asked.

Dani shifted uncomfortably in her chair and glanced out the window. "I don't know. Because she's been here the longest?"

That didn't sound like a very good reason for one accountant to get assigned all the new hires. It seemed to Savannah that Ashleigh had a pretty sweet deal going on here. She assigned all her files to the trainees, who worked dozens of hours of overtime to keep up with their own workload plus taking care of Ashleigh's returns.

"Nice work if you can get it," Savannah muttered under her breath as she pushed open the door to the office and stepped outside. The bright sunshine that greeted her conflicted with her dark mood, and she fought the urge to raise her fist and shout, "Enough already!" at the sky. The relentlessly cheerful climate here was beginning to grate on her nerves. It was almost as if she wasn't entitled to a black mood every now and then.

Screw that, she thought as she stomped down the street to Jilly's Lingerie. She was tired of being abused, ignored, and dumped on. Her new life wasn't turning out like she'd planned, and she was pissed off. How could someone change everything about herself and *still* not be happy?

She pulled open the door to the lingerie shop and took a deep breath, trying to calm down. Why wasn't her life getting better? Hadn't she done everything she was supposed to do? She'd thrown out her old self and started over from scratch. What more could she do?

"Ooh, this is too cute. I'll take it as well."

Savannah heard a familiar voice and ducked behind a row of see-through peignoirs. What was Ashleigh doing here?

"Is that all?" a salesclerk asked, sounding hopeful that Ashleigh would add a few more items to her stack of purchases.

Must be on commission, Savannah thought.

"Yes, that's it," Ashleigh said.

Savannah watched through a film of white lace as her coworker slid a piece of plastic across the counter. The clerk took the credit card, swiped it through a card reader, and handed it back to Ashleigh.

"Thank you, Ms. Coltrane," the clerk said.

Savannah's mouth dropped open. Ms. Coltrane? But Ashleigh's last name was Van Dyke.

"Good afternoon. Can I help you?" a tall woman with mocha-colored skin asked from behind her, making Savannah jump. She reached out to steady herself and knocked half of the peignoir sets onto the beige carpet.

"I'm sorry," she apologized, reaching down to pick up the nighties at the same time the clerk did. The clerk reached the hangers first.

"Don't worry about it," the woman said pleasantly. "I'll take care of it."

Savannah straightened. "Thank you. I'm sorry," she apologized again.

"What are you doing here?" Ashleigh asked, having turned away from the cash register at the commotion.

Savannah crossed her arms over her chest defensively. She was not in the mood to be put down by Ashleigh I'm-Marrying-Money-So-I'm-Better-Than-You Van Dyke. "I'm here to shop, just like you. And why did the clerk just call you Ms. Coltrane?"

Ashleigh looked at her, unblinking, for a long moment. Her green eyes seemed unfocused, as if her mind had just gone somewhere far away. She came back with a smile and a conspiratorial laugh as she dug the credit card she'd just used out of her purse and studied it. "Oh, my gosh. Mary Coltrane and I used to shop here together all the time. It looks like our cards must have gotten mixed up. I'll have to give her a call and let her know I've got this."

"Oh," Savannah said, surprised that Ashleigh admitted to being friendly with someone from the office. Maybe Ashleigh wasn't so bad after all. Maybe she had only distanced herself from the other accountants because they were jealous of her.

"Hey, listen. Why don't we grab something to eat when you're done with your shopping," Ashleigh suggested.

Savannah glanced at her watch. She only had thirty minutes until her appointment, and she *really* needed to get some new underwear. But wasn't this exactly what she wanted? The chance to become friends with someone like Ashleigh?

She noticed a rack marked with the word *sale* just off to her left. Maybe she could accomplish both of her goals here. "I'd love to," Savannah said.

Without looking at much more than the size, she hastily

grabbed four pairs of brightly colored panties from the sale rack and tossed them onto the counter. "I'll take these," she told the clerk.

"You don't want to try them on?" the woman asked.

"No," Savannah answered.

"They're not returnable," the clerk cautioned.

Savannah checked the sizes one more time just to be sure they'd fit. "I'll take them," she said again.

The clerk shrugged and ran the first garment past her scanner. Savannah handed her her debit card and silently prayed that this purchase wouldn't bankrupt her. How embarrassing would it be for her card to be rejected in front of the glamorous Ashleigh?

Fortunately, the card ran through, and the clerk handed it back along with a bag full of Savannah's new treasures. As she and Ashleigh walked back out into the ever-present sunshine, Savannah began to feel better about her prospects for a new life. Maybe she and Ashleigh would become friends, and Savannah would get invited to her wedding—maybe even be asked to fill in at the last minute when one of the bridesmaids got sick or disappeared like Trish had done at Savannah's wedding back in February. And maybe one of the groomsmen would end up falling in love with her as they danced the evening away under the stars.

Savannah sighed as she imagined herself being whirled around on the beach under a full moon, her bare feet sinking into the warm sand as waves lapped against her toes. She looked up, into the eyes of her fantasy man—

And tripped on a nonexistent crack in the sidewalk when she realized that the man she was dreaming of was Mike Bryson.

Savannah chewed on her bottom lip. She had to find some way to erase that fantasy, because it was only going to lead to heartbreak. Mike was not going to convert over to the hetero side for her, and she had to get it out of her head that he might. Besides, it wasn't like the poor guy had done anything more than kiss her, once, on the nose. Like a brother or a friend might. Other than that, he had shown absolutely no interest in her whatsoever.

Why, then, was she constantly fantasizing about him?

"Are you all right?" Ashleigh asked, looking at her strangely.

Savannah quit biting her lip. "Yes, sorry. I'm fine. Can we just grab a quick sandwich somewhere? I've got to be back in the office by one."

Ashleigh chuckled and waved one pink-polished nail in the air breezily. "Don't worry about that. Somebody will cover for you."

"Uh, I don't like to make people do that. There's a coffee shop up on the next block that has really good sandwiches. Let's get something from there."

Ashleigh tossed her dark hair over one shoulder with a flick of her head. "Fine by me," she acquiesced.

Once they had bought their lunches and were sitting down to eat at a table on the patio outside, Savannah decided to ask the question that had been bothering her since she'd told Justine she couldn't file her taxes for her. "Did you know that Justine was a prostitute and not a sex therapist?"

Ashleigh bit into her tuna on whole wheat, chewed, swallowed, and then wiped her lips with a napkin before answering. "I suspected it, yes."

"And you didn't tell Mary Coltrane that it would be wrong to file on her behalf?"

Savannah took a sip of her iced tea and let the cool liquid roll around on her tongue while Ashleigh took a moment to frame her answer. "Have you noticed all those President's Club awards on the wall in the consultation room?" she asked after a while.

Savannah pushed her turkey and provolone sandwich away, untouched. "Yes," she answered, wondering what that had to do with it.

"Len gets a bonus—a *big* bonus—for every one of those awards. He shares it proportionally with everyone in the office. At our staff meeting every Monday, he brings a list of where each accountant stands in relation to the others. As you know, we all make about the same salary. This is your only way to significantly increase your income. And you don't do that by turning away customers."

"Yes, but—"

"I got eighty percent of the bonus pool last year," Ashleigh interrupted, her even white teeth ripping off another bite of her sandwich.

"But we have a duty to do what's in the best interest of the government as well as to ourselves," Savannah protested. "And if we file taxes for people running illegal operations, we are helping to legitimize those operations in the eyes of the IRS. We should report people like Justine, not help them beat the system."

"I don't have any proof that Justine isn't a bona fide sex therapist," Ashleigh said, widening her eyes innocently.

"Mary Coltrane did. She even told Justine she should set herself up as an L.L.C."

"And Mary was fired at the beginning of the year when it was discovered that she was engaging in questionable practices. So what's the problem?"

"The problem is that you were her supervisor. Did you advise her that what she was doing was wrong?"

Ashleigh surprised her by leaning forward and patting her on the back. "Of course I did. But some people will do anything to get ahead, you know. Mary was just one of those people who thought the rules didn't apply to her. Now, me, I try to learn just as little about my clients as I need to know in order to file their returns. As far as I'm concerned, what I don't know can't hurt me. That philosophy has served me well over the years, and it's one you need to learn if you want to succeed in life."

Savannah sat back and slowly unwrapped the plastic from around her sandwich. "I can't turn a blind eye like that," she said. Just thinking about filing questionable tax returns and allowing fraudulent deductions made her stomach cramp. She took a bite of her sandwich, but it turned to dirt in her mouth, so she surreptitiously spit it back out into her napkin.

Ashleigh watched her, a serious look in her dark green eyes. "That's what I thought you'd say," she said, tilting her head and studying Savannah as if she were a butterfly pinned by her delicate wings under a piece of glass.

Savannah looked down at her blouse to make sure she hadn't dropped a glob of mayonnaise on her boob or something. "What?" she asked as Ashleigh continued to stare.

Finally Ashleigh shook her head and gave Savannah a

strange sort of half-smile. "Nothing." She paused, then continued gaily as if their previous conversation had never happened. "Hey, I have a great idea. My bachelorette party is tomorrow. Some friends and I are flying down to Key West for the night and staying in my fiancé's house down on Southard Street. It's within walking distance of all these great bars and it's going to be a blast. Would you like to come?"

It was Savannah's turn to stare. *Would she?* This was exactly the sort of thing that would happen to Vanna—last-minute invitations to weekend parties, jetting off to private villas in glamorous locales, pub crawling with rich and interesting friends.

There was only one problem: work. Savannah had a nine o'clock appointment tomorrow morning, not to mention the fact that she'd be back on the top of the walk-in list by the end of today. And with only three weeks until April 15, she was already drowning in 1040s that needed to be completed.

Oh, and then there was that other problem: money. How would she come up with the cash she would need to pay last-minute airfare down to Key West? Payday was Monday, but she needed that money to pay her rent and buy groceries. And she'd just used the last of her cash to buy new underwear. Underwear no one but she was ever going to see if things continued the way they were, Savannah thought glumly.

"I can't," she said, her shoulders drooping with disappointment. Didn't it figure? She finally had the chance to be the person she wanted to be, but her own stupid practical nature held her back. God, it was no wonder Todd hadn't fought for her—she was so boring that even *she* hated herself.

"Why not?" Ashleigh asked, taking a sip of her half-caf, no-foam latte.

Yes, why not? Savannah looked over at the table next to them as a cool breeze blew past, riffling through the fashion magazine the lone young woman had open on the table in front of her. It was this month's issue of *Glamour*—the one Savannah had given to Christina the other day. She grimaced, thinking about her plan to use magazine quizzes to change her life. The problem was, she was going through the motions— buying the new car, wearing the new clothes, moving to a sunny new locale—but she was the same old Savannah inside.

What she really needed was to let go of that part of herself that always made the sensible choice, always followed the rules, always worried about doing the right thing and not hurting anyone else's feelings.

Well, fuck that.

She finally—*finally!!!*—got it. It wasn't the car, or the clothes, or the address that needed to change. It was her entire personality.

So what if she called in sick tomorrow and others had to take on her workload? Hadn't she done the same thing year after year after year for slackers in the Maple Rapids office? Why did *she* always have to be the super-responsible one? It wasn't like the world would end if she missed a day of work.

And as for money, she'd call her mom and ask for a loan. What was so wrong with that? Her family always seemed to expect her to be a screwup, so why not start acting like one?

Savannah turned back to Ashleigh and narrowed her eyes with determination. "Forget it. I'll come," she said. "I'll call in sick. Everybody does it. Like you said, they'll just have to cover for me."

Ashleigh's face lit up when she smiled, and Savannah didn't bother trying to second-guess why it was so important to her that Savannah went to Key West. *Maybe she just likes you,* she told herself, wondering why that was such a difficult concept for her to grasp.

"That's great," Ashleigh squealed. "I haven't said a word about the party at the office. Ever since I announced that I was quitting, they've all turned on me anyway. If they'd been nicer, I might have invited at least some of them to the wedding, but . . ." Her voice trailed off as she shrugged one shoulder nonchalantly as if to say she couldn't care less about being snubbed. Which she probably didn't.

That was the difference between her and Ashleigh. It was eating at Savannah that her new coworkers were treating her like an outsider, but Ashleigh had so much confidence in herself that she really didn't care if people liked her. That was definitely an attitude Savannah wanted to adopt, starting right now.

Savannah checked her watch and saw that it was five minutes past one. This was it. Her first test. She was late for her one o'clock, but would she leap up from the chair and race back to the office?

No.

She slowly sipped her iced tea, willing her hands to stop shaking.

By seven past one, her knees were jiggling uncontrollably under the table, but Savannah remained seated.

At nine after she finally set down her drink and stood up to leave. Ashleigh had lit a cigarette and looked to be in no hurry to get back to the office.

"I've got to run," Savannah said. "What time shall I meet you at the airport tomorrow?"

"Ten A.M.," Ashleigh answered. "Don't bring anything fancy. Key West is a low-key kind of town."

"Great. I'm looking forward to it."

Then, without a backward glance, Savannah forced herself to stroll in a leisurely fashion back to the office, where her one o'clock appointment was waiting. She tried not to hurry in case Ashleigh was watching her but refused to look back. If she had, she would have seen Ashleigh staring at her, a deadly calculating look marring the perfection of her smooth, lightly tanned skin.

You Can't Always Get What You Want . . . Or Can You?

Some women seem to have a gift for getting what they want. The richest guys, the best jobs, the nicest apartments in the city. What's their secret? They decide what they want and then they go after it! So are you the type of girl who always gets what she wants? Take this quiz and find out!

You have a crush on your best friend's boyfriend—a successful investment banker who treats you like his kid sister. After they break up, you:

a. Give him a call and tell him you're "there for him" if he ever needs to talk.

b. Do nothing but pine away for what might have been. He became off-limits the minute he started dating your best friend.

c. Listen carefully to every reason he gave for breaking up with your best friend and then coolly and calculatedly insinuate yourself into his life, making sure to avoid all the behaviors he listed. After all, *someone* might as well learn from your girlfriend's mistakes, right?

What you A girls have just done is to give that guy an open invitation to use you for his booty calls. Get some self-esteem! You may get laid with this approach, but you'll never get a ring! Here's a halo for those of you Goody Two-shoes gals who chose B. We hope heaven is its own

continues on next page . . .

reward because you sure as hell aren't going to have any fun while here on earth! Those of you who chose C know how to get what you want. You wait until the time is right, you formulate a solid plan, and you go after your goal. Who says you can't have everything you want? And if you lose a friend or two along the way . . . Well, sometimes sacrifices must be made, right?

{twenty-three}

When Savannah called and left a message with the Refund City answering service the next morning that she was feeling ill, she wasn't lying.

Back when she was in the fifth grade, Savannah had a reading class with the teacher's daughter, Megan, who was a stellar student. To encourage the kids to read, Megan's mother had brought in a box of cards that had short stories printed on the front and five multiple-choice reading-comprehension questions on the back. For each test a student passed, she got one extra credit point added to her grade. The only trouble was, the answers to the tests were printed on the bottom of each card, so if a student wanted to cheat, all she had to do was to copy the answers into her notebook and show the teacher that she'd completed the test.

Around the same time that Mrs. Weinand brought the cards in, Megan had a birthday and Savannah accidentally overheard Mrs. Weinand telling Megan that she had to invite all of the students from class to her party. When Megan complained that there were certain students she didn't like—she actually named Savannah as one of the kids she wanted to exclude—Megan's mother patiently told her that it wasn't right to leave out certain people because it would hurt their feelings.

After overhearing that Megan didn't like her, Savannah

vowed to beat her at the reading challenge, no matter what she had to do to win.

And so, every afternoon when she left class, Savannah waited to be the last one to go and pocketed a handful of cards. Every night, she neatly numbered her notebook pages and copied down the answers to the tests. At the end of the year she won a blue ribbon for the most extra-credit points earned that year. Mrs. Weinand had even taken her aside and told her, obviously impressed, that Savannah had passed more than twice the number of tests than the second-place student, who just happened to be Megan.

Before Savannah left Maple Rapids, she'd run into Megan at the Super ShopMart one day. Savannah had heard through the grapevine (aka her mother) that Megan's husband, Greg, had left her for a woman he'd met down at Gold's Gym the day before Megan gave birth to their third child in four years. Megan, who hadn't worked since her part-time job at the Dairy Queen back in high school, had moved back in with her parents. Rumor had it that Megan's dad left her mother within the month.

As they'd stopped near the frozen fishsticks to chat in the awkward manner of people who had known each other nearly all their lives but never really liked one another, Savannah couldn't help but feel that Megan's current state of affairs could be blamed, at least in some small part, on that public defeat back in fifth grade, when Savannah had stolen victory right out from under Megan's nose. Savannah suspected that Megan had pursued Greg because she knew that Savannah had a crush on the fast-food restaurant manager they both worked for. Winning Greg's favor was Megan's way of getting back at her all those years later.

And the worst of it was that it had all been a lie. It was Megan who had really won. Twenty years later Savannah still felt a little sick whenever she thought about how she had cheated and how her actions had wreaked such havoc on Megan's life.

As Savannah left the message on the answering machine telling her coworkers that she wouldn't be in that day, that same sick feeling rolled through her, making her want to vomit.

"Yeah, that's sexy." Savannah mocked herself in the mirror after she hung up the phone and wiped the cold sweat off her brow.

Then, before she could change her mind and call back and tell them that she was already feeling better and would be in shortly, she grabbed the overnight bag she'd packed and repacked a hundred times that morning and headed out of her motel room, being careful to lock the door behind her. She didn't want to come back tomorrow to find her tub filled with rum and cockroaches again.

As she tested the door a third time to make sure it wouldn't budge, she couldn't seem to stop herself from glancing to her left at the darkened window of Mike Bryson's room. She'd heard him leave earlier that morning—with the paper-thin walls, she could pretty much hear it when he blinked his eyes, much less when he turned on the shower or closed his front door. She even imagined she could smell his cologne as he walked by her door, his footsteps slowing as if he were tempted to stop and kiss her good-bye.

Savannah sighed.

Once again her imagination was running away with her.

Stop fixating on the gay guy, she admonished herself as she headed down the stairs and out into the courtyard below, surprised to find that Christina and the gang were already up and beginning Day 6 in Partyville. Mike had said the students were leaving on Monday afternoon. She wondered if he was looking forward to their departure as much as she was.

As she walked out into the parking lot, she turned to find that James and Christina had followed her. James had his arms wrapped around Christina's chest, his hands resting right below her breasts, as they followed Savannah.

"Gotta get something out of the car," Christina explained, raising her car keys as if to prove it when Savannah raised her eyebrows at them.

"Sweet car." James let go of Christina and rocked back on his heels on the sidewalk, nodding approvingly as Savannah unlocked the door to her convertible.

"Thanks," Savannah said, resisting the urge to add "Dude" at the end of every sentence when talking to him. She tossed her bag into the back and pulled open the driver's side door.

The sun had already warmed the white leather interior to about a thousand degrees, so Savannah ooched and ouched as she slid into the driver's seat. For today's excursion, she had chosen a short green skirt and black tank top. She had put a sweater in her carry-on bag in case it got cold on the plane, but she didn't think to bring a towel to save her skin from being scorched by the seat of her car.

If it was this hot in late March, she couldn't imagine what August was going to be like.

"Hey, Savannah?" Christina said hesitantly as she paused near Savannah's door.

Savannah looked up from fiddling with the air conditioner to see that James had disappeared back into the courtyard of the motel. "Yes?" she asked. Warm air from the AC blasted her full in the face, and Savannah hoped it wouldn't take long to cool down. She felt like the Wicked Witch of the West when Dorothy threw water on her, sliding into a puddle on the floor crying, "I'm melting, I'm melting."

"I'm sorry about that tub thing. And about the ants. And your underwear," Christina added, her gaze resolutely fixed on a wad of blue gum that had bonded with the pavement.

Savannah glanced at the clock on her dashboard. If she didn't hurry, she was going to be late for her new life. "It's all right," she said, shifting the T-bird into reverse, but keeping her foot on the brake.

"No, I mean it," Christina said, looking down at Savannah remorsefully. "I was just trying to . . . I don't know. Get James to like me by showing him that I'm not a Goody Two-shoes, I guess."

Savannah cocked her head and looked at the younger woman. "Did it work?" she asked.

Christina shrugged almost sheepishly. "Yeah."

"You must be happy," Savannah said, thinking about how desperately she herself wanted to be seen in a different light and how good it would feel once people saw that she was fun and exciting and sexy, too.

"I got what I wanted," Christina acknowledged with a nod.

"Good," Savannah answered. Then she decided to take pity on Christina and said, "Look, don't worry about the whole bathtub episode. It was actually kind of funny." She shot the student a mock frown and added, "Just don't do it again."

"I won't. Thanks."

Christina smiled and waved as Savannah took her foot off the brake and backed out of the parking lot. It wasn't until about eight hours later, as she sat in a cold cell, shivering and alone and about to lose everything she held most dear in her life, that Savannah thought back to what Christina had said. When Savannah had asked if she was happy with the results of her own transformation, Christina hadn't answered yes. All she had said was "I got what I wanted."

And those two things—being happy or getting what you want—are two very different things, after all.

So You Wanna Be a Star?

You've always dreamed that one day you'd be in the front row at a concert and you'd get pulled up on stage and get your big chance to become a star. But, be honest, what would you do if that really happened?

a. Start warbling out the only tune that comes to mind— Barry Manilow's "Looks Like We Made It."

b. Stare out at the audience and freeze, then mumble an apology and jump offstage.

c. Are you kidding? You'd grab the microphone with both hands and belt out that tune you've been practicing in the shower for a decade. You can almost smell the star- dom right now!

If you chose A, you may dream of stardom, but you don't really want it. If you did, you'd be thinking about it all the time. You'd have every move down just in case your opportunity ever came. After all, ninety percent of success is just being prepared. Boo! Did we scare you B girls? We're not surprised. You're afraid of your own shadows! Bling, bling! Those of you who chose C are headed for stardom. Can we be part of your entourage when you become rich and famous?

{twenty-four}

Savannah, you made it!" Ashleigh squealed as if her life was now complete.

Savannah felt a warm glow in the pit of her stomach as Ashleigh embraced her in the boarding area of their flight to Key West, which was scheduled to depart in forty minutes. With her arm still around Savannah's shoulders, Ashleigh introduced her to all her friends—about ten in all—who looked as well groomed and expensively turned out as Ashleigh did. Savannah tried not to feel self-conscious about her own self-manicured nails and nondesigner clothes, not to mention the extra ten pounds hovering around her lower half.

After the introductions Ashleigh dragged her a little bit away from the group and asked, "Hey, do you want to get a little pre-party drink? There's a bar just two gates down."

Savannah had decided that her new mantra was going to be "What would Vanna do?" This was an easy one. Who cared if it wasn't even ten o'clock yet? Vanna would definitely be up for some pre-party partying.

"Sure," Savannah said, allowing Ashleigh to lead the way.

The bar was nearly empty, with a bored-looking bartender holding up the counter near a wall of mostly full liquor bottles. Savannah hopped up onto a stool, feeling a bit like a kid sitting at the grown-up table since her feet didn't even reach the top rung of the stool.

"Let's have a Sex on the Beach." Ashleigh giggled and jabbed her in the ribs as if they were in high school.

"Sure. Sex on the Beach," Savannah repeated with a smile.

The bartender rolled his eyes heavenward and shook his head, then went off to make their drinks. On the stool next to her, Ashleigh leaned forward conspiratorially. "Dani told me that you got Mr. CIA this year," she whispered.

Savannah's nose wrinkled as she scrunched up her face. "Huh?" she asked.

"Mr. CIA," Ashleigh repeated. "Guy comes in every year and acts like he's being followed. Says the IRS believes he's dead, like he's some kind of secret government agent or something." Ashleigh laughed.

"Oh, him." Savannah was relieved to find out that she wasn't the only one who had encountered Creepy Nameless Guy. "Yeah, he got me the other night. I was thinking . . . You know, after we talked yesterday . . ." Savannah paused, not quite sure why she was hesitating.

The bartender slid two pink drinks toward them. "That'll be sixteen dollars," he said.

Savannah gasped. Sixteen bucks for two drinks? Geez, it was a good thing she'd asked her mom to loan her a couple hundred dollars—and that Mom was kind enough to deposit the money right into Savannah's bank account the night before. *Thanks, Mom,* Savannah silently expressed her gratitude as she pulled out a twenty and said, "I got it."

Ashleigh seemed to take this as her due and didn't even thank her, instead fixing her green eyes on Savannah and prompting, "So what were you thinking about after we talked yesterday?"

"Well, it's about Mary. You know, how you said she sort of played fast and loose with the rules," Savannah said after sipping her drink.

"Yeah?" Ashleigh said, taking a swallow from her own glass.

"When Mr. CIA, as you called him, came to see me, he said a woman in our office had filed his taxes for him last year. I think . . . Well, when we get back—I mean, after April fifteenth, I'm going to go through our files and see if he was telling the truth. If he was, some poor taxpayer's relative out there may end up having to deal with an audit and it would be our fault."

"I'm sure Mary would have turned him away," Ashleigh said, spearing a piece of pineapple with her miniature Captain Hook sword and popping it into her mouth.

"But she told him she'd just file under one of our deceased clients' Social Security numbers. And he gave her the money to pay his taxes."

Ashleigh snorted. "And do you think that Mary really would have done that? I mean, why wouldn't she just have pocketed it? There'd be no way he could trace the money unless he wanted to go back to the IRS and admit he was still alive."

"My God," Savannah said, shaking her head as she reached for her drink. "You're right. That's probably what she did. I'm going to suggest to Mr. Leonard that we audit all of Mary's files to make sure that she didn't do something like this with her other clients."

Ashleigh slammed her drink down on the bar, making it slosh over the rim. "Do you have to be so fucking conscientious?" she hissed.

Savannah recoiled and nearly slid off her stool. "I'm s-s-sorry," she stammered.

Ashleigh closed her eyes and put the heel of her hand to her forehead for a moment. After a few seconds, she dropped her hand and smiled at Savannah as if nothing had happened. "No," she said, reaching out to pat Savannah's hand. "I'm sorry. I'm just tense about the wedding, and all of this talk about work is making me more stressed. Plus, I think I'm a little woozy from not having breakfast this morning. Would you mind grabbing that bowl of peanuts over there for me?" She pointed toward a wooden bowl of nuts that had no doubt been dipped into by countless travelers passing through this airport.

Savannah slipped off her stool and trotted over to grab the nuts. Anything to soothe the savage beast that had just come out of Ashleigh's mouth like that creature in *Alien*.

When she turned back toward the bar, Ashleigh suddenly straightened up as if someone had pulled a string attached to her back. *Weird*, Savannah thought, but she didn't think anything more about it as she clambered back up on the stool and set the nuts in front of Ashleigh.

"Well, let's finish our drinks and go join everyone else. We'll probably be boarding in a few minutes," Ashleigh said in an eerily cheerful sort of way.

Savannah downed her drink in one swallow. She feared that she was going to need it.

Somewhere over the Gulf of Mexico, Savannah lost her inhibitions. For some reason, the phrase "I'm too sexy for my seat belt, too sexy for my seat belt" started running through her head, and she giggled drunkenly as she flipped the buckle open and shut, open and shut, open and shut. She didn't realize that she was actually crooning the words until Ashleigh, who was sitting directly in front of her, turned around to look at her, a slow smile spreading across her face.

"Feeling festive, are we?" Ashleigh asked.

Savannah grinned and started waving her hands in the air, swaying in her seat. "I feel like dancin', dancin', gonna dance the night away," she said, feeling the sudden urge to get up and do just that.

So she did.

Her hips bumped the seat back of the man across the aisle, who shot Savannah a dirty look and went back to reading his newspaper. She reached out and grabbed the paper, pushing it down in the man's lap. "Sorry about that," she said, then giggled because his scowl suddenly seemed funny.

She lurch-danced a few more steps forward, toward the front of the small plane. She didn't really have a destination in mind; it just seemed like a good idea to get up and dance.

"Ma'am, are you all right?" a flight attendant asked, her smooth forehead wrinkling with concern.

"Hey, do you know Mike?" Savannah asked, her head bobbing to the tune only she could hear. "He's cute, isn't he?" She leaned forward, put a hand on the flight attendant's arm, and whispered loudly, "Too bad about that gay thing, though, huh?"

"Ma'am, I think you'd better take your seat," the flight attendant suggested.

"I feel woozy," Savannah said. The cabin of the plane had started to spin, and Savannah felt as though she were sitting in the middle of a dance floor while couples waltzed slowly past her. Around and around they twirled, but Savannah was the one getting dizzy. She put a hand to her head and closed her eyes, but the world kept spinning. It wasn't an unpleasant sensation, but Savannah was finding it difficult to keep her balance. She tried to frown, but her lips felt like they'd turned to rubber. What was wrong with her?

"I think I need to use the rest room," she said, opening her eyes again. Maybe she'd feel better once she splashed some cool water on her face.

The flight attendant stepped aside to let her pass, watching her as she weaved her way down the aisle.

As Savannah neared the front of the cabin, she saw a male flight attendant put a small microphone to his mouth and, a few seconds later, his voice flooded the cabin. Savannah smiled, or at least she thought she did.

Cool, she thought. In-flight karaoke!

The flight attendant finished his announcement about weather conditions in Key West and hung the microphone up on a hook near a stainless-steel coffeemaker. Then he made the critical mistake of turning his back and leaving the microphone unattended.

Savannah grinned, unable to contain her glee.

She reached out and grabbed the mike, then ducked into the tiny galley. Oh, this was going to be so great. She was going to impress Ashleigh and her new friends with her awesome singing ability. They'd see what a fun, hip person she was, and the invitations would come pouring in. Soon she'd be so busy leading her glamorous new life that her old, boring self would be nothing but a distant memory.

"All right. Let's do this," she said to herself, psyching herself up for the performance of a lifetime.

She lowered her head and stepped out of the galley. Reaching behind her, she flipped on the microphone and stood silently at the head of the plane for one perfect moment.

Then she began.

"Wa-ooh-wa-ooh-ah. Wa-ooh-wa-ooh-ah." She lifted her head and looked out over the passengers, imagining that they were a crowd of thousands; adoring fans here to see her perform.

She launched into "Livin' on a Prayer," doing her best to improvise her dance routine in the tight confines of the plane.

She had reached the first chorus, belting out, "Oh, oh, we're halfway there. Oh, oh, livin' on a prayer," with all the pent-up passion in her soul, when the first flight attendant tackled her.

"Wait, I'm not done yet," Savannah wailed as the man tried to snatch the mike from her hands.

She lurched backward and slammed into the closed cockpit door.

"Keep her away from the pilots!" one of the passengers in the front row screamed, as if Savannah were some kind of terrorist.

Savannah struggled to keep her balance, but her knees had gone wobbly and weren't cooperating. She slid to floor, listing to one side as the female flight attendant who had spoken to her earlier grabbed her arm.

Savannah's stomach gurgled unpleasantly, and she fought a wave of nausea as her suddenly nerveless hands dropped the microphone. The male flight attendant grabbed the mike from off the floor and latched on to her other arm. The two flight attendants were talking over her head in low, hushed tones, but Savannah couldn't make out what they were saying. Her stomach rolled over again and crashed against her rib cage. Savannah broke out into a cold sweat, her cheeks and hands damp and clammy. She tried to raise one hand to her forehead, but the flight attendants held her arms and wouldn't let her move.

"I think I'm going to be sick," Savannah whispered. At least, she thought she did, but the words didn't even reach her own ears.

Then she was being hauled up off the floor. Her legs didn't seem to want to support her, so she let herself be dragged along, her feet scuffing along on the carpet. The antiseptic smell of airline lavatory wafted out as the male flight attendant opened the bathroom door. Her stomach protested violently at the stench, and Savannah groaned as she tried to stop the bile rising in her throat.

Her world went dark as the door closed, and Savannah

flinched when she heard the lock sliding into place. Her head banged against the wall behind her as if her neck refused to support its weight any longer.

Everything was spinning, spinning, spinning, out of control. She couldn't seem to focus. Her eyes and body had gone numb. As she felt another wave of nausea wash over her, she tried to command her legs to move, to get up off the toilet and turn around so she wouldn't throw up all over herself, but her traitorous limbs would not obey.

Instead, all she could manage was to make her head flop forward as she vomited. When her stomach stopped heaving, Savannah started to cry, hot tears rushing down her cheeks and dripping into her lap. She closed her eyes, wondering what her mother, her sisters, her old friends would say if they could see her now. She could almost picture Miranda, looking down at her, shaking her head with disappointment.

"This would never have happened if you had listened to me," Miranda would say.

Todd would cluck his tongue and turn away from her, disgusted. "I told you that you weren't worth the trouble. Just look at you."

Savannah wrapped her arms around her waist and cried even harder, the tears coming faster now.

"You're taking too long. Let me do it."

"You're just a big baby. You don't know how to do anything."

Savannah put her hands to her ears, trying to drown out the disapproving voices from her past.

"You can't do anything right."

"You're a mess."

"You're not worth it."

"Stop it! All of you, stop it! Just leave me alone," Savannah sobbed, curling herself up into a tight ball on the cold airline toilet. And then, as the engines roared on, blessedly, she passed out.

How Can You Tell
If That Hot Guy Is Gay?

Some of us have finely attuned gaydar and can tell if a hot guy is gay at twenty paces. Others can't seem to read the signs, even if the fella in question is wearing a hot-pink silk Georgio Armani shirt and is draped over another guy at the bar. So, if you fall into the latter camp, how can you tell for sure if your guy is gay?

a· He has seen you nearly naked but never mentions that he'd like to see more.

b· He's kissed you once. On the nose.

c· He talks to his mother. A lot.

Yes, sadly, all three of these are signs that your hot guy may prefer members of the same sex. We're sorry to have to be the ones to break it to you. And, like you, we're just as pissed off that all the nice guys do seem to be gay these days.

{twenty-five}

Mike had just ordered a tall black coffee from Ralph at the Conch Republic Coffee Stand when his pager went off. He was scheduled to take a 12:43 flight from Key West back to Naples, with instructions to pay particular attention to the passenger seated in 8C. They suspected the woman would be given her "package" to carry up to Naples after she got through security. Mike would tail her from the time she checked in until she left the airport. At that point she would come under the jurisdiction of the Naples P.D.

He exchanged the paper cup full of coffee for two bucks, then unclipped his pager from his belt and read the display. He expected to be given the location of his suspect, but, instead, the message told him to return to the security office.

Hmm. What was up? Maybe the woman had canceled her flight. Or perhaps she'd been dumb enough to try to get the drugs through security and had been nabbed by the security agents on duty.

Well, he'd find out soon enough.

Mike hurried through the small airport, the sound of his footsteps echoing off the linoleum. Most everyone in the airport was dressed for vacation in khaki shorts and brightly colored tropical shirts. Even on Saturday morning, though, there were a couple of people dressed for business in suits or conservative dresses, all heading off to Orlando or Miami or Tampa to close real estate deals or banking transactions.

Mike pulled his ID card out of the breast pocket of his jacket and held it up to the magnetic key reader outside the security center. The reader beeped and the green indicator light came on, and Mike heard the unmistakable click of the locks sliding open. He tugged the door open and stepped inside.

The security office was an unremarkable space with gray carpeting on the floor and white painted walls. A central hallway cut through the office, with two rooms on each side. The first room on the right was filled with computers, monitoring equipment, television screens, and a loudspeaker system. The second room was a briefing room for the small security staff, and the room across from it was the office of the airport's chief of security. The room to Mike's left, the first one he passed as he entered the office, did double duty as an interrogation room and a holding cell for passengers waiting to be picked up by the FBI or the local police.

Mike turned toward the monitoring room, but no one was there, so he continued on down the hall to find out why he'd been paged. He could hear the faint sounds of someone—a female someone—crying in the interrogation room. Most likely, he figured, it was the woman he'd come to Key West to tail.

He popped his head inside the chief of security's office and found the man, Joe Daniels, sitting behind his desk.

"Hey, Joe. Did you page me?" Mike asked.

"Yeah. I got a call while you were out that a passenger on the 10:04 from Naples had flipped out and tried to break down the cockpit door. The flight attendants on duty were able to subdue her, but she's in a real state. Threw up all over herself—is probably on drugs. The group she was traveling with said they'd just met her that morning. One of the gals works with her and I thought maybe she'd know a little more. I asked her to wait a few minutes so you could talk to her. She's over in the briefing room."

"Thanks," Mike said.

Disorderly conduct was a fairly common occurrence on flights these days, but attempting to break into the cockpit was far more serious than mere disruptive behavior. He pulled an incident report from the stacks of forms neatly laid out on a table in the hallway and then opened the door to the briefing room.

"Good morning," Mike said, and the woman reading the Wanted posters tacked up along the far wall turned.

She looked vaguely familiar, a trim woman who looked to be in her early thirties with long dark hair and green eyes. She was dressed in a pair of white, cropped linen pants with a bright green tank top shrink-wrapped to her upper body. A lightweight white sweater was tied over her shoulders, the sleeves lightly knotted right between her breasts. She had the look of old money, and lots of it. Not uncommon for visitors from Naples.

"Good morning," she responded, taking a seat without waiting for him to offer.

As soon as she spoke, Mike remembered where he'd seen her—on one of his flights this week from Miami to Naples. She'd been traveling with a pack of well-heeled girlfriends and they'd all been a little drunk and she'd picked up on him. She didn't seem to remember, and it wasn't like it had been a life-altering event for him, either, so Mike didn't mention it as he pulled out a chair and sat down across from her. He set his coffee cup on the table and laid the incident report down next to it, then uncapped the blue pen he'd taken from his jacket pocket.

"My name is Mike Bryson. I'm a federal air marshal and I'll be handling the investigation into your friend's conduct on flight 622 today."

The woman across from him shook her head, her long hair sweeping her upper arms. "She's not my friend. I hardly know her. She just moved to Naples from Michigan and started working in my office a few days ago. We had lunch together yesterday, and . . ." The woman hesitated. Leaned forward. Batted her dark eyelashes at Mike. "Well, to be honest, I felt sorry for her. No one in the office seems to care for her and I was just trying to be nice by inviting her down to Key West with me. I didn't know she had a . . . a substance abuse problem."

Mike put the cap back on his pen. She was lying. He knew it as certainly as he knew his own name was Michael Ian Bryson.

"And your name is?" Mike waited for her to fill in the blank.

She smiled and held out her hand, knowing that Mike would have to get up in order to reach her. "Ashleigh Van Dyke. I work with Savannah at Refund City."

Mike dropped his pen.

Ignoring Ashleigh's outstretched hand, he repeated, "Savannah?"

Ashleigh let her hand fall to the table. "Well, yes," she said. "Savannah Taylor. Really, I had no idea she had a drug problem. I never would have invited her—"

"I need numbers where you can be reached, both here and in Naples," Mike interrupted.

Ashleigh Van Dyke gave him her cell phone number and sputtered when Mike told her he'd be in touch. "B-but I thought you were going to ask me more questions. About what happened, I mean." She leaned forward again in that way she had, as if she were graciously inviting him into her inner sanctum. She lowered her voice as she said, "I heard a rumor that she'd been arrested back in Michigan. By the FBI."

This was said with a sanctimonious nod that made Mike want to come across the table and strangle her with the sleeves of her sweater. He had no idea what made him feel so protective of Savannah. He knew she was on the verge of financial ruin, that she had some questionable run-ins with the law, and that she'd obviously moved down to Naples to get away from something bad in her past.

But even knowing all that, he liked her.

She had a good sense of humor and she was nice to the students—even after all the stunts they'd pulled. Plus, she was cute. Not in that plastic, don't-touch-me-I've-just-had-my-hair-done way, but in a completely touchable, completely kissable sort of way.

And, for some reason, this Ashleigh Van Dyke had it in for her. Too bad for her that Mike wasn't buying her act.

He stood up and pointedly held the door for her, repeating his warning that he'd be in touch.

She huffed past him, tossing her hair over her shoulder as if she were flipping him off. Mike watched her hips sway as she walked away, her high, tight buttocks and the white thong between them clearly visible through her white linen pants.

Mike waited until she was gone, the door securely locking into place behind her, before he opened the interrogation room with his card key. He hesitated for just a moment after the indicator light turned green, knowing that the ordeal ahead of him would not be pleasant.

As he pushed open the door, his nostrils were assaulted by the smell of stale puke and the lingering odor of airline lavatory. Savannah was seated in one of the two metal chairs in the room, her head resting on her arms on the stainless-steel table. She didn't lift her head when he came in, but she didn't appear to be crying any longer, which Mike took as a good sign.

The legs of his chair scraped loudly across the uncarpeted floor in the room. He wasn't certain why the other rooms were carpeted and this one wasn't. Most likely it was to make it seem as cold and inhospitable as possible.

He rested his elbows on the table and had to fight the urge to smooth Savannah's hair off her brow. First, he needed to find out what had happened on that flight this morning. Then he could decide what to do about his attraction to this woman.

"Savannah," he said softly. "I need you to talk to me. Can you do that?"

At the sound of his voice, Savannah lifted her tear-stained face out of her arms. The sight of him made her start crying again. "Mike? What are you doing here?"

She looked like she felt as bad as she smelled. Her makeup had long since been cried off, leaving only smudges of mascara and eyeliner pooled beneath her eyes and deposited in the tear tracks down her cheeks. Her skin was mottled from crying, but she had obviously tried to clean herself up a bit since her black shirt was still damp in places.

"Just a second," Mike said, pushing his chair back and wincing when Savannah flinched from the screeching noise. "Sorry. I'll be right back."

He went back to the briefing room and pulled his wallet out of the back pocket of his jeans. He peeled off a five-dollar bill and put it into the vending machine, then entered the codes for a bottle of water and a pack of spearmint gum. He would have bought her some crackers to settle her stomach, but the only ones that were stocked here were spread with an unnatural orange goo that was being passed off as cheese and would most likely make her feel sicker than she already did.

He rummaged around in the cupboards, trying to locate a spare T-shirt that someone might have left behind, and came up with a dark blue shirt with the letters TSA on the back. It was an extra-large, but it was the only thing he could find, so it would have to do.

He let himself into the interrogation room again, twisting off the top of the bottled water as he held it out to Savannah. "Here. Drink this," he ordered.

She took it and gratefully drank half the bottle in one long, thirsty swallow. She set the bottle down and licked her lips as if trying to capture every drop of moisture.

Mike handed her the T-shirt and the pack of gum. "I thought you could use these. If you want to change, I'll turn my back. Or, if you need to use the ladies' room, I can call a female security agent to escort you."

Savannah closed her eyes and shook her head ruefully. "No, I'm fine. Thanks."

Mike smiled kindly and turned his back so Savannah could change out of her soiled tank top and into the T-shirt which was way too large for her, but was clean, at least.

When she was done, Mike sat back down across the table from her. "All right," he said solemnly. "I need to hear your side of the story. What happened up there today?"

Savannah sniffed and rubbed her eyes with her knuckles. "I don't know what got into me," she said, her eyes filled with misery. "I only had one drink. At the bar in Naples. Before we even got on the plane. That's it. Then, about halfway through the flight, I just . . ." Savannah blinked rapidly, trying to hold back a fresh wave of tears. "I went crazy, I guess," she mumbled.

"What do you mean?" Mike asked, wishing he could take Savannah's hands in his but knowing things would go better for her if he maintained his professionalism throughout this interview.

Savannah bit her bottom lip and pushed a lock of hair behind her left ear. "I've never done anything like that before," she said with a watery half-laugh. "I know you probably don't believe me. I mean, every time you see me, I'm mixed up in something ridiculous. God, you might as well just send me to the electric chair right now."

"I'm hoping that won't be necessary," Mike said dryly.

Resting her chin in her hands, Savannah looked at him glumly. "Ever since I moved to Naples, my life has become one giant joke. I guess this is what I get for wanting to be someone I'm not. I should just go back to Maple Rapids and forget this whole thing."

"What whole thing?" Mike asked, completely confused.

"This whole trying-to-be-a-new-person thing," Savannah said, as if that explained everything. When Mike raised his eyebrows to show he was still in the dark, she lowered her gaze to a scratched spot on the table and rubbed the bridge of her nose. "It's a long story," she said.

Mike glanced at his watch. It was already past noon, and he wondered if Joe had assigned another agent to tail the suspected drug mule. Probably, since he knew Mike couldn't be in two places at once.

"Why don't you just tell me the parts that are relevant to what happened this morning?" he suggested. "We can save the rest for later."

Savannah nodded. "Well, the short version is that I moved to Naples because someone there stole my identity. She was running up all sorts of charges at the fanciest bars and the most expensive shops in town, but the FBI couldn't spare the manpower to investigate. By the time they arrested me for her crimes, she'd gotten smart and presumably moved on to another victim. I was able to convince the agent in charge of my case that I was innocent and all the charges were dropped. But I was curious about this woman. She was leading the kind of life I wanted to lead. She was out partying and having a great time, while I was stuck paying her bills."

"So that's why your credit is ruined," Mike said under his breath, as if he were talking to himself. "And why you've got that arrest on your record."

Savannah frowned. "How do you know about that? No official charges were ever filed against me. Agent Harrison said my record was clean."

Mike had the grace to at least look embarrassed. "I did a background check on you after my mother rented you a room. She's supposed to do that on anyone who wants something long-term, but until we got our report back on you, she seemed to think that her instincts were good enough."

"But that still doesn't—" Savannah began.

"My investigator has really good sources," Mike interrupted, knowing that Savannah wanted to know how he'd found out about her arrest since it wasn't part of her public record.

"So much for being innocent until proven guilty." She looked hurt, and Mike grimaced, sorry that he'd let on that he knew so much about her past. "Anyway," she continued, "I decided to move down to Naples to find this woman myself. I guess . . . Well, I guess I kind of admired her. I wanted to be more like her. Or maybe I just wanted to be less like *me*," Savannah confessed.

She looked so forlorn sitting there, buried in that too-large shirt, the sadness in her eyes so deep that Mike had to turn away and give her time to compose herself before he could bear to look at her again. Then, as if he couldn't help himself, he reached out and touched her hand. She looked up at him and their gazes locked, an electricity passing between them that seemed to shock them both.

"But I like *you*," Mike said.

Savannah didn't know what to say to that, so she just sat across the table from him and stared. If only things could be different between them. If only—

Mike cleared his throat. "Now why don't you tell me what happened today."

Savannah sighed and dropped her chin into her hands again. "Okay. So I moved to Naples and tried to find a more glamorous job, but you saw how well *that* worked out. I ended up going back to Refund City, which is the company I worked for back in Maple Rapids. This woman works there—"

"Ashleigh Van Dyke?" Mike interrupted.

"Yes. How did you— Never mind. Yes, Ashleigh Van Dyke. Ashleigh is really cool and glamorous, so I was thrilled when she invited me to come to Key West this weekend with her and her friends. I got to the airport this morning and everything was fine. I had a drink, like I told you earlier, and then we boarded the plane. After about twenty minutes, I . . . God, this is embarrassing," Savannah said, covering her face with her hands.

"It's all right. Just tell me what happened," Mike said calmly.

Savannah took a deep breath and let it back out again. "After about twenty minutes I got this sudden urge to dance. I don't know what came over me. It was like I was drunk or something, but I hadn't had anything but that one drink. The flight attendant suggested that I sit down, but I thought I should splash some cold water on my face because I was feeling so weird. As I headed up to the bathroom, another flight attendant made an announcement and I guess that's when I grabbed the mike and started singing."

"And did you get angry when the flight attendants tried to take the microphone away? Is that why you lunged for the cockpit door?"

Savannah lowered her hands and frowned at him. "I didn't lunge for the door. I lost my balance and fell."

"Did you try to fight back when they grabbed you?" Mike asked.

"No," Savannah answered, horrified. Goose bumps broke out on her arms when she realized that the flight attendants had thought she was trying to attack the pilots. "There's no way—no matter how out of it I was—that I'd ever do something like that. You have to believe me," she pleaded, reaching out to squeeze Mike's hand.

Mike nodded, but didn't squeeze back. "Are you in the habit of taking drugs?" he asked in a neutral tone of voice.

"No. I've never . . . not even occasionally," Savannah stammered.

Mike sighed and finally squeezed her hand before letting her go and leaning back in his chair. "Would someone have had an opportunity to slip you something? Did you leave your drink unattended at any time?"

Savannah's forehead crinkled as she tried to think back to the events of that morning, but her memory was all clouded and fuzzy. "I don't remember. It's like everything from the time I arrived at the airport this morning until I ended up here in this room is hazy."

"I think it's likely that you were drugged, although it will be difficult to prove. I'll have them pull the security tapes from the bar in Naples, but there's no guarantee I'll find anything."

Savannah felt her eyes filling with grateful tears and blinked several times in an attempt to hold them back. "Thank you so much, Mike. I could lose my CPA designation over this."

"I'll do my best," Mike said, then stood. "There's some paperwork I need to fill out, but I shouldn't have a problem getting you released into my custody pending the outcome of the investigation."

Savannah pushed her chair back from the table and stood, wrapping her arms around her stomach to stop from flinging herself into Mike's arms. She had never felt so thankful for someone's assistance in her life. She sniffled and tried to hold back the tears that threatened to start flowing again. "I never knew that flight attendants had so much influence over stuff like this," she said, silently sending up a prayer of thanks that they did. If she hadn't known Mike . . . or if he didn't work for the airlines . . . She shuddered and held herself even tighter, not wanting to think about how much worse the situation would be if airport security had gotten involved.

She looked up to find Mike watching her with a puzzled frown.

"What do you mean?" he asked. "The flight attendants from this morning will be interviewed, of course, but their version of events doesn't hold any more weight than a regular citizen's."

Savannah laughed at Mike's attempt at modesty. He had to know that he was saving her ass here. "No, silly. I mean you. Taking a look at the security tapes from the bar in Naples. Not to mention getting me out of here."

"But that's all part of my job," Mike said. Then his eyes widened as realization began to dawn. And then he smiled. Soon his smile turned into laughter, until in a few minutes he had to sit back down again because he was laughing so hard.

"What?" Savannah asked, somewhat grumpily. She didn't like being laughed at. Besides, what was so funny about him springing her out of here?

Mike looked up and wiped tears of mirth from his eyes. "You thought I was a flight attendant?"

Slowly Savannah uncrossed her arms. "Well, yes. I mean, your mother said . . ." Her voice trailed off as she thought back to their conversation. "Well, she didn't actually *say* that, but she certainly implied it."

Mike rolled his eyes heavenward. "Let me guess. She told you this the morning after you and the students went out to that bar, right?" He continued as Savannah nodded. "That was the day she saw the results of your background check. She probably thought that if you believed I was a flight attendant, you'd be convinced that I wasn't your type. We saw how large your debts are and most likely she figured that you'd be turned off because flight attendants don't make much money."

Savannah shifted her weight to the balls of her feet and glanced up at the gray ceiling, gnawing on the inside of her cheek. "I don't think that's what she was getting at."

Mike folded his arms comfortably on the table in front of him. "Oh?" he asked.

Savannah wasn't sure she should share her theory, but she couldn't think of a way out of it, so she blurted, "I think she wanted me to know that you're gay. Not that there's anything wrong with that," she added.

Mike opened his mouth. Squeaked as though trying to say something, but no words came out. "You think I'm gay?" he finally managed to say.

Savannah's mouth suddenly felt dry, so she reached out for the bottled water that Mike had brought her earlier. "Um," she said.

"Based only on my mother implying that I was a flight attendant? Or is there some other reason you think this?" Mike scratched the back of his neck and watched her intently. "Really, I'd like to know."

"Your mom said you liked strong, silent types. And the day we first met, when you saved me from the ice-cream cart. I saw you hugging another man," Savannah said. "And . . . that's it, I guess. That and . . . uh, I suppose you never really showed any romantic interest in me. Not that that means anything. I mean, you could just not be attracted to me." Savannah knew she was rambling, but the dark look on Mike's face was frightening her, so she took a step back until she was pressed up against the wall. "I think you're awfully handsome and really very nice and I thought, um, once or twice, that maybe I felt something between us when we touched, but it was probably just my imagination."

Mike stood up and stalked toward her like a cat after a mouse. She pressed her back harder against the wall, but there was nowhere for her to run.

When Mike grabbed her arm, Savannah felt a frisson of fear mixed with something much more pleasant, something very much like excitement. He loomed over her, his body just inches from hers. She could smell the clean scent of the soap he'd used that morning and felt the heat coming off of him as he leaned into her.

Slowly he lowered his head, until their mouths were separated by only a whisper.

Savannah's lips parted, her tongue moistening her bottom lip in anticipation of his kiss. She waited, desperately wanting his touch, and was just about to raise up on her tiptoes and claim him, when Mike turned his head and swore.

"What?" Savannah asked, nearly stomping her foot in frustration.

"Camera" was all Mike said as he stepped away from her. He ran a hand through his hair, let out a long-suffering sigh, and waved toward the upper right corner of the room.

Savannah looked up to find the steady eye of a camera recording their every move.

Mike strode to the door and opened it, then turned to spear her with a brooding look. "I get a hard-on every morning when I hear you singing in the shower. I imagine I'm in there with you, both of us naked and wet, only in my fantasy, you're not singing."

Savannah swallowed. "I'm not?" she whispered, hoping they weren't being audiotaped as well as videotaped. Surely Mike wouldn't say something like this if they were.

"No." Mike paused, holding her gaze. "But you're definitely making noise."

"I am?" Savannah asked, putting her palms against the wall behind her to steady herself since her knees had gone weak.

"I'm not a flight attendant, I'm a federal air marshal," Mike said in a low, husky voice that sent shivers up her skin. "And soon—very, very soon—my shower fantasy is going to become a reality. Any questions?"

Savannah pulled her bottom lip into her mouth and shook her head, incapable, it seemed, of talking.

"Good. Then just sit tight and I'll get you out of here as soon as possible. And tomorrow," he said, stepping through the doorway and forcing Savannah to lean forward to hear his words as the door swung slowly shut behind him, "I'm going to kill my mother."

Let's Talk About Sex, Baby!

Last night during sex, your boyfriend du jour asks you to try something you've never done before. You're a little uncomfortable with the idea but you do it anyway. Now you want to know if this thing is normal. Who do you call?

a• No one. Sex is a private matter between two people and should never be discussed outside the bedroom.

b• Your best girlfriend. She's told you all her dirty little secrets. It's time you shared one of yours.

c• Mom, of course. After all, Mother knows best!

Answer A should really be answer U for Uptight! Girl, you need to learn to loosen up those lips a little. We'll bet that "kinky" new thing your guy begged you for was probably anything besides the standard old missionary position you practice every time you hit the sheets together! B is a good answer, but remember that girlfriends sometimes give bad advice. They don't have the life experience that your mothers do. C is definitely our number-one choice! We're fortunate to have totally cool, hip moms who know their responsibility to educate their daughters didn't end with that birds-and-bees talk back in the seventh grade. When it comes to talking about sex, moms rule!

{twenty-six}

Home, sweet home. Savannah wearily closed her eyes and leaned forward to rest her head on the steering wheel of her convertible. The Sand Dunes Motel rose up in front of her like a fairytale castle made of sand and seafoam green taffy. She was so glad to be back in Naples, with the soft breeze tickling the nape of her neck, the air heavy with the scent of gardenias.

Being released from jail gave one a new appreciation for the simple things in life, Savannah supposed.

Her eyes jerked open when Mike opened the driver's side door and slid one arm beneath her knees and the other around her waist.

"Come on, Sleeping Beauty," he said. "Time to get you upstairs."

As Mike lifted her out of the car, Savannah thought about protesting that she was too heavy, but then decided to keep her mouth shut. No sense bringing to his attention the fact that she was ten pounds overweight. If he hadn't noticed it yet, she sure as heck wasn't going to tell him. Instead, she buried her nose in the clean-smelling T-shirt he wore and let herself enjoy the ride.

She had no idea how he was going to manage to unlock the door to the courtyard, but it turned out not to be an issue when a woman who lived in one of the downstairs motel rooms pushed the door open from the inside. Mike stood back as two young boys scampered noisily ahead of the woman into the parking lot. She held the door open for Mike and raised her eyebrows at him as he passed. Mike grinned in return.

"Hi, Mike," she said.

"Annie," Mike returned with a nod.

"Thanks for giving me a break on this month's rent," the woman Savannah presumed was Annie blurted.

Mike's cheeks colored. "Don't mention it. I know you'll get on your feet soon."

"Yeah. Well, thanks," Annie said again. Then, in a more cheerful tone she added, "You two be careful now. That's how I ended up with my twins." She gave them a wry smile as she hurried after her sons, letting the door slowly drift closed behind her.

Mike chuckled and made Savannah's pulse leap when he leaned down and whispered, "Not to worry. I have protection . . . and lots of it."

Savannah shivered at the threat—or was it a promise?—in Mike's voice.

She had no idea how he could find her attractive after seeing her at her absolute worst. She looked awful and needed serious quality time with some toothpaste and soap.

But Mike didn't seem to care, which made Savannah wonder if he had some sort of olfactory disorder. Not that that would stop her from finding him attractive. Who needed a guy with a sense of smell anyway? Especially if he had a knack for coming to your rescue when you most needed it.

Speaking of which, Savannah realized she'd never properly thanked him for freeing her back in Key West.

"Thank you springing me from jail," she mumbled into his shirt, wishing she could forget everything that had transpired earlier, but knowing she'd relive the scene over and over again until the day she died.

She felt Mike's chest rumble beneath her cheek when he laughed. "You weren't in jail," he said as he cleared the top step and walked out onto the second-floor breezeway, not even winded from carrying her up the flight of stairs.

"It sure felt like I was," Savannah said.

Mike stopped and stared down at her until she was forced to look up and meet his gaze. "Listen," he said softly, "I like you. I liked you even when I thought you had a murky past. But the last thing I want from you is gratitude. If that's why you're with me, we need to end this right now."

Savannah reached up and put a hand to Mike's cheek, his bristly stubble rough under her palm. Her chest felt tight, as if someone were hugging her fiercely and making it impossible for her to draw a full breath. "I like you, too. And I *am* grateful that you were there to help me today, but that's not the reason I'm attracted to you."

Mike nodded and started walking again. "Good, because that's no way to start a relationship."

"I agree," Savannah said as Mike stopped in front of his motel room door and slowly let her feet slide to the floor so he could get his keys out of the pocket of his jeans. With a grin, Savannah twisted so that her front was pressed up against Mike's right side. She let her left hand travel from his strong shoulders down past his waist and on to his firm butt. Playfully, she gave a little squeeze. "Believe me, it's not your assistance I'm attracted to."

Mike reacted so quickly that Savannah didn't even see him move. She blinked, surprised to find herself backed up against the wall with Mike looming over her, his hips pressing her against the warm stucco.

"Oh?" he mock-growled. "And what *would* you be attracted to then?"

Savannah felt her heart flutter. God, was he cute when he went all dark and dangerous like that. It was a good thing he had her pinned to the wall; otherwise, she wasn't certain her weakened knees would support her.

She slid her hands into his thick hair and raised herself up on tiptoes to lick the salty skin just under his ear. Then she softly bit his earlobe and whispered, "If you're good, I'll tell you in an hour."

Mike turned his head to capture her teasing lips with his, and Savannah heard her own breathy moan when he sucked her tongue into his mouth. He pushed one knee between her thighs and slowly inched his leg up, the worn material of his jeans rubbing against her bare skin. He stopped about an inch below where she wanted him to be, and she could feel the heat coming off of him, so close to her throbbing clitoris that she wanted to scream.

Savannah squirmed as Mike kept her immobile against the wall with his heavy body. Didn't he realize that there was a certain part of her body that needed touching *right now*?

He broke their kiss, his lips moving away from hers so he could nibble on her neck. When he got to her ear, he said something, the touch of his warm breath on her skin sending a shiver through Savannah's body. It took a few seconds for his words to register in her brain, and when they did, she smiled with all the satisfaction of a cat being presented with her very own cow.

"How about you let me know in two hours?" Mike said, then added, "I'm very, very good."

Two and a half hours later, Savannah lay in a boneless heap in the middle of Mike's bed, pondering how nice it was to find a man of his word. She stretched contentedly, feeling the soft sheets slide over her naked skin. Mike slept soundly next to her, his left arm resting on his chest. She yawned and was about to reach down for the T-shirt he'd discarded earlier—sexy or not, she couldn't sleep in the nude—when she heard the sound of voices outside Mike's door. Figuring it was the coeds on their way to their rooms, she scooted back under the covers in case someone happened to look inside and could see her in the crack between the curtains.

When she heard the jangle of keys and the sound of a door being opened, she froze.

That was *her* door that had just been opened. Someone was in her room.

Savannah leaned over and grabbed Mike's dark blue T-shirt off the floor. She threw it on over her head and turned to jostle him awake. She hated to wake him, but no way was she going over there alone when she had her own personal lawman right here in bed with her.

"Mike!" she hissed. "Wake up. Someone's next door."

Mike groggily opened his eyes and then closed them again. "Huh?" he asked, reaching out to grab her arm and tug her on top of him. Savannah felt the cool breeze on her bare rear end as the T-shirt rode up.

Then she squealed and toppled off the bed in her haste to hide when someone pounded on Mike's door.

"Mike, are you home?" Savannah heard a muffled woman's voice ask through the thin metal door.

"Just a second, Mom," Mike shouted before sitting up and rubbing the sleep out of his eyes. He yawned and scratched his chest and then stood up and reached for the jeans he'd slung over a chair.

Savannah had to drag her eyes from his gloriously naked body.

She shook her head, trying to clear it. Now was not the time to be thinking of Mike and his nakedness. She needed to . . . To what? It wasn't like they were naughty teenagers who had to hide from their parents. Still, she didn't exactly want to greet Mike's mother again wearing nothing but her son's wrinkled T-shirt and a self-satisfied smile, so while Mike went to answer the door, Savannah dashed into the bathroom and locked herself in.

The walls were so thin she didn't even have to press her ear to the door to hear their conversation.

"What's up?" Savannah heard Mike ask his mother.

"Savannah's not a criminal," Lillian answered, sounding as if she were about to do a little happy dance right there in the hall.

Savannah frowned. She'd forgotten that Lillian knew all about her so-called sordid past.

"I know," Mike said. "But if you have any intentions of fixing me up with her, there's something you should know . . ."

Savannah's eyes opened wide. Omigod. What was he going to tell his mother? That he already had another girlfriend? Or worse, a secret marriage his mom knew nothing about? That rat! That bastard! That rat bastard!

She jerked open the door and heard Lillian gasp with surprise just before Mike drawled, "I'm gay."

Savannah froze in mid-righteous anger. She closed her eyes. Shook her head. Then started laughing. If there was one thing she knew after the last couple of hours, it was that Mike was into women. Really, *really* into women.

He was just toying with his mother and, from the look on her face, she knew she'd been busted.

Lillian cleared her throat and kept her gaze fixed on a spot behind Mike's left ear. "I apologize for that little misunderstanding," she said.

"Misunderstanding, my ass," Mike muttered. Then he left the doorway, walked over to Savannah, put his arm around her shoulders, and squeezed. "And I'm not really gay."

"Not that there's anything wrong with that," Savannah hastened to add, just in case Lillian were to think she was a homophobe.

Lillian cleared her throat again, her cheeks tinged bright pink as she was faced with the evidence that her son indeed preferred women. "Of course not," she agreed. "Nice to see you again, Savannah."

"By the way, how do you know she's not a crook?" Mike asked.

Lillian clapped a hand to her forehead. "Oh my goodness. I completely forgot. Savannah, your mom and oldest sister are here. They told me the whole story of how you got your identity stolen and got arrested on your wedding day and everything."

"Your wedding day?" Mike asked, raising his eyebrows.

"It's another of those long stories," Savannah answered. "The short version is, I got arrested at the altar and my fiancé didn't care to reschedule. It turns out that he did us both a big favor. I can't imagine being married to him now."

"I'm glad you're not," Mike said, and squeezed her tighter.

Savannah smiled up at him and thought, *I could just fall in love with you right now.*

Then she heard a commotion from the next room, which reminded her that she had company. "Could you please tell my family that I'll be right over?" she asked Lillian, who nodded and disappeared.

Savannah reached down to scoop up her underwear. The skirt she'd worn this morning was too dirty for her to even think about putting back on and the rest of her clothes were over in her room, so her mom and sister were just going to have to deal with seeing her half-naked.

Mike was already tugging a black T-shirt on over his head as Savannah pulled on her panties. "Want to borrow some sweatpants?" he offered.

"Thank you. Yes," she answered gratefully. It was bad enough that his mother knew they'd just had sex. Her mother didn't need to know, too.

When they were both dressed, they went next door. Mike grabbed Savannah's hand as they stepped inside her room, and she had to resist the urge to curl herself around him. She was forced to let go of him, though, when her mother got up off the bed and threw her arms around her youngest daughter's shoulders.

"Baby! I was so worried about you," her mother said.

Savannah hugged her mother back, surprised at how good it felt to be enfolded in her mom's embrace. "Why? How did you find out about what happened down in Key West?" she asked, the words muffled since her face was buried in her mother's soft chest.

Linda Taylor stepped back, holding Savannah at arm's length as if to get a good look at her.

Savannah was surprised to see tears in her mother's eyes and threw herself back into her arms. "Oh, Mom. Don't cry. It hasn't even been two weeks since I left Maple Rapids."

"But you're my baby girl. I've missed you. And I knew something had to be wrong when you asked to borrow money. Savannah's never borrowed money from us," Linda added, obviously not talking to her daughter. "Miranda and Belinda both treated their father and me like unlimited ATMs in college, but not Savannah. She's always insisted on doing everything by herself."

"Mom," Savannah protested, embarrassed, but also surprised that her mom thought of her as someone capable and independent.

"We weren't that bad," Miranda said as she patted her youngest sister on the back affectionately. "And what's this about Key West?"

"You don't know?" Savannah asked.

"Know what?" her mom said.

Savannah turned to look at Mike, her eyes pleading for his silence. He frowned as if to say she needn't have asked. "Nothing," she said, breathing a silent sigh of relief that her latest humiliation was, for the moment at least, still a secret.

Her mother finally released her and Savannah introduced everyone. She was surprised when, after half an hour of small talk, Mike suggested they go to dinner down at the Fat Cat. The day had seemed endless, but it was only seven o'clock.

And when dinner was over and they were back at the motel, when Savannah laughingly noted how snug she and Miranda and Mom would be all curled up in bed together, her mother shocked her by raising her eyebrows, nodding in Mike's direction, and whispering, "Why in the world would you sleep with your sister and me when you've got *that* waiting for you next door?"

What Does Your Handwriting Say About You?

Handwriting analysts will tell you that your handwriting says a lot about you. When writing on a nonlined sheet of paper, do your words slant toward the bottom of the page? Then we'll bet you're a pessimist. What about those loopy l's that look like they were written by a third-grade girl? You're a dreamer. So what does your handwriting reveal about you? Read on and see!

Write the phrase "i love you" on a sheet of blank paper. Now tell me:

a· Did you dot your i with a little heart?

b· Is your v pointed at the bottom or round?

c· Did you add an exclamation point at the end of the phrase, even though we didn't tell you to do so?

If you dotted your i with a heart, excuse us while we gag. You're just too twee, aren't you? Why don't you go bake cookies for your sick neighbor or something? If your v is pointed, you're harsh and unrelenting. It's a good thing you love you, because it's not likely many others do. If you added an exclamation point at the end of the phrase, you're daring and have an adventurous spirit. It's amazing what your handwriting reveals, isn't it?

{twenty-seven}

The next morning, Savannah rolled over on Mike's king-sized bed and buried her face in his pillow. It smelled like him, with faint traces of the chocolate-flavored body oil he'd let her rub all over him early that morning. Savannah smiled and stretched, wishing he hadn't had to leave an hour ago for his next flight. Funny, but after only one night together, she already missed him.

She wished she could lie here all day, wrapped in the glow of truly mind-blowing sex. But if yesterday's fiasco had taught her anything, it was that she wasn't cut out to ditch her responsibilities. She knew that calling in sick yesterday had been wrong and—great sex with Mike notwithstanding—it was still very likely that she'd lose her CPA designation if he was unable to prove that she had not intentionally gone for the cockpit door.

It had occurred to her yesterday, sitting in the cold dark interrogation room in Key West, that those three little letters meant more to her than she'd ever realized. And why not? She'd worked hard to get the work experience and knowledge needed to earn them.

And what she did, as mundane as it might seem, really helped people. Why had she felt that she needed something different to be happy? She wasn't such a bad person. She was good at her job, she had friends and a family that loved her. So what if she didn't own the most expensive shoes or stay out partying until all hours of the morning? Was that really going to make her a better, more interesting, or more exciting person?

No. All it did was to make her into someone she didn't like or respect. If she spent all her extra money on shoes and clothes, she wouldn't have anything left to make a nice home for herself. And she had hated borrowing money from her parents. As for partying all night, that just made it more difficult to get up in the morning and be productive or to give 100 percent to the job she was paid to do. Besides, it was pretty hard to make good friends—*real* friends—when you had to shout to be heard over the loud dance music and all you had in common was a drinking problem.

Savannah stared up at the ceiling in Mike's room, startled to discover that she'd ended up right back where she'd started . . . and even more surprised to feel a sense of peace when she realized that she'd been the right sort of person all along.

Although, it certainly would have been nice—not to mention, less expensive—to have learned this lesson back in Maple Rapids. The thing is, she probably wouldn't have come to this conclusion without this move. She would never have been able to truly reinvent herself at home. Without the freedom to be whoever she wanted to be, she never would have realized that who she wanted to be . . . was herself.

Savannah took a deep breath and slowly released it. Then, because she knew it was the right thing to do (and because she finally understood that doing the right thing was what made her feel good about herself), she swung her feet to the floor and got out of bed.

With her mom and Miranda planning to spend the day shopping, it was time Savannah went to work.

She arrived at the office forty-five minutes later, expecting to be the only one there. On the walk from the motel, Savannah had noticed all sorts of things she hadn't seen before: a brilliant spray of bougainvillea spilling over the wrought-iron fence of a well-maintained house on the corner; a tree with fuzzy red blooms and another with purple flowers, both looking as if they'd sprouted from the pages of a Dr. Seuss book; the playground that she passed, the children outside enjoying the eighty-degree weather without galoshes or mittens or winter jackets buttoned up to the neck. It was as though, overnight, her world had gone from black-and-white to full living color.

Savannah stood outside on the sidewalk for just a moment, feeling the warmth of the sun's rays on her bare arms, warming her back. She heard the steady tinkle of water from the fountain just up the street and the laughter of a woman as her dog barked at a passing butterfly.

She unlocked the office door with her key and went in, pulling the door closed behind her. As she'd expected, the place was deserted.

Savannah went to her desk and powered up her computer, wincing when she saw a terse e-mail waiting for her from her coworker Lucy.

"Thanks for calling in sick yesterday," the message read. "Your nine o'clock appointment got shuffled to me, and I spent an hour with her, just to find out after all that work that she couldn't get her refund because she was a no-show at an audit appointment earlier this year. Then I got stuck listening to her cry about her financial woes and how she's going to lose the house she inherited from her mother and how she's working two jobs to help feed her sister's kids and blah, blah, blah. Just what I *didn't* have time to deal with in addition to my regular workload."

Savannah reminded herself that she deserved her coworker's hostility for calling in sick so close to April 15. Vowing that it wouldn't happen again, Savannah quickly sent a reply thanking Lucy for filling in and offering to take on some of her files in return.

In the meantime, she needed to see what was up with Jane Smith. Savannah picked up the file that Lucy had dropped on her desk.

She looked through the forms and Lucy's handwritten notes from yesterday, and then found the notice from the IRS explaining why they were holding Jane Smith's refund.

Savannah decided to check their records to see if Jane had

used Refund City to prepare her taxes the year that was being audited. If so, the least Savannah could do would be to check the return to see if everything was in order. If it was, she would call the client and assure her she had nothing to fear and urge her to reschedule her appointment with the IRS as soon as possible. And if something was amiss, then Savannah would do her best to remedy the situation.

It was the least she could do.

She brought the current year's file with her to the filing system along the back wall of the office. Paper returns were filed according to the taxpayer's Social Security number, so Savannah looked at the SSN on the return Lucy had filled out and searched for a match from the previous year's files. When she didn't find anything, she decided to check their computer system to see if perhaps the documents had been filed incorrectly or, even worse, if the 1040 itself had been submitted with the wrong SSN on it.

She moved her mouse to take her computer out of sleep mode, then entered her user name and password. She did a search on taxpayer name and city and found the record in the computer for the return in question. Refund City *had* filed a return last year for Jane Smith. So then, where was the file?

Savannah cross-checked the SSN to make sure Lucy had written it down correctly. It was a match, so Savannah went back to the filing cabinet to see if the folder had simply been misfiled. She found it stuck to another folder, five spaces from where it should have been. This sort of thing wouldn't happen once all their records were in the computer system and were organized electronically.

Shaking her head, Savannah brought the return back to her desk and opened it up to take a look. Only, just as she went to open a blank 1040 to check the previous accountant's math, she noticed that a second record had popped up for a Jane Smith at 716 Sandpiper Lane in Naples—a Jane Smith with a different Social Security number than the woman who had come in to the office yesterday.

Hmm. That was odd.

Savannah wrote down the SSN of Jane Smith 2 and walked back to the filing cabinet to see if Refund City had prepared this other woman's tax returns. There wasn't a file for last year, but there were 1040s going back seven years on Jane 2, who appeared to be about twenty years older than Jane 1.

Thinking that perhaps the elder Jane Smith was her client's mother, Savannah put the files back in the filing cabinet and locked it, but didn't throw away the Post-it with Jane 2's SSN written on it. After she checked and double-checked the numbers on the younger Jane Smith's file, Savannah felt ready to give the woman a call. She experienced a brief moment of unease when she saw that Jane's return had been filed by Mary Coltrane, but since the numbers all added up, she told herself to stop worrying.

She dialed the number Jane Smith had given her on Friday when she'd called to make an appointment, drumming the eraser of her mechanical pencil on her desk as the phone rang once, twice, then three times.

The phone was finally answered by a harried-sounding woman who mumbled as though she were balancing the receiver between her ear and her shoulder as she talked.

"Yes, hello," Savannah said. "Can I speak to Jane Smith?"

"This is she," the woman answered.

Savannah glanced at the open file in front of her and, to make sure she had the right Jane Smith, said, "This is Savannah Taylor down at Refund City. I'm trying to reach the woman who came into our office yesterday, but I noticed that there are two Jane Smiths listed at this address. Are the last four digits of your Social Security number 3131?"

"Yes," the woman answered. "And the other Jane Smith was my mother, who passed away two years ago."

"I'm so sorry," Savannah said, cringing.

"Thank you. It's . . . it's been a difficult time," the younger Jane Smith admitted.

Savannah cleared her throat. She hated to just switch the topic to business, but she didn't know what she could possibly say that would ease the other woman's grief, so she decided to just move ahead with the reason for her call. "I understand you came in yesterday expecting to get a refund for last year but that there was some trouble with the IRS."

"Yes. I—" Savannah heard the sound of a chair being dragged across a tile floor and the whoosh of air as Jane sat down and sighed. "I worried that your system might be hooked in with the IRS, but I had to try. I really need that money. The taxes are due on Mama's house and I can barely squeeze enough out of what I make to buy food for my sister and her family. I don't know what I'm going to do."

Ms. Smith was not the first client Savannah had ever had who was experiencing financial difficulties. The truth was, it happened a lot. People got behind and decreased their with-holdings to try to make ends meet, hoping their lot would im-prove by the time their tax bill arrived and not knowing what to do when it didn't. Savannah's approach had always been to try to take the emotion out of the situation and just focus on the numbers. That's what served her clients best, not allowing them to wallow in their misery, but to give them a plan—a way out of their rut.

"I understand you weren't able to get your refund because you didn't appear at an appointment with the IRS auditor in Miami. Was there some reason you didn't call to reschedule?"

Savannah heard Jane sigh again. "They told me I was go-ing to owe another two thousand dollars. That their prelimi-nary report showed I should have paid a higher rate than I did. I guess I just . . . got scared. I can't owe the IRS *another* two thousand dollars. I barely make twenty-five thousand dollars a year, and that's with me working two jobs. How can I owe that much?"

Savannah frowned and looked down at the tax return on her desk. In the "wages, salaries, and tips" box, Mary Coltrane had entered, very plainly, $0.

"The 1040 form that I have in front of me shows that you didn't earn any regular income," Savannah said.

"Why do you have my return?" Jane asked. "Did the IRS give it to you? They shouldn't do that. Not without my consent."

"What do you mean? We're required to keep a copy of all the returns we prepare here at Refund City."

"But you didn't do my return last year. My mama always thought an accountant could get her a bigger refund, but once she was gone, I decided to do it myself. I thought I'd done fine until I got that audit notice back in January."

Savannah rubbed her forehead and squinted down at the folder on her desk. "But I'm telling you, I have a return right here in front of me with your Social Security number on it. It shows interest income of twenty thousand dollars, but no wages, salaries, or tips. With your standard deductions, that would put you in the lowest tax bracket. But if you had another twenty-five thousand dollars of income, you'd owe a higher effective rate on a portion of the additional income. That must be the problem—you can't file one return for your wages and another for your investments. All of your income has to be combined," Savannah explained patiently.

"Investments? What investments? I tell you, the only investment I got is my mama's house, which I'm about to lose if I don't come up with the thirty-five hundred dollars I need to pay the real estate taxes. I'm being pounded into the ground by all these taxes. Everywhere I turn, I gotta pay a sales tax or real estate tax or income tax or turn-left-at-the-light tax. It's got to end. I just can't pay it all." On the other end of the line, Jane started to sob.

"Look, Jane," Savannah said gently, "I'm going to help you figure this out. I know it seems hopeless right now, but it's not. We'll get to the bottom of this." She flipped through the file to see if there was a copy of the 1099 from the financial institution that had reported the interest income.

Ah, there it was. She checked the Social Security number from the 1099 against the 1040 to make sure they matched. They did, but none of this made sense. In order to earn this much interest, Jane would have to have nearly half a million dollars in this account. If that were the case, she certainly wouldn't be crying about a $3,500 tax bill.

"Are you sure you don't know about an account at the First Bank of Naples? Maybe your mother opened an account in your name before she died," Savannah suggested.

"She might could have, I suppose," Jane said, sniffling. "She worked cleaning houses every day since I was little. But we were always strapped for cash. Sometimes, she even had to borrow my baby-sitting money to pay the bills. I can't imagine she ever found any extra to save."

"I find it hard to believe that she wouldn't tell you about it. This account must have about four hundred thousand dollars in it," Savannah admitted, then jerked upright in her chair when a loud crash sounded in her ear. There was a rash of clattering and then Jane came back on the line.

"Four hundred thousand dollars?" Jane repeated.

"Well, that's just an estimate. The 1099 only shows how much interest was earned, not how much is in the account," Savannah said.

"Four hundred thousand dollars," Jane said again, as if she were in a trance.

Savannah was pretty sure she wasn't going to get much more information from Jane, so she took control of the conversation. "Okay, here's what we need to do. First, we'll meet at the bank at nine A.M. tomorrow and see if we can find out who opened the account. It could just be a bank error that we can take care of right away. Next, if you bring me a copy of the return you filed last year, I can review that after we're through at the bank. Then we'll call the IRS agent you were supposed to meet with, and we'll reschedule your appointment. I can come with you if you'd like. You'll see—we'll get this all worked out," she said.

"Yes. Things are looking better already," Jane agreed absently. Then she confirmed that she'd meet Savannah at nine o'clock tomorrow morning at the First Bank of Naples before she hung up the phone.

For some reason, Jane's comment about things looking better already made Savannah feel uneasy, like there was more to this than just a simple mix-up. And maybe it was just her imagination . . . but then again, Savannah thought as she stared down at Mary Coltrane's signature on the 1040 on her desk, maybe, just maybe, it wasn't.

Do You Have a Good Sense of Humor?

Aside from firm breasts and shiny hair, one of the most important things a man looks for in a woman is a good sense of humor. So when it's time to show those pearly whites, how well do you rate?

One of the pranksters in your office loves to play practical jokes on people. You mostly think he's funny, but sometimes he goes too far. One Monday morning the cute guy from Sales you've had your eye on for months just happens to be hanging around your cubicle when you come in. You don't realize he's been clued in that the joke's about to be on you until you smile and sit down and realize the Mr. Practical Joker has rigged an airhorn to your seat. After you make certain you haven't just suffered a heart attack from the surprise, you:

a· Screech, "I am going to kill that asshole!" and grab the sterling-silver letter opener you got for being with the company for five years to do the deed.

b· Mumble, "I don't think that was very funny," and then burst into tears and run to the ladies' room.

c· Put one hand to your chest and hold the other out for Mr. Cute Guy in Sales to take to help you up off the floor. Then you laugh and smile up at Mr. Sales and say, "I just love a good joke, don't you?"

continues on next page . . .

Maybe you A girls didn't read our introductory paragraph closely enough. Guys are not looking for women with good aim. They want women who can laugh at themselves. If you chose B, you need to stop taking things so seriously. So someone made you look silly for a minute? Was it the end of the world? Lighten up! Those of you who chose C know how to turn a situation to your advantage. Not only have you proved to Mr. Cute Salesguy that you have a sense of humor, you've created the perfect opportunity to flirt and let him know you're interested in him. Way to go!

{twenty-eight}

$\mathcal{S}$avannah rubbed her aching neck as she parked her car in front of the Sand Dunes Motel. The dark night enveloped her in its soft embrace, the warm air gently licking her skin. She wished that it were Mike's arms holding her, his tongue on her skin, but he'd left that morning with a long good-bye kiss and a regretful apology that he was scheduled for an overnight flight this evening and wouldn't be back to Naples until tomorrow morning. Since tomorrow was Monday, Savannah would be at work all day, so she wouldn't see him again until the evening. Although, now that she thought about it, she realized he hadn't said anything about seeing her again.

Now that they'd slept together, maybe he wouldn't want to see her again. Maybe—

"Okay, stop," Savannah admonished herself as she pushed open the driver's side door. This whole agonizing self-doubt thing had to end. Maybe things would work out with Mike and maybe they wouldn't. But never again would she let herself believe that if some guy dumped her, it meant there was something wrong with her. All it really meant was that they weren't right for each other. And better to know that before they were forever (well, these days *forever* was a relative term) joined in matrimony than to keep pretending, as she had with Todd, that things were great when they weren't.

She unlocked the courtyard door and stepped inside to find her mother, Miranda, and Christina all draped over lounge chairs near the edge of the pool. Her mother and Christina were chattering away while Miranda buried herself in what Savannah guessed was the latest issue of *Stylish* magazine.

"Hi, all," she said, flopping down in a chair as she squinted at the headlines to see if there were any good articles this month.

SEXY MOVES HE'LL GO WILD FOR

12 TIPS TO RELIEVE STRESS

HELP! MY BOYFRIEND'S CHEATING ON ME— WITH ANOTHER MAN!

GET FLAT ABS IN FIVE MINUTES

MAKEUP TRICKS YOU NEED NOW

FASHION TRENDS HOT OFF THE PARIS RUNWAY

NEW HAIRSTYLES FOR A NEW YOU!

COULD YOU BE A SUPERSTAR? TAKE OUR QUIZ AND FIND OUT!

As Savannah stared at the cover, she couldn't help but wonder if this was what she really wanted her life to be about: hair, makeup, clothes, boyfriend, sex? What about being a good friend? What about raising a family? Making a difference—no matter how small—in the world? Where was the advice on those things?

Yeah, okay, so looking the best you could and feeling good about yourself weren't bad things. But where was the balance? These magazines were all about getting a guy's attention and keeping it, and that didn't leave any room for other things in life that mattered just as much, if not more.

Only, it wasn't the magazine's fault that she had lost her perspective. It was *her* fault for thinking that all of life's answers could be found inside those glossy pages, when, instead, the real answers were in her own heart. No magazine could tell her how to be the person she wanted to be. She had to figure that out for herself.

Savannah sighed and closed her eyes for a moment. It was a shame that she'd had to risk the things that were most important to her to figure out who it was she really wanted to be.

"I'm through with this. Do you want it?" Miranda asked, pushing the magazine in Savannah's direction.

"I'll take it if you don't want it," Christina said. "I need something to read on the plane tomorrow."

"It's all yours," Savannah said, holding up her hands as if to ward off an evil spirit. She looked over at Christina as she reached out for the magazine, surprised to find the young woman dressed in a pair of baggy black shorts and a worn T-shirt. The comfortable clothes were a far cry from the coed's typical barely there attire.

"Where's everybody else?" Savannah asked.

"Oh, they went out," Christina said, but didn't elaborate.

Savannah leaned back in her chair and looked up at the black sky dotted with pinpricks of light. The moon smiled down at them, bathing them in its glow. It was so nice to be outside at this time of year without having to bundle up in twenty-three layers of clothing just to keep warm. Of course, she figured she'd be missing Michigan along about July, when temperatures in Naples climbed toward a hundred. But maybe not. It wasn't like she had to work outside in the full noonday heat. She had a convertible. And air-conditioning. Maybe she'd make it through the hot Florida summer just fine.

"Don't frown like that. You'll get wrinkles," she heard her mother say and looked over to see Christina scowling at the flat surface of the pool.

"What's wrong?" Savannah asked. "You seem upset. Are you sad because you and James are going back to different schools tomorrow?"

"No. I just—" Christina stopped and turned to Savannah with a look of frustration. "You know how it is when you think someone's a certain way and then you find out, once you really get to know them, that they're completely different? Completely *not* who you expected at all?"

Savannah laughed and reached out to squeeze Christina's hand. "Oh, boy, can I relate," she said, thinking about how Ashleigh had thrown Savannah's own bleeding body to the sharks back in Key West. Some glamorous and fun-loving friend *she* turned out to be.

"And it's like, I did all this stuff to change and I'm still not happy," Christina wailed.

Savannah leaned forward and grasped Christina's hand in her own. "Yes, but aren't you glad you know that about yourself now?" she asked. "If someone can't like you for who you are, that doesn't mean he's right and you're wrong. The only person who really has to like you is you."

"Yeah, well, it gets awfully lonely being your own best friend sometimes," Christina said with a sigh.

Savannah squeezed Christina's fingers sympathetically as they watched an ominous-looking black cloud come out of nowhere to blot out the moon. "I know it does," she said quietly. "But it's even lonelier when you try to be someone you're not and you find out that even *you* don't like the person you've become."

"I'm glad you finally realize that," her mother said softly, and Savannah smiled when she felt Mom's strong fingers clasp her own.

Her smile widened when Miranda rolled her eyes at them all and stood up. "All right, enough of this Dr. Phil crap. What do you say we order a pizza and whip up a batch of margaritas and have a little fun here? I'm on vacation."

Savannah was putting a second coat of mascara on her eyelashes the next morning when she heard a commotion outside Mike's motel room. She tried to ignore the shouts, figuring it was just the students up to one last silly prank. She was too interested in making certain she looked her best to care what they were up to. Mike had mentioned yesterday morning that his flight got in around eleven A.M., and she wasn't taking the chance that she might run into him on the street looking like she had down in Key West.

She jumped and poked the mascara wand right into her eye when someone started pounding on the door.

"I am so glad you all are leaving today," she mumbled, grabbing a piece of toilet paper to dab at her leaky eye.

She marched to the door of her room and flung it open, prepared to lay into whoever was standing there. She closed her mouth when she saw Christina draped over James's shoulder, fireman style, her face bright red.

"Put me down, you cretin!" Christina yelled, pounding James ineffectually on the back.

"What's going on here?" Savannah asked with a stern frown. As the oldest one there, she felt some responsibility to be the token authority figure.

"I'm sorry, Savannah. I tried to stop them, but James locked me in a closet downstairs and it took me an hour to get out." Christina pounded once more on James's back, but he still didn't put her down.

"James, put Christina down before I call the police and have you arrested for assault," Savannah said calmly in a voice that told him she wasn't kidding. Christina didn't act like this was some big joke. As a matter of fact, she looked as if she were about to cry.

James turned toward Savannah and then slowly lowered Christina's feet to the floor when he saw that she wasn't joking about calling the police.

"Now, what's going on here?" Savannah asked again.

Christina blinked and two fat tears slid down her cheeks. "They ruined your car," she said.

"What?" Savannah dropped the mascara tube she'd been holding in her left hand.

"It's just a joke," James said with a curl of his lip and a nonchalant shrug that made Savannah want to deck him.

She picked up her purse and pulled the door shut behind her. Christina trotted to catch up with her as she headed down the breezeway. She heard another door open and Miranda shouted, "What's going on?"

"I'm not sure," Savannah called back without slowing down.

"I'm so sorry," Christina kept saying, which just made the rock in Savannah's gut grow bigger with every step.

She flung open the door leading out into the parking lot and, staring at her car, stood rooted to the spot as if the hot pavement had melted the soles of her shoes. Slowly she turned to look at James, who was swaying from one bare foot to the other, trying not to laugh.

"I am going to sue you and your parents for every last cent of the damage," she said in a deadly voice that frightened even herself. "And if there is any justice in the world, I hope your folks make you take a job cleaning gas station toilets to pay them back."

Then she flipped open her cell phone, dialed 911, and told the operator who answered, "Yes, I'd like to report a case of vandalism. What? Do I know who did it? Yes. The little prick is standing right here."

Are You a Killer Date?

You make plans to meet someone, but you're running late, and when you arrive at your meeting place, he's already gone. You take this as a sign that:

a· You're not worth waiting for.

b· Someone more fun and interesting came along.

c· Who cares? If someone can't wait a few minutes for you, they obviously don't realize how great you are.

We hate to tell you A gals this, but if you think you're not worth waiting for, then you probably aren't. If you chose B, maybe you need to work a little harder to become more fun and interesting so your dates don't stand you up, eh? You C girls have the right attitude. If someone doesn't get how fabulous you are, why waste your time on them? If they'd waited around, they would have seen what a killer date you can be!

twenty-nine

I'm sorry," Christina said for what had to be the thousandth time that morning.

"Stop apologizing. It wasn't your fault. You tried to stop them," Savannah assured the younger woman as they watched the uniformed police officer finish taking statements from the other students who had helped James fill her car with water and release the baby alligators they'd bought at the pet store that morning.

She wondered if, one day, she'd look back on this incident and laugh.

After giving it some thought, she really doubted it.

Even worse, she was already half an hour late to meet Jane Smith down at the bank. She'd left a message on Jane's home number, and hoped Jane wouldn't think that she had stood her up. She'd also arranged for AAA to tow her car to a mechanic once animal control got through fishing out the baby alligators. Although her insurance would pay for the damage, James's complete lack of remorse really ticked her off. It was as if he didn't care one bit that his prank had damaged her car, that it had inconvenienced her, that she was going to have to come up with the money to pay her deductible, that if she hadn't carried full coverage she may have had to write her car off as a total loss, that—

And then it struck her. She was feeling all this righteous anger toward James for what he had done, and yet she had actually *admired* Vanna for her actions, which had hurt her even more. How could she have ever felt that way about the woman who had stolen her identity? Vanna was not the sort of person to emulate. She was selfish and uncaring and immature, and she should be locked up behind bars and reviled, not revered.

"Have you called AAA yet? What about animal control? And your insurance agent. I can take care of it if you want me to," Miranda offered, interrupting Savannah's thoughts.

Savannah knew this disaster wasn't her sister's fault, but Miranda's constant questioning of Savannah's abilities suddenly made her furious. She rounded on her sister and, through clenched teeth, said, "I can take care of it myself."

"But I'm happy to—" Miranda began.

"What part of 'I can do it myself' don't you understand?" Savannah asked, knowing she was close to shouting but unable to lower her voice. If she tried to rein it in, she was afraid the top of her head might blow off.

"You don't have to yell." Miranda got that hurt look on her face that Savannah knew all too well. This is what happened every time Savannah tried to declare her independence from her oldest sister. She was subjected to the dreaded guilt-trip routine.

"I'm not yelling!" Savannah yelled. "I'm saying that I can take care of this myself."

Miranda shook her head. "Of course you can. I know that. But I like doing things for you. You've never understood what it's like to be a big sister. When you were a baby, Mom needed me to help look out for you. It was my job to protect you and I always thought of you as my special baby sister. I never wanted to see you struggle or get hurt. I can't just turn that off now that we're adults."

Savannah stared at her sister, her mouth hanging open in shock. She felt a curious stinging in her eyes and blinked back the tears that had gathered there. "But you—" she began, then discovered that her mouth was too dry to talk so she had to swallow several times before starting over. "But you think I'm incompetent. That's why you're always trying to do things for me," she protested.

Miranda just looked at her without saying anything, her own eyes suspiciously moist.

Savannah rubbed her forehead with one hand. "I can't believe I've had things so wrong all my life," she said.

Miranda attempted to remain aloof, but her resolve didn't last longer than a couple of heartbeats once Savannah threw her arms around her and gave her a hug.

"It's okay. I love you anyway," Miranda said, hugging her back.

"I love you, too," Savannah said. They finally broke apart when the officer who had responded to the 911 call said, "I'm done here. You're free to go."

"Great. If only I had something to go in," Savannah muttered beneath her breath as the patrolman got in his car and headed out of the parking lot.

"You can borrow our rental car. Mom and I can see the Everglades some other time," Miranda offered. They had a tour scheduled that morning and would be late if they didn't get moving soon.

"Do you need a ride somewhere?" Christina asked, overhearing her. "I have to return my rental car to the airport by noon, but I'm happy to drive you wherever you need to go before then."

"Well, how am *I* going to get to the airport?" James asked from beside them.

Both Christina and Savannah glared at him with such venom that he backed up a step. Miranda joined in as a show of solidarity.

"According to your birth certificate, you're supposed to be an adult by now. You figure it out," Christina said. Then she turned her back on him, dismissing him quite effectively. "Let's go," she said to Savannah, pulling her car keys out of the pocket of her shorts. "I was loading my bags into the car this morning when I found out what James was up to. I'm more than ready to get out of here."

Savannah glanced at her watch. She was now thirty-five minutes late to the bank, and it would take at least another twenty minutes for a cab to get here. Not to mention that a taxi would cost money she didn't have. Besides, Christina *had* offered.

"Thank you," Savannah said. "I'd love a ride."

She hugged Miranda again and wished her a fun day with the gators, trying not to think of the ones still swimming in her car. Then she promised to be home early so they could have a nice dinner together, and Miranda left to round up their mom.

Christina popped open the locks to her Ford Taurus and they were soon speeding down Sunshine Parkway toward the First Bank of Naples, where Savannah hoped Jane would still be waiting.

"So," Savannah said as the silence in the car lengthened uncomfortably. "James turned out to be different than you expected, huh?"

"Pardon me?" Christina asked.

"Last night you said that you thought James was a certain way and then you found out that he's completely different," Savannah reminded her.

Christina laughed and turned one of the air conditioner vents so that it was aimed directly at her face. "I wasn't talking about James. He's exactly how I thought he would be."

"Oh." Savannah blinked several times as they turned left at the intersection of Sunshine Parkway and Main Street. "Then who did you mean?" she asked.

"Nathan," Christina answered. "I always thought he was sort of quiet and shy, the kind of guy who was happy being in the shadows. But yesterday we all went to the beach and were playing volleyball—James and I against Nathan and Liz—and James was being kind of a show-off. Well," she corrected with a derisive snort, "he was actually being an asshole. We were just playing for fun, but he kept spiking the ball right at Liz's face and laughing when he hit her. And Nathan stood up to him. He wasn't even a jerk about it. He just told James to knock it off with this quiet authority, like in the movies when the geeky guy goes and learns karate or something and he knows he can kick the bully's ass, but in the end he learns that just knowing that he can beat him is enough to make the bully back down. Yeah," Christina said, nodding with a faraway look in her eyes. "That's exactly how it was."

Savannah had to chew on the inside of her bottom lip to keep from smiling. Then she waved frantically and said, "Oops, here it is. On the left."

Christina went up to the next block and hung a U-turn at the intersection, then eased the Taurus into a parking spot near the entrance to the bank.

"I shouldn't be more than fifteen minutes," Savannah said, grabbing her purse and the folder containing Jane Smith's tax return from the previous year.

As Savannah stepped out of the car, Christina busied herself searching for a new radio station. Cold air enveloped Savannah as she stepped inside the quiet, single-story bank. Like churches, everyone seemed to speak in hushed tones inside banks, so Savannah—who had no idea what Jane looked like—felt awkward as she raised her voice and said, "Jane? Jane Smith? Are you here?"

The half-dozen people in line as well as the tellers and the loan officers at their desks all turned to look at her. Even the drive-through teller poked her head outside her cubbyhole to stare.

Savannah shrugged and tried to cool her face down by fanning herself with Jane's file. When no one stepped forward, Savannah guessed that Jane had gotten tired of waiting for her and left. But Savannah was curious about how much money was in the account under Jane's name, so she got in line behind a woman with a sticky-faced toddler and waited for her turn with a teller.

The line moved quickly and it didn't take long for Savannah to reach the front. When a young man with curly brown hair and an eyebrow ring waved her forward, Savannah smiled politely and set her file on the counter.

"I'd like to inquire about a balance on an account," she said.

"Do you have your bank card? You can get that information at the ATM in our lobby," the man said.

"I don't have a card. I just have the account number. And the Social Security number associated with the account."

"Do you have ID?" the man asked.

"I'm not trying to make a withdrawal," Savannah protested. "I just want to know how much money is in this account." She pushed the 1099 toward him, but he didn't even look down at it.

"I'm not authorized to give you that information," the man said. "You have to use your bank card. Or you can call customer support from that phone over there. They're available twenty-four/seven."

"Why can they give me the information but you can't?" Savannah asked. Banks these days were about as flexible as the IRS with their ten-day holds on checks and charges for coming inside the bank to talk to a live teller.

The man behind the counter said, "Those are the rules," as if he didn't understand them any more than she did.

Savannah let out a frustrated breath. Okay, fine. She'd just call in her request. She located the beige phone near the bank entrance that had a direct connection to customer service. When it rang, she pressed a sequence of numbers that was like unscrambling a strand of DNA, and was happy to finally reach the part where she was to enter the account number she wanted the information for. She carefully entered the number using the Touch-Tone phone and then pressed the pound sign as instructed.

After a few seconds of Muzak, she was surprised when a man came on the line and asked for the last four digits of the SSN on the account. His voice sounded familiar and Savannah's entire face squinched up in a disbelieving frown when she turned to see that the teller who had turned her away was on the other end of the line.

"You've got to be kidding," Savannah said.

"The SSN?" the teller repeated, giving her a little wave from across the lobby.

Savannah gave him the last four digits of Jane's Social Security number and rolled her eyes so far back in her head that she could almost see the roots of her hair. Talk about asinine rules.

"I'm sorry, ma'am, this account's been closed," the teller said.

"When?" Savannah asked.

"This morning," the teller answered.

"Well, how much was in it before it was closed? Wait—" Savannah interrupted before he had a chance to answer. "Let me rephrase that. What was the amount of the last transaction?"

"A withdrawal in the amount of four hundred forty-three thousand, two hundred and seventy dollars and sixty-two cents posted this morning at 9:03 A.M."

"Thank you," Savannah said absently as she hung up the phone and stared at the light blue fuzzy wallpaper on the wall in front of her. Without any identification to prove that she was Jane Smith, she knew she'd never get the teller to let her see the paperwork from when the account was opened. She wasn't even certain it would tell her anything, but she had a hunch that the handwriting on the bank's signature card would match that of the accountant who had signed the tax return in the folder she was holding.

She glanced at the file on the counter in front of her. The 1099 showed a post office box as the account holder's address, but the actual tax return had a street address that Savannah hoped would be Jane Smith's real address.

At least, she hoped that was the case. She wasn't about to believe that whoever had really opened that account in Jane's name had picked this morning of all mornings to come clean out the account. That meant Jane had taken the money . . . and Savannah knew that Jane would be in real danger once her theft was discovered.

She was certain of this because she'd spent hours at the office yesterday pulling Mary Coltrane's files and had uncovered some startling information. First, Mary Coltrane appeared to have two very different signatures. Second, a suspiciously disproportionate share of her clients had only interest income to declare to the IRS. Third, the 1099s for all of these interest-only clients were mailed to the same post office box in Naples.

And, fourth—and, perhaps most important—all of the 1099s had been sent to dead people.

If You Were a Heroine in a Movie, What Role Would You Play?

If you could play any part in a movie, what would it be?

a. The cute but shy girl next door.

b. The rowdy party girl who's irresistible to men.

c. The alluring private detective who solves the case and wins her man in the end.

Get out the kittens and kiddies for all of you who chose A! You're destined to play supporting roles for the rest of your lives. If you chose B, you're used to having lots of fun . . . maybe too much fun! You may need to remember to balance all that hard play with some hard work every once in a while. You C women have it all—brains, beauty, and the guts to tackle anything!

{thirty}

"Step on it," Savannah urged as the digital clock on the dashboard of Christina's rental car added another minute to the time. She leaned forward, straining at her seat belt as if that would make the car go faster and ignoring the warning taped to the back of the sun visor that told her to sit at least twelve inches away from the airbag. This was no time to heed practical advice.

"Okay," Christina said. "But do you mind telling me what's so urgent all of a sudden?"

"Someone's life could be in danger, and it's all my fault," Savannah answered. She didn't have time to elaborate as they pulled into the driveway at 716 Sandpiper Lane. Before Christina had a chance to put the car in park, Savannah was already out of the car, heading up the cracked walkway that led to the front door of the two-story white clapboard house. The paint was chipped in places, and the house had the same look as Savannah's fingernails five days after a manicure.

She pounded on the door after pressing the doorbell and not hearing any sound from inside the house.

When no one answered, Savannah leaned over to look through a crack in the curtains shading the front window. Inside was a living room, the floor and furniture strewn with boxes and toys and bolts of fabric. Savannah couldn't tell if the mess was there because the inhabitants of the house were just untidy or if there was something more nefarious afoot.

She turned to the front door and tried the knob, but it was locked. Well, this was no time to play by the rules. Jane was in real trouble here.

Savannah walked around the front of the house to the chain-link fence guarding the backyard. She was about to lift the latch when Christina appeared beside her and asked, "Do you think they have a dog?"

With a grimace, Savannah scanned what she could see of the lawn. It was brown and patchy in places, but there were no dog toys lying about, no holes in the dirt, and no "Beware of Dog" sign posted anywhere she could see. "I hope not," she said as she slowly pushed the gate open, the metal hinges squeaking in protest.

"Here, puppy," she called out, just in case there was a dog and it was inclined to look favorably on intruders who seemed friendly.

"Come on, doggie." Christina got into the spirit and whistled as they eased their way to the sliding glass doors at the back of the house.

Fortunately, the Smiths didn't appear to have a dog, so Savannah and Christina stepped up onto the concrete patio and pressed their noses to the sliders in the back, cupping their hands on the glass to see inside the darkened interior of the house.

After a few moments Christina asked, "What are we looking for?"

"I don't know," Savannah answered, worried that they were going to find a pair of women's legs lying somewhere they shouldn't be. In all the cop shows on TV, the murder scene almost always showed a pair of legs lying halfway out of a room or sticking out from behind a Dumpster. That's how you knew someone had been murdered.

Savannah tried to open the sliders, but they were locked. She was about to suggest that they break something when Christina pointed to an open window about four feet off the ground.

"We can get in there," she said.

"Good thinking," Savannah answered, dragging a plastic

lawn chair under the window. She got up on the chair and looked into what appeared to be a child's bedroom. The floor was littered with stuffed animals and toys, and there was a brightly colored coatrack attached to the wall with wooden letters that spelled out the name Dylan.

Savannah made quick work of pushing the screen out, throwing one leg over the window frame, and dropping down to the floor below. When Christina's face appeared in the window, Savannah asked, "Are you sure you want to do this? We could get in trouble."

"Sure. I've got two hours until my flight," Christina answered with a shrug.

They made their way through the house, jumping at the sound of every creaking board or scuffling of birds up on the roof. Once, when a tray of ice cubes dropped into the tub below the icemaker in the freezer, they both screamed and leaped into each other's arms.

But they weren't accosted by any madmen hiding under the beds or body parts lying anywhere they shouldn't be. Instead, after a thorough search of the entire house, the only thing they'd found of interest was a sealed note propped up by the telephone in the kitchen with the name Roni written on the front in green ink. Next to the phone was a framed photo of two dark-skinned women with the most beautiful eyes Savannah had ever seen.

"I wonder if that's Jane and her sister," she said, pointing to the photo with the index finger of her right hand.

She was running out of ideas, so she tapped the note on the edge of the counter and held it up to the light, but she couldn't read any of the words written on the paper inside.

"Ah, to hell with it," she cursed, slipping her thumb under the seal and ripping the envelope open.

"What does it say?" Christina asked eagerly, caught up in the excitement.

Savannah quickly scanned the message and sighed, handing it to Christina so she could read it for herself. "At least she was smart enough to not tell her sister where she was going," she said.

Christina took the note while Savannah sat down heavily on a stool in the kitchen, trying to think about what to do next.

The police would think she was nuts if she called them and told them that Jane's life was in danger. She had nothing—no proof that the money Jane had taken didn't belong to her, no idea where Jane might go, no nothing.

"'Dear Roni,'" Christina read aloud, as if Savannah hadn't just read the letter for herself. "'Something happened and things are going to be so much better for us all now, but I've got to leave town. I'll call you tonight when I get to where I'm going. Hug Dylan for me and tell him Auntie Jane is going to miss him. I love you. Jane.'" Christina put the note down on the counter. "You're right," she said glumly. "That's no help at all."

"How can we find her?" Savannah asked, rubbing her temples with her index fingers as she urged her brain to think.

What would she do if she were in Jane's situation? Savannah closed her eyes. Jane was running away to protect her sister, that much was clear. But where would she go? And how would she get there? A car would be the easiest way to go and the least traceable, but it wouldn't get her far away very quickly. Plus, during their search of the house, Savannah had noticed a car in the garage. She didn't think it was likely that Jane had an extra one, since she probably would have sold it for cash before now if she had.

No, the most likely scenario was that Jane had left the car here for her sister to use or sell and had taken a cab to the airport or train station.

But which cab company would she have called? There had to be at least two dozen here in town, and—

Savannah snapped her fingers, opened her eyes, and grabbed the cordless phone off its charger. Then she hit Redial and waited impatiently for it to start ringing.

"Blue-top Cab," a bored-sounding man on the other end of the line answered on the second ring.

Savannah jumped off the stool and nearly screamed in the man's ear when her hunch proved correct. "Yes," she answered, trying to keep her voice calm. "My name is Roni Smith and I live at 716 Sandpiper Lane. I called earlier to arrange for a taxi to come pick up my sister, and I wanted to make sure your driver arrived on time."

The man clicked a few keys on a keyboard and made Savannah's pulse race when he said, "The cab got there at nine forty-seven."

"Great," Savannah said, reaching out to squeeze Christina's arm as she asked her final question. "And did they get to the airport okay?"

"My driver just dropped her off," the dispatcher assured her.

Savannah thanked the man and hung up, a wide grin slowly spreading across her face. "Come on. We've got to get to the airport," she said.

As Christina followed her out the front door, her car keys jiggling in her hand, she said, "Wow, you're really good at that."

Savannah's chest puffed up with pride. What could she say? Everyone liked a little praise now and then. "Which part do you mean?" she asked. "The fast thinking? The creative problem solving?"

"No," Christina said as she closed the door behind her. "I meant the lying."

Do You Know How to Fend Off an Attacker?

Sorry to turn serious on you, girls, but we know that life isn't always about wearing the right lipstick or knowing the hottest new trend in shoes. Yes, sometimes, life can be—gasp!—downright ugly. Last month we asked readers to tell us their worst fear. Not surprisingly, since most of you are women, your Number 1 fear was being attacked from behind. So would you know what to do if it happened to you? Take our quiz and find out!

You're walking to your car when you hear footsteps behind you. You've done everything right—your hands are free and you have your keys out and ready—but none of that seems to matter when a man grabs you. What do you do?

a· Stomp with all your might on your assailant's instep.

b· Scream "Fire!" as loud as you can.

c· All of the above.

There are two approaches that might work here. First, try to get away from your attacker by stomping on his instep. If that doesn't work, use your keys to jab at his eyes or neck. And, of course, the testicles are always the best place to launch a counterattack if possible. Second, to bring help onto the scene, try screaming "Fire!" That's much more effective than yelling for help because, oftentimes, people don't want to get involved with something that might endanger themselves. However, everyone loves a fire, so by alerting them that there's a good show to be had, anyone within earshot will come running. C is definitely your best answer!

{thirty-one}

"Come on, pick up. Pick up," Savannah urged into the phone. Mike's plane was scheduled to land in Naples at 10:42 and, according to the clock on the dashboard of the Taurus, it was now 10:47, but her call rolled directly into voice mail, so Savannah assumed he still had his phone turned off.

"Mike, it's Savannah," she said after the beep. "I don't have a lot of time to explain, but I need your help. There's a woman named Jane Smith and I think she's in real danger. She took some money that isn't hers and booked herself on a flight out of Baxstrom airport. I don't know where she's going, but she's there now and I've got to stop her. Christina and I are in the rental return lot now and we're going in to look for Jane. If you get this message . . . Well, I don't know what you can do without any evidence, but I sure could use your help."

Savannah ended the call and stepped out of the car to join Christina in the parking lot just across the street from the entrance to the airport. Unlike the big airports like Tampa International that had multilevel garages, this airport had one level of open-air parking a short distance from the terminal. Savannah guessed that Jane was using this small airport as her jumping-off point to Miami or Tampa, where she could board a flight to anywhere in the world.

While Christina struggled to strap on a heavy-looking

backpack, Savannah pulled the younger woman's duffel bag out of the trunk and shook her head with amazement at all the stuff Christina had loaded onto her back. There was a bottle of water in one pouch of her backpack and a bag of pretzels in another. The magazine Miranda had given her last night was rolled up, cover side out, in another pocket. Savannah briefly wondered why students these days lugged so much stuff around like pack mules. By the time they reached forty, they'd all have compressed vertebrae and be two inches shorter than they were now. Hmm. If she were still looking for a different career, she ought to think about chiropractics. In two decades she'd be rich.

Once Christina had loaded up, she and Savannah raced across the parking lot and into the terminal building. There were sitting areas near the entrances with television monitors mounted about eight feet above the ground. Savannah studied the one nearest them for a moment, trying to figure out which flight Jane might be on.

"She's probably on the earliest one," Savannah said aloud. That's what she'd do if she thought someone was after her. She'd book herself on the first flight out of Naples and then lose herself in the crowds at one of the bigger airports. And while in Naples, where there were no hordes of people to hide in, she'd hang out in the one place no one would bother her— the ladies' room.

"I have my boarding pass for my flight, but how are *you* going to get through security?" Christina asked.

Savannah frowned. Huh. Good question. Then she held up one finger as a thought occurred to her. "Wait a second," she said, rummaging through her purse and pulling out a slip of paper that was stuck on the bottom. "I have my boarding pass from the flight to Key West on Saturday. Do you have a black pen? I'm going to change the dates."

Christina turned her back to Savannah and craned her neck to look over her shoulder. "There should be one in that bottom pocket."

Savannah unzipped the pocket Christina had indicated. She pulled out a box of raisins, three yellow highlighters, a ruler, a chain of safety pins, a handful of Band-Aids, a mini-office kit with scissors, a stapler, and tape, and a lip gloss.

"You're a girl after my own heart," Savannah said, impressed, as she dug in for a second round. This time she found what she was looking for—a plain black ballpoint pen. She took the pen and her used boarding pass over to an empty spot on the Skyway Airlines counter and tried not to wonder what the repercussions of being caught tampering with an official federal document might be. Would this fall under the jurisdiction of the FAA? Would Mike be the one who had to arrest her? Savannah cringed at the thought of Mike tossing her in jail. Her fantasies about Mike and handcuffs did not include a cold dark cell or iron bars.

When she was finished, she held the boarding pass up to the light and studied it. There was no way it would stand up to intense scrutiny, but it was the best she could do on such short notice.

"Come on, let's go see if we can find Jane," she said.

As they headed toward security, Savannah took a deep breath and reminded herself that she had to stay calm if she wanted to save Jane. She had a feeling that the person who had put that money in the bank in the first place would be relentless about tracking the person who had taken it. She also had a feeling that the accounts she'd discovered yesterday were only the tip of the iceberg—which meant that the mastermind behind this plan had millions of dollars at her disposal, millions of dollars that could be used to hack into airline records or bribe a low-paid ticket agent to find out where Jane's journey was going to end. Jane had no way of knowing that the money she'd taken was just a tiny slice of the pie; a tiny slice that someone might stop at nothing—not even murder—to get back.

"How are you today?" the security officer checking boarding passes asked as Savannah and Christina approached the checkpoint.

Savannah forced her mind to become a blank. She *had* to make it through security. Jane's life depended on it.

"We're great," she answered cheerfully. "It was my cousin's spring break, so I flew up from Key West to meet her here in Naples. This is such a lovely town. We had a great time. Didn't we Christy?"

Christina turned the full measure of her charm on the

agent. "Oh, yes. I love it here. When I get out of school, I'm thinking of moving here," she gushed.

"Well, you two gals have nice flights home," the agent said, waving them through.

Savannah let out the breath she'd been holding. "Great job," she whispered as they put Christina's bags and her purse onto the conveyor belt at security, and then took off their shoes and pretty much everything but their underwear and loaded it on, too.

Something in Christina's clothes made the metal detector beep, so Savannah told her, "There's a flight leaving out of Gate 16 at ten fifty-seven. I'll meet you there after you get wanded."

Christina nodded and sat down to wait for a female agent to come and do the full-body wand-and-grope routine, while Savannah headed off down the terminal to find Jane. Her high heels clicked on the linoleum floor, and Savannah wished she'd opted for flats today, but she'd actually found that she liked at least some pieces of her new wardrobe. She wore her Kate Spade knockoffs with a short red skirt, black tights, and a lightweight black sweater that would have been perfect for the air-conditioned office. Now, however, it was making her sweat.

Boarding had just begun when Savannah reached Gate 16. She hurriedly scanned the crowd milling about waiting for their rows to be called, but didn't see any sign of Jane. "Hurry, hurry," she urged silently to Christina, watching the terminal for any sign of the younger woman. There was another flight leaving in ten minutes out of Gate 24 and it would probably begin boarding shortly. She couldn't stand here and watch to see if Jane came out of the ladies' room just in time to get on the flight at Gate 16 and also check out Gate 24, so she figured she'd just have to check the bathroom and then move on down to Gate 24.

She dashed into the ladies' room, bending over to peer under the stall doors for the telltale sign of feet. One stall was occupied, so Savannah turned and pretended to wash her hands until she heard the toilet flush. When the woman emerged from the stall a few moments later, Savannah let out a disappointed breath. Dang. It wasn't Jane.

She grabbed a paper towel and dried her hands, then ran back out into the terminal. There was still no sign of Christina, so she hurried to Gate 24 alone. As she approached the gate, the tiny hairs on the back of her neck started to prickle. She slowed her steps, warily searching the boarding area for whatever threat her body had subconsciously picked up on.

Then, from behind her, she felt something cold and hard being poked into her back. A strong hand grabbed her upper arm. "You know, you really should learn to mind your own business," a man whispered into her ear as his fingers dug painfully into her arm.

Savannah opened her mouth to scream, but clamped it shut again when the man laughed and said, "Do it and your little friend Miss Janie dies."

"I don't even know her," Savannah said, turning her head to get a look at her captor. He towered over her own five-foot-four-inch frame, and the dark look on his face was menacing, as though he would have been happier to kill her than to let her go.

"Then go ahead and scream," he said with a mocking sneer.

Savannah ground her teeth together. Bastard. How did he know she wouldn't do just that?

Of course, she didn't scream. Jane was in this mess because of the information Savannah had given her. She felt responsible for getting Jane into trouble, and it was up to her to help get her out.

Her cell phone rang just then and Savannah's heart leaped. *Please, let it be Mike,* she prayed, reaching for her purse.

The man behind her jammed what she assumed was the barrel of a gun into her kidneys. "Answer it and die," he said.

"Aren't you being a little melodramatic?" Savannah asked. Odd, but the fear she should be feeling had been replaced by a sense of bravado that Savannah would never have thought herself capable of.

"Just try me," the man muttered, then pushed her forward and said, "Move."

They started walking back toward security, Savannah dragging her feet while she tried to formulate a plan. When she saw Christina coming toward her, her mind raced. She had to think of some way to enlist Christina's aid without alerting her captor. The last thing she wanted was to get Christina harmed, too.

"Savannah? What's going on?" Christina asked as they got within shouting distance.

"I've got two more men watching us," the man behind her growled. "You tip her off and we'll nab her, too."

"Yeah, I figured as much," Savannah muttered. She had no way to know if he was bluffing about having backup, but she couldn't take the chance that he was telling the truth. "Hey, Christina," she called as the younger woman approached. "This is Adam, a friend of mine from work. He's going to help me find Jane, so you can go. I don't want you to miss your flight or anything. Thank you so much for your *help*." She grinned with a faux-cheerfulness that made her molars ache and swallowed a grunt of pain when the guy behind her jabbed her again with his gun. She guessed that he had noticed her emphasis on the word *help* . . .

"Hi," he said, raising his free hand just above Savannah's shoulder.

"Hi," Christina said, looking confused. "Are you sure you don't need me? I've got another half hour before my flight boards."

"No, no. You just go back and visit with your friends," Savannah said. "I'm sure you and Mike have a lot to catch up on."

"Mike?" Christina asked. "Don't you mean James?"

From the corner of her eye, Savannah could see the suspicious way the man's eyes narrowed and figured she'd better cover her intentional mistake. She laughed gaily. "Oh, yes. Sorry. I meant James. You go on and have a good flight home now. It was great meeting you." So as not to alarm her captor, she slowly reached out to give Christina a hug. Her arms bumped into the bulging backpack Christina wore on her back and she heard a faint rustling sound when her hand brushed over the magazine in the side pocket.

Suddenly her eyes widened. The magazine. Yes. That was it. She pulled the latest issue of *Stylish* out of Christina's backpack, and it unrolled in her grasp.

She backed up a step, bumping right back into the gun.

"Hey, do you mind if I take this back? I forgot that there's a quiz in here that I wanted to take."

Christina frowned, her nose wrinkling at Savannah's odd behavior.

Savannah pointed to one of the headlines on the front cover. "It's this one," she said, watching as realization dawned in Christina's eyes. When the man behind her leaned over to see what she was pointing at, Savannah's finger slipped from "HELP! My Boyfriend's Cheating on Me—With Another Man!" to "Could You be a Superstar? Take Our Quiz and Find Out!"

"Well, we'd better get going," the man prodded.

Savannah nodded. "Yeah, okay. Bye, Christina." She waved as her captor frog-marched her down the terminal, hoping that Christina would take her earlier hint and try to find Mike. She was surprised when they turned right before reaching security. She had assumed the man was going to take her out of the airport. Instead, they walked down a quiet hallway, still inside the secured area of the terminal.

"Where are we going?" she asked.

The man ignored her and kept walking.

Savannah looked outside the floor-to-ceiling windows and saw what appeared to be small, private planes sitting out on the tarmac. Uh-oh. If they got her on a plane, they could disappear anywhere and no one would ever find her.

She licked her lips and grasped the magazine tighter, wishing that she'd taken a "What to Do If You Ever Get Kidnapped" quiz instead of ones about sex and beauty.

The man came to the end of the hallway and entered a code on a keypad next to a door that read "Warning. Do Not Open. Alarms Will Sound." She heard a clicking sound and the man pushed the door open. Unfortunately, an alarm did *not* sound.

Savannah was slapped full in the face with a blast of hot, humid air as she stepped out onto a metal grate twenty feet above the ground. Jet engines roared and baggage carts buzzed around the terminal, driven by men in blue coveralls with orange headphones covering their ears.

The man behind her nudged her toward a flight of metal stairs leading down to the tarmac. If she screamed now, she doubted anyone would hear her. Besides, Jane was still in danger, and Savannah couldn't just leave her to fend for herself. So she walked down the rickety stairs, doing her best not to get her heels stuck in the grating.

Once they reached the ground, the man shoved her in the direction of a medium-sized Learjet that had a set of movable steps next to it, leading up to the cabin.

Savannah took a deep breath and marched forward, straightening her shoulders as she went.

This is it, Savannah thought as she put her hand on the cool metal railing and began her ascent. Time for the final showdown with her arch enemy.

She knew that only one of them could triumph. Savannah gritted her teeth and took another step upward, toward the battle of her life.

And as she stepped inside the plane, her feet sinking into the plush pile carpeting beneath her feet, Savannah fleetingly wished she had a more potent weapon than the fashion magazine she clutched tightly. But suddenly she realized that she already had all she needed to wage this war. She didn't need a complete life makeover or some dark, mysterious stranger to swoop in and fix what was wrong. She was perfectly capable of handling her own problems by herself.

Slowly she lowered herself into a beige upholstered chair and crossed her legs, setting the magazine down on a small round table to her left. Then she smiled at the woman sitting across from her on a matching sofa, her own green eyes meeting those of her alter ego as she said, "Well, hello, Ashleigh. Or"—she paused for effect, then continued—"should I say Mary? Or Savannah? Or . . . hmm, let's see. Who, exactly, might you be today?"

Are You Worth the Trouble?

Let's be honest, there are times when we're high maintenance—when we cry for no reason, when we overdraw our bank accounts, when we swear we saw a mouse run into the closet and can't sleep until you (we apologize in advance to those of you who are squeamish) bring its tiny little head to us on a platter. But if you're worth it, your guy will comfort you, give you money, and, yes, even conquer rodents for you. So how do you know if you're worth the trouble? Take our quiz, of course!

Your guy works in airport security, and you just made the teensy, tiny mistake of making what you thought was just a harmless joke about having a bomb hidden in your underwire bra. When your fella finds out, he:

a· Swears he doesn't know you.

b· Tells his fellow officers that he always suspected you were a terrorist.

c· Takes your bra off himself and runs it through the X-ray machine to prove that you were just kidding.

If your answer was A, your guy definitely does not think that you're worth the trouble. Now it's up to you to figure out why you think that is—and whether you should stay with someone who thinks so poorly of you. You B gals are even lower on the "not worth it" scale. You need to dump this guy and consider yourself well rid of the creep! If you chose C, you'd better hang on to your man. He's willing to risk his job for you, and that tells us that he believes you're worth every ounce of trouble that comes his way.

{thirty-two}

The phone to Mike's left started to ring as he watched Ashleigh Van Dyke lean forward and drop something in Savannah's drink.

"I knew it!" he said triumphantly as he paused the security tape, picked up the phone, and identified himself.

"This is John Harrison with the FBI," a man on the other end of the line said. "We're working a money-laundering case, and our sweepers just discovered that a critical person of interest in the case has booked a ticket on Skyway Airlines flight 642 to Tampa leaving Naples at 11:07 this morning. We need to stop this woman from leaving town. We believe she may be carrying a significant amount of cash and that her life could be in danger."

Mike was already pulling up the passenger manifest for the flight in question, which, according to the flight schedule on another screen, was in the process of boarding out of Gate 24. He leaned over to switch the security system to focus on the boarding area and asked, "What's the subject's name?"

"Jane Smith. I'm faxing you a photo of her right now."

The fax machine beside him in the "war room" of the Baxstrom Airport security office began to whirr as Mike searched the passenger records for the flight. "Looks like she checked in at the main ticketing counter at 10:19 and got her boarding pass, but she hasn't yet boarded the plane," Mike said.

"Good. We need to make sure she doesn't get on that flight. The people she's up against have serious ties to the criminal world, and according to the information we were provided with yesterday from our main source on the case, they're very well funded. Ms. Smith doesn't realize it, but she needs protection, and she needs it now. I've just sent one of our local guys out to watch her family."

Mike picked up the fax that had just finished printing and looked at the photo of the subject—a mid-thirties African American woman with almond-shaped eyes. He looked back to the screen showing the boarding gate, but didn't see anyone milling around who matched the woman in the photograph. Since she hadn't boarded yet, Mike figured she was most likely hiding out in the gift shop or the lavatory until the last minute, although he could have told her she would have been safer had she already gotten onboard. Of course, there was another alternative. While people coming into the terminal could be tracked according to when and where they'd received their boarding passes, there was no guarantee that Ms. Smith hadn't been intercepted somewhere between the ticketing counter and the main terminal.

He tapped a few keys on the keyboard of another computer and thanked God for technology as the security video behind the ticketing counter at Skyway Airlines started replaying from 10:18 A.M. He put the video on fast-forward and watched Ms. Smith get her boarding pass and head toward security. Mike punched in the sequence of commands to change to the next camera. Jane Smith looked around nervously as she approached the security agent and handed him her ID and boarding pass. The man waved her through, and Jane passed through baggage screening without incident.

After going through the metal detector and retrieving her carry-on items, Jane headed for the gift shop just inside the terminal entrance. The camera inside the gift shop captured her flipping through a stack of magazines and looking at the back cover copy of several books. She kept her back to the entrance and her head down, as if she had a feeling she was being followed. Mike flipped to the camera out in the terminal and scanned the video for anything suspicious, but didn't see anyone who looked out of place.

He toggled back to the gift shop footage and watched as Jane purchased two books and a magazine. She paused and looked right at the camera as she turned back toward the terminal, and Mike could easily read the apprehension in her eyes.

"I've picked her up on the security tape," Mike said to Agent Harrison as he explained what he'd seen so far. The video continued to roll as Jane made her way to the gate, seating herself in the first row of seats next to the boarding door. She opened her magazine and pretended to read, but as the elapsed time on the tape ran to seven minutes, she didn't turn the page even once.

The boarding area began to fill up, but no one sat next to Jane, who had put her purse and coat on the seat next to her. That is, until a brawny man of about six feet two carrying a leather jacket swooped Jane's belongings off the chair and sat down. Mike saw Jane's eyes widen and the tiny braids on her head began to shake. Whatever the man said had obviously frightened her.

"Wait a minute, I've got something," Mike told Agent Harrison as he paused the video at a frame that clearly showed the man's face. He mouse-clicked on the picture and sent it to the fax machine to see if Agent Harrison could identify the man in question. Then he clicked Play again and watched as Jane and the man stood up, the man standing slightly behind and to the left of Jane. "I think he got her out of the boarding area by holding a weapon on her. Who knows how he got it through security," Mike added with a frustrated sigh. It seemed as though no matter how sophisticated they got with their detection devices, determined criminals always found a way to bypass the system.

"This isn't good," Agent Harrison said over the sound of crinkling paper.

"What?" Mike asked.

"This guy is Roman Sweeney. He's been on the DEA's watch list for years, but they've never had enough evidence to arrest him. He came to my attention yesterday, when my source in Naples led us to him through a coworker of hers who appears to be helping this guy launder his drug money. His girlfriend is an accountant and she's got this sweet scheme going. She sets up bank accounts in the names of former clients of her accounting firm who have died and makes frequent deposits into each account. She keeps the deposits under ten thousand dollars each, so the activity doesn't come under federal scrutiny. Then she files tax returns on the interest income and slowly drains the accounts of all the cash that's in them by investing in legitimate businesses her boyfriend owns.

"By this time, the money is as clean as the driven snow. Only she made a mistake with this Jane Smith and accidentally opened a savings account using the Social Security number of a dead woman's daughter, who is still very much alive. That's how our source figured out what was going on. I've got to hand it to her, she was really thinking outside the box on this one. I never would have put this all together without her help."

Mike was only half-listening to Agent Harrison as he tracked the progress of Jane Smith and Roman Sweeney as they headed back toward security. He expected Sweeney to guide her out of the airport, and was surprised when, instead, they turned toward the smaller gates set up for the many private and corporate jets that flew in and out of Baxstrom airport.

"Only, I'm a little worried about this source of mine," Agent Harrison continued. "I've been trying to reach her ever since we got the alert that Miss Smith was on her way out of town, but she's not answering her cell phone. I've got an agent down there looking for her, and I hope she turns up soon."

Mike frowned as Agent Harrison mentioned cell phones and looked down at his own phone, clipped to his belt. He'd been so caught up with his mission to prove that Savannah had been drugged before her flight to Key West that he'd completely forgotten to turn his own cell back on after getting off the flight from Atlanta this morning. He reached down and turned it on, not expecting to see the red light indicating that he had messages waiting. He checked his incoming-call log to see who had called. When Savannah's number was displayed, Mike felt the first stirrings of unease. He didn't know why he felt his stomach clench—it wasn't like he had any reason to suspect that Savannah was mixed up in all of this. She'd probably just called to say hello or to see if he wanted to go to lunch today.

So then why was his heart pounding against his rib cage?

He pushed the Speaker button on his cell and retrieved his messages while, at the same time, asking the question he almost dreaded to ask. "This source of yours . . ." He paused and cleared his throat as the voice-mail recording told him he had one new message. "Please tell me it's not Savannah Taylor," he continued.

Then he heard her voice. She sounded rushed and excited and frightened all at once as she said, "Mike, it's Savannah. I don't have a lot of time to explain, but I need your help. There's a woman named Jane Smith and I think she's in real danger. She took some money that isn't hers and booked herself on a flight out of Naples. I don't know where she's going, but she's at the airport now and I've got to stop her. Christina and I are in the rental return lot now and we're going in to look for Jane. If you get this message . . . Well, I don't know what you can do without any evidence, but I sure could use your help."

"Yes, that's her. How did you know?" Agent Harrison asked.

Mike hurriedly flipped the security video back to Gate 24 and fast-forwarded it about twenty minutes ahead of when Jane Smith had been abducted. Then he saw exactly what he had dreaded he was going to see—Savannah with her back to the camera, a large man coming up behind her, and then the scared but determined look on her face as she nodded and preceded Roman Sweeney down the deserted hallway that Jane had traveled twenty minutes before.

Sweeney opened a door at the end of the hallway, and Mike watched as Savannah straightened her shoulders and stepped outside. As the drug dealer went to follow her, he dropped his leather coat and for a brief second Mike saw sunlight glinting off the barrel of a gun.

Mike didn't waste time explaining to Agent Harrison what was going on. Instead, he dropped the phone, pressed his arm against his side to feel the comforting jab of his pistol in its holster, and raced out of the security office, stopping dead in his tracks when he barreled into the armed man on the other side of the door.

"Why did she give me that hint about Mike?" Christina muttered to herself as she paced the floor at her boarding gate. It was obvious that Savannah wanted her to help, but what was she supposed to do? And what did the motel manager have to do with it?

Christina had already called the motel, but she'd just gotten a recording. She didn't know what else to do. She'd tried telling the ticket agent at the gate that something was wrong, but the woman had just looked at her as if she were nuts.

"Hey, Christina. I missed you last night," Nathan said from behind her, startling her so much that she had to swallow a surprised scream as she spun around.

As her best friend's brother's best friend, Christina had known Nathan for more than half her life, but as she looked at him in the airport that day, it was as if she were seeing him for the very first time. Gone was the skinny boy who had dipped her training bra in water and put it in the freezer when she was twelve. In his place was a man with intelligent brown eyes and broad shoulders and a sense of maturity that was utterly lacking in his best friend.

"I heard about what James did to Savannah's car this morning. I'm really sorry. If I'd known—"

Christina grabbed Nathan's arm urgently and interrupted. "Can we talk about that later? I really need some help. Savannah's in trouble and I don't know what to do. She sort of hinted that I should go to Mike for help, but what can he do? He's just the manager of a motel."

Nathan's eyes crinkled as he smiled down at her. "No, he's not. He's a federal air marshal. You know, like Wesley Snipes in *Passenger 57*."

Christina inhaled sharply. "Omigod. That's why she wanted me to find him. Do you think he's here now?" she asked, tugging on Nathan's arm. She didn't wait for an answer as she mentally thwacked herself upside the head. Airport security. Of course. Why hadn't she thought of that before?

She took off running down the terminal, uncaring that she'd left her backpack sitting on the floor outside the gate.

"Where are you going?" Nathan called.

"To get help," Christina called back, without slowing down. She didn't take time to second-guess her plan as she headed straight toward security. She stopped when she was about twenty feet from the nearest TSA agent and put her hand under her shirt.

"I've got a gun!" she shouted.

The startled security agent put a hand to her own weapon, and Christina prayed that she wouldn't get herself shot as she turned and started running down the hallway where Savannah had disappeared with the guy who had said he was her coworker.

She didn't even see the man step out of a doorway to her right, but she sure felt him as he tackled her, his heavy body slamming her to the ground. Her chin hit the linoleum, and she tasted blood as she lay there, unable to move. She could feel the firm weight of a gun pressing into her side as the man grabbed for her hands.

"Hold it right there," he said. "You're under arrest."

Christina felt like sobbing. "No, you don't understand. I need you to follow me," she said frantically.

"Stop right there," Christina heard a woman say as Nathan's tennis shoes appeared in her line of vision.

"We're looking for Mike Bryson," Nathan pleaded.

The man who had tackled Christina slipped a pair of handcuffs on her wrists and helped her awkwardly to her feet. "Well, now you're looking at jail time," he said sternly.

"Are you traveling with this woman?" the female security officer asked.

Christina expected Nathan to lie and say he'd never seen her before in his life, but instead, he answered, "Yes. She's my girlfriend. We're in this together."

"Then get your hands behind your back," the female agent ordered, leveling her gun at Nathan's chest.

"You didn't have to do that," Christina whispered.

"Don't worry. We'll get through this. We'll find Mike and help Savannah," Nathan answered as he, too, was handcuffed.

The agents directed them down the hallway and then told them to stop outside a heavy metal door with a keypad at eye level. The male agent was in the middle of keying in a security code when the door was flung open from the other side and

Mike Bryson came charging out, running right into the other agent and knocking him to the ground.

"Shit," Mike said, holding out his hand to help the guy up. "I'm sorry."

"Mike!" Christina said from behind him.

Mike whirled around, surprised to find two of the students from the motel standing there, their hands cuffed behind their backs. "What's going on?" he asked, then waved his hand and said, "I don't have time for this right now. I've got to go find Savannah."

"I know," Christina said. "Some guy came while we were looking for this other woman, and he gave me some lame story about helping Savannah to find her, but then she pulled out the magazine she'd given me and pointed to the word *help*. We've got to save her."

Mike shook his head. Not one word of what Christina had just said made any sense.

"I could use your help," he said to the two security agents as he started down the hall toward the door Savannah had disappeared through.

"What should we do with these two? They could be dangerous," the female agent said.

"They're harmless. Let them go," Mike said, then glanced back at Nathan and Christina. "Thanks for the warning, but I've got it from here. You two go get on your flight back home."

He reached the end of the hallway and quickly keyed in the security code to open the door. He stepped out onto a metal platform and looked around the tarmac, wondering where Savannah had gone from here. The security cameras outside the terminal were much more sparse than the ones inside, the theory being that if you were out here, you had a security clearance and didn't need such close monitoring. As with all security measures, it was a delicate balance to provide the best protection while remaining within the confines of a budget. Sometimes, compromises had to be made.

Therefore, Mike had no idea where Savannah had gone once she and Roman Sweeney had exited the terminal.

His gaze roved the array of small jets scheduled to fly this morning. Several had their doors open while their pilots went through preflight checklists. Others were still and silent. There were about a dozen planes there—too many for him to check out by himself, so he was relieved when the two security agents followed him out the door. His relief dissipated when Christina and Nathan slipped through the door behind the agents.

"I thought I told you two to go back to your boarding gate," he said with a disapproving glare.

"We want to help," Christina protested.

"Then stay out of the way," Mike said as he and the other agents started down the stairs. Just then a portable jetway was pushed away from one of the planes as its cabin door was closed. Mike squinted at the cockpit window, his eyes widening when the pilot turned to look at him. The pilot smiled slowly at Mike as he gave a jaunty wave accompanied by the roar of a jet engine.

As he dropped his hand, Mike swore under his breath. It appeared that Roman Sweeney was about to get away.

Who's Your Perfect Match?

Do you really think a magazine quiz is going to provide you with the insight you need to find your perfect match? No magazine, no self-help book, not even the best advice from your friends can do that. To find your perfect match takes a lot more than that. It takes asking yourself if the man you love makes you a better person. Does he believe in you? Does he support your dreams? Does he laugh about your silly habits—your singing in the shower, your addiction to fashion magazines, the way you have to be allowed to ingest two cups of coffee in the morning before he's allowed to speak to you?

Do you want the same things out of life? What are the five most important things to him right now? What will be important to him in five years? In ten years?

How does he treat you when you're sick? When you're broke? When you're sad? How about when you're happy? Does he celebrate your successes as much as he would his own?

Is he respectful of the people you care about? Does he love your cat, or does he at least pretend to?

Does he always want what's best for you? Does he trust you to make your own decisions?

Would your world be darker without him in it? Would his be darker without you?

continues on next page . . .

Your perfect match doesn't need to be perfect. He only needs to be perfect for you. And no quiz is going to give you the answer to that one. To find your perfect match, you're going to have to trust your heart, instead.

{thirty-three}

"You always were annoyingly smug," Ashleigh said, calmly leaning back on the sofa with a freshly lit cigarette.

"Where's Jane?" Savannah asked, ignoring Ashleigh's comment for the moment.

"Back there," Ashleigh answered, waving her cigarette toward a closed door at the rear of the plane. "Drugged, just like you were on our trip down to Key West. I'm disappointed in her, though. She's not nearly as entertaining as you were."

This last was said with a look of such mocking disdain that Savannah was tempted to leap out of her seat and go for the woman's throat. But instead, she took a slow deep breath and forced herself to bide her time. She had to figure out something that would disable Ashleigh and keep the plane on the ground so Savannah could get both herself and Jane to safety. With the gun in Ashleigh's lap pointed at Savannah, she didn't think now was the right time to attack. She had to do it soon, though. The man who had kidnapped her had gone up to the cockpit and turned on the plane's engines. It wouldn't be long before they took off.

Savannah prayed that Christina had been able to reach Mike, but she knew she couldn't count on anyone coming to the rescue. She had to get out of this mess by herself.

"So, why did you choose my identity to steal? Have we

met somewhere before? Because if we did, I have to say you didn't make much of an impression," Savannah said coolly.

Ashleigh laughed a tight, ugly laugh. "I'm going to enjoy killing you," she said. Then, as if unable to stop herself, she blurted, "We've never met. You wrote those stupid articles for the monthly newsletter at Refund City last year. The ones about organization and automation. You made it sound like filing people's tax returns was *so* important. It got on my nerves. That's why I decided to ruin your credit and set you up with the IRS for tax evasion. I can't tell you how much pleasure I got from fucking with your life."

Savannah chuckled because she knew it was the last response that Ashleigh expected from her. "I remember the look on your face when I showed up at the office in Naples and introduced myself. You just about peed your pants."

Ashleigh took a drag on her cigarette and then tapped the ash off into an ashtray on the table beside her. "I was surprised, I'll give you that. But no more surprised than you were to see me here today, I'll bet," she said with a smug smile.

"Actually, I knew you were the one behind the money in Jane's account," Savannah said, turning her left hand to study her fingernails.

"That's bullshit." Ashleigh picked up the gun and waved it at Savannah. "You don't have the imagination to have figured out my plan. Even Roman was impressed, and he's one of the most intelligent men I know."

"What part do you think I didn't get?" Savannah asked, sliding the magazine she'd dropped on the coffee table onto her lap with a nonchalance she didn't feel. "The part about scanning the obituaries for Refund City clients who had died and using their Social Security numbers to open bank accounts in their names? The part about putting just enough in the accounts to make it so the interest income wouldn't exceed the lowest tax bracket? The part about how you kept the deposits into each account low enough that no one would alert the federal government? Or was it that you didn't think I could compare the handwriting on the bogus tax returns you filed under Mary Coltrane's name with your own files? I don't know, Ashleigh, none of it seems all that innovative to me," she said.

Ashleigh narrowed her eyes at Savannah, who was now leaning forward in her chair, clutching the magazine in her lap with both hands.

"You know," she continued, figuring she might as well say what she wanted to say until Ashleigh gave her the opening she needed. "I looked at all the stuff you charged to me—the expensive clothes and the designer shoes and all that—and I thought that those things made you a better person than me, but I was wrong. You think you're a mink, but the truth is, you're just a rat with a nice coat. A nice coat that really belongs to me," Savannah added with a snort.

Then she opened the magazine to an article about the dangers of unsafe manicures, yawned, and said, "By the way, I hope this isn't going to be a long flight. This is all I brought to read."

Ashleigh sneered and stood up, shaking the wrinkles out of her skirt as she walked to the front of the plane, turning her back on Savannah for just a second. "You have no idea where we're going, so even if you did alert the authorities to our little plan, they have no way to track us once we get out of U.S. airspace. Besides, I'm sure you didn't consider that Roman and I will be taking on new identities once we reach our destination. They'll never find us. And they'll never find you, either. Because you'll be dead." Ashleigh laughed and sat back down on the sofa. "So it looks like you're not as smart as you think you are," she taunted.

"No, I guess not," Savannah said, then looked right into her alter ego's eyes as she added, "But, then again, neither are you."

Mike started sweating as the plane taxied toward the runway. He had to do something to save Savannah—not just because it was his job, but because he'd realized the moment he found out Savannah was in danger that he'd fallen in love with her.

She may not know this yet, but he would never give up on her. No matter what.

But what could he do? Calling Air Traffic Control wouldn't help. By the time they got through to local law enforcement or the military, Sweeney's jet would already be in the air. And if the private plane flew below the radar—and if Sweeney had been smart enough to turn off his transponder, which signaled groundspeed and course projection information to Air Traffic Control—they'd get away before Mike could stop them.

He had to stop Sweeney's plane from taking off. But how?

Mike watched a slow-moving baggage cart weave its way toward one of the commercial airliners and an idea struck him. His eyes narrowed as he measured the distance between the cart and the plane moving toward the runway. Yes. Maybe, just maybe, it might work.

He started toward the cart and saw a flash of movement out of the corner of his eye. Christina and Nathan had been standing at the top of the stairs, watching him, but now they were racing down the steps and toward a group of baggage carts parked on the tarmac. The other two security officers were too far away to hear Mike if he yelled, so he gave up trying to stop the students. He couldn't stop them *and* help Savannah at the same time, so he focused all his attention on doing the latter and prayed the teens wouldn't get hurt.

Mike sprinted toward the moving baggage cart, leaping onto one of the cars when it came within reach. He pulled himself up onto the top of the car and ran to the front, leaping across the gap and onto the next car as he headed toward the man driving the truck.

When he got to the front, he crouched down and shouted "Move over" to the driver, who looked back at him with surprise etched on his face. Mike didn't give the man time to consider his options. Instead, he jumped from the top of the first baggage car into the crowded space behind the driver's seat.

"Federal air marshal on official business!" he yelled as he vaulted over the seat and pushed the other man aside, pressing his foot to the accelerator. The baggage cart bucked forward as Mike stood up, urging the vehicle to go faster.

The plane carrying Savannah slowed to make a turn in order to get into position for takeoff. Mike grimaced when another baggage cart sped past him, its empty cars whipping around like the caboose on a toy train. He saw Christina hunched over the steering wheel like a jockey intent on winning the Triple Crown.

"Come on. Hurry," he muttered under his breath as the plane in front of Roman Sweeney's took off. He had only about a hundred feet to go, and Mike kept his gaze steady on the wheels of that Learjet.

Seventy-five feet.

The Lear's engines whined.

Mike cranked the wheel to the right, trying to get as close to the jet as he could.

Only twenty more feet.

The Lear started rolling forward.

Through sheer force of will, Mike's baggage cart passed Christina's, the one being driven by Nathan in third place behind them.

"Surround them!" Mike shouted as he motioned to indicate what he meant in case he couldn't be heard over the roar of the jet engine. Christina nodded and eased back on her accelerator.

Mike pulled even with the plane's cockpit and waved at the pilot to stop the plane. Roman Sweeney did a double-take when he saw the baggage cart alongside him, but he just flipped Mike off and kept going.

"Asshole," Mike grumbled, praying that the drug dealer would stop when Mike drove the cart into his path. He winced and tried not to think about how this stunt might affect his career.

When the man on the seat next to him realized what Mike was about to do, he shot him a wild-eyed look and said, "Buddy, you're nuts." Then he leaped from the baggage cart, rolling over and over until he finally lay still on the brown grass beside the runway.

Mike spared a glance in the side mirror just in time to see the man sit up and dust himself off, shaking his head as he continued to watch the runaway baggage cart. Mike stood up and waved again for Sweeney to stop the plane, but the drug dealer kept his gaze focused straight ahead. The plane was gaining speed and Mike knew he had to make his move right now, so he closed his eyes and jerked the steering wheel hard to the right. Tires screeched and brakes whined as metal hit metal. Mike smelled heat and smoke and burning rubber and he felt the baggage cart being propelled forward on the runway. He felt the truck's two passenger-side wheels lift from the tarmac, and he held on, praying the vehicle wouldn't overturn and crush him.

But he wasn't that lucky. The vehicle started to tip and he

held on to the steering wheel with all his might as it went over. His back hit the pavement and he struggled to keep his legs inside the vehicle as the plane dragged the cart along the runway.

The awful screeching and groaning of metal seemed to go on for hours, but it was probably only seconds. When the noise finally stopped, it was so quiet that it was as if all life had ceased.

Mike opened his eyes and stared at the seat of the vehicle, which was lying above him, blocking out the sun. The seat was blue-gray leather with white stitching, and there were several cigarette burns in the upholstery.

"Don't they know smoking can kill you?" Mike mumbled, not quite sure why he felt compelled to say it.

He tried to wiggle his feet and was surprised to find that he could. He coughed and realized that he was still clutching the steering wheel, so he let go, his aching arms falling to the pavement beside his chest. Well, if he hurt, he couldn't be dead, right?

"Mike? Are you all right?" he heard Nathan ask.

"Yeah, I'm okay," he answered as he rolled himself over and crawled out from under the smoking baggage cart. The sudden sunlight nearly blinded him and he squinted, glad to see that both Nathan and Christina were unharmed. He looked up at the plane, wondering just how the hell he was supposed to get the cabin door open, when it slid open with a *whoosh* and a gush of black smoke.

A yellow emergency slide inflated, and Mike watched as a woman stumbled and then fell headfirst onto the plastic, her long, dark hair flopping forward to cover her face. Mike's heart stopped. Had they killed Savannah?

He pushed past Nathan and Christina and ran to the bottom of the slide. He hesitated for just a second before lifting the woman's shoulders and looking into her green eyes.

Thank God. It wasn't Savannah.

The woman groaned and her eyelids fluttered for a second before she passed out.

"Here comes Jane," Savannah said from the top of the slide as she gently lowered a groggy-looking Jane Smith onto the yellow plastic.

Mike moved Ashleigh Van Dyke out of the way and reached out to help Jane as she reached the bottom. Then he grabbed the side of the slide and pulled himself up into the cabin of the jet. Savannah met him at the top, her face covered with black soot. Her hair looked as if it had been burned off in chunks and her eyes were red-rimmed, but Mike thought she was the most beautiful sight he had ever seen.

He grabbed her around the waist and pulled her to him so tightly that neither of them could breathe.

"Are you okay?" he asked after a moment, moving away just enough so that they could both get some air.

"Yes, but I was pretty scared there for a while," she admitted.

"You're not the only one," Mike said dryly. "What happened here?"

"Ashleigh turned her back on me for a second, and I grabbed her lighter and set the latest edition of *Stylish* on fire. I knew those fashion magazines would change my life one day," Savannah said with what sounded like a smile.

Mike finally looked around the cabin, at the torched drapes and burned spots on the carpet.

"None of this stuff burned all that well, but the smoke was enough of a distraction for me to get the gun away from Ashleigh and knock her out. I was going for her boyfriend when we crashed."

Mike shook his head. He had to give it to her, nothing ever seemed to keep Savannah Taylor down. "Where's Roman Sweeney? The guy who kidnapped you?" Mike clarified in case they hadn't been properly introduced.

Savannah shrugged toward the cockpit. "In there," she said, then held up a gun. "He hit his head on the dashboard when the plane stopped, and I just left him there unconscious and took this. The idiot wasn't wearing his seat belt." She clucked her tongue, then ruined the effect by coughing so hard that tears came out of her eyes.

Mike patted her back and forced himself not to crush her in his arms again, trying to stem the tide of emotions that welled up and threatened to choke him like the smoke that rolled out of the airplane. Savannah wiped her eyes as her cell phone started to ring, and she pulled herself out of Mike's grasp.

"Hello?" she answered tentatively, as if afraid the phone might explode in her ear.

Mike left her saying, "Yes" and "Um-hmm," and went up

to the cockpit to handcuff Roman Sweeney. The man was heavy, so Mike left him there as he radioed for a security team.

When he went back out into the cabin, he couldn't resist taking Savannah into his arms again. She looked stunned, as if this whole nightmare had finally taken the spirit out of her. "Don't worry, baby," he whispered soothingly in her ear. "Everything's going to be okay."

Savannah nuzzled her face into his chest and said, "You're right. It is. I just got a call from the FBI. They offered me a job."

Mike blinked several times. "What?" he asked.

"Agent Harrison from the FBI—he's the one who arrested me back in Maple Rapids—that was him on the phone. He said he was so impressed with my work on this case that he brought it to the attention of his superiors, and they told him they could use creative thinkers like me on their team. Can you believe it?"

Mike started to laugh. And laugh. And laugh. Until tears were streaming down his cheeks and he had to sit down on the blackened sofa.

Savannah punched his arm and looked offended. "It's not that funny," she said.

"No, I'm sorry," Mike said, wiping his eyes. "It's just that you seem to come out of all this manure smelling like a rose. I've never met anyone like you."

Savannah sniffed haughtily. "Well, actually, if you're going to start comparing me to flowers, gerbera daisies are my favorite."

Mike grinned and reached out for Savannah's hand, pulling her down on his lap so he could feel her body next to his. "I'll keep that in mind," he said, gently pushing a lock of singed hair behind her ear with one hand as he stroked her back with the other. "What am I going to do with you?" he asked, fearing that his heart wasn't big enough to contain the way he felt about her.

Savannah sighed and slumped against him, nestling against his shoulder as she wearily shook her head.

"I know," she said. "I'm sorry to be so much trouble."

And, although Mike had no way of knowing it at the time, he stole Savannah's heart at that moment when he lifted her chin with the fingers of one hand, looked deep into her eyes, tenderly kissed the tip of her soot-blackened nose, and said, "That's okay, Savannah. You're worth it."